"A discovery of the first importance. . . . Professor Gates's masterful reconstruction of the historical background of Hannah Crafts's story is in itself a compelling narrative."
—Lawrence Buell, professor, Harvard University,
and author of *Writing for an Endangered World*

"Remarkable . . . winning."
—*Publishers Weekly*

"A truly unique, paradigm-changing text, unprecedented in nineteenth-century American literature by blacks or whites. . . . Compelling evidence identifying Hannah Crafts as the earliest known African American novelist."
—William I. Andrews, E. Maynard Adams Professor of English, University of North Carolina-Chapel Hill

"A vivid, compelling narrative . . . intriguing . . . engrossing . . . surprising."
—*Booklist*

"A wonderful, intriguing read and exciting detective work . . . worth the 150-year wait."
—www.nighttimes.com

"Remarkable for its historical value. . . . A first for American literature, THE BONDWOMAN'S NARRATIVE promotes the dignity of the race as an integral part of the plot. . . . At the same time, the book exhibits extraordinary narrative skill. . . . Professor Gates, once again, has made an important contribution to the literary story of American literature and to African American literature in particular."
—Augusta Rohrbach, author of *Truth Stranger than Fiction: Race, Realism and the U.S. Literary Marketplace*

"Remarkable . . . richly written . . . should be endeared as a treasured piece of American history."
—*Upscale Magazine*

ALSO BY HENRY LOUIS GATES JR.

The Signifying Monkey: A Theory of African-American Literary Criticism

Thirteen Ways of Looking at a Black Man

The African-American Century: How Black Americans Have Shaped Our Country (with Cornel West)

Colored People: A Memoir

Africana: The Encyclopedia of the African and African American Experience (with Kwame Anthony Appiah)

EDITED BY HENRY LOUIS GATES JR.

Our Nig; or, Sketches from the Life of a Free Black by Harriet E. Wilson

HIGHEST ACCLAIM FOR
THE BONDWOMAN'S NARRATIVE

Selected as One of the Best Historical Fiction Books of the Year
by *Black Issues Book Review*

"Immensely entertaining and illuminating . . . probably the first novel written by a black woman. . . . Rich in insight . . . a credible and compelling commentary on life under slavery."
—*New York Times Book Review*

"Compelling . . . a work of sagacity and moral purpose . . . likely will be the high-water mark of the year in American studies . . . and a bright light for years to come in African American literature."
—*Dallas Morning News*

"Remarkable . . . engaging . . . harrowing and memorable scenes . . . [and] exhibits a strong social critique . . . eloquent and persuasive."
—*New York Newsday*

"Engrossing."
—*Entertainment Weekly*

"A real find . . . a compelling, exciting, and moving story."
—Nina Baym, professor,
University of Illinois at Urbana-Champaign

"Entertaining. . . . Has the arresting ring of authenticity. . . . It is impossible to read Crafts's story and not admire her independent mind."
—*Cleveland Plain Dealer*

"American and African American literature are indebted to Henry Louis Gates Jr. . . . [This novel] offers readings of race that recall Toni Morrison's *Paradise*. Framed by Gates's masterful critical edition, [this] is another permanent text in the African American literary tradition."
—Rudolph P. Byrd, professor, Emory University

"Inestimable."
—*New York Daily News*

"A feat of extraordinary sleuthing . . . [a] scholarly coup . . . engages readers with two compelling stories, Crafts's search for independence and Gates's search for Crafts."
—*Boston Magazine*

"Crafts's manuscript contradicts, challenges, and confounds many prevailing notions about form, content, and intent of nineteenth-century women's fiction."
—**Frances Foster, professor, Emory University**

"Convincing domestic details . . . a sharp observer of character."
—*Newsweek*

"A treasure of great value. . . . Once again, the field of black literature and culture is the beneficiary of Professor Gates's incredible investigative talents."
—**Nellie Y. McKay, professor, University of Wisconsin, Madison**

"Unique . . . revealing . . . provides a window into the psychology and perspective of a slave woman."
—*New York Times*

"One of the year's most interesting books. . . . Its grounding in actuality gives it uncommon power. . . . Crafts's picture of slave life and her insights into the psychology of the enslaved are fascinating."
—*San Jose Mercury News*

"A milestone in African American and women's studies . . . probably the first novel by a black woman, and certainly the first by a former slave."
—**Vincent Carretta, professor, Department of English, University of Maryland, College Park**

"A major feat of literary sleuthing and editorial advocacy. . . . Crafts offers an invaluable view of slavery from the inside out."
—*San Francisco Chronicle*

"From calamity to coincidence . . . Crafts [is] a sly social commentator."
—*People*

The Bondwoman's Narrative

HANNAH CRAFTS

Edited by
HENRY LOUIS GATES JR.

With a New Introduction by
HENRY LOUIS GATES JR.
AND GREGG HECIMOVICH

GRAND CENTRAL

New York   Boston

Copyright © 2003 by Henry Louis Gates Jr.

New introduction for this revised edition copyright © 2025 by Henry Louis Gates Jr. and Gregg Hecimovich

Cover copyright © 2025 by Hachette Book Group, Inc.

Hachette Book Group supports the right to free expression and the value of copyright. The purpose of copyright is to encourage writers and artists to produce the creative works that enrich our culture.

The scanning, uploading, and distribution of this book without permission is a theft of the author's intellectual property. If you would like permission to use material from the book (other than for review purposes), please contact permissions@hbgusa.com. Thank you for your support of the author's rights.

Grand Central Publishing
Hachette Book Group
1290 Avenue of the Americas, New York, NY 10104
grandcentralpublishing.com
@grandcentralpub

Originally published in hardcover in 2003

This Revised Trade Edition: June 2025

Grand Central Publishing is a division of Hachette Book Group, Inc. The Grand Central Publishing name and logo is a registered trademark of Hachette Book Group, Inc.

The publisher is not responsible for websites (or their content) that are not owned by the publisher.

The Hachette Speakers Bureau provides a wide range of authors for speaking events. To find out more, go to hachettespeakersbureau.com or email HachetteSpeakers@hbgusa.com.

Grand Central Publishing books may be purchased in bulk for business, educational, or promotional use. For information, please contact your local bookseller or the Hachette Book Group Special Markets Department at special.markets@hbgusa.com.

Library of Congress Control Number: 2001098325

ISBNs: 978-1-5387-7351-2 (trade paperback), 978-0-4464-0562-1 (ebook)

Printed in the United States of America

LSC-C

Printing 1, 2025

In memory

of

Dorothy Porter Wesley,

1905–1995

on whose shoulders

we stand.

CONTENTS

INTRODUCTION xi

THE BONDWOMAN'S NARRATIVE   Hannah Crafts   1

TEXTUAL ANNOTATIONS   247

APPENDIXES

    A. Authentication Report—Dr. Joe Nickell   319

    B. Testimony of Jane Johnson

        Version 1   355

        Version 2   357

    C. John Hill Wheeler's Library Catalogue,

        Compiled by Bryan C. Sinche   361

A NOTE ON CRAFTS'S LITERARY INFLUENCES   373

BIBLIOGRAPHY   375

ACKNOWLEDGMENTS   379

"The Abolitionist preference was for facts, facts, facts: not for fantasy, which can be forged. Slave writers were urged to be specific, to skewer names and dates and places, as protection against the owners' frequent allegation that slave narratives were the product of white Northern do-gooders with too little information and too much imagination. In her preface, Hannah declares her book to be a 'record of plain unvarnished facts,' but a glance at any page shows it to be something far more artful. So why did Hannah choose to write a novel, not an autobiography? She prefers to tell a story about herself, and perhaps that story had been necessary for her psychological survival. Long before she was free in fact, she had escaped in imagination. She had extracted herself from degrading circumstances and inserted herself into others, more flattering, as a persecuted heroine in a romance. The novel shows us that she has been able to protect her psyche and keep its core intact; an autobiography would merely assert it. Autobiographies display the triumph of experience, but novels are acts of hope."

—Hilary Mantel, "The Shape of Absence,"
London Review of Books August 8, 2002

INTRODUCTION

In 1857, Hannah Crafts escaped enslavement on a North Carolina plantation and fled to a farm in central New York. In freedom she worked on a manuscript that would make her famous, but that fame would not come until long after her death.

With a dash of her pen, Crafts struck out the name that she had been disguising throughout her narrative as "Wh—r." She dipped her pen, drew up fresh ink, and took a risk: next to the marked-out passage, defiantly she wrote, "Wheeler" (MS 190). With the ink still fresh on her quill, she backtracked through the manuscript, returning to every page on which "Wh—r" appeared, thus identifying her enslavers. "Their names are Wheeler" (MS 159), she wrote, darkening the missing letters over the dash so there would be no mistake: "Mrs. Wheeler informs..." (MS 159), "Mrs. Wheeler came..." (MS 184), "Mrs. Wheeler complained..." (MS 184), "Mrs. Wheeler sent for..." (MS 185).

Up to this point, the author had obscured her story so that she could not be easily traced. As she knew too well, the Wheelers prosecuted escaped slaves and their abettors.

Once again, Hannah Crafts dipped her pen and constructed a new scene, boldly marking the name of her enslaver (MS 193). This time, she told the story of Mrs. Wheeler suffering a bout

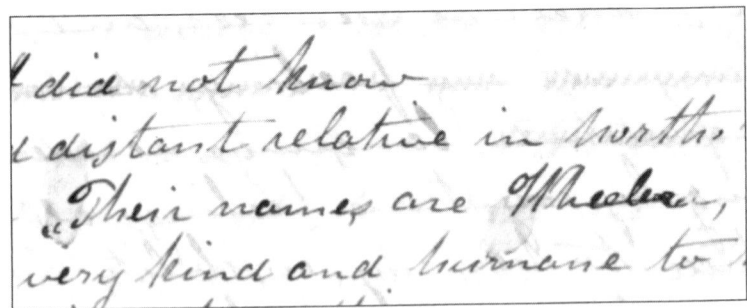

Figure 1: Detail of *The Bondwoman's Narrative* MS 159

of constipation: "I was the attendant of *Mrs. Wheeler*," she wrote, "though it is impossible to say how irksome the duty had become." This was the kind of insolent power a formerly enslaved woman could possess—one who was a nascent author, writing her "self" into being, as it were. From this point on, the Wheelers are named precisely throughout the manuscript, and their activities in Washington, D.C., and North Carolina figure strongly.

As she pressed on, Crafts disclosed the truth for all to see: Mrs. Wheeler was "a bigot in religion," and her "notions of religion and truth were highly improper for one in her station." She even hinted at the deepest wound: "compelled to sacrifise" [sic] to a "gentleman" and the loss of "honor and virtue" (MS 192–93). In reanimating her mistress, Crafts showed Mrs. Wheeler to be a hypocrite.

When the author completed the manuscript in 1858, she added a title page: "The Bondwoman's Narrative by Hannah Crafts a Fugitive Slave Recently Escaped from North Carolina." This is the closest she came to identifying herself. The stitched and bound manuscript then disappeared from literary history until 2001, when Henry Louis Gates Jr. purchased the work at auction, authenticated it, and published it to great acclaim. In April 2002, Hannah Crafts became a *New York Times* bestselling writer. Against all odds, the first Black woman to write a novel had gained an astonishing level of literary celebrity, seemingly overnight. And yet the full scope of her life remained unknown. Now readers have the opportunity to read Crafts's novel in a richer context.

In 2001, Henry Louis Gates Jr. began his quest to uncover Hannah Crafts's life story after coming upon the author's manuscript in the catalogue of the Swann Auction Galleries. Each February, the Swann holds a public sale of "Printed & Manuscript African-Americana" in New York City. Among the hundreds of documents and photographs and memorabilia on offer, one entry in particular stood out to Gates. It was lot 30, an "Unpublished Original Manuscript" whose provenance was believed to be "circa 1850s," New Jersey, from the private collection of Dorothy Porter Wesley, the esteemed librarian and historian at the Moorland-Spingarn Research Center at Howard University, indeed one of the foremost Black librarians of the twentieth century. Porter Wesley and Gates had long been friends, and on occasion she had taunted him by claiming to have in her possession a treasure far rarer and more unconventional than even the 1859 novel of Harriet E. Wilson, *Our Nig*, which Gates had unearthed, authenticated, and published in 1982. Was this item that treasure to which Porter Wesley had tantalizingly referred? Gates decided to purchase the manuscript.

The item was marked as "a fictionalized biography...purporting to be the story of the early life and escape of one Hannah Crafts, a mulatto, born in Virginia." These words came from the 1948 catalogue of the manuscript's original owner, the bookseller Emily Driscoll, but the following singular observation came from Porter herself: "The important point about this fictionalized personal narrative is that, from internal evidence, it appears to be the work of a Negro and that the time of composition was before the Civil War."[i]

In 2001 it was only a guess that *The Bondwoman's Narrative* was quite possibly the first novel written by a Black woman, and certainly the first by a Black woman who had been enslaved. Up to that point, Harriet E. Wilson held the former distinction. But the more Gates investigated the narrative, the more he came to believe that Dorothy Porter Wesley had gone to her grave believing that this unpublished novel, in a holograph manuscript, had actually been written by a formerly enslaved Black woman.

But was Crafts's manuscript fact or fiction? Gates and the initial readers of the work noted the amalgam of literary conventions from gothic novels, sentimental novels, and slave narratives. Without knowing the details of Hannah Crafts's life it was impossible to categorize. Early critics wondered about Crafts's voice, which ranges from what the critic Ann Fabian calls both "clumsy" and untutored, based on the mechanics of her writing, to sophisticated and strikingly authentic, in a powerfully compelling first-person voice. The narrative incorporated elements of travelogues, religious and abolitionist literature, and the sentimental novel; it ends with the equivalent of "and they lived happily ever after." She was clearly well read, adding literary epigraphs at the beginnings of chapters. She understood the slave narrative genre, taking pains to explain to readers how she became literate, a signal feature of virtually all slave narratives since Frederick Douglass.

And most important, Crafts's language indicated that she herself was Black by depicting Black people as simply "people," without a racial modifier. Crafts's Black characters, as Dorothy Porter's stunning insight underscored, were first and foremost human beings; their race did not determine their character, as was customary in the writings of Harriet Beecher Stowe and virtually every white author, including (maybe even especially) white abolitionists. In fact, the Blackness of the characters inhabiting Crafts's work was the *default*, and while her descriptions were colorful and revealing, they did not necessarily include outright indications that a particular character was Black. Yet the author was keenly attuned to class distinctions. Gates viewed her frank disdain for field laborers and her unusually detailed attention to sensory perceptions, like the odor of the quarters in which the enslaved were forced to live, as compelling signs that the author was a Black person and that the writer viewed the world through the lens of a subject position as an enslaved woman working in the house and not in the field.

In short, before we knew anything about Crafts's life and history, her raw and uninhibited writing style, the freedom with which she wrote of Black characters, and the specificity and intimacy with which she detailed the power dynamic between enslaved and enslaver were among the elements that led one of Black America's most accomplished bibliophiles, Dorothy Porter, to guess that Crafts was indeed a Black writer who had formerly been enslaved. Knowing that propelled Gates to embark on the search to prove, or disprove, Porter's instincts and suppositions.

The search for Hannah Crafts involved multiple paths: the scientific work of authenticating her manuscript, the search for her name in census records, and literary analysis to see how her work fit with other texts. In the late 1980s, Gates had used census data and other indices now well known (in part through the wide popularity of Gates's PBS series *Finding Your Roots*) as the tools of the genealogy trade to authenticate Wilson's *Our Nig*. In 2001, the work of authenticating *The Bondwoman's Narrative* moved from library to laboratory, from microfilm to microscope.

Based on the analysis by Harvard College Library's curator of manuscripts, Leslie A. Morris, of the manuscript's physical form and by Harvard University Art Museums' deputy director of conservation, Craigen W. Bowen, of the "paper, binding, and ink," the date of publication was determined to be mid-nineteenth century, 1850s to 1860s. Wyatt Houston Day, who had initially authenticated the manuscript for Swann Galleries, leaned toward the earlier part of that decade, using the "style of the narrative, the handwriting and most important, the tone of the ink and type of paper," as well as the absence of any mention of the Civil War or secession, to place the date "probably [in] the first half of the 1850s." Next, Kenneth Rendell, a dealer in historical documents, confirmed that Crafts's manuscript was written before the start of the Civil War, possibly as early as 1855, based on the sort of ink that was used: iron-gall ink, which was widely in use until 1860.

The self-described "investigator and historical document examiner" Dr. Joe Nickell, a writer who exposed the diary of Jack the Ripper as a fraud, noted that text references in Crafts's manuscript, such as one to an "equestrian statue of Jackson" that was erected in 1853, and non-references to secession definitively placed the time of writing between 1853 and 1861. He also analyzed punctuation irregularities (the author never used periods), handwriting style (far less delicate and "diminutive" than if she had been a white middle-class woman), variety and sophistication of vocabulary (multisyllabic words and misspellings permeate the manuscript), and literary "thefts" from white authors (learned references, including both single sentences and full paragraphs, to classics and other literary works typically found in a white, middle-class mid-nineteenth-century home library) that pointed to an autodidact, a self-taught someone unaware of the accepted rules of citation and attribution. These findings, coupled with details such as thimble marks impressed on correction slips and the handling of the racial identities of characters that matched the writer's self-identification as female and light-skinned, establish the foundations of the author's personal story.

A picture began to emerge after this arduous authentication process. With Gates's careful analysis and summary, *The Bondwoman's Narrative* was published along with his findings in a detailed annotated edition in 2002. (In addition, a facsimile edition of the holograph manuscript was published as well in an effort, Gates hoped, to facilitate additional research into the author's identity by other scholars.) The work debuted to extraordinary sales and a solid place on the *New York Times Best Seller* list. Even without knowing the precise identity of the author, readers and scholars marveled at the powerful way Crafts reveals the sexual exploitation of women in her narrative. Yet the question remained: How might knowing the full story of the writer open up her novel even further? Who was this amazing writer?[ii]

In the search for Hannah Crafts, it is no surprise that literary scholarship was the key. While Gates had traced the novel's indebtedness to other slave narratives, Hollis Robbins was the first scholar to contact Gates to point out that the novel "borrowed" from popular novels of the day, most notably Charles Dickens's *Bleak House* and Walter Scott's *Rob Roy*. Other scholars dove into Crafts's borrowings of *Jane Eyre, Uncle Tom's Cabin,* and *The House of the Seven Gables*. William L. Andrews's work clarified the minute class and racial elements of the novel, while also pointing to the strangeness of the work's "happy" ending. Robert S. Levine explored the essentializing traps of racial identity keyed to Black and white, both inside and outside the work. Lawrence Buell, William Gleason, Augusta Rohrbach, Karen Sanchez-Eppler, Bryan Sinche, and Ann Fabian spelled out, in rich and diverse ways, the material contexts of the novel's production: the narrative's position in the literary marketplace (Buell, Fabian, and Rohrbach), its genre conventions (Sanchez-Eppler and Sinche), and even its architecture (Gleason).[iii]

All of this work pointed to an author clearly surrounded by books and literature. Did she have access to her enslaver's library? Did she tiptoe in and read widely and surreptitiously? For twenty years, Gregg Hecimovich—a scholar initially skeptical of Gates's conclusions—pulled these and many other threads, focusing on the broader Wheeler family, the patriarchs of which were cruel slaveholders even while cultured and literary men. Was Crafts an enslaved woman inside this family structure? It turns out she was. Over two decades, Hecimovich meticulously uncovered and documented the author's experiences and in 2023 published *The Life and Times of Hannah Crafts*, a definitive account of her life, drawing on interviews with descendant communities and a rich array of public and private records (letters, diaries, ledger accounts, court cases, census and property records). In short, Hecimovich has firmly established the author's identity and reconstructed her personal journey, verifying Gates's initial claims.

Here is what we now know about the author of *The Bondwoman's Narrative*, the novel you are about to read. Hannah Crafts was born in 1826 as Hannah Bond on the plantation of Lewis Bond in Indian Woods, North Carolina, a child of rape by a white father, the planter Lewis Bond, and her mixed-race mother, called Hannah Sr. in estate inventories. Orphaned when she was separated from her mother at the age of ten, the author was trained to be a house servant. During her childhood she began to "steal" literacy, to borrow Frederick Douglass's famous metaphor, a practice she continued when she came to serve female college students in nearby Murfreesboro, North Carolina. Like Frederick Douglass, Crafts learned her letters despite laws prohibiting literacy among the enslaved. In 1856, in Washington, D.C., she began writing a novel on paper that she stole from her captor, the diplomat and politician John Hill Wheeler.[iv]

She entered service to the Wheeler family upon the marriage of her first mistress (and her half sister), Lucinda Bond, to Samuel Jordan Wheeler. Before her escape, the author's life had centered on the household of John Hill Wheeler in Washington, D.C., and in the all-Black Baptist church that she attended. But in the spring of 1857, the author was removed from her privileged role as the Wheelers' lady's maid in Washington, D.C., and returned to North Carolina. Here, she was forced for the first time to live among the enslaved people who resided in the Wheelers' squalid field huts, intentionally to be exposed to rape by another bond person. It was then, to protect control over her own body, that she ran.

The brutality that suffuses the early chapters of Crafts's narrative mirrors the violence that formed the circumstances of her childhood in Bertie County, North Carolina, and might properly be read as autobiographical. Crafts's enslaved community knew racist cruelty intimately. Her family lived through the public executions of eight neighbors accused of plotting a rebellion in 1802, called the Bertie Conspiracy, more than two decades before Crafts was born. The Bertie conspirators were hanged from the so-called Gospel Oaks, a well-known Indian Woods crossroads a stone's throw from the author's slave cabin. Then, in 1822, after her sale to Jacob R. Pope, Crafts's grandmother Rosea Pugh was hanged on a nearby plantation. The community also suffered the reprisal violence that followed Nat Turner's bloody slave revolt in nearby Southampton County, Virginia, in 1831. The legacy of such violence darkened the author's childhood, inspiring the signature scene of Crafts's narrative in which Sir Clifford De Vincent ties an enslaved female domestic named Rose to a tree and then, from his front porch, listens serenely to her slow asphyxiation.[v]

Crafts frames the story as one that "we had heard... told in the dim duskiness of the summer twilight or by the roaring fires of wintry nights" (*TBN* 25):

> "Now take this old witch, and her whelp and gibbet them alive on the Linden" [Sir Clifford De Vincent] said his features distorted and his whole frame seeming to dilate with intensity and

passion...An iron hoop being fastened around the body of Rose she was drawn to the tree, and with great labor elevated and secured to one of the largest limbs. And then with a refinement of cruelty the innocent and helpless little animal, with a broad iron belt around its delicate body was suspended within her sight, but beyond her reach.

And thus suspended between heaven and earth in a posture the [sic] most unimaginably painful both hung through the long long days and the longer nights. Not a particle of food, not a drop of water was allowed to either, but the master walking each morning would fix his cold cruel eyes with appalling indifference on her agonised countenance, and call to inquire whether or not she was ready to be the minister of his vengeance on the dog. For three consecutive days she retained the strength to answer that she was not.

While early critics, searching the text for signs of "authentic" detail, found Rose's death unconvincing at best, if not unbelievable at worst, readers now can stop and wonder why Crafts added all the creaky gothic machinery to the scene: why the literary evocation of *The House of the Seven Gables* as a ghostly power "loosen[s]" the portrait of her master "from its fastings in the wall"; why the "decayed branches of [the linden tree]" clatter at the master's window ("Whence is that frightful noise?") (*TBN* 29–30). The spectral presence of the murdered slave haunts the text. Before knowing the life of the author, readers—underestimating both the range of texts to which an enslaved person could be exposed and the literary talent necessary to engage in intertextual riffing such as this one, asked: Could an enslaved person, admittedly one who had grown up in the shadow of the Gospel Oaks, actually have written this? Now that we know that yes, an enslaved woman did write this, based on a true story, we can ask new questions, such as: Why did the author shape her narrative as autobiographical fiction?[vi] Are all of her characters based in fact? Where is she taking a leap, and why?

The choices Crafts made in forming her novel were shaped intimately by life experience. We now know that her narrative came to reflect the specific conditions of her enslavement and her wish to transcend the circumstances of her birth. Crafts's book is, in effect, an act of freeing herself from the imposed trauma of her childhood and adolescence.

The kinds of memoirs popular today, exploring trauma and abuse, were not known in Crafts's day, and a writer, Black or white, could not imagine an audience for such direct revelations of private suffering. The likeliest path was the slave narrative genre established by Douglass and other formerly enslaved writers. But there was no place, even in slave narratives, for an enslaved woman trying to tell the story of sexual abuse. As physically abused slaves, Harriet Jacobs and Harriet Wilson would follow Crafts in turning to autobiographical narrative.

When Hannah Crafts was ten years old, her mother, Hannah Sr., was taken from her and given to her enslaver Lewis Bond's daughter-in-law as a wedding gift. Crafts's mother was then forced to move hundreds of miles to western Tennessee. The estrangement produced by this rupture understandably marked the author more than any other loss in her life. In many ways, it is reasonable to assume the novel that Crafts wrote drew from her need to reconcile and compensate for this loss. Perhaps it is not surprising, then, that she ends her novel with an act of fictional wish fulfillment that the reality of slavery had rendered impossible: Hannah and her mother are happily reunited in freedom in Crafts's manuscript.

In real life, Crafts's separation from her mother in childhood was part of the exploitative treatment many enslaved females suffered beginning near adolescence. The sexual exploitation and assault the author endured directly affected not only the shape of her psyche and personality but also the form, rhetorical strategies, and themes that comprise *The Bondwoman's Narrative.*

For a period after her mother's forced relocation to Tennessee, Crafts served at the neighboring plantation of Thomas Bond Jr. and his wife, Sawyer P. Rascoe. Thomas Jr. was Lewis Bond's nephew, and it appears that Crafts was placed on his property to avoid a legal claim. There she provided domestic help and childcare to the growing family—six children under the age of ten. By the 1840s, she became a permanent fixture in Thomas Jr.'s household, where it seems likely that he raped her at will.[vii]

Crafts writes the experience into her narrative with the introduction of a light-skinned, unnamed bride who, it turns out, is passing—a small woman "with a profusion of wavy curly hair, large bright eyes, and delicate features with the exception of her lips which were too large, full, and red." The following is quite possibly a description of Crafts herself when she was coerced into serving Thomas Jr.: "She dressed in very good taste and her manner seemed perfect but for an uncomfortable habit she had of seeming to watch everybody as though she feared them." In the novel, the protagonist Hannah becomes the shadow self to this unnamed mistress as the two plot to free themselves from bondage: "I fancied then that she was haunted by a shadow or phantom apparent only to herself, and perhaps even the more dreadful for that" (*TBN* 27).

As an enslaved woman, Hannah Crafts seems to have inhabited both these roles of slave and mistress: she was a light-skinned woman who could have passed for white, but instead she became a trafficked daughter. Her betrayer, perhaps even her father, never acknowledged his paternity, and he even allowed her to be sexually abused by his nephew. These experiences, unbearably traumatic, were thematized at the center of Crafts's novel. Crafts used gothic literary conventions to expose the dark heart of the American slave system.

Crafts gives voice to the views of her enslaver through the reflections of the character Hannah: "Slaves were slaves to him, and nothing more. Practically he regarded them not as men and women, but in the same light as horses or other domestic animals." The text continues, "He supplied their necessities of food and clothing from motives of policy, but [di]scounted the ideas of equality and fraternity as preposterous and absurd" (*TBN* 6). Strangely, just as the identity of the mistress is never disclosed in the novel, neither is a name provided for Hannah's original enslaver; rather, the character is presented only as a male presence. Perhaps both are obscured, like Crafts's personal experience, as a way to convert painful memories into art. Hannah the heroine is allowed to escape what Hannah the enslaved bore.[viii]

At the age of twenty-four, Crafts became the property of Esther Bond, a daughter of her original captor, and in 1852 she was forced into the role of maidservant to another daughter, Lucinda Bond Wheeler, wife of Samuel Jordan Wheeler of Murfreesboro, North Carolina. In her late twenties, between 1852 and 1856, Crafts lived at Wheeler House in Murfreesboro, where she had access to a college library and to the young college women that she served who were boarding with the Wheelers. It was here, it seems, that she helped herself to the world of literature.

But how did an uneducated enslaved woman become a novelist? Surprisingly, much of Crafts's journey to authorship can be traced in fascinating detail.

Direct evidence demonstrates that the Wheeler family and their relatives prized literacy as a trait among at least some of their domestic slaves. For instance, Samuel Jordan Wheeler, the occupant of the Wheeler family residence in Murfreesboro, kept a domestic body servant named Moses who also served as his secretary. Not only was Moses literate, but he was also a correspondent of the Wheeler children.[ix] Born at Willow Hall plantation in Indian Woods, Moses was likely a relative of the author.

Nor was literacy an aberration for the enslaved persons in the extended Wheeler family despite persisting myths. In 1849, for example, John Wheeler Moore, the diplomat John Hill Wheeler's nephew, brought his body servant, Harvey, to the University of North Carolina at Chapel Hill to assist him with his studies. Harvey, like Moses, was an enslaved man who served as Moore's personal secretary.[x] Even the Wheelers' children at times dictated their letters to enslaved women and men working in their household. Julia Wheeler, daughter of Samuel Jordan Wheeler and Lucinda Bond Wheeler, employed an enslaved "amanuensis," or dictation assistant, while attending Chowan Baptist Female Institute (the future Chowan University) in 1860.[xi] It would appear that the fictional Ellen Wheeler, in assigning Hannah to take dictation of her letters in *The Bondwoman's Narrative* (157), is only exercising what was, at least occasionally, a literal occurrence in the Wheeler and Moore families: the enslaved functioned as amanuenses, performing their literacy as part of their duties to their owners. In these highly literate homes, a slave's value could in fact depend in part on their literary skill.[xii]

Crafts's labor within the Wheeler household proved formative. In Murfreesboro, she assisted students who attended the adjacent female college, Chowan Baptist Female Institute. Evidence suggests that composition exercises assigned to young college students shaped aspects of Crafts's manuscript. Samuel Jordan Wheeler's daughter, Kate, preserved her English composition notebook from this period. In 1854, she composed various exercises for her English classes. The exercises required students to reflect on common aphorisms, or proverbs, and to expound on these according to personal observation. Among the documents preserved by Kate are compositions based on poetic verses and reflections such as

"How blessings brighten as they take their flight" (September 15, 1854), "Know Thyself," taken from the most famous of the philosophical maxims at the Temple of Delphi (September 22, 1854), "Novel Reading" (September 29, 1854), "When is the time to die" (October 6, 1854), and "The value of knowledge" (October 18, 1854). Young Kate Wheeler observes in her "value of knowledge" composition:

> How inestimable is knowledge! Its value is infinitely greater than other earthly treasures, yea: "nothing of this earth that can be desired is to be compared to it." Only by hard study & perseverance can we become the possessors of it. "Wealth may take not unto itself wings & fly as an eagle aloft towards heaven." Comfort is but temporary and friends may forsake, but this is a durable treasure, for as it cannot be given by an earthly hand so it cannot be taken by one & it will not forsake us until God think best to dispossess us of it. Then seeing its priceless value we should seek more earnestly for it & avail ourselves of every opportunity afforded us for acquiring it.[xiii]

Note the absence of citation of Kate's quoted sources, a practice that Hannah would also embrace throughout her text. If there was a distinctly forced quality to such exercises, they also developed a habit of mind. When Crafts came to write her novel, she knitted together similar kinds of expressions as a part of her narrative.

Take, for instance, an early passage in *The Bondwoman's Narrative* in which Crafts describes the power of nature to overcome ignorance. The framing and reflection match Kate Wheeler's responses in her composition lessons. Crafts writes early in her narrative from the perspective of her heroine, Hannah:

> Can ignorance quench the immortal mind or prevent its feeling at times the indications of its heavenly origin[?] Can it destroy that deep abiding appreciation of the beautiful that seems inherent to the human soul? Can it seal up the fountains of truth and all

intuitive perception of life, death and eternity? I think not. Those to whom man teaches little, nature like a wise and prudent mother teaches much. (*TBN* 18)

Further, Crafts observes:

It sometimes seems that we require sympathy more in joy than sorrow; for the heart exultant, and overflowing with good nature longs to impart a portion of its happiness. Especial[l]y is this the case with children. How it augments the importance of any little success to them that some one probably a mother will receive the intelligence with a show of delight and interest. But I had no mother, no friend.

The tone, scope, and length of these passages resemble those of the exercises Kate Wheeler recorded a few years earlier. But Crafts punctures the convention: "But I had no mother, no friend" (*TBN* 8). Aphoristic comfort breaks down in the face of the pain inflicted by the inhumane and cruel order of things common to "the peculiar institution."[xiv]

Crafts's genius for reworking literary influences extended beyond those college composition exercises. She also appears to have remade important elements of racist minstrel theater. John Hill Wheeler's diaries show that he and Mrs. Wheeler frequently attended minstrel shows during the same period Crafts served the family. In these shows, white actors in blackface lampooned enslaved men and women through caricature, musical performances, and variety acts. The typical program included popular songs like "Dixie" and skits and jokes whose humor hinged on the stereotypically inferior intellectual abilities and immorality of southern Black people, and commonly featured the wildly popular minstrel figures "Jim Crow" and "Zip Coon." Such shows, rife with racist caricature and ridicule, which Crafts may have even witnessed from the segregated balcony, comprised farce and physical humor, climaxing in a parody of the cakewalk called a "walk-around," in which each actor in blackface thrilled the audience with his specialty while troupe members clapped in unison to the accompanying songs.[xv]

Even though most blackface performers and composers had little to no direct experience with either the South or slavery, blackface minstrelsy centered simultaneously on a romantic portrayal of life on southern plantations as well as a perniciously distorted one, valorizing slavery at the expense of the humanity, and complexity, of the enslaved. Sometimes minstrel shows incorporated characters from popular literature. For instance, John Hill Wheeler appears to have been fond of Frank Bower, a lead performer in the traveling Sanford's Minstrels, based in Philadelphia. Wheeler's diaries show him attending Bower's performance in Philadelphia in 1856 and in Washington, D.C., in 1857. Significantly, Bower's specialty was his "Happy Uncle Tom," a parodic song-and-dance routine widely celebrated in its day. The troupe's director, Frank Sanford, wrote the piece and sold scripts of "Sanford's Southern Version of Uncle Tom" to other minstrel troupes. Its surviving images and lyrics reveal demeaning caricatures that reduced African Americans to childlike figures content with their enslavement, a common trope in both popular and scientific discourse at the time.

"Sanford's Southern Version of Uncle Tom" is largely lost to us, but one short scene was preserved and published in the *Daily Delta* of New Orleans (February 16 and 17, 1854). The setup for the minstrel identifies "Harriet Screecher Blow" as the author and then opens with a "Canadian snow scene" where, "amid old pines bending under waves of snow and glittering ice, the [Negro] fugitives long to get home." A group of white people in blackface portray fugitives from *Uncle Tom's Cabin*, singing, "Carry me back to Old Virginny, / To Old Virginny's Shore." A more detailed passage is copied in the paper, apparently original to Sanford's script:

> (Scene: Uncle Tom, shivering and forlorn amid the inclemencies of a Canadian winter. A Philanthropist approaches.)
>
> **Phi.:** Well, Uncle Tom, you seem to be in trouble. What do you want?
> **Uncle Tom:** Donno, Massa.
> **Phi.:** Do you want a house?
> **Uncle Tom:** No, Massa.
> **Phi:** Do you want clothes?
> **Uncle Tom:** No, Massa.
> **Phi:** Well, what do you want?
>
> *(In the distance, the strains of "Old Folks at Home" are indistinctly heard, and* **Uncle Tom,** *listening with tears in his eyes, breaks out, saying):* "Massa—that's what I want!"[xvi]

"This point in the drama," the reviewer in the *Daily Delta* commented, "...brought tears to the eyes of about every one [sic] present, in the same manner as other points produced irresistible laughter." Further, this scene, he said, was "quite melodramatic and also exceedingly correct."[xvii]

During those appalling performances, it would be surprising if Crafts failed to ask herself what a minstrel show would look like if the satire were reversed and focused instead on the mocking of white people. This is precisely what she did in her chapter "A Turn of the Wheel," a clever play on both her enslavers' surname and on the chorus of the astonishingly popular white minstrel performer T. D. Rice's song sensation "Jump Jim Crow," which caught fire in the early 1830s: "Weel about and turn about and do jis' so / Eb'ry time I

Introduction   xxix

weel about I jump Jim Crow." As Hannah observes after unwittingly blackening Mrs. Wheeler's face, "I had never seen her look better" (*TBN* 170). In the novel, Mrs. Wheeler's minstrel performance is a surprise, especially to herself, as the reader will see.[xviii]

The blackface scene in chapter 13 of *The Bondwoman's Narrative* is only the most dramatic example of Crafts's ingeniously signifying on, and self-consciously echoing, familiar literary texts in fascinating acts of interracial intertextuality.

As Hollis Robbins first noted, Crafts makes expansive use of Charles Dickens's *Bleak House* (1852–53). While Crafts served the college women boarding at Wheeler House during her enslavement there between 1852 and 1856, one of the key texts they studied was this extraordinarily popular novel, which, as Robbins and Gates noted, Frederick Douglass serialized in his newspaper, *Frederick Douglass' Paper*. Like the college composition exercises and minstrel performances she reimagined, Crafts also formally revised what must have been a closely read, treasured copy of *Bleak House,* perhaps acquired from a student boarder.

Crafts's narrator, Hannah, begins by introducing herself modestly: "It may be that I assume to[o] much responsibility in attempting to write these pages. The world will probably say so, and I am aware of my deficiencies. I am neither clever, nor learned, nor talented." Yet for one in her condition, Hannah maintains surprising optimism: "The life of a slave at best is not a pleasant one, but I had formed a resolution to always look on the bright side of things, to be industrious, cheerful, and true-hearted, to do some good though in an humble way, and to win some love if I could" (*TBN* 11). The narrative voice is compelling on its own, but it also displays a different kind of repetition and revision.[xix]

Here Crafts draws directly from the words of Esther Summerson, who introduces herself at the beginning of chapter 3 of *Bleak House*: "I have a great deal of difficulty in beginning to write my portion of these pages, for I know I am not clever. I always knew that." Hannah is writing herself out of Esther Summerson's monologue: "I often thought of the resolution I had made on my birthday to try to be industrious, contented, and true-hearted and to do some good to some one and win some love if I could."[xx]

If Hannah's fictional persona in Crafts's text owes its genealogy to Dickens and his character Esther Summerson, it is because for some reason Crafts identified with and admired Esther's temperament and sensibility, as well as Dickens's mastery of his craft and style of writing. Esther Summerson appears to have served as a model for Crafts as Crafts established her voice as an author, and she passed on those qualities to her protagonist, Hannah. In short, Crafts discovered in the figure of Esther both an anchor, a guidepost, for her authorship as well as a model for her own autobiographical protagonist—if not quite a doppelgänger, then at least a source for her to channel. Esther and Hannah's similarities are compelling. Both are orphans; both find their births to be stigmatized by sexual transgressions whose details are withheld from them. For Esther, her mother, Lady Dedlock, conceives her out of wedlock with a mysterious figure called Nemo (Latin for "nobody"). Meanwhile, for the autobiographical Hannah, she is separated from her mother early in life, and her white father is never identified. Hannah Crafts, the reader, found imaginative fellowship with Dickens's Esther Summerson, so much so, in fact, that she, the writer, then adopted part of Esther's narrative into her story.[xxi]

As perhaps one of the few books, if not the only one, the author possessed while she was enslaved, given the care with which she transposed its passages, *Bleak House* and Esther Summerson became important imaginative companions for Hannah Crafts, "inter-texts," as it were. They were imaginative maps that guided the fledgling author's foray into fiction. Crafts may even have modeled parts of her personal behavior on Summerson's—or at least her autobiographical heroine does. Like Esther in Dickens's novel, Crafts's Hannah is deeply religious, and her faith sustains her. Hannah and Esther are fastidious about comportment; both are modest and kind to others, even as they struggle to live generously in a world hostile to their presence.[xxii]

Crafts's lack of citation when she threads other narratives into her autobiographical story resembles a nineteenth-century literary practice that can confuse contemporary readers taught to be hypervigilant about noting sources. Like William Wells Brown, Kate Wheeler, and any number of American writers at the time, Crafts wove contemporary sources into her narrative without direct attribution because in her day that was acceptable literary practice.

Not only is a kind of literary genealogy traceable in Crafts's text, but even the reason for her escape and the route she took to freedom are recoverable through hints in her novel and fragments of the historical record. Beginning in 1856, Hannah Crafts was forced to serve in the household of John Hill Wheeler in Washington, D.C. Here she found community with other worshippers at the First Colored Baptist Church, an all-Black congregation near her enslaver's home. The church was an active organizing hub for an important Underground Railroad network, where Crafts would find allies as her efforts to find her written voice slowly developed.[xxiii]

During the year Crafts spent in the Wheelers' D.C. home, Wheeler, when he was not seeking employment through his connections, regularly sat in his study writing a manuscript, *The History of Nicaragua*. Ironically, it seems to be partly from the large stock of paper Wheeler bought to use for his Nicaragua history/

memoir that Crafts lifted some on which to write her novel. On paper resourcefully purloined from his library, Wheeler's racism, made patently clear in his own writing, would also be on full display in Crafts's manuscript.[xxiv]

In March 1857, Crafts journeyed with the family by steamboat, train, and carriage to Wheeler House in Murfreesboro, North Carolina. The family's two-month stay there can be sketched from the abbreviated notes Wheeler kept in his diary for the duration of the visit. The Wheelers moved among relatives and family properties including Wheeler House, Liberty Hall, and Maple Lawn. They also visited Willow Hall, the site of the author's childhood and the model for Lindendale in the novel. The sojourn lasted from Sunday, March 22, to Tuesday, May 5, when Mr. and Mrs. Wheeler returned to Washington, D.C.

While the family was in North Carolina, Wheeler traveled to Lincolnton to collect money owed to him from the sale of Ellangowan, his plantation near Charlotte. He was absent from the family from April 9 to April 30. In May 1857, Crafts was demoted from her role as lady's maid and sent to live in the family's slave huts in North Carolina, where she was forcibly exposed to a field hand, intentionally to be raped, as punishment for insolence. The author did not return with the Wheelers to Washington at the end of their stay in early May. Instead, Crafts was left at the family's Liberty Hall plantation outside Murfreesboro.[xxv] As John Hill Wheeler's account book shows, upon their return to the District in May 1857, the Wheelers immediately hired two Irish servants to take Crafts's place. The only other time the family hired white servants was following the ingenious and subsequently well-publicized escape in 1855 of the enslaved Jane Johnson. Jane's replacement, the doomed Irish servant Margaret Benn, brought on to join them in Nicaragua, died of cholera shortly after disembarking in the city of Granada.[xxvi]

As they were for Hannah in the novel, these events seem

Introduction xxxiii

to have been decisive in Crafts's determination to escape. "[C]ondemned to receive one of [the field hands] for my husband my soul actually revolted with horror unspeakable" (*TBN* 211). In Hannah's voice, Crafts goes on to say that "to be driven in to the fields beneath the eye and lash of the brutal overseer, and those miserable huts, with their promiscuous crowds of dirty, obscene and degraded objects, for my home I could not, I would not bear it" (*TBN* 213).[xxvii] It was this scene that first convinced Gates of the novel's authenticity, because of the explicit honesty, the bluntly "politically incorrect" (to be anachronistic) frankness of these observations. In contrast, no similar scene describing the sensory nature of enslavement—the way slavery "smelled," to take just one example—appears in any writings by white abolitionists.[xxviii] Nor was there anything even close, in the heavily regulated publishing industry in which the genre of the slave narratives unfolded, in those texts by fugitive slaves. Only someone outside of the abolitionist circle's editorial strictures would have dared to include such explicitly unfavorable descriptions in the first and final version of her text. The abolitionists' charge was to be "real," to be "true to nature"—but not this real.

The author fled from the Wheeler plantation near Murfreesboro in May 1857. John Hill Wheeler's account books and diaries, as well as private papers left behind by a nephew, corroborate this. Crafts's time in Washington, D.C., in 1856 and 1857 had brought her into contact with the Underground Railroad operators Paul and Desdemona Jennings as well as others familiar with the fugitive network organized by parishioners at the First Colored Baptist Church. Like Jane Johnson before her, Crafts enlisted the parishioners' help, seeking refuge upon her escape. Her D.C. contacts directed Crafts—still called Hannah Bond at the time—to

New York Central College in McGrawville (now called McGraw). Her route to freedom passed from the Wheeler plantation near Murfreesboro to Washington, D.C., and then to Craft Farm near McGrawville, likely via the agency of the Jenningses' longtime collaborator William L. Chaplin, who lived near the central New York town. The evidence is circumstantial, but the record strongly supports this assumption.[xxix]

Crafts's first opportunity to edit her work substantially seems to have occurred after she found safe shelter with Horace Craft and his family in August 1857 in rural Cortland County, New York, just north of McGrawville, over two hundred miles from New York City and thirty-five miles south of Syracuse. She carried with her the draft of the manuscript that she had started writing in slavery. At the time, the Craft family consisted of Horace (age forty-five), Harriet (forty-two), James (twelve), Mary (eight), and Alice (four). Tax records reveal the modest nature of the Crafts' property: twenty acres of farmable land and an additional thirty acres of "unimproved" property. Even the wooded acreage was a source of income. In addition, the family harvested substantial quantities of syrup each year from the black and red maple trees on the land. Harriet possibly directed these operations with the help of the children. Among this mostly self-sufficient Quaker family, the fugitive Hannah Bond seems to have found a home as she waited out the efforts of the Wheeler search party.[xxx]

It remains unclear precisely how long the author stayed at the Crafts' farmhouse—for the sake of safety, she appears to have prolonged her stay from late summer to early fall as she arranged a new destination[xxxi]—but her time there must have been consequential and meaningful. Her choice to assume the Craft surname suggests an intimacy forged between the author and the family during her stay. It is likely that the author felt secure on this remote property, concealed from even the most intrepid slave catcher. There was little chance that a willing informer would even know about the insular Craft Farm miles outside McGrawville. And the handful of faculty, staff, or students who encountered the author at New York Central College, a famously abolitionist institution "founded on the principle that all qualified students were welcome," could be trusted not to divulge her presence in the area.

From his diary records, we know that John Hill Wheeler, now ill, had given up his search for Crafts by August 31, returning to Washington, D.C. empty-handed.[xxxii] Safe at last from the Wheelers, Crafts specifically renounced the paternity and possession of the name Bond. Instead, like her fellow fugitive author William Wells Brown, she adopted the patronym of the family now sheltering her: the Craft family. She embraced "Crafts" as her nom de guerre and nom de plume, taking the plural form possibly because she wanted to honor both Horace and Harriet, who risked punishment by shielding her on their twenty-acre holding.

Then she went further. Now out of her captors' reach, the author specifically identified the Wheelers by name in her novel, returning to the manuscript to fill in the missing letters of their surname. With these changes, Crafts realized and declared her liberty, defying at once the will of her pursuers and the laws of a country that had defined her as property from birth.

And what became of Hannah Crafts after her escape to freedom? Her journey led her first to the all-Black town of Timbuctoo in New Jersey, just as she states in her novel, and then on to Burlington, New Jersey. She provides no specific details beyond the hint that her autobiographical protagonist, Hannah, took "refuge among the colored inhabitants of New Jersey." Again, the details in the narrative of Hannah's life seem to merge with Crafts's here. At this point, Crafts was a fugitive, seeking to avoid notice and trying to turn the page on a life stolen by slavery. In many ways, by completing *The Bondwoman's Narrative*, the author was closing the book on her experiences in enslavement. Her life in New Jersey as a free woman would be a new chapter.

How do we know that Hannah Crafts left central New York for New Jersey? She reveals as much in her autobiographical narrative. In Crafts's novel, a real couple named Thomas and Hannah Vincent match the description of characters in Crafts's autobiographical narrative and seem to offer a glimpse into the author's life after freedom, as Gates had speculated when he published the novel's first edition. Thomas Vincent (1822–1883) and Hannah Vincent (1826–1905/10?) are noted in census records, residing in Timbuctoo in 1857 and 1858 and then in Philadelphia briefly, in 1860, before returning to live permanently in Burlington.[xxxiii] Remarkably, a couple fitting this description is also recorded in Joseph H. Morgan's *Morgan's History of the New Jersey Conference of the A.M.E. Church, from 1872 to 1887* (1887), with Hannah Vincent noted as a "Stewardess" and "Sunday-School Treasurer" and "Teacher," similar to Crafts's Hannah, who "keep[s] a school for colored children" in an unnamed, all-Black town in New Jersey (*TBN* 244).[xxxiv]

Available evidence paints a picture that even more closely pairs the actual Hannah Vincent with the author. The African Union School was unique as the only all-Black institution chartered by the AME Church in New Jersey to teach the children of Black parents in the region. As Crafts writes in the novel, "[I] keep a school for colored children." She continues, "It is well attended, and I enjoy myself almost as well imparting knowledge to others, as I did in obtaining it when a child myself" (*TBN* 244). If the author did escape slavery and become a teacher at an all-Black school in New Jersey, it must have been at this singular African Union School seven miles away near the larger town of Burlington.[xxxv]

If Crafts's intimate glimpse of "another companion quite as

Introduction

dear—a fond and affectionate husband"—is based on her union with Thomas, which seems very likely, then circumstantial evidence suggests Crafts completed her novel within a year of her escape in 1857. The dating of the paper and ink for the closing chapters of her narrative suggests that the manuscript was completed in 1858, when Crafts bound the work with thread and marked "farewell" on the last page. Pen, ink, and paper forensics match the textual evidence of Crafts's narrative, pointing to a wedding date for Thomas Vincent and Hannah Crafts before December of that year, suggesting that the marriage occurred before the work's completion. Her marriage to Thomas Vincent, then, must have taken place in 1858, almost certainly at Bethlehem AME, the Reverend Vincent's home parish. Bethlehem AME and the close-knit African American community there would come to anchor Thomas and Hannah Vincent for the balance of their lives.

Although her condition in bondage at the time of writing distinguished her from other writers, Crafts wrote her novel for the same reason many people write novels and read them: she yearned to transcend her world by living imaginatively and intimately within a story she could form. In many significant ways, the reimagined journey to freedom she portrays in *The Bondwoman's Narrative* helped her realize the life she came to possess. The Thomas Bond Jr. who forced sex on the young author was superseded by another man named Thomas, a man who proved worthy as a husband, who recognized and valued Crafts's personhood.

Wondrously, the author found her faith rewarded in the same way that she imagined for her characters. The bond Crafts seems to have formed with her stepson, Samuel Vincent, must have been strong. Even after the death of her husband, Thomas, in 1883, Samuel continued to live in the same household with Hannah

Vincent. If Hannah Vincent lived out her life as did the heroine, Hannah Crafts, the author grew old not only content in an apparently loving relationship with her husband, but also with the support and care of an adoptive son. Bereft for most of her life of family ties, including the infant she lost in slavery, the author seems to imagine and then forge the loving family she always sought.

Why Crafts never published her work has always been a mystery. After all, it is written in an episodic and exciting fashion so well wrought that, even 150 years later, when it was published in 2002, it became a *New York Times* bestseller. Crafts may have kept her work private for any number of reasons, but the simplest might be that she felt no need to share her efforts beyond friends and family because she did not need the money. She may well have written the book with an audience in mind when she started it, but by the time it was completed, she appears to have felt comfortable keeping it to herself and to those she invited to read it. Indeed, she certainly had little to gain in drawing attention to herself before 1865, and after the war or for the rest of her lifetime, her exposé of white male predation of enslaved Black females did not hold promising prospects as a publishing venture. As William L. Andrews, a leading scholar of African American autobiography, has noted, only four narratives by formerly enslaved women appeared in print between 1866 and 1880, and of these, only one was written by the author herself: Elizabeth Keckley's *Behind the Scenes: Or, Thirty Years a Slave, and Four Years in the White House*, in 1868. Roundly criticized in the press as unseemly, the work sold poorly.[xxxvi] Conversely, during the same period, twenty-four men published ex-slave narratives that enjoyed enormous popularity.

Still, one can easily imagine Crafts reading her own work to her husband. Indeed, she writes such a scene into the novel ("...there, there my dear. I fear you grow prosy...," she has him say). Her beloved stepson also probably read the work, a safe opportunity for Crafts to share her experiences of slavery without the mental trauma of relating her sexual abuse or details about the infant she lost before her new life in New Jersey. Even if she had decided to seek publication as Hannah Vincent, Crafts, as an ordinary woman with no access to the means of production, faced steep odds. The short window that would have been available to her to market her book after the Civil War closed to most Black writers with the rapid rise and fall of Reconstruction, between 1866 and 1877, at least for works marketed to both Black and white audiences. A surge in the publication of Black creative literature, especially works by Black women authors, wouldn't occur again until the 1890s, named by Black feminists at the time the "Woman's Era."

Shortly before her death sometime in the first decade of the twentieth century, perhaps Crafts had the opportunity to open the pages of the manuscript she had stitched together so many years earlier, to reflect on her long life in bondage and beyond. If she did so, she would have encountered her preface, where she writes, "[P]ious and discerning minds can scarcely fail to recognise the hand of Providence in giving to the righteous the reward of their works, and to the wicked the fruit of their doings." As Hannah Vincent surely realized, and as her life made clear, only the inspired love of humans for other human beings can ensure salvation; only by those means can God deliver "to the righteous the reward of their works, and to the wicked the fruit of their doings." Her life and her novel are a testament to this deep faith.[xxxvii]

And what of her title, *The "Bondwoman's" Narrative*? Before she escaped the Wheeler House shortly after her thirtieth birthday, still under the name Hannah Bond, she was no doubt frequently called, in the manner common to plantation slavery, either "the Bond woman" or "the Bonds' woman."[xxxviii] All along, then, the title of her book was a clever pun, a veiled clue to her hidden identity left in plain view for a century and a half for any of her potential pursuers to see, one more sign of her authorial ingenuity and one more example of her subtle wit and sense of humor. Hannah Crafts's life and work, lost for so long, have now been found, brought to light for a new generation of readers.

Henry Louis Gates Jr. and Gregg Hecimovich

Notes

i. Dorothy Porter Wesley Papers, James Weldon Johnson Memorial Collection in the Yale Collection of American Literature, Beinecke Rare Book and Manuscript Library, Box 22.

ii. Gregg Hecimovich, *The Life and Times of Hannah Crafts: The True Story of The Bondwoman's Narrative* (New York: Ecco, 2023), 2–5.

iii. Also indispensable was the work of skeptics including Nina Baym, Thomas Parramore, and R. J. Ellis. Their chief argument maintained that no antebellum slave "recently escaped from North Carolina" could have possessed the literary skill to write a novel so notable for its studied allusiveness. Their skepticism helped guide the path to identifying the author. Nina Baym, "The Case for Hannah Vincent," in *In Search of Hannah Crafts: Critical Essays on The Bondwoman's Narrative*, ed. Henry Louis Gates Jr. and Hollis Robbins (New York: BasicCivitas, 2004), 321.

iv. Thomas Pugh, last will and testament, dated August 1806, proved November 1806, North Carolina, Bertie County, Will Book F/26 (CR 5200.10.1346): 16–31; Bertie County Estate Records, Box 9 (Martha Bond, Catherine Turner, and Thomas Bond Sr. folders) and Box 81 (Catherine Bond, Colonel Thomas Bond, and Lewis Bond folders) (CR 010.508), North Carolina State Archives, Raleigh, N.C.; Pugh Family Genealogical Records, E. W. Pugh Papers, 1855–1899, Private Collection 1631, North Carolina State Archives, Raleigh, N.C. This constellation of records is primary in establishing the identity of Hannah Bond and her family members and their ties to the Pughs and Bonds of Indian Woods, North Carolina. We also used family trees and genealogical documents provided to us by Mack and Clara Bell of Windsor, North Carolina.

v. Hecimovich, *Life and Times*, 23–29, 106–10.

vi. Hecimovich, *Life and Times*, 53–59. As the scholar Teresa A. Goddu has noted, the gothic genre is not a pathway to escapist fiction but rather "a primary means for speaking the unspeakable in American literature." See *Gothic America: Narrative, History, and Nation* (New York: Columbia University Press, 1997).

vii. Bertie County Estate Records, Box 9 (Martha Bond, Catherine Turner, and Thomas Bond Sr. folders) and Box 81 (Catherine Bond, Colonel Thomas Bond, and Lewis Bond folders) (CR 010.508), North Carolina State Archives, Raleigh, N.C.; Hecimovich, *Life and Times*, 137.

viii. Hecimovich, *Life and Times*, 125-36.

ix. Correspondence in the Kate Wheeler Cooper Papers housed at East Carolina University helps to demonstrate the point. In a letter dated June 27, 1861, Samuel Jordan Wheeler notes that Moses has received Kate's letter: "I read the letter that you [Kate] wrote to him [Moses], in which you charge him to take good care of his master." Samuel Jordan Wheeler to Catherine Wheeler, June 27, 1861, Folder D, Box 1, Kate Wheeler Cooper Papers, J. Y. Joyner Library, East Carolina University (hereafter cited as Kate Wheeler Cooper Papers MSS). The fact that the Wheeler children were corresponding by letter with one of their slaves suggests an acceptance and encouragement of literacy very different from the legal tradition and conventional wisdom.

x. As Moore studied law and other subjects, he taught these subjects to Harvey. Indeed, after the Civil War, Moore suggested that Harvey move north to try his own career at law, which he did, setting up a successful practice in Philadelphia. The John Wheeler Moore Papers collected at the Southern Historical Collection at the University of North Carolina–Chapel Hill detail this unique literary friendship. See in particular Folders 1 and 31. Also see Sally Moore Koestler's Elizabeth Jones of Maple Lawn, Pitch Landing, Hertford Co., North Carolina, Hertford County Public Library, Winton, N.C., 15.

xi. In a letter dated July 20, 1860, a friend of Julia Wheeler observes of Julia's body servant, "By the way, who is that attaché of yours who is so kind as to direct your letters +c? He must be very convenient—I'd like very much to have an amanuensis, particularly if he wrote such a pretty hand as yours does." Fonte Bella Hooper to Julia Wheeler, July 20, 1860, Folder C, Box 1, Kate Wheeler Cooper Papers MSS.

xii. Hecimovich, *Life and Times*, 10-11.

xiii. Box 2 ("School Records" folder), Kate Wheeler Cooper Papers MSS.

xiv. Hecimovich, Life and Times, 143-44.

xv. See William J. Mahar, *Behind the Burnt Cork Mask: Early Blackface Minstrelsy and Antebellum American Popular Culture* (Urbana: University of Illinois Press, 1998).

xvi. Daily Delta (New Orleans), February 15, 1854, 3. See also Joseph P. Roppolo, "Uncle Tom in New Orleans: Three Lost Plays," *New England Quarterly* 27, no. 2 (June 1954): 213-26.

xvii. *Daily Delta* (New Orleans), February 17, 1854, 5.

xviii. Hecimovich, *Life and Times*, 232–36.

xix. Hollis Robbins, "Blackening *Bleak House*: Hannah Crafts's *The Bondwoman's Narrative*," in *In Search of Hannah Crafts*, 75.

xx. Robbins, "Blackening *Bleak House*," 75.

xxi. Robbins, "Blackening *Bleak House*," 75–76.

xxii. Robbins, "Blackening *Bleak House*," 76. See Gates's "A Note on Crafts's Literary Influences," 373–74 of this volume, for further passages of Dickens that the author remade in her own image. Also see Hecimovich, *Life and Times*, xv–xvi, 141–43, 149–50, 229–30, 236–39, 241–52, and 344–45.

xxiii. Hecimovich, *Life and Times*, 209–10, 216–18, 265–66, and 306–15.

xxiv. "History of Nicaragua MS," Box 21, John Hill Wheeler MSS. Also see Parramore, "Keystone Konquistadores," 14. Hecimovich, *Life and Times*, 309–11.

xxv. Box 1, John Hill Wheeler MSS.

xxvi. Hecimovich, *Life and Times*, 268.

xxvii. Hecimovich, *Life and Times*, 316–19.

xxviii. Crafts reworks a passage from Charles Dickens's novel *Bleak House* in describing the Wheeler family's slave huts. She embroiders on Dickens's depiction of London slum dwellings to emphasize the terrible odor of slavery in the slave quarters. Dickens writes:

> Now, these tumbling tenements contain, by night, a swarm of misery. As, on the ruined human wretch, vermin parasites appear, so, these ruined shelters have bred a crowd of foul existence that crawls in and out of gaps in walls and boards; and coils itself to sleep, in maggot numbers, where the rain drips in; and comes and goes, fetching and carrying fever. (BH chap. 16)

Crafts reworks the passage thus:

> There was not that division of families I had been accustomed to see, but they all lived promiscuously anyhow and every how; at least they did not die, which was a wonder. Is it a stretch of imagination to say that by night they contained a swarm of misery, that crowds of foul existence crawled in out of gaps in walls and boards, or coiled themselves to sleep on nauseous heaps of straw fetid with human

perspiration and where the rain drips in, and the damp airs of midnight fatch [fetch] and carry malignant fevers. (TBN 204–5)

Note that Crafts does not echo Dickens's depiction of "maggot numbers," but instead humanizes the slave huts by emphasizing "human perspiration."

 xxix. Hecimovich, *Life and Times*, 254–60, 315–25, 328–30.

 xxx. New York State Census 1855, Selected U.S. Federal Census Non-Population Schedules, 1850–1880, Census Year 1860, Taylor, N.Y., Cortland County.

 xxxi. Hecimovich, *Life and Times*, 322–24.

 xxxii. Box 1, John Hill Wheeler MSS.

 xxxiii. 1860 United States Federal Census, Ward 10 East District, Philadelphia, Pa., NARA; 1870 United States Federal Census, 2nd Ward, Burlington, New Jersey, NARA; *Burlington County Directory for 1876–77 Containing the Names of the Inhabitants of Bordentown, Burlington and Mount Holly, Together with a Business Directory of Burlington County and Much Useful Miscellaneous Information* (Burlington, NJ: James Shaw, 1876), 141; 1880 United States Federal Census, 2nd Ward, Burlington, New Jersey, NARA; 1885 New Jersey State Census, 2nd Ward, Burlington, New Jersey, New Jersey State Archives, Trenton; 1895 New Jersey State Census 2nd Ward, Burlington, New Jersey, New Jersey State Archives, Trenton; *Boyd's Directory of Burlington County New Jersey, 1905–1906* (Philadelphia: C. E. Howe, 1905), 146.

 xxxiv. Joseph H. Morgan, Morgan's History of the New Jersey Conference of the A.M.E. Church, from 1872 to 1887 (Camden, NJ: S. Chew, 1887), 65.

 xxxv. Hecimovich, *Life and Times*, 325–28.

 xxxvi. William L. Andrews, email to author, September 24, 2022.

 xxxvii. Hecimovich, *Life and Times*, 337–42.

 xxxviii. Henry Louis Gates Jr. preface, *Life and Times*, xvii.

A Note on Punctuation and Spelling

Throughout the text, every effort was made to print the novel as it appeared in the original holograph. Hannah Crafts's spelling has been retained, though, on occasion, a bracketed insertion has been added to aid readability (e.g., "to[o]"); the use of [sic] has been restricted to syntactical matters.

Periods at the end of sentences have been inserted globally; question marks after interrogatory sentences appear only where Hannah Crafts put them; crossed-out words indicate Crafts's own revisions. Bracketed quotation marks have been added around dialogue where their absence would impede the readability of the narrative.

The Bondwoman's Narrative

By Hannah Crafts

A Fugitive Slave Recently Escaped from North Carolina

Preface

In presenting this record of plain unvarnished facts to a generous public I feel a certain degree of diffidence and self-distrust. I ask myself for the hundredth time How will such a literary venture, coming from a sphere so humble be received? Have I succeeded in portraying any of the peculiar features of that institution whose curse rests over the fairest land the sun shines upon? Have I succeeded in showing how it blights the happiness of the white as well as the black race? Being the truth it makes no pretensions to romance, and relating events as they occurred it has no especial reference to a moral, but to those who regard truth as stranger than fiction it can be no less interesting on the former account, while others of pious and discerning minds can scarcely fail to recognise the hand of Providence in giving to the righteous the reward of their works, and to the wicked the fruit of their doings.

CHAPTER 1

In Childhood

Look not upon me because I am black; because the sun hath looked upon me.
SONG OF SOLOMON

It may be that I assume to[o] much responsibility in attempting to write these pages. The world will probably say so, and I am aware of my deficiencies. I am neither clever, nor learned, nor talented. When a child they used to scold and find fault with me because they said I was dull and stupid. Perhaps under other circumstances and with more encouragement I might have appeared better; for I was shy and reserved and scarce dared open my lips to any one I had none of that quickness and animation which are so much admired in children, but rather a silent unobtrusive way of observing things and events, and wishing to understand them better than I could.

I was not brought up by any body in particular that I know of. I had no training, no cultivation. The birds of the air, or beasts of the feild are not freer from moral culture than I was. No one seemed to care for me till I was able to work, and then it was Hannah do this and Hannah do that, but I never complained as I found a sort of pleasure and something to divert my thoughts in employment. Of my relatives I knew nothing. No one ever spoke of my father or mother, but I soon learned what a curse was attached to my race, soon learned that the African blood in my veins would forever exclude me from the higher walks of life. That toil unremitted unpaid toil must be my lot and portion, without even the hope or expectation of any thing better. This seemed the harder to be borne, because my complexion was almost white, and the obnoxious descent could not be readily traced, though it gave a rotundity to my person, a wave and curl to my hair, and perhaps led me to fancy pictorial illustrations and flaming colors.

The busiest life has its leisure moments; it was so with mine. I had from the first an instinctive desire for knowledge and the means of mental improvement. Though neglected and a slave, I felt the immortal longings in me. In the absence of books and teachers and schools I determined to learn if not in a regular, approved, and scientific way. I was aware that this plan would meet with opposition, perhaps with punishment. My master never permitted his slaves to be taught. Education in his view tended to enlarge and expand their ideas; made them less subservient to their superiors, and besides that its blessings were destined to be conferred exclusively on the higher and nobler race. Indeed though he was generally easy and good-tempered, there was nothing liberal or democratic in his nature. Slaves were slaves to him, and nothing more. Practically he regarded them not as men and women, but in the same light as horses or other domestic animals. He ~~furnished~~ supplied their necessities of food and clothing from ~~the same~~ motives of policy, but [di]scounted the ideas of equality and fraternity as preposterous and absurd. Of course I had nothing to expect from him, yet "where there's a will there's a way."

I was employed about the house, consequently my labors were much easier than those of the field servants, and I enjoyed intervals of repose and rest unknown to them. Then, too, I was a mere child and some hours of each day were allotted to play. On such occasions, and while the other children of the house were amusing themselves I would quietly steal away from their company to ponder over the pages of some old book or newspaper that chance had thrown in {my} way. Though I knew not the meaning of a single letter, and had not the means of finding out I loved to look at them and think that some day I should probably understand them all.

My dream was destined to be realized. One day while ~~I was~~ sitting on a little bank, beneath the shade of some large trees, at a short distance from my playmates, ~~when~~ an aged woman approached me. She was white, and looked venerable with her grey hair smoothly put back beneath a plain sun bonnet, and I recollected having seen her once or twice at my master's house whither she came to sell salves and ointments, and hearing it remarked that she was the wife of a sand-digger and very poor.

She smiled benevolently and inquired why I concealed my book, and with child-like artlessness I told her all. How earnestly I desired knowledge, how our Master interdicted it, and how I was trying to teach myself. She stood for a few moments apparently buried in deep thought, but I interpreted her looks and actions favorably, and an idea struck me that perhaps she could read, and would become my teacher. She seemed to understand my wish before I expressed it.

"Child" she said "I was thinking of our Saviour's words to Peter where he commands the latter to 'feed his lambs.' I will dispense to you such knowledge as I possess. Come to me each day. I will teach you to read in the hope and trust that you will thereby be made better in this world and that to come.["] Her demeanor like her words was very grave and solemn.

"Where do you live?["] I inquired.

"In the little cottage just around the foot of the hill" she replied.

"I will come: Oh how eagerly, how joyfully" I answered "but if master finds it out his anger will be terrible; and then I have no means of paying you."

She smiled quietly, bade me fear nothing, and went her way. I returned home that evening with a light heart. Pleased, delighted, overwhelmed with my good fortune in prospective I felt like a being to whom a new world with all its mysteries and marvels was opening, and could scarcely repress my tears of joy and thankfulness. It sometimes seems that we require sympathy more in joy than sorrow; for the heart exultant, and overflowing with good nature longs to impart a portion of its happiness. Especial[l]y is this the case with children. How it augments the importance of any little success to them that some one probably a mother will receive the intelligence with a show of delight and interest. But I had no mother, no friend.

The next day and the next I went out to gather blackberries, and took advantage of the fine opportunity to visit my worthy instructress and receive my first lesson. I was surprised at the smallness yet perfect neatness of her dwelling, at the quiet and orderly repose that reigned ~~in~~ through all its appointments; it was in such pleasing contrast to our great house with its bustle, confusion, and troops of servants of all ages and colors.

"Hannah, my dear, you are welcome" she said coming forward and extending her hand. "I rejoice to see you. I am, or rather was a northern woman, and consequently have no prejudices against your birth, or race, or condition, indeed I feel a warmer interest in your welfare than I should were you the daughter of a queen.["] I should have thanked her for so much kindness, and ~~interest~~ such expressions of motherly interest, but could find no words, and so sat silent and embarrassed.

I had heard of the North where the people were all free, and where the colored race had so many and such true friends, and was more delighted with her, and with the idea that I had found some of them than I could possibly have expressed in words.

At length while I was stumbling over the alphabet and trying to impress the different forms of the letters on my mind, an old man with a cane and silvered hair walked in, and coming close to me inquired "Is this the girl ~~mother~~ of whom you spoke, mother?" and when she answered in the affirmative he said many words of kindness and encouragement to me, and that though a slave I must be good and trust in God.

They were an aged couple, who for more than fifty years had occupied the same home, and who had shared together all the vicissitudes of life—its joys and sorrows, its hopes and fears. Wealth had been theirs, with all the appliances of luxury, and they became poor through a series of misfortunes. Yet as they had borne riches with virtuous moderation they conformed to poverty with subdued content, and readily exchanged the splendid mansion for the lowly cottage, and the merchant's desk and counting room for the fields of toil. Not that they were insensible to the benefits or advantages of riches, but they felt that life had something more—that the peace of God and their own consciences united to honor and intelligence were in themselves a fortune which the world neither gave nor could take away.

They had long before relinquished all selfish projects and ambitious aims. To be upright and honest, to incumber neither public nor private charity, and to contribute something to the happiness of others seemed to be the sum total of their present desires. Uncle Siah, as I learned to call him, had long been unable to work, except at some of the lighter branches of employment, or in cultivating the small garden which furnished their supply of exce[l]lent vegetables and likewise the simple herbs which imparted such healing properties to the salves and unguents that the kind old woman distributed around the neighborhood.

Educated at the north they both felt keenly on the subject of slavery and the degradation and ignorance it imposes on one portion of the human race. Yet all their conversation on this point was tempered with the utmost discretion and judgement, and though they could not be reconciled to the system they were disposed to stand still and wait in faith and hope for the salvation of the Lord.

In their morning and evening sacrifice of worship the poor slave was always remembered, and even their devout songs of praise were imbued with the same spirit. They loved to think and to speak of all mankind as brothers, the children of one great parent, and all bound to the same eternity.

Simple and retiring in their habits modest unostentatious and poor their virtues were almost wholly unknown. In that wearied and bent old man, who frequently went out in pleasant weather to sell baskets at the doors of the rich few recognised the possessor of sterling worth, and the candidate for immortality, yet his meek gentle smile, and loving words excited their sympathies and won their regard.

How I wished to be with them all the time—how I entreated them to buy me, but in vain. They had not the means.

It must not be supposed that learning to read was all they taught me, or that my visits to them were made with regularity. They gave me an insight to many things. They cultivated my moral nature. They led me to the foot of the Cross. Sometimes in the evening while the other slaves were enjoying the banjo and the dance I would steal away to hold sweet converse with them. Sometimes a morning walk with the other children, or an errand to a neighbors would furnish the desired opportunity, and sometimes an interval of many days elapsed between my calls to their house.

At such times, however, I tried to remember the good things they had taught me, and to improve myself by gathering up such crumbs of knowledge as I could, and adding little by little to my stock of information. Of course my opportunities were limited, and I had much to make me miserable and discontented. The life of a slave at best is not a pleasant one, but I had formed a resolution to always look on the bright side of things, to be industrious, cheerful, and true-hearted, to do some good though in an humble way, and to win some love if I could. "I am a slave" thus my thoughts would run. "I can never be great, nor rich; I cannot hold an elevated position in society, but I can do my duty, and be kind in the sure and certain hope of an eternal reward.["]

By and by as I grew older, and was enabled to manifest my good intentions, not so much by words, as a manner of sympathy and consideration for every one, I was quite astonished to see how much I was trusted and confided in, how I was made the repository of secrets, and how the weak, the sick, and the suffering came to me for advice and assistance. Then the little slave children were almost entirely confided to my care. I hope that I was good and gentle to them; for I pitied their hard and cruel fate very much, and used to think that, notwithstanding all the labor and trouble they gave me, if I could so discharge my duty by them that in after years their memories would hover over this as the sunshiny period of their lives I should be amply repaid.

What a blessing it is that faith, and hope, and love are universal in their nature and operation—that poor as well as rich, bond as well as free are susceptible to their pleasing influences, and contain within themselves a treasure of consolation for all the ills of life. These little children, slaves though they were, and doomed to a life of toil and drudgery, ignorant, and untutored, assimilated thus to the highest and proudest in the land—thus evinced their equal origin, and immortal destiny.

How much love and confidence and affection I won it is impossible to describe. How the rude and boisterous became gentle and obliging, and how ready ~~they~~ all were to serve and obey me, not because I exacted the service or obedience, but because their own loving natures prompted them to reciprocate my love. How I longed to become their teacher, and open the door of knowledge to their minds by instructing them to read but it might not be. I could not have even hoped to escape detection ~~would have~~ and discovery would have entailed punishment on all.

Thus the seasons passed away. Summer insensibly melted into autumn, and autumn gave place to winter. I still visited Aunt Hetty, and enjoyed the benefits of her gracious counsels. Seated by the clear wood fire she was always busy in the preparation or repair of garments as perfect taste and economy dictated, or plying her bright knitting needles by the evening lamp, while her aged companion sat socially by her side.

One evening I was sitting with them, and reading from the book of God. Our intercourse had remained so long undiscovered that I had almost ceased to fear disclosure. Probably I had grown less circumspect though not intentionally, or it might be that in conformity to the inscrutable ways of Providence the faith and strength of these aged servants of the Cross were to be tried by a more severe ordeal. Alas: Alas that I should have been the means.

The door suddenly opened without warning, and the overseer of my master's estate walked into the house. My horror, and grief, and astonishment were indescribable. I felt Oh how much more than I tell. He addressed me rudely, and bade me begone home on the instant. I durst not disobey, but retreating through the doorway I glanced back at the calm sedate countenances of the aged couple, who were all unmoved by the torrent of threats and invectives he poured out against them.

My Master was absent at the time, ~~over~~ the overseer could find no precedent for my case, and so I escaped the punishment I should otherwise have suffered. Not so with my venerable and venerated teachers. It was considered necessary to make an example of them, that others might be deterred from the like attempts. Years passed, however, before I learned their fate. The cruel overseer would not tell me whither he had removed them, but to all my inquiries he simply answered that he would take good care I never saw them again. My fancy painted them as immured in a dungeon for the crime of teaching a slave to read. Their cottage ~~of~~ home remained uninhabited for a time, and then strangers came and took possession of it. But Oh the difference to me. For days and weeks I was inconsolable, and how I hated and blamed myself as the cause of their misery. After a time the intensity of my feelings subsided, and I came to a more rational and consistent manner of thinking. I concluded that they were happy whatever might be their condition, and that only by doing right and being good I could make anything like an adequate return for all they had done and suffered for me.

Another year passed away. There was to be a change in our establishment, and the ancient mansion of Lindendale was to receive a mistress. Hitherto our master had been a bachelor. He was a portly man, middle-aged, and of aristocratic name and connexions. His estate had descended to him through many generations, and it was whispered though no one seemed to know, that he was bringing his beautiful bride to an impoverished house.

~~holidays and the time for warming fires to be kindled in the~~

~~dusty chimneys of southern chambers It was then that our master brought home his bride~~ The remembrance is fresh to me as that of yesterday. The holidays were passed, and we had been promised another in honor of the occasion. But we were not animated with the idea of that half so much as because something had occurred to break the dull monotony of our existence; something that would give life, and zest, and interest, to one day at least; and something that would afford a theme for conversation and speculation. Then our preparations were quite wonderful, and the old housekeeper nearly overdid herself in fidgetting and fretting and worrying while dragging her unwieldly weight of flesh up and down the staircases, along the galleries and passages, and through the rooms where floors were undergoing the process of being rubbed bright, carpets were being spread, curtains shaken out, beds puffed and covered ~~and~~ furniture dusted and polished, and all things prepared as beseemed the dignity of the family and the fastidious taste of its expected mistress. It was a grand time for me as now I had an opportunity of seeing the house, and ascertaining what a fine old place it was. Heretofore all except certain apartments had been interdicted to us, but now that the chambers were opened to be aired and renovated no one could prevent us making good use of our eyes. And we saw on all sides the appearance of wealth and splendor, and the appliances to every luxury. What a variety of beautiful rooms, all splendid yet so different, and seemingly inhabited by marble images of art, or human forms pictured on the walls. What an array of costly furniture adorned the rich saloons and gorgeous halls. We thought our master must be a very great man to have so much wealth at his command, but it never occurred to us to inquire whose sweat and blood and unpaid labor had contributed to produce it.

The evening previous to the expected arrival of the bridal party

Mrs Bry the housekeeper, announced the preparations to be complete and all things in readiness. Then she remembered that the windows of one apartment had been left open for a freer admission of air. ~~It must be closed~~ They must be closed and barred and the good old dame imposed that duty on me. "I am so excessively weary or I would attend to it myself" she said giving me my directions "but I think that I can rely on you not to touch or misplace anything or loiter in the rooms." I assured her that she could and departed on my errand.

There is something inexpressibly dreary and solemn in passing through the silent rooms of a large house, especially one whence many generations have passed to the grave. Involuntarily you find yourself thinking of them, and wondering how they looked in life, and how the rooms looked in their possession, and whether or not they would recognise their former habitations if restored once more to earth and them. Then all we have heard or fancied of spiritual existences occur to us. There is the echo of a stealthy tread behind us. There is a shadow flitting past through the gloom. There is a sound, but it does not seem of mortality. A supernatural thrill pervades your frame, and you feel the presence of mysterious beings. It may be foolish and childish, but it is one of the unaccountable things instinctive to the human nature.

Thus I felt while threading the long galleries which led to the southern turret. The apartment there was stately rather than splendid, and in other days before the northern and eastern wing had been added to the building it had formed the family drawing room, and was now from its retired situation the favorite resort of my master; when he became weary of noise and bustle and turmoil as he sometimes did. It was adorned with a long succession of family portraits ranged against the walls in due order of age and ancestral dignity. To these portraits Mrs Bry had informed me a strange legend was attached. It was said that Sir Clifford De Vincent, a nobleman of power and influence in the old world, having incurred the wrath of his sovereign, fled for safety to the shores of the Old Dominion, and became the founder of my Master's paternal estate. ~~When the~~ When the house had been completed according to his directions, he ordered his portrait and that of his wife to be hung in the drawing room, and denounced a severe malediction against the person who should ever presume to remove them, and against any possessor of the mansion who being of his name and blood should neglect to follow his example. And well had his wishes been obeyed. Generation had succeeded generation, and a long line of De Vincents occupied the family residence, yet each ~~one~~ inheritor had contributed to the adornments of the drawing-room a faithful transcript of his person and lineaments, side by side with that of his Lady. The ceremonial of hanging up these portraits was usually made the occasion of a great festivity, in which hundreds of the neighboring gentry participated. But my master had seen fit to dissent from this custom, and his portrait unaccompanied by that of a Lady had been added to the number, though without the usual demonstration of mirth and rejoicing.

Memories of the dead give at any time a haunting air to a silent room. How much more this becomes the case when standing face to face with their pictured resemblances and looking into the stony eyes motionless and void of expression as those of an exhumed corpse. But even as I gazed the golden light of sunset penetrating through the open windows in an oblique direction set each rigid feature in a glow. Movements like those of life came over the line of stolid faces as the shadows of a linden played there. The stern old sire with sword and armorial bearings seems moodily to relax his haughty ~~brow~~ aspect. The countenance of another, a veteran in the old-time wars, assumes a gracious expression it never wore in life; and another appears to open and shut his lips continually though they emit no sound. Over the pale pure features of a bride descends a halo of glory; the long shining locks of a young mother waver and float over the child she holds; and the frozen cheek of an ancient dame seems beguiled into smiles and dimples.

Involuntarily I gazed as the fire of the sun died out, even untill the floor became dusky, and the shadows of the linden falling broader and deeper wrapped all in gloom. Hitherto I had not contemplated my Master's picture; for my thoughts had been with the dead, but now I looked for it, where it hung solitary, and thought how soon it would have a companion like the others, and what a new aspect would thereby be given to the apartment. But was it prophecy, or presentiment, or why was it that this idea was attended to my mind with something painful? That it seemed the first scene in some fearful tragedy; the foreboding of some great calamity; a curse of destiny that no circumstances could avert or soften. And why was it that as I mused the portrait of my master ~~changed~~ seemed to change from its usually kind and placid expression to one of wrath and gloom, that the calm brow should become wrinkled with passion, the lips turgid with malevolence—yet thus it was.

Though filled with superstitious awe I was in no haste to leave the room; for there surrounded by mysterious associations I seemed suddenly to have grown old, to have entered a new world of thoughts, and feelings and sentiments. I was not a slave with these pictured memorials of the past. They could not enforce drudgery, or condemn me on account of my color to a life of servitude. As their companion I could think and speculate. In their presence my mind seemed to run riotous and exult in its freedom as a rational being, and one destined for something higher and better than this world can afford.

I closed the windows, for the night air had become sharp and piercing, and the linden creaked and swayed its branches to the fitful gusts. Then, there was a sharp voice at the door. It said "child what are you doing?["] I turned round and answered "Looking at the pictures."

Mrs Bry alarmed at my prolonged absence had actually dragged her unweildly person thither to acertain the cause.

"Looking at the pictures" she repeated "as if such an ignorant thing as you are would know any thing about them."

Ignorance, forsooth. Can ignorance quench the immortal mind or prevent its feeling at times the indications of its heavenly origin. Can it destroy that deep abiding appreciation of the beautiful that seems inherent to the human soul? Can it seal up the fountains of truth and all intuitive perception of life, death and eternity? I think not. Those to whom man ~~learns little nature~~ teaches little, nature like a wise and prudent mother teaches much.

CHAPTER 2

The Bride And The Bridal Company

When he speaks fair, believe him not; for there are severe abominations in his heart.

PROVERBS 26:25

The clouds are not apt to conform themselves to the wishes of man, yet once or twice in a life-time the rain falls exactly when we wish it would, and it ceases raining precisely at the right time. It was so at our place in Lindendale. The weather had been rainy for many days. Mrs Bry looked over her gold spectacles and through the windows where the rain-drops pattered incessantly and assured me that she had never known such a season since that very unfortunate year which witnessed the loss of her husband's India ship, and his consequent failure in business; a circumstance that broke his heart and reduced her to the extremity of accepting the situation of housekeeper. She hoped, however, that the weather would improve before the arrival of the bridal party, but had no expectation that it would. It was so apt to rain just when a clear sky was most wanted, and would be best appreciated. The servants were of the same opinion. Of course it would rain; it always did when they desired fair weather—their holidays had been spoiled by rain no one could tell how often. But it left off raining at last and Lindendale revived beneath the cheering influences of wind and sunshine. For the greater honor of the distinguished event, and the brilliant guests expected to grace the occasion with their presence the broken trillis-work of a bower was repaired, though a vine to adorn it was out of the question, the leaves were gathered from the garden-alleys where the wind had carried and left them, and the broken stalks of faded flowers removed from their beds as untimely and out of place. The clear cold sunshine glancing down the long avenue of elms saw nothing but moving shadows of the leafless branches, and heard nothing but the roaring wind as it passed among the trees.

What strange ways the wind has, and how particularly anxious it seemed to enter the drawing-room in the southern wing, rattling the shutters, and shrieking like a maniac, and then breathing out a low gurgling laugh like the voice of childhood.

But whether it laughed or shrieked the wind had something expressively ominous in its tone, and not only to me; for all observed it, and Mrs Bry said that it filled her with awe and dread, because it had just such a voice on the day during which her poor husband was shipwrecked. Then the linden lost its huge branches and swayed and creaked distractedly, and we all knew that was said to forbode calamity to the family. "It should not be so" said Mrs Bry, impressively. "It should not be so to[-]night when the morrow is to bring a mistress to Lindendale. Ah me: I fear—" but she left the sentence unfinished ~~and the wind blew and the linden creaked~~.

The servants all knew the history of that tree. It had not been concealed from them that a wild and weird influence was supposed to belong to it. Planted by Sir Clifford, it had grown and flourished exceedingly under his management. But the stern old man was a hard master to his slaves and few in our days could be so cruel, while the linden was chosen as the scene where the tortures and punishments were inflicted. Many a time had its roots been manured with human blood. Slaves had been tied to its trunk to be whipped or sometimes gibbeted on its branches. ~~the master belonging their agonies from the drawing room windows and doubtless enjoying the sigh On such occasions he would drink wine or coolly discuss politics with an acquaintance, pausing prob~~

On such occasions, Sir Clifford sitting at the windows of his drawing room, within the full sight and hearing of their agonies would drink wine, or coolly discuss the politics of the day with some acquaintance, pausing perhaps in the midst of a sentence to give directions to the executioner, or order some mitigation of the torture only to prolong it.

But his direst act of cruelty, and the one of a nature to fill the soul with the deepest horror was perpetrated on the person of an old woman, who had been nurse to his son and heir, and was treated with unusual consideration by the family in consequence. Whether Sir Clifford thought that severity to her would teach the others a lesson of obedience, or whether he had conceived an especial ~~delight to the~~ dislike against the poor old creature it is impossible to determine; not so the fact of her unnatural and unmerited punishment. She had it seems a little dog, white and shaggy, with great speaking eyes, full of intelligence, and bearing a strong resemblance to those of a child. But this dog, so singularly beautiful and innocent in his helplessness, was bound to Rose, as she was called, by yet other ties. He had been the pet and favorite of her youngest daughter, and that daughter now languished out a life of bondage, in the toiling in the rice swamps of Alabama. On the day of her departure she had given the dog to her mother with a special request that the latter would never cease to care for it, though of that injunction there was little need. As the memorial of her lost one her heart clave to it with the utmost tenacity of tenderness. It fed from her hand, slept in her bosom, and was her companion wherever she went. In her eyes it was more much more than a little dumb animal. It had such winning ways, and knew so well to make its wants understood that it became to her what a grandchild is to many aged females. The heart must have something to love, something to which its affections may cling, something to cherish and protect. It may perchance be a tree or flower, perchance a child or domestic animal, with poor old Rose it was her little dog. Then, too, he was her treasure, and sole possession, and the only earthly thing that regarded her with fondness, or to whose comfort her existence was essential.

But this poor little animal was great enough to incur the wrath of Sir Clifford, and Sir Clifford in all his state and haughtiness could demean himself sufficiently to notice the trespass of a little dog. He at once commanded Rose to drown it under pain of his displeasure. Had he commanded any thing else, however unpleasant the duty she would doubtless have obeyed, but that she could not do. As soon would a mother drown a favorite child. She wept, she entreated, she implored, kneeling at his feet, that he would remit the sentence, but in vain. Sir Clifford made it a boast that he never retracted, that his commands and decisions like the laws of the Medes and Persians were unalterable and so he bade her rise and do his bidding at once, or that in case of refusal he should enforce her obedience by a punishment of which she had no ~~conception~~ idea. Calmly and resolutely the old woman arose with something of the martyr spirit burning in her eye. To his inquiries she answered plainly that she should not and could not obey his orders, that—

"By heavens you shall" he cried interrupting her. "You shall see him die a thousand deaths, and vainly beg the priveledge of killing him to end his tortures": and he knocked loudly against the window sash, which was his manner of summoning the servants. They soon came.

"Now take this old witch, and her whelp and gibbet them alive on the Linden" he said his features distorted and his whole frame seeming to dilate with intensity of passion. The obsequious slaves rudely seized the unresisting victims. An iron hoop being fastened around the body of Rose she was drawn to the tree, and with great labor elevated and secured to one of the largest limbs. And then with a refinement of cruelty the innocent and helpless little animal, with a broad iron belt around its delicate body was suspended within her sight, but beyond her reach.

And thus suspended between heaven and earth in a posture the [sic] most unimaginably painful both hung through the long long days and the longer nights. Not a particle of food, not a drop of water was allowed to either, but the master walking each morning would fix his cold cruel eyes with appalling indifference on her agonised countenance, and calmly inquire whether or not she was ready to be the minister of his vengeance on the dog. For three consecutive days she retained strength to answer that she was not. Then her rigid features assumed a collapsed and corpse-like hue and appearance, her eyes seemed starting from their sockets, and her protruding tongue refused to articulate a sound. Yet even in this state she would faintly wave her hand towards the dog and seemed in commiseration of his sufferings to forget her own.

It was enough, they said, to have melted a heart of stone to hear her talk to that affectionate and equally tortured favorite so long as she retained the power of speech, as if she sought by such demonstrations of tenderness to soothe her own misery and mitigate his sufferings. How she seemed to consider him a being who could know; and think and reason, and as such assured him of her undying love and regard, entreated him to be patient, and to bear with fortitude whatever the wickidness of man imposed, and strove to solace him with the certainty that a few more hours would finish all their woes, and safely confide them to the place where the weary rest.

And when her voice failed she would turn her eyes with looks of unutterable tenderness on her equally failing companion, and who shall say that he did not perceive and appreciate the glance. The Lady of Sir Clifford besought him with tears and prayers to forgive the old woman in consideration of her great age, her faithful services, and her undying affection for the little animal. Her entreaties were seconded by those of their son, who was nearly frantic at such barbarous treatment of his kind old nurse, but the hard-hearted man was obdurate to all. She then desired that they might be put to death at once, as she declared that the sight of their agonies and the noise of their groans would haunt her to her dying day, but this he refused on the plea that he never changed his plans.

After they had hung in this manner five days, and till their sinews were shrunk, their nerves paralysed, their vital energies exhausted, their flesh wasted and decayed, and their senses gone, a dreadful storm arose at night. The rain poured down in torrents, the lightning flashed and the thunder rolled. And the concussion of the elements seemed partly to revive their exhausted natures. The water that moistened their lips and cooled their fevered brains restored their voices and renewed their strength. Through the din and uproar of the tempest could be heard all night the wail of a woman the howling of a dog, and the creaking of the linden branches to which the gibbet hung. It was horrible: Oh how horrible: and slumber entirely fled the household of Sir Clifford. His Lady heretofore one of the gayest of women was never seen to smile afterwards. The next morning when the storm had past away, and

Nature resumed her usual serenity he went forth again to interrogate his victim. But the helpless object of his wrath had already ceased to breathe and the delicate limbs were rigid in the cold embrace of death. He surveyed it a moment contemptuously and then turned to Rose. She was yet alive, but wan and ghastly and hedeous in countenance, and either to sport with her sufferings or for some other unknown purpose he proposed to have her taken down. ~~But the~~ At the sound of his voice she opened her bloodshotten lack-lustre eyes, —and her voice as she spoke had a deep sepulchral tone. "No" she said "it shall not be. I will hang here till I die as a curse to this house, and I will come here after I am dead to prove its bane. In sunshine and shadow, by day and by night I will brood over this tree, and weigh down its branches, and when death, or sickness, or misfortune is to befall the family ye may listen for ye will assuredly hear the creaking of its limbs" and with one deep prolonged wail her spirit departed.

Such was the legend of the Linden as we had heard it told in the dim duskiness of the ~~twilight~~ summer twilight or by the roaring fires of wintry nights. Hence an unusual degree of interest was attached to the tree and the creaking of its branches filled our bosoms with supernatural dread.

~~But as the rain had ceased so did the wind though not a moment sooner as later on account of our wishes~~

But the wind ceased to blow and the linden branches no longer creaked, yet the air was sharp chilly and bracing just enough so perhaps to give freshness to the cheek and an edge to appetite. All day long we had been looking for the bridal party. Time and again and perhaps a dozen times had some of the younger ones climbed the trees and fences and a neighboring hill in order to descry the cavalcade at a distance and telegraph its approach. Times without number had Mrs Bry taken the circuit of the drawing rooms, din-ing rooms and parlors to make certain that all was right. Over and over again had she summoned the servants and made the same inquiry probably for the hundredth time and received as often the same answer—that the fires were all lighted in the various apartments—that the feast ~~is~~ was ready for the table, and everything ~~in~~ in a due state of preparation, even to the children's hands and faces.

At last they came, at last after the sun had set, and the twilight faded, after eyes had been dimmed with looking and ears wearied by listening for them. Through the sharp chill night they came with their bridal company. Yet the twinkling lamps of their traveling chariots gave warning even at a distance of their approach. Then there was great bustle and confusion. Lanterns were lighted and rooms illuminated; doors flung open and chambers hastily surveyed. The stately mansion is no longer a darkening mass of front, but looks most imposing to the brilliant circle as they descend from their carriages and move on towards it. Mrs Bry, however, was mentally grieved at one thing, and so were the servants. She had planned that the entire troop of slaves, all arrayed in the finery of flaming Madras handkerchiefs and calico blazing with crimson and scarlet flowers, should be ranged on either side of the graveled walk leading to the mansion, with due regard to their age and character, and thus pay homage to their master and new-found mistress. But the night to their great disappointment forbade this display, and the ceremonial of reception was confined to the housekeeper. And well she discharged it. The deferential grace of her manner being only equaled by the condescending politeness of the master and mistress, the latter of whom immediately asked to be shown to her rooms. Excusing herself Mrs Bry deputed me to bear the light, and the bride escorted by the bridegroom moves on along the passage, ascends the oaken staircase, and pauses at length before a door carved and paneled in the quaint old style.

~~These rooms~~ "This door opens to your rooms, my dear, I hope you will like them" he said. "Hannah attend your mistress."

Her favorite waiting maid had been detained by sudden sickness. I opened the door, and we entered, but my master, saying that he would call and lead her down to supper in an hour immediately retired to his apartment. My mistress required little assistance and I had full leisure to examine and inspect her appearance. Slaves are proverbially curious, and while she surveyed with haughty eyes the furniture and dimensions of the rooms or opened and shut bureau-drawers, or plunged into caskets and jewel-cases, I was studying her, and making out a mental inventory of her foibles, and weaknesses, and caprices, and whether or not she was likely to prove an indulgent mistress. I did not see, but I felt that there was mystery, something indefinable about her. She was a small brown woman, with a profusion of wavy curly hair, large bright eyes, and delicate features with the exception of her lips which were too large, full, and red. She dressed in very good taste and her manner seemed perfect but for an uncomfortable habit she had of seeming to watch everybody as though she feared them or thought them enemies. I noticed this, and how startled she seemed at the echo of my master's footsteps ~~when~~ when he came to lead her down stairs. I am superstitious, I confess it; people of my race and color usually are, and I fancied then that she was haunted by a shadow or phantom apparent only to herself, and perhaps even the more dreadful for that.

As one of the waiters I saw the company at supper. There were jeweled ladies and gallant gentlemen. There were youthful faces and faces of two score that strove to cheat time, and refuse to be old. There was a glare and glitter deceitful smiles and hollow hearts.

I have said that I always had a quiet way of observing things, and this habit grew upon me, sharpened perhaps by the absence of all elemental knowledge. Instead of books I studied faces and characters, and arrived at conclusions by a sort of sagacity that closely approximated to the unerring certainty of animal instinct. But in all that brilliant ~~I had only eyes and ears for one man~~ company I had eyes and ears for only one man, and that man the least attractive of any in the throng. He was a rusty seedy old-fashioned gentleman with thin grey locks combed so as partly to conceal the baldness of his forehead, and great black eyes so keen and piercing that you shrank involuntarily from their gaze.

Yet it was not his singular features, or the peculiar expression of his ~~imperturbable~~ countenance that puzzled and interested me, but his manner towards my mistress so deferential and defiant, and her equally remarkable bearing in his presence. They never conversed except to exchange a few customary courtesies, never seemed to note or regard each other, but somehow and quite intuitively I arrived at the conclusion that each one watched and suspected the other, that each one was conscious of some great and important secret on the part of the other, and that my mistress in particular would give worlds to know just what that old man knew.

The bridegroom was probably too happy, and the company too gay to note all this. They saw not how carefully and studiously she avoided him, or how rarely he looked at her, how without seeming to intend it he was ever near her, and with an outward manifestation of indifference was really the most interested of all.

At length the supper was concluded, and the guests arose. Should there be singing or playing, or dancing? My master had ordered a splendid piano for his bride. It stood in the drawing room—who would give them music? No one. They could, however, take a promenade to survey the rooms, ~~especially that~~ especially the one that the family portraits adorned. "And we will have music and dancing there" said the host. "Twill be such a novelty" and thither he conducted the glittering train across the hall, and along the passages, and through the rooms, and up the staircase to the illustrious presence of ancestral greatness. I saw my mistress sweep gracefully along in her bridal robes, and following close behind like her shadow was the old gentleman in black. She passed on to examine beneath a broad chandelier the portrait of Sir Clifford. The image regards her with its dull leaden stare. She turns away and covers her eyes.

Meanwhile the weather has changed. The moon shined only through a murky cloud, and the rising wind moaned fitfully amid the linden branches. Then the rain began to patter on the roof, with the dull horrible creaking that forboded misfortune to the house. The cheek of my master paled. I saw that; saw, too, that his gayety was affected, and that when he called for music, and prepared to dance he was striving to obliterate some haunting recollection, or shut from his mental vision the rising shadows of coming events.

Though not permitted to mingle with the grand company we, the servants, blockaded the halls and passages. We cared not, why should we? if the fires went out, the chambers were neglected and the remnants of the feast remained on the table. It was our priveledge to look and listen. We loved the music, we loved the show and splendor, we loved to watch the twinkling feet and the graceful motions of the dancers, but beyond them and over them, and through the mingled sounds of joyous music and rain and wind I saw the haughty contenance of Sir Clifford's frowning pictured semblance, and heard the ominous creaking of the linden tree. At length there was a pause in the music; a recess in the dance.

"Whence is that frightful noise?" inquired one of the guests.

"It is made by the decayed branches of an old tree at the end of the house" replied my master. "I will order it cut down to[-]morrow."

The words were followed by a crash. Loosened from its fastenings in the wall the portrait of Sir Clifford had fallen to the floor. Who done it? The invisible hand of Time had been there and silently and stealthily spread corrupting canker over the polished surface of the metal that supported it, and crumbled the wall against which it hung. But the stately knight in his armor, who placed it there had taken no consideration of such an event, and while breathing his anathema against the projector of its removal dreamed not of the great leveler who treats the master and slave with the same unceremonious rudeness, and who touches the lowly hut or the lordly palace with the like decay.

CHAPTER 3

Progress In Discovery

Surely every man walketh in a vain show: surely they are disquieted in vain.

DAVID

Coming events cast their shadows before.

CAMPBELL

The days flew past in a succession of rejoicings and festivities in which all belonging to the place alike participated. Sounds of music and mirth came from every hut while the great house assumed a conviviality of appearance and manner that seemed almost unbecoming in a mansion so ancient and respectable. From morning to night and night to morning it was thronged with guests. Carriages came and went incessantly up and down the long avenue of oaks. Gentlemen on horseback crossed and recrossed the lawn. The window shutters were all thrown back, for not a room ~~was~~ was tenantless, not a mirror blank. ~~We the servants liked it We liked the fun and frolic, the show the novelties and the servants of the glorious feasts We like the days of hilarity and the nights of revelry though ever and when the mirth was we would hear the doleful creakings of the Linden tree~~

Amid the stylish and splendid groups of ladies and gentlemen Amid the servants, loungers, dependants, and cousins of my master for the twentieth time removed came and went the old gentleman in black. They called him Mr Trappe, and it was easy to percieve that he was there for some purpose of an uncommon nature. He seemed to stand alone. He never mingled with the dancers, laughed with the gay, or conversed with the talkative, yet all treated him with deferential consideration, as he was understood to be a lawyer of wealth and ~~consideration~~ position.

I said he came and went, that is he was only visible at times, and then you would see him ~~leaning speechless against a pillar or sitting silently in a corner~~ perhaps leaning speechless against a pillar, or sitting silently in a corner. And sometimes you would encounter him in some lonesome passage, or near the door of the drawing room when my mistress was within. Of course in this society she reigned supreme. She was beautiful, intelligent, accomplished and all seemed to know it, but it became a marvel to me that her manner should so instantly change when that old man was near. Usually kind and amiable she wrapped an air of insolent grace about her as if it were a mantle when he approached. In his presence, too, she smiled the sweetest and looked the prettiest. Were these smiles and looks put on for the occasion or not?

At length the feastings and festivities ceased, the guests departed, and things resumed their usual course. Mr Trappe, however, was domiciled in the family. He claimed to have been the guardian of my mistress previous to her marriage, and as such was probably invited to prolong his visit. My master evidently regarded him as eccentric, and deficient in certain conventionalities usual in good society, yet perfectly genteel and respectable. He appointed servants to attend him, though Mr Trappe rarely if ever required their services, and a vacant place was reserved for him at the table ~~which he seldom occupied~~ to which he seldom came. And then the meals were ordered to his room, a plainly furnished chamber on the second story, old-fashioned like himself and having a quiet ~~irresponsive air~~ impassive air.

As the waiting maid of my mistress I was always near to attend her, and soon ascertained that she was not happy. She gave no outward manifestation or sign of grief. She never wept and seldom sighed, but there was an air of restlessness and unquiet about her the very reverse of that placidity which always accompanies a state of mental repose. She seemed to be always looking for somebody and expecting something that never came. Though she never said so I knew that she feared the approach of a stranger, and that the receipt of a letter was to her a cause of alarm. Then how little she slept of nights, and I felt that the burden of her sorrow must indeed be great, and that she was nearly overwhelmed by it, ~~when it led~~ for up and down, up and down in light or shadow I could hear her pacing the chamber floor for hours.

After the arrival of her first maid we were both attached to her person, and Lizzy, as she was called, being very communicative I learned from her many particulars about my mistress, her former life and situation, and her mysterious connection with the old man of the name of Trappe, though of this last circumstance Lizzy knew no more than I did myself. That is, she could never fathom the secret, or arrive at the bottom of the affair, but she told of many inexpliccable and current events relating to it, which sharpened our conjectures as to what the end might be.

Lizzy was much better educated than I was, and had been to many places that I had never even heard tell of. She had also a great memory for dates and names which I invariably forgot. She was a Quadroon, almost white, with delicate hands and feet, and a person that any lady in the land might have been proud of. She came, she said of a good family and frequently mentioned great names in connection with her own, and when I smiled and said it mattered little she would assume an air of consequential dignity, and assert that on the contrary it was a very great thing and very important even to a slave to be well connected—that good blood was an inheritance to them—and that when they heard the name of some honorable gentleman mentioned with applause, or saw some great lady flaunt by in jewels and satins the priveledge of thinking he or she is a near relative of mine was a very great privelage indeed. And then I said "Of course" which mollified her rumpled vanity.

But Lizzy, notwithstanding her good family, education and great beauty, had been several times under the hammer of the auctioneer, had passed through many hands, and experienced all the vicissitudes attendant on the life of a slave. She had been the pet of a rich family and the degraded drudge of another, had known alternately cruelty and kindness, and suffered the extremes of a master's fondness, a mistress's jealousy and their daughter's hate. She could tell tales that of slavery that made the blood run cold to hear. She had been, she said, with our present mistress for a period of ten years, and was very thankful after all her woes and wanderings to find so good a place. She remembered our mistress's father and his mournful death-bed in the presence of Mr Trappe, who sate [sat] looking on, cold, silent, and impassive as ever. Then he became the executor of the dead man's will and had access to his papers, in which Lizzy verily believed that he discovered some important secret, as from that time his manner towards her mistress changed, and her manner changed to him, and each appeared to be watching the other, though wherefore or why was past finding out. "I know" continued Lizzy "that he is the shadow darkening her life, and I can well believe that she married Master purposely to escape his persecutions."

"Perhaps he wished to marry her himself" I suggested.

"Impossible" she answered. "It is much more probable that he wished to sell her."

"Sell her—what do you mean?"

"What I say, neither more nor less."

"But Mistress is not a slave.["]

"I suppose not" and then she stopped short, and refused to give any explanation, assuring me that she knew nothing; and only remarked as she did in a jesting joking way. But I knew better there was too ~~When our mistress descended to the breakfast room one morning at an early hour, and we in her train~~ much earnestness in her voice and manner.

I need hardly say that our mistress in her great goodness and kindness of heart treated us rather as companions than servants. She seldom went out, or received company, but remained nearly all the time in her own apartments. Yet she could not bear the companionship of her thoughts, and would request us to sit with her, and divert her mind by conversation. Sometimes she asks to hear the legend connected with Sir Clifford's portrait, which has been restored to its usual place on the drawing-room's wall, or speaks gloomily of the linden and its dreary creak.

But she shuns Mrs Bry, and that good lady is not over fond of her. Perhaps she fears that Mr Trappe has taken her into his confidence, or perhaps it is something else. Who can tell?

It was now spring, and Mr Trappe had been living in the family all winter. Generally in his room, but sometimes descending to the library, and making himself at home among the books and papers. It is seldom that he speaks, or is spoken to; all feel his uncommunicative irresponsive air.

Our master was an easy good sort of man, fond of his wife, but not given to habits of observation. It never occurred to him that the burden of a great misfortune was on her mind, or that other causes than ill health occasioned her lowness of spirits, her avoidance of society, and long detention in her rooms. He never suspected—how could he? that the figure of that old man, with his dark clothes, and darker eyes was incessantly haunting and pursuing—that a voice was forever crying in her ears "I'm in the secret, I know all about it, more perhaps than you do. I could tell if I chose, and shall tell when it suits me, which will be whenever I can turn it to profit and advantage." He never dreamed of the dread, the doubt, the uncertainty that clouded her whole existence. He knew that she occupied a brilliant position, but he did not know that she had no assurance of holding it for another day.

One day the postman brought a bundle of letters. There was nothing singular in that. I received them on a silver salver and presented them to her. They bore the superscription of master, of herself, and of Mr Trappe. At the last she looked narrowly as if examining the hand writing, looked eagerly, and then remarked impulsively "Well, I would give half my fortune to know the contents of that letter."

"I presume Mr Trappe would gratify your curiousity for much less" answered Lizzy.

Mistress shook her head, and turned her eyes to the floor with a cold vacant stare.

"Or perhaps your letters may throw some light on the subject, you have scarcely looked at them" continued Lizzy.

Thus reminded she took the missives, broke the seals, and soon seemed lost in their perusal.

"Take that letter to Mr Trappe" she directed ~~on~~ ceasing to read, "and much good may it do him."

Yet the calmness of her voice was strange and unnatural, and her countenance wore an expression of indefinable dread as if she knew that the worst was coming, and was not prepared to meet it.

My mistress was very kind, and unknown to Master she indulged me in reading whenever I desired. The next morning I descended to the parlor, and seated myself with a book behind the heavy damask curtains that shaded the window. In this situation I was entirely concealed. In a few moments the echo of a light footsteps [sic] was heard on the stair; then the door opened, and mistress entered. She looked thin, and weak, and ill. A night of utter irretrievable misery had wrought the effect of years on her frame, and in her appearance. She was bent as if with age, her eyes were sunken and heavy with midnight watchings, and the pallor of her countenance was like that of death.

Gliding in after her, and so close behind her that he might have touched her robe came Mr Trappe. Dressed in seedy black as usual, his keen eyes gleamed with an expression of unwonted satisfaction as taking a chair at a little distance from the sofa on which she sat, and regarding her with a steady gaze, he observed "You desired this interview I think."

"I did."

"I am very much surprised that you should" he answered "because you must be aware that I could not approve of the course you have taken."

"What course?"

"That is a singular question, indeed" he replied. "What was my agreement and your promise before your marriage transpired. Were you not to maintain an equal impassive serenity, and not betray by look, or word or deed the least discomposure in my presence. Were you not to treat me on all occasions with due deference and respect, and was I not to receive a monthly stipend from your income, and knowing as you do that this stipend has not been paid, I am surprised that you can have the face to meet me, much surprised that under the circumstances you can ask or expect a favor.["]

"I have neither asked nor expected any."

"There is no use for equivocation or denial" he continued, not noticing her last remark, and slightly raising his voice. "You well know and I know that our agreement being broken, the engagement terminated. That we are placed in a new position, and that you can have no further claim to forbearance on my part.["]

"~~And~~ But I have a claim, never had a greater. It was not my fault that the bank ~~broke~~ which contained my property broke, and that consequently I became unable to pay your monthly allowance, but have you not been well supplied and cared for in my husband's family? I think you have."

"Yet even that—my staying here, and being cared for, as you have expressed it, was a violation of our agreement. You was [sic] to have provided me with a house and servants in the City."

"Well"

["]And then after the loss of your property, and when you invited me to become one of your family I consented simply because I had a part to play and a prize at stake."

"I do not understand you."

"Very likely, and yet I have spoken plainly."

"You say" observed my mistress "that you do not approve of the course I have taken, and it is a clear case that I do not comprehend the motive of yours. Why have you kept my secret so long only to reveal it now—and why did you wish me to marry only to break my husband's heart?"

["]Why bless my heart, madam" he replied. "You are simple as a child. Why did I do these things?—and your secret How ridiculous. It is not your secret, but mine, and may be your husband's before another day, as any former reason that I might have, and did have for keeping it have [sic] ceased to exist.}

"That scarcely explains your inconsistency."

"I am very consistent, madam" he replied, placing an ironical emphasis on the last word. "Very consistent in view of the plan marked out for myself. I wished of course to turn my knowledge of your birth to my own advantage. Had I betrayed what you really were I should have gained nothing by it. Had I opposed your marriage it would have been a barren speculation, but as you offered me a snug little sum to keep the first safe I consented to do so under certain stipulations; and as I was confident that your husband, if you had one, would give still more to preserve himself and his family from so horrible a disgrace, and misfortune I favored your marriage as would inevitably result from your exposure. I favored the marriage of yourself and now as the heirs and creditors of your father still continue pushing their claims, and since they anxiously desire to ascertain whether he had not other property than that given up, while I know that such property, and valuable property, too, really exists, who shall prevent my making such use of the knowledge as the occasion demands. It would be very different were you in a situation to fulfill your first engagements, or were your husband in affluence, but I have found out that his property is mortgaged to its fullest extent, and that notwithstanding his position he is in fact a poor man."

During all this long speech my speech mistress had remained silent and passive, shading her face with her hand. Once or twice she had lifted her eyes to look at him, but dropped them again beneath his gaze. He regards her as he did at first eagerly, but without pity. My own situation was becoming each moment more awkward and embarrassing. Unintentionally I had been made the witness of a private interview, and overheard conversation designed to be entirely confidential. It seemed that without intending it I had acted a dishonorable part, but I could not recede without exposure, and I was not prepared for that.

Finding that she remains silent, and is likely to remain so Mr Trappe proceeds, and again with reference to the past.

"You recollect my first overtures."

She remembers them perfectly well.

["]And how scornfully you rejected them—how you taunted me with being an old man, and said that you would rather be the veriest slave in existence than wed a man you could not love, you remember all this?"

She gives a slight motion of assent with her eyes rather than with her head.

"And as you would not spare the old man, can you expect the old man to spare you?"

"I do not wish you to spare me from mere personal considerations, but my husband and his family. Oh: that I had never married."

"Why yes" he answered, in his cold imperturbable manner. "Of course that is something to be thought of, but since he cannot redeem you it is a mere secondary consideration that cannot in the least affect the regular details of business. Pecuniary interests are to[o] valuable to be set aside because somebody's honor may be compromised. Don't you see it so."

She spoke not, but sighed or rather gasped like the gasp of death.

"You must, you do see it so" he continued. "Had you treated me—"

She made a slight gesture of impatience.

An ineffable shade of scorn, hate, or passion, or all three combined passed over his face, and he resumed. "Had you treated me in a different manner, your fate would have been different—remember that I have seen the time when I could have stooped to kiss the hem of your garment."

She looked at him, her eyes actually blazing, but the fires momentarily died out.

"Yes," he continued, rising and promenading the room. "Yes, once you were the leading star of my destiny, the light of my life, and I may yet possess you on my own terms."

She said nothing, she seemed even incapable of speech and both remained silent for a time.

At length she spoke. "I think this interview were better ended. I have no more to say."

"But a little more to hear" he replied.

"Say on, then" she answered, something of her old defiant manner coming over her.

"Last night I received a message" he said "a message on business connected with yourself."

"Will you explain its purport?" she inquired, an apparent tremor in her voice.

"I cannot, madam" he answered "besides it is quite unnecessary. Anything I could reveal would not mend the matter in the least, though it might increase the difficulties of your position. I say it might though I am not certain even of that."

He pauses, and she inquires "Have you done torturing me? if so—"

He interrupts her coolly and calmly. "I have not. By that message I am summoned away. I shall go this day, this very hour, perhaps, how soon I may return, or how long I may be gone it is impossible to say. I shall not inform your husband of the complicated circumstances in which we are placed, because it would not answer my policy to do so. When I return it may be necessary."

She breathes quickly and heavily, but answers not.

"There is one thing more that I have to say" he resumes ["]and then I have done. I have to caution, to entreat, if entreaty is a proper word, to command you to restrain and compose yourself during my absence. Why woman you are losing all your beauty, you look older by ten years than you did a month ago. There is no occasion for so much moping and pining, no occasion at all for anything of the like. Be to your husband what you were during the time of courtship. Avoid doing or saying anything to attract observation or excite suspicion. These are my commands do you promise to obey them?"

"Why should I promise?"

"Because matters are not yet ripe for a full denóument that will come soon enough at all events. Do you promise?" he inquires again.

"I will not bind myself" she replied, glancing mechanically at the bell-wire. I read in an instant the association of ideas in her mind. She was thinking of a certain resting place "where the wicked cease from troubling." The eyes of Mr Trappe followed the direction of hers. For a moment his countenance changed. Goading her on to despair and madness he was not prepared for that contingency. He stood for a few moments steadily contemplating her, and probably debating in his mind whether or not to allude to her secret thoughts and deciding in the ~~negative~~ affirmative he resumed. "Neither will you lay violent hands on yourself." She started as if surprised that he should know of what she was thinking. "Why should you?" he proceeded. "Life should have charms for a beautiful woman, and then the avenging Deity."

She repulses his advice with a disdainful wave of the hand.

"Do we part as friends or enemies?" he inquired.

"Either, it matters not."

Was he surprised at the frozen coldness of her despair? did he fear that to escape him she would rush into the cold embrace of death, or was it possible that he was touched with something of pity or remorse, but a softening expression came over his face, and melted in his voice. "If the difference is nothing to you, it is something to me" he said. "Let us part as friends," and he extended his open hand. With an apparent effort she laid her small fingers in his palm. He held them a moment, lifted them to his lips, and breathing rather than speaking "farewell" left the apartment.

CHAPTER 4

A Mystery Unraveled

The sins of the fathers shall be visited on the children.
MOSES

When he was gone, when his retreating footsteps sounded no longer in the hall, nor on the stair my mistress arose with apparent composure, and retired to her room. Yet I perceived perfectly well that the calmness was all forced, there was such wild disturbance in her eyes, and something so unnatural in her carriage and manner. I knew it better when half an hour afterwards I stole softly to her room, not because I was summoned, not ~~because~~ because I supposed that she desired my presence, neither was it through vain or idle curiosity, but because I could not bear that in her great agony of spirit she should be alone, and no friend near to sympathise or condole with her.

Noiselessly and unobserved I entered the chamber. She was pacing the floor up and down, up and down—her hair in the wildest disorder flung back from her brow over which was spread a deathly pallor, her bosom heaving with stifling sobs, and her whole frame writhing as if in mortal pain. A slight noise informed her of my presence. Her face flushed a moment, and she articulated "Hannah." That was enough. Flinging myself at her feet, and clasping her hands I bathed them with my tears.

"My dear, good, kind, indulgent mistress" I said. "You will forgive me when I tell you that I know all you have suffered and are suffering from that heartless cruel man—when I tell you that I overheard your conversation with him just now, not intentional[l]y but by the merest accident, and when I implore you to confide in me, to entrust me with this dreadful secret, that knowing I may more deeply sympathise with your woes and wrongs."

I cannot tell why it was that I forgot that moment the disparity in our conditions, and that I approached and spoke to her as though she had been my sister or a very dear friend, but ~~when~~ sorrow and affliction and death make us all equal, and I felt it so the more when she sunk down beside me on the floor in her deep distress, clasped me in her arms, and rocking her frame to and fro, entreated me to pity and save her if I could. And then in broken and incoherent sentences she related the story of her life— ~~A dark one it was, though not on her part~~ how she had been brought up, and educated by a rich gentleman, whom she called father, and by whom she was introduced into society as his daughter—how she had been taught by him to consider her mother as dead, and how she had since ascertained through Mr Trappe, that whoever might be her paternal relative, her mother was a slave then toiling in the cotton feilds of Georgia. The[n] she clasped her hands, and moaned and sorrowed, refusing to be comforted.

"Can you be certain that his information is correct" I inquired "and that he does not merely seek to torment and trouble you?"

"It is true, all true, I have had sufficient proofs. Only one thing is wanting to complete the chain of evidence, and that is the testimony of an old woman, who it seems was my mother's nurse, and who placed me in her lady's bed, and by her lady's side, when that

Lady ~~Lady~~ was to[o] weak and sick and delirious to notice that the dead was exchanged for the living.

"It seems that my mother, or the nurse, or some one privy to the affair preserved a record of these facts, and carefully concealed it among my father's papers. I much doubt that he ever discovered it. My confidence in his affection induces me to believe that had such been the case he would have executed a deed of manumission in my favor. At any rate I was publicly known and received in society as the daughter of his legitimate wife, as such I succeeded to his property as heiress, and never knew a care till that old man discovered the secret of my birth."

"That old man—have you long been acquainted with him."

"Yes: yes very long. He was my father's solicitor, and had a room at our house, but I never liked him. Even when a child the shadow of his presence occasioned within me a thrill of dread and fear. As I grew older he professed a fondness for me, he even sought my hand in marriage, and my refusal made him an enemy. He had been in the secret for some time before he gave me any intimation of it, and then he did it to extort money. He has made a fortune that way. He has spent his life in hunting, delving, and digging into family secrets, and when he has found them out he becomes ravenous for gold.

["]I well remember the time when he first made known to me his discovery. I had long noticed something singular in his manner and general bearing towards me. I felt, too an indefinable presentiment of evil in his presence, though we had little intercourse—no more indeed, than was actually necessary in the details of business."

One day contrary to his usual custom he requested the pleasure of seeing me in his room. Trembling with apprehension I ascended the staircase, passed through the hall, and stood before him. He was seated at a low table, upon which lay a great pile of books and papers that he seemed particularly interested in examining—so much so indeed as ~~at first~~ not to notice my presence. This gave me an opportunity to look around his apartment. Its chief furniture was books and bundles of papers. There were books on the floor, books in the corners, and books heaped up and piled up in an antique cupboard. Some of them seemed to have been recently used, but on others the dust had thickly accumulated. I touched one of them; it fell with a rattling sound, still he did not look round, and I began to construe his silence into studied neglect.

"I have come, Sir, according to your request" I said rather impatiently perhaps.

"Be not impatient, Madam" he answered. "What I have to say concerns yourself closely, and is of such a nature that after hearing it you will thank me for deferring the communication as long as possible." His voice, his manner, above all his singular words quite overcame me, and I ~~was obliged to~~ leaned for support against the table. He noticed my emotion, and with a gleam of something like pity or remorse on his countenance, arose from his seat, went to the cupboard, and took thence a bottle of wine, from which he poured ~~out~~ a glassful, and presenting it entreated me to drink. I replied by pressing him to let me know the worst at once.

"Not till you have drank."

I pressed the glass to my lips, and returning it again demanded to know the worst.

["]Now I wish you to inform me of all that you know about a slave woman belonging to your father, whose countenance was nearly white, and whose name was ~~Charlotte~~ Susan. You must remember such an [sic] one, for she was very fond of you."

"Yes, I remember her; she was very beautiful; and father sold her."

"Contrary to her wishes, I believe."

"Very much so. They were oblidged to use force to carry her away, and then she shrieked and screamed in the wildest manner."

"And did she not, previous to her departure clasp you in her arms, kiss you, weep over you, and call you her darling?—Did she not do all this?"

"She did, Sir, but what of it?"

"Much very much.

"Well now" he said as he touched a secret drawer in the table that opened with a spring, and drew thence a portrait. "Well now I wish you to look at this."

I did so.

"Do you know it."

"It resembles me" I answered "though I have never sate [sat] for my likeness to be taken."

"Probably not, but can't you think of some one else whom it resembles?"

["]The slave Charlotte Susan.["]

"And it was hers, and it is yours; for never did two persons more resemble each other, and now I wish you to examine this paper.["]

He held a paper towards me old, and torn, and yellow with age. I took it and commenced reading. At first I could make nothing of it. I could not understand the horrible truth thus presented to me. I read and re-read but by degrees the mystery unfolded. I perceived the worst and what I was, and must ever be. Then I fell to the floor without sense or motion.

"And after that"

["]Of what happened after that for a long a very long time I have only a confused recollection. My thoughts were in Chaos. I was half mad, half-wild, and then Mr Trappe who had occasioned all my misery undertook to console me—said that no one but himself and two or three other obscure persons were informed of the secret and that gold would shut the mouths of all.

["]And thus I bribed him to secresy, but you know the rest you know the horrible foreboding that renders my very existence a curse—and now what shall I do? Oh what shall I do?"

She ceased speaking, and it was my turn to say something. I saw that her only chance was in flight, flight immediate and precipitate.

"You have inquired what you shall do" I began "and though it becomes not a slave to advise I think the question might be satisfactorily answered."

"How—how?"

["]You must fly from this house, from this place, from this country, fly immediately—to[-]night—or stay. I have a better plan. My master as yet knows nothing of it. Mr Trappe is gone you can go away in open daylight and in your carriage giving out that you design to visit a relative.["]

My mistress was delighted with the plan. Her first thought was to escape from the horrible doom impending over her, and she eagerly grasped the least shadow of hope. She thanked me, she kissed me, and for the first time she wept over me.

["]And you will go with me?["] she inquired.

"I will, my dear mistress."

["]Call me mistress no longer. Henceforth you shall be to me as a very dear sister" she said embracing me again. "Oh: to be free, to be free."

There was something ominous to me in the transports of her joy. Her eyes were illuminated and her countenance shone. The transition was sudden and complete, but it is ever thus with impulsive natures.

"My dear Mistress."

"There: there, mistress again when I have forbidden it."

"Well then, my dear friend, let us weigh this matter well. I advise flight by all means, yet the time, the way, the route should all be duly considered. You have relatives residing near the Steamboat landing on the James River?"

"I have."

"We will talk of going there to spend a week."

But a revulsion was taking place in her feelings, and she burst into tears. "My husband" she said "how can I bear to deceive him so."

"Your flight will occasion less trouble to him when he comes to know the truth than any other course that you could take."

Again she wept and moaned, while I comforted and consoled her, and sought to imbue her with the idea that it was a time for thinking and acting rather than giving way to overstrained sensations of any kind.

"Oh I will try, I will try" she would say, when I thus reminded her. "I will to be composed, but you know not, you cannot know, nor even imagine the mental agony that I have suffered. You will forgive me but I must weep" and then she would burst into such a passion of tears, and wild hysterical sobbing that it alarmed me. After a few hours, however, she acquired serenity of mind and greater fixedness of purpose. Yet she was impatient to be gone, but declined the project of visiting as she said her husband would certainly wish to accompany her.

"How then?" I inquired.

["]Why we will just go away, leave the place altogether. We can reach the river by morning I think, if we start at midnight, and once there a steamboat will soon convey us beyond the reach of our pursuers."

"And Lizzy."

"I shall leave her."

It was now near night, and the glorious summer sunset never looked more beautiful, yet my reflections were meloncholy, though not so much on my own account as that of my mistress. How would she bear the exposure—how endure the fatigue?, but relaxation of purpose I never thought of. I knew that degradation and disgrace awaited her if she remained, and that she would be tortured by a suspense more horrible than the worst reality. In a short time, probably her escape would be rendered doubly difficult, if not impossible.

Thus I reasoned with myself while the shadows fell and night slowly gathered over the landscape. ~~At the usual time I went to the room of my mistress The still still night very quiet and beautiful and~~ The still still night on the dusty roads, and over the quiet woods over the gardens and the feilds I lifted the window and looked out with a feeling akin to regret. Lindendale had been the home of childhood, and with it was connected all the associations of my riper years. Within its shadows, though a slave, I had known many happy days. I had been the general favorite of the young people on the estate, but though I loved them much, I loved my mistress more.

She had excused herself from meeting her husband at supper, and Lizzy had been dismissed to attend a dance in the neighborhood, but we considered it expedient to defer all preparations till the house became quiet. How slowly the hours passed away—how long the servants lingered in the kitchen. How long it seemed before the lights were extinguished in the surrounding cabins, but little by little the voices, hum and confusion ceased; one by one the cabins were darkened. The time had arrived.

Silently I went to the room of my Mistress, and as silently entered. There was a dim light burning on the table, yet so shaded as not to be seen from the window. She was dressed and vailed, and she rose to meet me with more composure than I had expected. "My dear good Hannah" she said "I think you had better stay. You are of great use here. What will the old people, and the children—the weak helpless ones do without you—what—"

But I interrupted her. "And leave you to go forth alone. My dear indulgent mistress—never, never."

Just then the rising wind howled mournfully around the house, and the Linden creaked audibly. I shuddered at the sound.

"If you will go, if you really wish to go" she resumed ["]if you desire freedom for its own sake, far be it from me to speak a word of discouragement, but we may be pursued, and overtaken and brought back, and then."

"I know."

"I would not be the means of your going, and that you should be exposed to punishment for my sake."

"Say no more, my mind is fixed. We will go and trust in heaven."

She extinguished the light and all was darkness. Hand in hand we listened, all was still; we went down stairs softly, the hall was deserted; we opened and shut the door—again listened and looked, but no one was near—then paused, lingered a moment, turned to the house with a farewell glance, and then ~~left~~ turned to the wide expanse of feild and forest and meadow, crossed by intersecting roads, and hurried away.

CHAPTER 5

Lost, Lost, Lost

When men say peace and safety sudden destruction cometh
                                                    BIBLE

We took the road leading to the river, and walked hastily forward. It was not a time to loiter or linger, freedom, happiness, everything perhaps life was at stake. We trembled at a sound, a shadow filled us with alarm. Trees in the dusky gloom took the forms of men, and stumps and hillocks were strangely transferred into blood-hounds crouching to spring on their prey. Every one must be aware that in the southern states a person traveling at night, especially a female, would be certain to excite observation. We came near being betrayed on two or three occasions. Once we heard the distant murmur of voices and the tramp of horses' feet, evidently approaching at a rapid pace. There was not a moment to be lost. To pass them without exciting suspicion would be impossible. True my mistress was well known in that neighborhood, but what excuse could she frame for being out there at the dead time of night. Nothing but concealment presented itself, but where how could we find a place. The whole country was an open common. ~~They're~~ There was neither wood, nor tree, nor fence. To increase our difficulties the moon which had been concealed behind a cloud shone out brilliantly. Meanwhile the voices and the trampling feet grew nearer and nearer, retreat was impossible, to advance would be fatal to our hopes, and ~~wrapping our cloaks~~ muffling our heads and faces, and hands in our cloaks we crouched on the ground in terror determined to abide the worst. As it terminated this was the wisest course we could have taken. They glanced casually towards us, and probably mistook us for cattle sleeping on the common. ~~passed a~~

Again we were overtaken by a physician, who had been summoned to attend a sick-bed, and yet again we came near encountering a planter who was returning from some distant expedition to his home. His blood-hound sate [sat] at his feet in the carriage, and passing near where we lay behind some bushes, we distinctly heard his fierce growl, and saw the fiery gleaming of eyes. We heard his master inquire, "What do you see, Cesar?" and then sharply eyeing the clump of cedars, and ~~seeing~~ only seeing the thick dark branches, he continued addressing the dog "You thought you scented a Negro. I suppose but there is nothing there."

To our unspeakable relief he was soon out of sight.

We went on for several hours and were greatly fatigued. Towards morning, I knew the time by the stars and the fresh breezes my mistress declared that she could go no farther, and that she must rest.

"But, my dear Mistress are we not near the river. We must be there by morning to meet the boat. Lean on me if you are weary. I am much the stronger."

She was nervous and excited; at one moment bouyed by hope and exultant, the next overcome by the deepest despondency, and though endeavoring to do my utmost to soothe and comfort her I felt my own strength giving way under the increasing weight of a dreadful suspicion.

It had occurred to me once before, and where the roads intersected each other that we were going wrong. This became more apparent every moment, yet I feared to communicate the painful truth to her. She might bear it heroically, or she might sink beneath it, and so I determined to stop, wait for the morning light, and ascertain the fact. There was a wood near by, thick, dense with undergrowth, and thither I led my mistress, prepared for her a mossy seat, wrapped my own cloak around her; then seating myself behind her I drew her head to my bosom, and bade her sleep.

At first she was painfully awake, and would start and shudder at the least sound. I well knew the soothing and comforting influences to be derived from reading portions of the Holy Scripture, in times of trouble and affliction, and so commenced repeating many beautiful passages from the Psalms.

"God is our refuge and strength, a very present help in trouble."

"Therefore we will not fear though the earth be removed and the mountains carried into the midst of the sea."

"God is our refuge in distress, an ever present help in times of trouble."

"He is indeed" she softly murmured.

And then while I continued the blessed insensibility of sleep slowly locked her senses in oblivion.

I determined to watch and wait. But weary nature will have her rights. By degrees the scenes and objects in which I had mingled through the day recurred to my memory in a manner confused and indistinct, and I soon lost all recollection of where and what I was.

It was bright fresh morning when I woke, the leaves were whispering and the birds singing. So profound had been my slumber that it required an effort to recall the events of the preceding day, or to understand fully my situation. I looked around for my companion. She had awakened first, and deeming my posture uncomfortable had gradually lowered me to the ground, formed a pillow of leaves for my head, and covered me with our cloaks. She smiled, but sadly and wearily, at my look of surprise, and coming towards me expressed her gratitude that I had slept so well.

I arose with a feeling of weakness pervading my whole frame, and my head swam with a strange sensation of giddiness. I well knew the cause. Without any appetite I apprehended the necessity of food. We had made no provision for this contingency, because we had anticipated reaching the boat by morning, and now what next?

Before proceeding farther it was necessary to hold a consultation. To procure food was out of the question except such as nature spontaneously afforded, and I dismissed the thought. My mistress for the time seemed incapable of action or decision. She reclined wearily on a mossy knoll, her face buried in her hands, and tho she said nothing I felt that she must be aware how far we had wandered from the right way.

"My dear Mistress" I said approaching her. "We have certainly been going from the river instead of towards it. Don't you think so?"

She nodded in the affirmative.

"Have you any idea what part of the country we are in?"

She shook her head.

"Were you ever here before?"

"Never."

"Then what shall we do?"

"Just sit down and die here" she replied, with a sort of shriek.

"It is horrible, dreadful to be sure, but better after all than to be sold for a slave."

I saw that one of her nervous excited spells was coming on, and felt all the more the absolute necessity for strong resolution and courage on my own part. I spoke up cheerily, and how my cheerfulness belied my real feelings. "We will do no such thing. I will climb yonder hill. Perhaps I can thence obtain a view of some village, or river, or something else that will show us where we are."

She quietly acquiesced in my proposal, and I ascended the hill. There was a house, but no village in the distance. There were men laboring in the adjacent feilds and I heard the barking of a dog. I gathered a few berries, carried them to my companion and entreated her to eat. She refused, saying that she had no appetite.

"But you are weak and faint. Eat my beloved mistress for my sake if not your own."

Thus I plead[ed] with and entreated her, and finally prevailed. She partook a small quantity.

We lingered in the woods till nearly noon uncertain what course to pursue. To our confused intellects even the sun appeared to occupy a wrong position in the heavens. Oh: the horror the bewilderment of being lost. After a time, however, I felt a new confidence springing up within me. I felt that we had one friend and protector and that One the greatest and the best. We could not be utterly forsaken, and hopeless and helpless when God was near. We had committed no crime and what had we to fear? We had not the appearance of fugitives from slavery. No one there could recognise who and what we were. We could easily reach the house I had discovered, where perhaps we could ascertain all we desired to know.

This plan I communicated to my mistress. At first she hesitated, declaring that detection would be worse than death.

"But there can be detection" I replied.

"Oh: I don't know I don't know" she answered wringing her hands.

"I can see no reason why we should fear it. We will represent ourselves as poor women who have become accidental[l]y lost."

"Which will be no more than the truth" she said with a sudden energy.

"Certainly it will be truth, and as such we will tell it. Now let us go."

I took her hand, and she arose, but her apparent weakness really surprised and alarmed me. I could not fully appreciate all she had suffered; for tho' a slave myself I had never possessed freedom, wealth, and position as she had, but I saw its effects in the utter prostration of her nervous system, her trembling limbs, and tottering steps.

Determined not to be again misled; for the second time I ascended the hill, took good notice of the direction, and then went down. She was sitting where I had left her at the foot. I assisted her to rise, gave her my arm, bade her be of good courage, and led her unresistingly across the plain.

It was farther to the house than I had at first supposed; and we were obliged to cross a small stream where some boys were fishing. They regarded us with evident surprise, and one of the smaller boys called out to his companions that two crazy women were coming.

"Not exactly that my good little fellow" I said soothingly. "Not exactly that, but almost as bad; we are lost, ~~give~~ can you give us the direction to the village of Milton to which the steamboat runs.["]

"Bless you, Madam, he can't tell you anything about it. He is too little. I am bigger you see," and the little fellow assumed an air of childish importance really laughable to behold.

"Well" I said "as you are bigger, perhaps you can tell us."

"To be sure I can" he replied "but Missus it is a long road."

"Think so?"

"Yes, and yonder are some boys bigger still than I am, and may be they could tell you still better."

"Perhaps they could" I answered "but who lives in that large house yonder?"

"Why father lives there."

"And what is your father's name?"

"Frederick Hawkins, but they call him Colonel sometimes."

"And do you suppose that we could get some food; and rest for a short time in your father's house before we proceed?"

"Oh: I know very well that you could. I will go with you and tell him that you have been lost, and that you are hungry and weary."

I looked at my mistress. She said nothing but shook her head. I hesitated I [sic] [a] minute or two and then decided that probably, in view of all the circumstances, it would be better to go on directly to the village. We obtained the necessary information and started off, traveling through fields and along by roads in order to escape observation. But we made slow progress. Unaccustomed to fatigue, or any continued exercise my dear companion could not bear it, and she was often very often compelled to stop and rest. On such occasions I could scarcely tell which predomderated predominated—her great fear and horror of discovery, or her affectionate tenderness to me.

"My dear Hannah" she would say "what a great trouble I be to you—how you are obliged to wait on me, and to wait for me. Oh, if I was only strong, if I could only walk on fast and briskly like you can, if I could bear exposure and want as you bear them, how rejoiced I should be."

And then I would soothe and compassionate with her, and tell her how much I loved her, and how pleasant her society was to me; that even there and then I found motives for consolation and encouragement, that we must exercise faith and patience and an abiding trust in God. Oh, the blessedness of such heavenly trust—how it comforts and sustains the soul in moments of doubt and despondency—how it alleviates misery and even subdues pain.

Towards night we approached a farm-house in the outskirts of the village. It was a happy-looking rural, contented spot, wanting, indeed, in the appearances of wealth and luxury, but evidently the abode of competence and peace. I felt that the possessors of such a humble comfortable place must be hospitable people, that they would have a care for two weak weary wandering women, and so exhorting my mistress to be of good cheer and strong in hope, we entered the gate, and advanced by a neatly graveled walk towards the dwelling. Every thing seemed imbued with a quiet air of domestic happiness. Even the little dog came ~~running wagging~~ to meet us wagging his tail and frisking as if we were old acquaintances. A benevolent-looking middle-aged ~~old~~ Lady came out into the porch as we approached, and politely inquired our wishes. We told her briefly as possible that we were two poor women, who in seeking to find the village of Milton had become bewildered and wandered from the way; that we were weary and hungry, and though we had no claim on her hospitality save that of distress, we should be greatly obliged if she would grant us shelter for the night.

"Come in, and I will ask father" she said, and we entered the house.

An old man, with grey hairs and of the most venerable appearance was sitting near the open window reading the Bible. He looked up, and bowed slightly.

"Father" said the woman, approaching him "here are two poor women, who have been lost in the woods, and who desire to stay with us all night. You have no objections?"

~~Again he~~ He glanced inquisitively towards us, and seeming satisfied with our appearance replied "Not the least in the world."

Her countenance was irradiated with a benevolent smile of joy, as she requested us to be seated and make ourselves at home. The old man continued reading.

"You will excuse father" said the good dame, addressing us. "He always spends the hour of sunset in reading the Bible. I call him father, though he is my husband it seems so natural like."

We replied as well as we were able—that we should be sorry to disturb him.

There was a charm about this house and its appointments. It was very plainly, yet neatly furnished and through it breathed and moved an atmosphere of love. It was the sanctuary of sweet home influences, a holy and blessed spot, so light and warm and with such an abiding air of comfort that we felt ~~so~~ how pure and elevated must be the character of its inmates.

She was one of those old-fashioned women it does one's heart good to behold. Her brown hair, ~~just~~ slightly silvered by time was smoothly parted, and put back beneath a plain cap of snowy whiteness. A neat handkerchief encircled her neck with its snowy folds, and ~~being~~ then crossing her bosom was fastened on one side with a silver pin. Her dress was perfectly in taste, being neither too light nor too dark, too gay nor too sombre, and her apron of black silk pleasantly rustled as she moved about genially like the breeze of summer and beneficently as the sunshine.

Slavery dwelt not there. A thing so utterly dark and gloomy could not have remained in such a place for a day.

Soon there was the hospitable jingle of preparation for supper in another apartment.

"I hope we are giving you no trouble" I ventured to suggest.

"Trouble, Oh no, it is our supper time, and you must partake with us."

"You do us great honor" I responded. And when the table was spread we all sat down together.

It was not such a board as we were accustomed to see spread at my master's house there was nothing that could minister to luxurious habits, or delight an epicurean fancy, but white bread and golden butter, some cherries fresh from the tree, and sweet milk formed the frugal repast. Before tasting it, however, the venerable man invoked the blessing of heaven upon it, and when we had finished he modestly returned thanks.

During supper our hostess became pleasantly talkative. She had a very soft voice, and her conversation was seasoned with cheerful gayety. It seemed to invite confidence, and she was evidently a little curious about the two wanderers thus strangely thrown on her hospitality. It was not strange that she should desire to know our names, and something connected with our former condition, before introducing us to her chambers, and giving us for the night the freedom of her house, yet the revelation might involve us all in danger and difficulty. It could not be made.

"Madam" I said revolving these things in my mind. ["]I trust you will not attribute to any improper motive our hesitancy to reveal what you wish to know. Of one thing you may rest assured whatever we are, or have been we have committed no crime. We have been unfortunate not guilty."

A gleam of intelligence flitted over her face, but gave way in a moment to a look of the deepest compassion, and she said "I see how it is, tell me no more. I do not wish to know."

There were voices in an adjoining room. The face of my mistress paled with fear.

"It is only my brother" said the hostess, probably noticing her look of alarm. "He is a lawyer, and has a room here, but being very retired in his habits we see little of him."

A lawyer, and retired in his habits—could it be possible? but no, and why should we torment ourselves with unnecessary fears? Since sufficient for the day is the evil thereof.

The good dame now led us into a room more retired and secluded than the former ones, but having the same air of orderly neatness, comfort, and perfect taste. It contained a bed very white and sweet, some chairs nicely cushioned, a small bureau, a very little stand, and a table. There was one window, only one, and that was low, little and half-curtained by whispering leaves. Stems of sweet lavender and rose-leaves were lying about, but the air seemed sultry, and going to the window I opened it, and looked out on the night.

It was a starlight night, but the air being soft, and balmy and hazy the stars seemed to look down upon you through a misty veil. They are shining here as they shine over the splendid mansion of my master. And what do they see there? Do they see the house in confusion, the servants alarmed, the master distracted. Have the large rooms been overturned, the galleries explored, the chambers searched? Has there been a hurrying to and fro, a racing and chasing around the country, notices posted up, and rewards offered. Perhaps. Or it may be that fearing the exposure and disgrace the master has hushed up all rumour and concealed the flight of his wife, vainly supposing that she will soon return; that he thinks of her moodily and wonderingly, sitting alone in the drawing room, while the shadows darken and thicken around him and the linden creaks.

Our hostess came in with a light. It was a lamp very little and pleasantly shaded, that diffused a soft illumination through the apartment, not enough to overpower the gloom, but sufficient to melt and soften it.

Regarding us compassionately she said pointing to the bed "You can rest there, and you need not fear disturbance. You have my best wishes" and she passed from the room, leaving gloom where the light of her presence had been.

My dear companion had taken a low seat, and remained silent and passive. We were alone, yet it seemed to me that the shadow of an evil presence was near us, that some evil eye was noting our doings, and that evil plans were concocting against us. Our benevolent hostess and her husband were above suspicion, but the old lawyer of retired habits, I was not so sure of him. The leafy curtaining of our window was slightly rustled, yet there was no breeze. I looked towards it; my companion trembled. Again there was a slight rustle, and I distinctly saw a human hand cautiously parting and pushing aside the leaves. The large white fingers were certainly those of a man. No less certainly was it a man's face that appeared there in another moment, the keen black eyes taking in the room and us at a glance. A keen black eye, and sharp angular features, though I obtained only a glimpse of them—but such an eye, only one person in the world possessed it, and that was Mr Trappe.

"Did you see him?" said my mistress, clasping her hands in agony. "Oh say, did you see him, or am I dreaming?"

"I saw something, or somebody" I replied

"It was his eyes, it was him. We are discovered" ~~said~~ she said with a suppressed cry of utter despair.

For a time I could say nothing to comfort her. I needed a comforter myself. He was then watching us, dogging our footsteps, and would be haunting us everywhere. By a natural instinct I turned towards the bed. Go to bed, to sleep, to rest without fear of being disturbed. How utterly impossible. Would there be rest or quiet anymore for us in this world? Were we ever again to sleep in peace? It seemed not. We must fly again. That very night we must set forth. We must leave the hospitable cottage and its inmates without thanks or ceremony. Under the broad heaven, with the free air, the free leaves, the free beauties of nature about us, we could breathe freer than there, but could we hope to escape?

My companion arose from the floor with tolerable composure. She was strong as persons have sometimes exhibited strength on the rack, as fever, delirium, or mortal agony makes strong. "What shall we do, what can we do?" she inquired hoarsely.

"Go to bed, and put out the light" I answered.

"Do you think that I could sleep, that I could shut my eyes after what I have seen?"

"I do not suppose that you would, neither should I, and yet our only chance of escape is in that project.

"There is no doubt that our enemy is this moment in the house. He has discovered us, our safety rests in his believing that we did not discover him. We will retire as if nothing had happened, and wait till in the late hours of night all becomes quiet, till even his restless brain is overpowered by slumber, and then we will go."

I said this calmly, for a sort of desperation had given me calmness. She acquiesced in the scheme. Silently we laid aside our outer garments, extinguished the light and retired to bed. Need I describe how painfully awake we were, how we were sensitive to the smallest sound, or how long and wearily the hours dragged on.

Once or twice we distinctly heard a door open and shut, and a man's step in the passage, then all became perfectly still.

About midnight I arose and looked softly out. Not a star was in sight. The heaven was overcast with clouds and the wind moaned heavily. I thought of the Linden and its creaking limbs, thought of those who enjoyed their luxurious beds in pleasant dreams of home and friends, thought of ourselves, who without crime were hunted from place to place, and obliged to seek safety in darkness and obscurity.

Thinking that the time had come, and trusting in Heaven we arose, put on our clothes, carefully hoisted the window, pushed aside the leaves, and crept through the aperture. We reached the ground without harm, or making a noise. Quite as cautiously and silently we scaled the low board fence opposite, and were once more in the wide broad field. This advantage trifling as it was afforded us inexpressible relief. We fancied that we were leaving our enemy behind, ~~and~~ that every step increased the distance between us, and thus strengthened we hurried on. But whither? Our plans were all disconcerted now. He would intercept us at the village, he would be before us in the boat. Our only chance lay in concealment, and how were we to effect that? A deep, dark wood presented on our right hand, and thoughtless of superstitious dread, careless of fatigue, anxious only to escape our dreaded enemy into it we plunged. Over the logs, through the brushwood, tearing our garments, mangling our feet. On, on we went, how far we cared not only the farther the better. At length my beloved companion sank down by the side of a huge log, and declared that she ~~must rest~~ could not surmount it, that she must rest. Almost equally overcome I crouched beside her, and there in that position we remained till day. We then retired still farther into the woods, making our breakfast on some wild fruits, and quenching our thirst at a small rillet, that meandered among the shades. Gloomy, indeed, was our walk, but gloomier were our thoughts. Serpents, wild beasts, and owls were our companions, yet our horror was of man.

Towards noon the clouds blew off, and the sun came out. The young leaves whispered and talked, the birds sang, and the winds laughed among the trees. There was mirth and music around us; there was youth, and love, and joy for all things, but our troubled hearts.

Suddenly we were surprised and alarmed by emerging into a small clearing, in which stood an old cabin. A moment[']s survey, however, convinced me that it was uninhabited. The paths leading to the entrance were choked with weeds, and all appeared forlorn and desolate. Cautiously we advanced, ~~and entered~~ as cautiously we entered. It had been the residence probably of some forester, and was formed much as Indians formed their wigwams. There was neither floor, door nor window, an old bench, of which one leg was broken, a broken iron pot, and some pieces of broken crockery were scattered about. In one corner was a heap of damp mouldy straw that had probably served as a bed, and in another was a bundle of old clothes. I feared to examine them; for I thought, but wherefore I know not that they might be connected with some deed of crime. As there were no traces of recent inhabitants we determined to abide there for a few weeks. True, a more lonely and desolate place could not well be imagined, but loneliness was what we sought; in that was our security. We could gather our sustenance from the forest, we could quench our thirst at a neighboring spring, and at least we should be free.

And there we remained for many days: how many I cannot tell. But the fruits and berries that were hard and green ~~on our arrival~~ when we arrived there became juicy and mellow and finally departed before we left. The flowers that were just budding, opened, ripened, and dropped their seeds, and the birds that were busily employed all day long, singing and building their nests, hatched and matured their offspring.

I had long thought that the cabin had been the theatre of fearful crime, and subsequent discoveries tended to confirm this opinion. There was a dark deep stain on the ground that I could not divest from the idea of blood, and when we removed the straw in the corner the spears were matted and felted together as if blood had been spilt over and then dried upon them. Removing the bundle of clothes we found a hatchet, with hair yet sticking to the heft, and while searching for berries discovered the remains of a human skeleton which the dogs and vultures had disentombed.

In consideration of these discoveries a superstitious horror took possession of my dear companion[']s mind. The scream of a nightbird, or the howl of a wolf, even the voice of the wind filled her mind with terror. The sounds of the night she interpreted into utterances from the unseen world, and the shadows flitting across her path she regarded as things of eternity made visible. In vain ~~Towards Autumn, so fe~~ I besought her to banish these gloomy apprehensions. In vain I strove to support her with the reflection that whatever might have been done as we were innocent of crime no harm could come to us, but though her reason consented to all I said, her terrors were unconquerable.

Towards Autumn we began to think of changing our habitation, but where to go, or how to go was a serious question. Our garments were torn, our shoes worn out, and we could not hope to escape observation in so miserable a plight. But to remain there through the winter was impossible. The frost would destroy our supplies of food, and then we had neither fire nor the means of obtaining any. All these things we carefully revolved, and in our extremity sometimes half resolved to throw ourselves on the mercy of our enemy, and know the worst.

The difficulties of my situation were increasing daily. The mind of my companion became seriously effected. Want, fatigue, exposure, and the long long agonies of mental torture, had deeply wrought on her physical constitution, and impaired her intellect. She became querelous and complaining, upbraided me as the cause of all her difficulties, and heaped the strangest accusations of conspiracy on my head. This seemed the bitterest cup of all and I was ready to cry in the language of the Saviour "Father, if it be possible let this pass from me" but through his infinite goodness I felt to add likewise "Not my will but thine be done."

After a time my mistress became decidedly insane, and her insanity partook the most painful character. She fancied herself pursued by an invisible being, who sought to devour her flesh and crush her bones. She would scream with affright, and cowering to the ground crouching to the earth point with her finger to the ob dreadful creation of her distempered fancy. "There; there it is, it is coming, keep him off, keep him off won[']t you? Oh horrible. He tears my flesh, he drinks my blood. Oh; oh" then falling to the ground in a paroxysm of the wildest fear. She would remain insensible for a long time. At intervals, however, the light of her mind, struggling struggled through its enveloping clouds, and she would converse rationally as in former times.

One morning I was surprised by the barking of a dog, and the shouts of men. The sounds were evidently near and probably proceeded from a party of hunter's [sic]. In a few moments more three men emerged from the wood, and advanced directly towards our cabin. Flight, had we been so disposed was out of the question, and so cowering in a corner we determined to abide our fate, or rather I did; for my companion seemed incapable of any connected thought. I heard them talking as they approached.

"Well, it is strange anyhow, but this Cabin must certainly have been inhabited recently. The paths are well worn, and, by Jove, here's the print of a footstep too" said one, in a loud coarse voice.

"Where? I can't see any" said another.

"There in the dew on the grass. Don't you see it now?"

"Yes, and a woman's too."

["]Some runaway Negro, perhaps, hope we can catch him" and he called his dog.

"No Negro never made such a track as that."

"I dare say by looking round we shall find out who made it. They can't be far off" said the third.

"Well we'll look here first" and suiting his actions to the word he advanced to the door and looked in, but hastily drew back on seeing us.

"What is it?" inquired his companion.

"Lord help me if I know what it is. Look for yourself."

The two others now thrust in their heads, took one look at us, and drew back. Had we indeed lost all resemblance to human beings. We were crouched in the corner beneath our cloaks, and our head the only parts of our persons visible, were disfigured by matted masses of hair, which feel [fell] over and vailed our faces.

"Shoot at it" said one.

"I believe in my soul, it's a woman" exclaimed another as my companion slightly moving revealed a part of her person.

With that I threw off the cloak, rose to my feet, and moved towards them. "Gentlemen" I said "we are two poor women, who lost our way last spring, wandered off here, and here took up our abode, because we could find no other home."

"A[i]n't you runaway slaves?" suggested one.

They were hard featured men with little in their appearance to recommend them. I tremblingly answered that I was or had been a slave.

"And what is she?" they inquired alluding to my companion.

"She was my mistress."

"Your mistress" and he burst into a loud guffaw.

"A fine story you are telling me, mistresses don't go wandering about in that manner."

"Stop" said another one of the trio "there is some mystery here. I heard something about it last spring. What was your master's name?"

Not perceiving that any good could come of concealment I told him.

"Yes, that was the name. It is just as she says" he continued addressing the others.

"How long have you been here?" inquired another.

"All summer nearly."

"Faith, I wouldn't stay here a night for all ~~your master's~~ that was once your master's fortune."

"May I inquire the reason why?["]

"Because it is said that a beautiful girl was once murdered here, and that the place is haunted. Haven't you found it so."

I replied that a good conscience was a sure protector, and that no spirit had troubled me.

"Well, who would have imagined that our gunning expedition would have been so profitable. Why these gals will be worth more to us than all the game in the woods."

"My mistress is sick and deranged. She has suffered so much" I said. "You will deal tenderly with her."

"Certainly, if she behaves herself" he answered dryly.

Fortunately ~~she was in a bo~~ her mind was in a lucid interval, and she maintained surprising composure, remarking only that the bitterness of death was past, and that whatever might be her destiny her sufferings could not exceed those she had already felt.

"I make no appeal to your sympathy" she said. "I say nothing of horror or alarm. I do not ask you to consider that possibly some great misfortune may happen to you, and you may need friends as we need them now. I do not ask you to consider all this, well knowing that were I not dumb you would be deaf, that neither tears, nor prayers, nor entreaties of ours could move your purpose whatever that may be."

"You think meanly of us, Madam" said one of the men. A smile rested on the countenances of the others, perhaps that he should designate such a miserable looking person by such a term. He observed it.

"Smile if you please" he said "but that woman once graced an exalted station, and I pity the misfortune which seems beyond hope of remedy."

"Heaven I fear has turned against us" continued my mistress mournfully. "There is no use battling against fate. Henceforth come what will I am resigned."

The passiveness of a settled despair was apparent in all her words and movements.

"Then you will go with us peacefully" said one.

"Whither" she inquired, coming forward, and fixing her large sad eyes with an expression of mournful interest on the speaker's face. ["]Will you take me to my father? Heaven knows how gladly I would go to him."

Her senses were wandering.

"Not to your father, dear Madam" replied the one, who had formerly addressed her thus, and whom his companions called Horace "not to your father, but where you will be taken care of."

"To my husband, then?"

"We could not."

"Why not?" inquired one of the others.

"He is dead" answered Horace in a low voice. "At least that old lawyer who knows or seems to know everything told me so."

She caught the word lawyer. An expression of unutterable agony flitted over her ~~face~~.

"Not to him" she almost shrieked. "Indeed I cannot go to him."

"And you shall not, you shall not," said Horace pityingly. "I will see to that."

Presently the three men withdrew to a little distance, where they stood and talked, and whispered. I thought that Horace remonstrated with them, that he objected to some proposal, but I caught only one sentence of their conversation and that was something about a large reward.

Then they returned to us, and we were led away as sheep are led to the slaughter unresisting, uncomplaining and uncertain of our fate.

I am half-inclined to believe that my overtaxed brain became bewildered at times like that of my poor dear mistress. I am sure that they talked of us, tho' I failed to comprehend the words. I heard them. I understood their meaning, but could attach to them no sense in any other connection. I had heard them say "He is dead" and yet failed to realize at first that it was my master of whom they spoke. Then slowly, yet certainly the overpowering conviction was forced upon me, but how did he die?

We were walking along a narrow wood-road—all except my mistress. She was incapable of the exertion, and so they had formed for her a sort of rude litter which they carried alternately, two at a time, leaving one ~~at freedom~~ unemployed to prevent my escape. An unnecessary precaution, since even my strong desire for freedom, now become the object of my life, could not have induced me to abandon her. The man Horace was walking with me. He looked sad and sympathising. I might venture to inquire of him "You said, I think, that my master was dead, will you tell me how he died?" I asked.

"By his own hand, in the drawing-room—that ancient one where hung the family pictures" he replied.

"And the mansion?" I inquired.

"Has already with the servants passed into other [hands].["]

From all I could gather it appeared that on the next day but one succeeding that of our escape Mr Trappe unexpectedly returned. Enjoying as he did the freedom of the house he went directly to the apartments of my mistress which he found vacated. Descending again he encountered Lizzy in one of the passages who in a great state of consternation and alarm informed him that her mistress had gone no one knew whither. Whether he was prepared for such a contingency, or whether he was betrayed from his usual calm indifference into something like surprise it is impossible to say, but he made inquiries for my master, and proceeded to ~~have~~ hold [an] interview with him.

He was in the south drawing-room, and of course Mr Trappe was admitted to his presence. What might have been the tenor of their conversation, what secrets were revealed, what disclosures made must remain a mystery. Who can doubt the painfulness of their character, or the depths of disgrace and exposure that were laid bare? The interview was long, very long, and then Mr Trappe came gliding out. His seedy black clothes, and blacker eyes gleamed a moment in the passage. The echo of his stealthy step was first heard on the porch, and then his retreating form passed rapidly down the long avenue of oaks, and he was seen no more. The evil his presence always brought with it had been accomplished there. He had brought misery and destruction on the household. Was not that enough?

Silent and solitary in his apartment, the linden creaking beneath the window remained my master. No one ventured to intrude on his privacy. Was there no voice in all that sumptuous dwelling with its luxurious appointments to meet the servants going to and fro, or passing in and out with the whisper "go to him." Is there no influence there to prefigure even to Mrs Bry what is then passing in his room, and beneath that roof? Is there no significance in the hours as they pass away, and still he comes not forth? His dinner is waiting, a sumptuous dinner served on massy plate. The delicate viands breathe a delicious flavor, the wine leaps and sparkles. His carriage is waiting, he had ordered them to have it in readiness by four o clock. Four o clock in the afternoon, and that hour passed. It is a long time for him to linger in his room. I never know him to remain so long before, mused Mrs Bry.

Five o'clock, and still invisible. Something must be wrong. Mrs Bry goes around the house, and looks up at the window; the shutters are closed. She returns enters the house and seeks the door of his apartment; it is fastened within, and even the keyhole closed up by bits of crumpled paper. She listens; there is noise. She knocks; there is no answer. She becomes seriously alarmed and the other servants catch the contagion. There is hurry and confusion, and a great scampering about the rooms. No one could tell what they are doing or trying to do. On that point they have no definite idea themselves. However they all say that something is wrong, and it really seems as if they designed that since insuperable obstacles prevented getting where the wrong apparently was, they would go at random where it was not.

There is a sort of scream, and a voice in one of the lower rooms. "My God, what is this?"

Mrs Bry hastens; others run to ascertain the nature of the discovery. "It is water" said one "nothing—somebody has spilt some water."

"Do you call that water?" inquired the discoverer holding up her finger stained with a dark red substance. "It is blood, that's what it is, and so is this, and this."

And sure enough on the floor were several little pools of clotted gore. Mrs Bry looks upward at the ceiling; that is bloody too. She comprehends it all in a moment. ~~immediately above this is the apartment~~ In great alarm and agitation she rushes out, summons the overseer of the estate, who quietly hears her story, looks at the blood, remarks that it is very strange, and then forces open the door of my master's room.

What find they there? The master fallen from his easy chair; fallen on his face to the floor, his garments and the carpet saturated with the red stream that still oozed slowly from a ghastly wound in his throat.

CHAPTER 6

New Places

Lo; the wicked bend their bow, they make ready their arrow on the string.

PSALMS

Leaving the woods we advanced along an open plain, and thence entered a well-beaten road that led through the midst of a well-populated district. Our conductors laughed and joked on the strange appearance we all presented and the curiosity of the people, who sought to discover who and what we were. The novelty of our situation seemed to have wrought favorably on my mistress. She remained passive and silent, only inquiring now and then where they were taking her, or what they designed to do with her. And when they answered her evasively she would laugh with a short hysterical sob, and then relapse into silence.

We traveled slowly. The men soon wearied beneath their burden, and my weakened limbs and attenuated frame could ~~barely~~ hardly support the exercise of walking, even with long and frequent intervals of rest. At length, and just as night was shutting over the landscape, the patter of a mill, the spire of a church, and the distant hum of voices gave indication that we approached a village. The houses were soon in sight, some of them in a sort of dusky gloom that was neither light nor darkness, but the most with lights twinkling at the windows, ~~that look~~ and all wearing a placid look of peace and content.

One of the men went forward, as I supposed to herald our arrival, and to see that some place was prepared for our reception, my heart told me too well what place that would be.

He returned speedily, whispered that it was ready, and on we went into the village, along a street, past a tavern where many lights were burning and a great many people standing by a store whose broad glass windows were richly illuminated besides being garnished with a great variety of goods—and to a large building that seemed to blockade the street as it loomed dark and gloomy and in perfect contrast to the surrounding objects. They paused before this building, and one of ~~them~~ them tapped at a little low window, which like the others, was garnished with iron gratings. A few words were exchanged in a low tone with some one within, and the bolts revolved, an iron door swung heavily open and we stood within the vestibule of a prison.

It was a small, but strong guard room, from which a narrow stair case led upwards, and two low entrances conducted to cells or apartments on the ground floor, all secured with the tyrant strength of bolts and bars. The bleak walls otherwise bare were not unsuitably furnished with iron fetters, and other uncouth implements, designed for still more inhuman purposes, interspersed with broad bowie knives, guns, pistols, and other weapons of offence and defence.

At finding ourselves, ~~thus suddenly~~, and without having committed any crime, thus introduced into one of the legal fortresses of a country celebrated throughout the world for the freedom, equality, and magnanimity of its laws, I could not help reflecting on the strange ideas of right and justice that seemed to have usurped a place in public opinion, since the mere accident of birth, and what persons were the least capable of changing or modifying was made a reason for punishing and imprisoning them.

At our first entrance I turned an eager glance towards my mistress, and our conductors, but the lamp in the vestibule was too low in flame to afford my curiosity any satisfaction. Had her countenance expressed all the horror in the world, or theirs all the sympathy I could not have discerned it by the dim uncertain rays. Presently the jailer lit a small tallow candle, which he found after along search on a little shelf, and I obtained a distinct view of his uncouth features and wild appearance. His hair was red as fire, and being brushed back from his equally red face stood all on end. His eyes were blood-shotten, and various small red pimples disfigured his nose. He seemed to understand perfectly who and what we were, and made sundry remarks at our expense.

"Gals runaway—couldn't afford to lose 'em—bring heaps of money—one of 'em sick, eh."

He then bade us follow him.

"You will make them comfortable as you can, poor things" said Horace.

The fellow grinned an affirmative.

"And keep them here, till we have time to notify their owners and receive our reward" suggested another.

Another ghastly grin, and then he marshaled us up the stairs, and along a narrow gallery, which had several doors opening into it, that apparently communicated with other cells and passages. Then coming to a dead halt, he applied a key to ~~the lock of~~ the lock of a door so low and narrow that no one could pass through it erect, or without turning side-foremost. The door flew open.

"Now walk in there, one at a time" he said eyeing us closely.

We obeyed in silence, and he was about closing the door upon us when I inquired if we couldn't have a light.

"A light, faith, and what do you want of that?" he answered roughly.

"To see by, of course; it is very dark in here" I replied.

"There isn't much to see, I guess" he said with a low chuckle "but I shall be back directly to bring you some supper" and the door shut with a bang.

We were now in almost Egyptian darkness, and the hot stifling air had a suffocating stench. We could only cling to each other, and group [grope] our way ~~around the cell~~ with outstretched hands around the cell.

It contained no furniture with the exception of a low wooden stool, and a cot-bed or pallet very narrow and exceedingly filthy. Stumbling over these we were both seated when the jailer returned.

"Making yourselves at home a[l]ready" he said in a half-cheerful half sneering manner. "Here is your supper and ~~hope you~~ I hope you won't ~~many~~ make any disturbance, or try to get out, because you see it isn't pleasant to have a muss, specially with women."

Telling him not to give himself uneasiness on that score I again besought him to leave us a light.

"If it wasn't gin the rules" he began.

"Who cares for the rules" I said interrupting him. "You must certainly be an independent man, you can tell, you know very well what is necessary. We have not been placed here for punishment but only safe-keeping." And thus by alternately coaxing and flattering him he was induced to leave the candle with us, muttering meanwhile to himself that he wasn't sure it was all right.

The food he brought us was coarse and unpalatable. It consisted of some hard, dry mouldy bread, some cheese alive with vermin and some water so ~~me~~ warm and fetid that we could scarcely drink it. We only ate a few morsels, and then retired to our humble bed.

It is said that persons have been known to sleep on the rack, and even when exposed to the keenest agony of torturing fire. Worn out with fatigue and harrowing anxiety I sank into a painful and uneasy slumber. It was not rest, for I was wearied and tortured by a frightful dream. It was not the blessed oblivion that locks the senses when peace and happiness surround us, but a sort of lethargic stupor, the result of over-taxed exertion mental and physical.

Then came a sensation of bodily pain, and presently a consciousness that some animal was trying to devour me. I started up in horror and grasped a huge rat that was nibbling at my cheek. Releasing him as quickly he ran frightened into his hole, which the faint rays of the lamp rendered visible in the farthest corner of the cell.

With the contingency of being devoured before my eyes, I could not shut them again, but lay painfully awake, while my terrified imagination began to conjure strange fancies. I had heard of rats in prisons and ancient charnel-houses, that ~~banqueted~~ banqueted hediously on the dead, or that assailing even living men and women by thousands gnawed the quivering and palpitating flesh from their bones. Such a fate was too horrible to contemplate. I gazed in fascinated horror at the cavity, whence now and then the creature would stick its head, glance around with its eager eyes, and then draw back suddenly.

At length to my inexpressible horror and alarm the candle which had burned low in the socket suddenly flickered, wavered, went out and we were involved in darkness. A cold sweat rose to my forehead, and I trembled with excess of nervous agitation, when a voice seemed to whisper to my soul ~~one word only~~ "God" and immediately, like light breaking in the darkness I felt a comforting a heavenly assurance of his protection and presence. "Cast all your care upon him, for he careth for you." "The hairs of your heads are numbered your tears are in his bottle." These and the like consoling passages of Scripture strengthened and supported me. Then I thought of the Saviour and his agony and drew comfort from the assurances of his dying love. I felt that the God of Israel was my refuge, that underneath me were his everlasting arms, and I felt rebuked in conscience for my doubts and fears and despondency, and that I had forgotten him so long.

I embraced my dear companion, though she slumbered heavily, kissed and wept over her, and then endeavored to compose myself. I succeeded. A pleasant slumber sealed my eyelids, and I enjoyed a blessed dream of my mother, whom I had never seen. My angel mother; I loved then, I still love to fancy that she was near me at the time; that a spirit herself she influenced me spiritually, and that her blessed and holy presence was made the medium of my consolation.

When the jailer came round in the morning we implored for more light and liberty. It was reluctantly granted and the range of a few small cells accorded us. They were all equally miserable and discomfortless, but they added a fellow prisoner to our society. She was a little old woman, withered and skin-dried and having altogether the most singular appearance. Yet her countenance was benevolent, and she had a soft low voice, though sorrow and confinement had impaired her intellect. She was the victim of mental hallunciation, and strangely enough believed that these miserable cells were palace halls, in which she acted the character of hostess and received us as guests. Her bows, and smiles, and courtesies were painfully amusing as she extended her hand to receive us, and observed with an air of great politeness "Very happy, I am sure, but whom have I the honor of addressing?"

The jailer, who was present, looked at me, touched his forehead, and said half-aside "Not quite right here, but perfectly harmless. They can amuse each other" and he pointed to my mistress.

"I see you are strangers here" continued the old lady whose name was Wright. "I was a stranger here myself, and it was sometime before I learned to appreciate all the comforts of the place. I have the honor of living here now, and I live well and easy too. The state cares for me, provides for me, furnishes me a home—very motherly and good is the state." Then glancing at my companion she inquired "Be you sisters?" I shook my head. "Only friends.["] "Friends" she repeated after me. "Well, I had a friend once. I had a lover once. I had children once; I had a husband once, but I have nothing now, neither friend, nor lover, nor child, nor husband; all all deserted me when I came here, but misery dwells in palaces I always heard that" and her eyes wandered over the rough stone walls, and the high dark ceiling with an admiring and complacent look.

I felt a strange curiosity to ascertain what grand or beautiful semblances her diseased fancy had given to the hard coarse stones, filthy with accumulated dust and clothed with the webs of spiders.

"They brought me here" she continued "they told me it was necessary that I should stay. I couldn't see it so at first but after a time I—I—grew more reconciled. And now I call it my palace, and that man, who comes in once and awhile is my groom of the ceremonies, and I have guests occasionally as I have now."

"But why did you come here?" I inquired "You certainly would have preferred staying with your husband and children."

I had struck the right chord in her memory, and she answered perfectly rational.

["]It's a long story. I don't know that I can tell it all; for sometimes I forget, or I cannot recall names and events in their proper places."

I told her that made no difference; she only need give me the outline of her history. I should be quite satisfied with that.

It seemed as near as I could gather from her disconnected and disjoin[t]ed statements that she had been well to do in the world, and greatly esteemed and beloved by her neighbors. Her woman's heart was brimful of love and kindness for all, but most especially for the oppressed and afflicted. She had a great fondness for little children, yet one, and that one a slave child, shared particularly her love and tenderness. The kind good-hearted soul had never learned the cold lesson of the world that slaves were made for toil, not love, and that it was a waste of affection to lavish it on them.

In her earlier years and before she was able to work Ellen was suffered to visit Mrs Wright whenever she pleased, and to stay as long as she desired. Then she made one less about the grounds, she obtained food and many little things of which the mistress took account, but when she grew older, and her labor became desirable she was forbidden to visit the house of her friend. But habits of intimacy once acquired are not readily broken off. Ellen felt that she must go, and go she would and did. She had attained her fifteenth year, and was really a beautiful girl, in complexion approaching the Spanish with dark sparkling eyes, and a profusion of hair, jet black, and curling around a neck and over shoulders of exquisite grace.

A slave-trader was around. He was selecting and purchasing beautiful girls for the New Orleans market. Ellen attracted his attention, and he determined to obtain her if possible. ~~Readily and willingly~~ Readily and willingly, for the consideration of a good sum in money, her master yeilded to his wishes. He felt no compunction in dooming the beautiful girl to a life of misery ten times more horrible than a death of torture. He reck[on]ed not that she was a woman of delicate sensibilities and fine perfections—she was a slave, and ~~no more~~ that was all to him.

When the news of her dreadful fate reached the ears of Ellen, she fled in horror and consternation to Mrs Wright. That good lady was filled with almost equal grief and astonishment. It seemed that duty, love, religion, humanity everything and every generous sentiment urged her to preserve the beautiful victim from such a miserable doom. Perhaps she exercised too little discretion, but moved by the considerations of mercy and tenderness, and above all by the tears and prayers and entreaties of Ellen she resolved on a desperate expedient, no other than smuggling the terrified girl out of the country.

Without consulting her husband, or informing her children, she retired with Ellen to a private room, cut off her long beautiful hair, and disguised her in the garments of a boy. Then leaving a note for her family, she ordered her carriage, mounted it took Ellen by her side and drove away.

Unfortunately, however, the flight of Ellen was immediately discovered by her master. He traced her to the dwelling of Mrs Wright, and there discovered her beautiful hair and cast-off garments, ascertained, too, that the good lady had taken a boy into her carriage and driven away. They followed with all speed, overtook and arrested her, carried Ellen back and sent Mrs Wright to jail. She was tried for kidnapping convicted and sentenced to a long imprisonment.

Thus the matron was torn from her home, the wife from her husband, the mother from her children for no crime but yeilding to the dictates of humanity. For a time she brooded in hopeless sorrow, and to aggravate her punishment as much as possible she was doomed to a solitary cell, and forbidden ~~the society of her husband~~

~~and e~~ to receive the visits of her husband and children. Even the comforting influences of nature were withdrawn. The sunshine, the free winds, the blessed face of heaven were denied her. For two long weary years she only beheld one human face, and that one the jailer[']s. Then, wherefore wonder that her mind failed? or that premature age and imbecility stultified her faculties, and she became little better than an idiot?

At length their resentment softened in some degree. Little by little she was allowed more light, more air, and more liberty. Meanwhile an epidemic ravaged the country; her husband and children all died, her property passed into other hands, and she ceased to be spoken of even by those who had experienced the most of her kindness.

By constant habit and association likewise her ~~home had~~ prison had become pleasant. She connected it with ideas of home, a home that the state with great trouble and expense prepared for her, even as it makes provision for its acknowledged head.

All this she told me, bowing and smiling in a way that would have been diverting, had I not reflected on all she must have suffered before her mind gave way.

"I used to hate slavery" she continued "born in a slave state, educated in a slave state, with slavery all the time before my eyes I could see no beauties in the system. Yet they said it was beautiful, and many thought me a fool for not seeing it so, but somehow I couldn't; no I couldn't" and the old creature sighed.

"Have you ever seen it so?" I inquired.

With a bow and a smile, a peculiar turn of the head and twist of the eye as much as to indicate that she did not tell any longer all she or [sic] knew she said

["]Oh you must not ask me such questions, indeed you must not. It might involve us in a great deal of trouble. I have learned what all who live in a land of slaver[y] must learn sooner or later; that is to profess approbation where you cannot feel it; to be hard when most inclined to melt; and to say that all is right, and good; and true when you know that nothing could be more wrong and unjust.["]

CHAPTER 7

Mr Trappe

I have done judgement, and justice; leave me not to my oppressors.

DAVID

An accumulation of misfortunes, differing in cause and character distract and divert the mind by their contrary operation. Thus a change however painful may prove an essential benefit. After our imprisonment the insanity of my beloved mistress assumed a milder character, and finally sunk into a sort of meloncholy. She would sit for hours watching the motions of a spider, or waiting the appearance of a mouse. I strove to draw her out in conversation, tried to amuse or interest her, but in vain. A physician had been summoned to her aid, by whom I never knew. He said that time and quiet would effect her cure, ordered the jailer to ~~permit her~~ allow her all necessary indulgences, and to furnish her with books and other means to enliven her solitude. Was it humanity or policy that prompted them to obey.

We now had the range of an apartment which contained two or three windows, that though heavily grated, admitted light and air and sufficed to give a limited view of the street. This was a great improvement in our condition. We could see ~~the bright shar~~ softly smiling between the bars the quiet and beautiful stars; the moonbeams sometimes checkered our floor, and the free winds lavished a tribute of flower-scents from the groves and fields.

Hitherto we had seen nothing of Mr Trappe. Once or twice, indeed, I had just caught a glimpse of a rusty black coat that reminded me of him, but the idea that he was hovering near us, modulating the degrees of our torture, and waiting till circumstances should admit his striking with most effect, took firm possession of my brain. Then, too, we often received little presents from som[e]body; good clothes had been provided us, though whence they came, and at whose instance we were still confined in the prison remained alike mysteries. But I determined to sound the jailer. That individual had become social and even communicative. Notwithstanding the repulsiveness of his appearance there was something genial and clever in the man. Long habits of association with the vile, and accustomed to witness all the varied exhibitions of possible depravity his manners were uncouth and awkward, his speech always rough and sometimes harsh, ~~yet beneath~~ his countenance expressive of anything but gentleness, yet beneath this unpromising exterior, like the pearl in the unseemly shell of the oyster was concealed a really kind and obliging disposition. One day he came in with a small present of fruits and sweet meats.

"These are really delicious" I observed. "Will you permit Mrs Wright to share them with us?"

He shook his head mysteriously.

"Why not, pray?"

Because it would be contrary to orders.

"At least I may ask whence you received them?"

"Which, the orders, or the sweetmeats?"

"Both."

Another shake.

"Well sir" I observed "I can describe the man exactly. He is rather aged, though he has only a matured look. His eyes are very keen and black; he wears a suit of black like himself old but well-kept; he has a sort of stealthy pace as if feeling the way before him, and he is a lawyer."

The fellow grinned, and said "You've hit it."

"And he sent us these clothes" I continued "he is always hovering near us; he comes to the prison at least once a day."

"Once a week" said the jailer correcting my last sentence. "He was awfully concerned about the other one. He said that she could be cured, that she must be cured, or it would be as good as two thousand dollars out of his pocket. He told the doctor so I heard him."

"The wretch" I muttered half unconsciously.

["]He fears that she will lose her beauty, and then,["] continued the jailer "she would be much less valuable."

Could the heart of a man be capable of such depravity. All these little favors that might be interpreted as symptoms of regard proceeded from the most selfish the most detestable policy. In the power of such a man we had nothing to hope.

I cannot tell how long we remained in the prison, or in what season my mistress began to exhibit symptoms of decided improvement. Slowly and gradually the clouds cleared from her mind, and she regained the full exercise of her mental faculties. The past seemed all like a dark deep dream over which she wept and shuddered, but her very soul revolted at the future before her.

The jailer came in one morning and announced "good news." Mrs Wright as usual smiling and bowing inquired "if it was for her?"

"It is for these" he answered, pointing to us "you are to get yourselves ready to leave the prison."

"And whither are we going?"

"Wherever your master directs of course.["]

However I was delighted with the idea of being once more at large, of revelling in the free wild winds, and possessing even that share of liberty allotted to a slave. Mechanically my dear companion rose. Mrs Wright bade us farewell with a formal ceremony of bowing, curtisying and shaking hands. Bade us receive her blessing, hope we would be very happy, and ended by declaring how happy she should be, and how much she should think herself honored by receiving a visit from us at some future time.

"Oh get along old lady" said the jailer "your [you're] tiresome, come: come."

We glided along the passages, slowly descended the ~~windy~~ winding staircase, and stood in the vestibule of the prison. "Here they be" said the jailer addressing a sharp-looking man, who regarded us intently for a moment or two.

"These are the birds, then, eh; faith they be pretty ones" he said, approaching us with a familiar demonstration.

We retreated a step or two.

"I see" said the man "that they don't incline to be gentle; and now, good ladies" he continued "just let me tell you what's what. I am about to carry you away from this place, agre[e]ably to the commands of your present owner. I want to do so without noise or disturbance. I don't want to employ violence of any kind. You need not be nervous or apprehensive as no harm will be offered you, unless indeed you attempt to escape, and then, I have this" and he displayed the handle of a revolver.

"They're sensible women" said the jailer. "You'll have no occasion for that.["]

"Can't tell" returned the man. "Nothing like being prepared. And now, my dears, pray sit down on that step."

"Why should we sit down there?" inquired my companion.

"Because I tell you to, if for no other reason" returned the man. "Now I want to treat you well, if you will let me. I should like to be polite if I can under the circumstances. If I can't that's another thing, but whether I am so, or otherwise depends on you. So now I command you to set down there."

"You're wrong there, Hayes" said the jailer. "I have had some little experience of mankind, and human nature that you will allow—and I have always found that the simplest request ~~has more power to obtain what you~~ goes farther than the loudest command. If a woman is stubborn or obstinate ask her as a favor, coax her, flatter her and my word for it she'll be pliable as wax in your hands."

"They must mind me either way" answered Hayes.

To me, who had been all my life a slave the idea of obedience was not repulsive, but it galled exceedingly the proud spirit of my companion. I saw from her countenance that she was inclined to rebel, but prudence finally triumphed, and she complied.

"And you, too, by her side there" continued Hayes.

I sat down.

"Now you behave something like" he said. "And just for no other reason in the world than to prevent your being exposed to the temptation of running away, and me from being obliged to shoot you I must put these manacles on your feet. Just thrust them out a little further, hold still. I shall not hurt you."

My companion was deeply affected with a mingled sense of shame, horror, and indignation.

"Why, bless my soul" said Hay[e]s. "This is nothing, nothing at all. I've often seen women as proud and handsome as you subjected to much worse treatment. Now hold out your hands."

Again we complied as resistance would have been worse than useless.

He clasped handcuffs on our wrists.

"Now get up."

We rose manacled together.

The jailer opened the prison door, and Hay[e]s conducted us to the wagon, our chains clanking at every step. Sinking down in the bottom of the vehicle we remained in gloomy silence. That our meditations were of the most painful character no one can doubt. In the language of the prophet "the thing we greatly feared had come upon us." Our situation even precluded hope, that balm to so many sorrows, but we had at least one comforting assurance. We knew that God was with us, and that when earthly friends and protectors failed we should find in Him a sure and certain refuge.

"Are you comfortable" said Hay[e]s turning sharply round. "I mean are you cold, or dry, or hungry?"

Thus recalled to myself, as my companion said nothing I answered for both that we were neither dry nor hunger[sic].

"But you are cold, you look cold. Now wrap up well in this" and he threw a large buffalo robe towards us. "Or stay. I will do it for you" he said, suddenly recollecting our manacled hands.

And with apparent kindness, he tucked the warm furs about us, told us to keep a good heart, and not be disconcerted at trifles. ["]I've had my orders to make you comfortable and I mean to do so, if I can."

But we were not comfortable, with the past behind us, the dark the dreadful future before us, and the present the bitterest and darkest of all.

Had we been less confused and troubled our ride would probably have been pleasant. The sharp frosty air was clear and bracing, and the sunshine had a warm summer time look, really delightful. Then, too, the country through which we passed had such a cheerful appearance with rickyards, milestones, farm houses, wagons, swinging signs, horse troughs, trees, fields, fences, and the thousand other things that make a country landscape. Our conductor stopped once or twice to look at the advertisements which were stuck up on wide boards at the corners of the roads, and which with large black letters on a red or yellow [back]ground made a most conspicuous appearance.

I inquired to what they referred when he informed me that there was to be a great sale of slaves on the morrow. of which ["]Oh: you needn't tremble and turn pale" he continued. "I am not taking you there."

On several occasions he stopped and got out at little country inns; went familiarly into the bar-rooms laughed, chatted; took something to drink, and generally came out with something warm and good for us, a little aniseed or toddy, that he entreated us to drink holding the glass, to our lips, and telling us how much better we should feel for it, always saying in conclusion "I've had orders to make you comfortable, and I'm bound to do so if I can."

The manacles on our wrists grew very painful, and I entreated him to take them off.

"I've had my orders" he replied briefly.

"That we should be chained and fettered like the vilest criminals?" said my companion inquiringly.

"Not exactly that, but much the [same] thing."

After much persuasion and entreaty he consented to remove our fetters, and we solemnly engaged to conform in all things to his requirements.

The sun was probably an hour high when we caught the

glimpse of a white house through some trees on the top of a hill before us. Our conductor pointed to it with his whip, and said "There's your journey's end." Then putting his horses into a canter he took us forward at a great rate, though it was up-hill, and the poor beasts were already tired with our long drive. Presently we lost the house, presently saw it, lost it again and again saw it; then turned into an avenue of cedar, and drew up before a fine cottage residence. Our hearts beat wildly, tumultuously as an old man came hobbling out on a crutch towards the wagon. Age sits beautifully on some ~~and the least farm~~. The frame bent with years, and the dark locks frosted with silver give the possessor a more interesting appearance, than all the flush of youth and beauty. Smile not, when I say that many old men are decidedly loveable, but the one who approached us was not of that sort. His forehead was bald, his eyes blear and very large and round, and not being relieved by eye-lashes which had fallen off, they really looked ogreish. He had a prominent nose, high cheek bones, and black ugly teeth slightly protruding from his mouth at all times, but having the most disagr[e]eable appearance when he opened his lips to speak. But it was the expression of his countenance after all that made me shrink from and fear him. It was so dark, so sinister and sneering. It told so much of malice, of hate, of dislike to the beautiful the good and true. There could be nothing of sunshine to his spirit, nothing of love in his soul.

"Heaven preserve us, if that man is to be our master" whispered my companion. It was the first word she had spoken for a long time.

"He is not your master exactly" said Hay[e]s "but rather your master's steward, a sort of overseer when he is absent."

Removing the manacles from our limbs Hay[e]s bade us alight. We obeyed him.

"You may tell your master" he said, addressing the old man "that I obeyed his directions to the letter. I first made them safe, then I made them comfortable, now have brought them here, and finally deliver them over to you. You are henceforth accountable for their safe-keeping."

The old man replied to this harangue by a sort of leering assent. That of course Mr Hay[e]s knew as well as any man when he had done his duty, and as to our safe-keeping he shouldn't stand on ceremony with us. He never did with that kind of cattle.

"Have you many on hand at present?" inquired Hay[e]s.

["]Not one. The last went off day before yesterday. Master made a pretty speck on her—bought her at auction for five hundred dollars and sold her for fifteen hundred."

"That's what I call doing business" said Hay[e]s. "But take your gals into the house and make them comfortable as I did. They're cold I'll warrant. Get out."

This last was intended for the horses, who seemed to understand it perfectly, and started off at a brisk pace.

Attended by the old man we went to the house, and entered it by a large door heavily paneled that shut with such a bang and woke so many echoes I half fancied that all the doors in the house were shutting. It was still broad day, but all shutters were closed over the high windows with their tops, which gave the rooms a gloomy uninhabited air.

We were ushered into a large apartment that furnished in better taste would have been handsome. As it was a bright fire on the hearth communicated to all around a warm and hospitable glow.

"This room" said the old man, glancing around him "you are to consider yours till further orders, and that ~~one~~ door, there, you see by the chimney leads to another you can occupy for a bed-room. If at any time you want anything you can pull that bell-wire. I shall be always at hand."

I nodded assent and he retired, but returned again in a moment to inquire if he should bring us some supper. I replied affirmatively, and he again disappeared bolting the door behind him.

It was evident that we had only been transferred from one prison to another. The several doors leading from our apartment to others were all fastened on the outside. The window shutters were secured in the same manner, indeed there was a general air of security about the dwelling well calculated to excite apprehension. We were amazed at the deep and utter silence that prevailed. Not the sound of a voice, not the echo of a footstep. Was the house uninhabited except by us? We were almost tempted to ask the old man when he came with our suppers, but his forbidding aspect seemed to repel conversation, and sitting the tray with refreshments on a small walnut table he departed without saying a word.

And here in this dull place we remained a month. I could not even if I wished describe the tedious monotony of our existence, or what we suffered in racking suspense. True, the wants of our nature were all supplied. We were provided with delicate food, were furnished with books and embroidery, and ~~might~~ so far as outward appearances were concerned ~~have been~~ we might have been happy. But those who think that the greatest evils of slavery are connected with physical suffering possess no just or rational ideas of human nature. The soul, the immortal soul must ever long and yearn for a thousand things inseperable to liberty. Then, too, the fear, the apprehension, the dread, and deep anxiety always attending that condition in a greater or less degree. There can be no certainty, no abiding confidence in the possession of any good thing. The indulgent master may die, or fail in business. The happy home may be despoiled of its chiefest treasures, and the consciousness of this embitters all their lot.

During all this time we saw not a human face with the exception of that old man's. He came and went mechanically never smiling, and seldom speaking. To our tears and entreaties he was immovable. To our questions he gave no answer. Had he been deaf as an adder he could not have manifested a greater insensibility to our words. At length we became aware that another person was in the dwelling. We heard the distinct utterance of ~~two~~ voices as if two persons were conversing in a low tone. We were confident that after the old-man's step in the passage there came another, unlike the first yet resembling it in certain particulars, for both seemed stealthy and had the soft gliding sound betokening privacy. We were likewise sensible of more noise in general. There was more opening and shutting of doors, more ascending and descending stairs, and more of everything accompanying the presence of free life. Some one had evidently arrived, and without knowing why we felt interested in the event.

The old man came at night with our suppers. For the first time a gleam of intelligence lightened his stolid face as he said "You will be wanted in an hour?"

"By whom?"

"Master."

"But who is master?"

He shook his head, clapped his finger to his ear—his usual manner of expressing deafness, when asked questions he did not choose to answer, then repeating "Remember in an hour" he passed from the room. Wanted in an hour by master; then our suspense would be resolved into certainty.

In an hour, though it seemed two or three to us, the old man came to our apartment and bade us follow him. He regarded us with a look of curious surprise, as we had neither changed our dresses, nor arranged our hair. Unadorned we went not expecting to ask favors or receive them. My companion trembled so that I found it necessary to support her ~~frame~~, as we ascended the stairs; the old man gliding before with his light, and pausing now and then to look back at us. Perhaps he feared that even then we might give them the slip. From the stair case landing we passed along a close uncomfortable passage to a small door that opened at the farther end and which on the present occasion stood slightly ajar. The old man paused before it, but did not enter, and we hesitated.

"Go on: Go on," he said with corresponding gestures.

We advanced, entered the room, and stood in the presence of Mr Trappe. He was sitting beside a table on which a small lamp was dimly burning. At his elbow stood a decanter of old wine, and by it was placed a glass that had been lately used. He looked calmly, though searchingly towards us ~~as we entered~~ and I detected an expression in his face at once complacent and self-satisfied. Not that he seemed exultant or triumphant. He was too strictly too severely self-repressed to exhibit much feeling of any kind, but he can chuckle a little, a very little over a good bargain, and now he felt an increased sense of his own power, importance, and strength of purpose now that our destinies for time I had well nigh said for eternity were in his hands. He was sedately pleased and looked just as one may be supposed to look when some great work is accomplished. Perhaps he thought that he had been doing a great work—there is no telling.

Carelessly holding his green spectacles in one hand, and adjusting the leaves of a book in which he had been apparently reading with the other, he seemed waiting for my companion to speak. Finding, however, that ~~would be obliged~~ she will not break the silence he does so very leisurely and quietly by saying "It is a long time since we met."

She inclines her head and would say "yes" but has no voice. The past comes rushing over her with its tide of memories moved and swayed by his presence. She remembers all she has been, she thinks with horror of what she is. His manner is different, too. He evidently feels that she is a worm beneath his feet to be crushed or preserved. ~~as he~~ Time was when he would have brought her a chair with obsequious politeness, now he does not even invite ~~us~~ her to be seated.

"It is a long time since we met" he repeated. "May I inquire in a friendly way how you have enjoyed yourself?"

She looked at him intently, her countenance very pale, and her whole frame trembling with excessive agitation.

He looks at her no less intently, and the muscles of his mouth twitch slightly with inward satisfaction. "Did you find a good home and pleasant company more desirable than the one so resolutely abandoned contrary to my expressed will and pleasure. That was a very bad move, very bad indeed; it hastened matters much, brought affairs to a speedy crisis, and ~~had almost disastrous~~ was attended with most disastrous consequences to your husband. It hurried him to the grave, it hurries you to slavery."

My companion gasped and trembled. It became necessary to support her to a seat. I led her to an old-fashioned sofa that stood in a little recess. She sunk down upon it, and buried her face in the cushions. He had no mercy, no pity, love of gold had turned his heart to stone, long accustomed to witness human sufferings he was stolid indifferent, apathetic to them, and he coolly went on.

"There is no need of your taking on so, no use at all in it. You have long known the condition of life to which your birth subjected you, and you ought by this time to have become reconciled to it. Lord bless me, it is nothing so bad after all. We are all slaves to something or somebody. A man perfectly free would be an anomaly, and a free woman yet more so. Freedom and slavery are only names attached surreptiously and often improperly to certain conditions ~~and in many cases the slave possesses more~~. They are mere shadows the very reverse of realities, and being so, if rightly considered, they have only a trifling effect on individual happiness."

He said this composedly as if she were a mere machine that he was discussing and analysing.

There was a gasp and a sob; otherwise she was silent.

"You will blame me, no doubt" he continued "you will curse me, you will regard me as an enemy, as one who embittered your existence, and dashed the cup of pleasure from your lips, yet in doing so you will be unjust. Rather blame the world that has made me what I am, like ~~Like yourself~~ yourself the victim of circumstances. It was not my fault, but rather the result of accident that made me acquainted with your lineage. Indeed I had my suspicions for a long time—for days, weeks, months, and years, but who can help their suspicions. I was not accountable for the idle words and looks of others that still contributed to feed them, and when I made it my business to find out, and clearly ascertain the whole affair I did it because it was in my line."

"I don't apprehend your meaning" she said with great effort.

["]I mean my line of business. You are not the first fair dame whose descent I have traced back—far back to a sable son of Africa, and whose destiny has been in my hands as clearly and decidedly as you must perceive that yours is now. Many and many are the family secrets that I have unraveled as women unravel a web. You may think of it as you please, you may call it dishonorable if you like, but it brings gold—bright gold.["]

["]But does it happify the conscience, or bring that sweet peace which passeth understanding?"

"My conscience never troubles me" he replied, with an expression which in countenances more variable and impulsive would have been a sneer.

"My conscience never troubles me" he repeated. "The circumstances in which I find people are not of my making. ~~If a beautiful woman is sold and sells cheap~~ Neither are the laws that give me an advantage over them. If a beautiful women [sic] is to be sold it is rather the fault of the law that permits it than of me who profits by it. If she sells cheap my right to purchase is clear; and if I choose to keep her awhile, give her advantages, or otherwise increase her attractions and then dispose of her again my right is equally unquestionable. Whatever the law permits, and public opinion encourages I do, when that says stop I go no further.

"You, Madam" he continued, after a short pause "should be the last to blame me for the turn affairs have taken. You were well married. I approved of the match, and with me the happiness of your husband was something of a consideration. Something, I say, though nothing very important. When I talked of undeceiving him, it was only to try you. I had not the remotest intention of so doing, and should not have done it had not your precipitate flight rendered such a course necessary. But I wished to see you humbled at my feet as I had been at yours. I wished you feel yourself standing on the brink of a precipice, and know that my hand could thrust you down to certain destruction, or pluck you back to safety."

Absorbed she listened to him, and now and then her lips moved as if in replying, but they emitted no voice. It was clear that she heard what he was saying that she repeated his words in her mind, and understood what they meant of themselves, but it was not so evident that she attached meaning to them in any other connection, or felt their intimate relation to herself.

["]But there is no use of lingering over the past. We have to do with the present now, and of the present I would speak. It is not my intention to expose you in the public market for slaves, but rather to dispose of you in a private manner, as I am now your legal owner. To[-]morrow morning you will receive the visit of a gentleman who proposes, if pleased with your appearance, to become your purchaser. You must look your best, as he is extremely fastidious ~~in his taste~~. You must—"

He was interrupted by a slight scream from his victim ~~and the sofa pillows and cushions~~ and the next moment I discovered that the sofa pillows were tinged with blood that bubbled from her lips. Quick as thought I sprang to her side and supported her fainting head. Her excessive agitation had ruptured a blood-vessel, and she was fast approaching that bourne where the wicked cease from troubling and the weary are at rest. Mr Trappe arose from his chair, and came slowly forward, but started when he discovered her dying state. I half fancied that a deeper shadow passed over his countenance, that his eye for an instant grew dim.

Was conscience thus late awakened, or was it a vision of pecuniary loss that flitted before him?

"Hannah, darling."

The blood gushed afresh, staining my hands and clothes, as I stooped yet lower to embrace her, and kissed her pallid brow, now damp with dews of death.

"The Lord bless and sustain you" she articulated whispering with the greatest difficulty.

"Don't speak dearest, it will make you worse."

A gleam of satisfaction shone over her face. There was a gasp, a struggle, a slight shiver of the limbs and she was free.

CHAPTER 8

A New Master

Arise, Oh Lord; Oh God, lift up thy hand forget not the humble.

DAVID

My beloved companion, my idolised mistress I know not where they laid her. I know not whether it was consecrated ground, whether the holy ritual of religion was celebrated over her remains, or whether she was borne away unceremoniously and with little thought to an unblest tomb. The poor priveledge of weeping over her lifeless form was denied me, and as if to augment my misery I was ordered back to the apartment we had inhabited together. Could it be that the events of the past few hours were not a horrible dream? Every thing wore its old familiar face, the chairs, the table, the walls, the ceiling, the bed, the books in which she had read, the embroidery we had wrought together, but I was alone. No kind compassionate countenance beamed upon me, no sweet familiar voice greeted my ear, yet weeping, sighing, moaning in utter loneliness I felt in my heart that it was better much better for her. She had escaped wo[e] and oppression, and insult, and degradation. Through death she had conquered her enemy, and rose triumphant above his machinations, and I longed to follow her. ~~Life had no m~~ Doomed to slavery, hopeless unmitigated slavery, subjected to the power of one so cruel and unrelenting I even prayed for death, prayed that the great Creator in his infinite mercy would take me to himself. But my days of probation were not destined to be thus soon and happily ended. I had yet other toils and trials to endure, other scenes of suffering and anguish to pass through, no doubt for some wise purpose to be known in that world which solves the enigma of this.

After exhausting a sleepless night in vain efforts to compose my mind and become reconciled to the fate that probably awaited me I arose in the morning really ill, nervous, and disheartened ~~with a despondency~~. The old man servant came with my breakfast. It was good, but I could not eat. Mental anxiety precluded the gratification of the senses, and I turned with loathing from the snowy bread and golden butter. It seemed like preparation for the sacrifice.

"You had much better eat" he said "as there's a long journey before you to[-]day.["]

"What kind of journey?" I inquired.

"Why you're sold" he answered in evident surprise that I was unaware of such an important change in my affairs.

"To whom?"

"Why to Saddler, the slave-trader but maybe I hadn't ought to tell you" he continued.

"Are you sure of this?"

"Surtin [certain] I am" and a grinning a sort of demoniacal smile he carried away the breakfast things.

In most cases there is something horrible in the idea of being bought and sold; it sent a thrill to my heart, a shiver through my brain. For a moment I felt dizzy, but a moment only. I had experienced too much trouble and anxiety to be overwhelmed by this. Then, too, I thought that though my perishable body was at their disposal, my soul was beyond their reach. They could never quench my immortality, shake my abiding faith and confidence in God, or destroy my living assurance in the efficacy of the dying Saviour's blood.

The old man, however, was mistaken. I was not sold, ~~though~~ though every thing was tending to that consummation. Towards noon I heard the roll of wheels and the tramp of horse's feet, evidently approaching the house. To these noises succeeded the echoing footsteps of a man, then there was a murmur of voices in an adjoining apartment and presently the door communicating with mine was thrown open; while some one said audibly "There she is." I knew the voice to be Mr Trappe's, but a stranger a answered "Why Trappe I thought you said that she was beautiful; in my eye she's excessively homely."

"But you ~~haven't seen the good~~ haven't seen her good points yet" said Trappe "walk in and take a fair estimate of her attractions, they are neither small nor few."

Both men came in, while I shrunk into a distant corner.

"Nay: Hannah, that won't do" said Trappe. "Come out here and show yourself. I don't think Mr Saddler ever saw a better looking wench. Come out I say.["]

I obeyed reluctantly.

"Now I'll tell you what" said Trappe. "You won't find a nicer bit of woman's flesh to be bought for that money in old Virginia. Don't you see what a foot she has, so dainty and delicate, and what an ankle. I don't see how in conscience you can expect me to take any less. Why you'd make a small fortune of her at that rate."

"How you talk" said Saddler. "I've bought finer wenches often and often for less money. Then you see she's skittish which makes some difference. However as I'm making up a gang I wouldn't mind having her. But I think you told me that you wanted to dispose of two. Where is the other one?"

"Dead."

Saddler received this announcement with a look of profound surprise and repeated "dead."

"As a door nail" said Trappe.

"Why? how? what was the matter?" inquired Saddler. ["]If my memory serves me right you said that she was well only two or three days ago."

["]She did not die of disease. The truth is she broke a blood vessel. I reckon it a clear loss of one or two thousand."

"How unfortunate" said Saddler. "But these wenches will die. I have sometimes thought that accidents happened to them oftener than to others. I have lost much in that way myself; probably ten thousand dollars wouldn't cover the amount. If the business in general had not been so lucrative it would have such things would have broke me up long ago. You see my trade is altogether in the line of good-looking wenches, and these are a deal sight worse to manage than men—every way more skittish and skeery [scary]. Then it don't do to cross them much; or if you do they'll cut up the devil, and like as anyhow break their necks, or pine themselves to skeletons. I lost six in one season and out of one company. I had orders to fill at New Orleans and all for young and beautiful women without children. Now a woman of eighteen or twenty without a child, and a slave, is not so easy to find, to say nothing of looking for fifty or a hundred."

"Rather a difficulty I should think" said Trappe. ["]I've had some experience of that kind myself."

Trembling with fear I shrank back into the corner, while the gentlemen having seated themselves pursued the conversation. Mr Trappe meanwhile keeping his eye on me.

"At last I concluded" continued Saddler "to take the women with or without children, and get clear of the brats somehow, in any way that offered. But heavens, how they did carry on, and one, Louise by name, and the freshest and fairest in the gang, actually jumped into the river when she found that her child was irretrievably gone. Another one escaped and ran off to the place where she supposed her boy to have been carried. The overseer was the first to discover her, and knowing her to be a stranger, he lugged her off with the blood-hounds. They were real devils fierce, eager, and fiery—they tore her dreadfully, spoiled all her beauty, rendering her utterly unfit for my traffic; and so I sold her for a song. Now this one—what's her name?"

"Hannah."

"Thank you; now Hannah."

"Has no child" suggested Mr Trappe.

"Has no child" repeated Saddler "which is great advantage, but it seems that she's given to running away."

"Not at all" returned Trappe. "No one could be more peaceable and contented than she is. That running away was altogether the fault of the other one, and something Hannah would never have thought of had she been left alone."

"Is she good-tempered?"

"Lord love you, the best tempered in the world, kind trusty, and religious."

["]Bah: I hardly think that religion will do her much good, or make her more subservient to the wishes of my employers. On the whole I should prefer that she wasn't religious, ~~but I suppose that they can drive it out of her~~ because religion is so apt to make people stubborn; it gives them such notions of duty, and that one thing is right and another thing wrong; it sets them up so, you'll even hear them telling that all mankind are made of one blood, and equal in the sight of God."

"There may be something in that" said Mr Trappe.

"There is something in it, there's a great deal in it" pursued Saddler "give me a handsome wench, pleasant and good-tempered, willing to conform herself to circumstances, and anxious to please, without any notions of virtue, religion, or anything of that sort. Such are by far the most marketable, provided they have health, are young and show off to advantage."

"Well, Hannah does show off" answered Trappe. "Come out here again, and walk across the room. No disobedience, mind that:"

I walked forth.

"There's a gait for you" said Trappe. "Few women can walk well, but Hannah does. She holds her head gracefully. Don't you think so?"

"Tolerable" said Saddler.

"She has a fine shape, good teeth, beautiful hair and fair complexion; is young; in high health; has good spirits and amiable disposition. Why fifteen hundred dollars is nothing, nothing at all put in the scale against such a woman. She'll bring you two thousand easy."

"I'm not so certain of that. She might possibly, provided I had her there, and she might not. It all depends on how she stands the journey. She may look old, worn and faded, and then I could scarcely ~~one thousand for her However at a risk I will give you twelve hundred~~ realize one half that sum. However I'll give you twelve hundred at a risk."

"Say thirteen and take her" said Trappe.

"Sorry that I can't" answered Saddler "but twelve hundred is really too much. Only think of my expense in getting her to the market, to say nothing of the risk. I think it would be a wise plan to have the lives of such wenches insured.["]

"Oh you'll have no risk with her on that score. Not a bit of it. Just get her into the wagon, put on the cuffs and she'll be safe enough."

"And you'll take twelve hundred?"

"Suppose I must though I am very certain it is not enough."

Saddler drew a leather wallet from his pocket, slowly counted out the money, and laying it on the table requested Mr Trappe to see that it was right. He examined it, pronounced it good, and proceeded to make out a bill of sale. That concluded, Trappe came to where I stood weeping.

"What the devil are you crying for?" he asked "Are you then so sorry to leave me?"

"No sir, I am not" I faltered.

Saddler laughed as if he thought my reply a good joke.

"What is the matter then."

"Oh never mind" said Saddler. "These women with their whims, and caprices, and tears, and fooleries are the greatest plagues imaginable. Why they'll cry a dozen times a day, and you'll know no more than the dead what ails 'em. They puzzled me terribly for awhile and then I found out that the best plan was to just let them alone. If they wanted to cry why let 'em and pay no attention to it."

Saddler laughed again. No so with Mr Trappe. He never laughed. You might as well have accused him of love or sentimentality as of laughing. His countenance seldom if ever relaxed into a smile. His lips could curl with disdain, his brow lower with hate, his eye sparkle with revenge, but he could not laugh.

Again he began in his cold ironical tone. "You know Hannah that it is a lawyer's business to give advice."

"Certainly it is" said Saddler.

I had no voice to speak.

["]And such being the case I propose to bestow about five dollars' worth on Hannah, as a parting gift that she can keep by way of remembrance.["]

His manner more than his words vexed and irritated me. He seemed so sedately satisfied, so calmly pleased. Passion gave me strength to speak.

"I want none of your gifts. Were such a thing possible I would forget your name and existence; for I feel that the thought of you must always be a haunting curse to my memory" and again I burst into tears.

There might have been a slight contraction more than usual on his brow, and a rapid gleam of hate or satisfied malice shone in his eye, but quickly passed and his countenance became like a frozen lake when lit by moonlight, cold, unimpassioned, and utterly dead to all feelings of sympathy as he began.

["]I shall tell you nothing that you are not old enough to know without my telling it. Good sense must long ago have taught you that obedience was the chief essential to one in your condition—that you must never dream of sitting [sic] up an independent will—must have no mind, no desire, no purpose of your own. You will find few masters like Mr Vincent, and where you are going other duties and services, and those perhaps more irksome than those required in his family will be expected of you, but never for a moment forget that submission and obedience must be the Alpha and Omega of all your actions."

Though this advice was probably well adapted to one in my condition, that is if I could have forgotten God, truth, honor, and my own soul; it was manifestly not given with any kind intention. He loved to probe the human heart to its inmost depths, and watch the manifestations of its living agony. He wished to vary the modes of my mental torture, and to make me realize that in both soul and body I was indeed a slave.

I turned from the cold icy glitter of his eye, and he went on.

"But whatever you do, whatever you be, or whatever hardships you meet never think of running away. No good could come of it in any case. You would almost certainly be caught, and if not, you would be certain to perish miserably, perhaps hunted and torn to pieces by dogs, or perhaps eaten alive by the vultures when reduced by famine and privation to a dying state. You must bear what you have to bear, and that's the long and short of the matter."

Saying this he really seemed pleased, but miserable as I was, helpless, ~~hopeless~~ almost hopeless and a slave I felt that my condition for eternity if not for time, was perferable to his, and that I would not even for the blessed boon of freedom change places with him; since even freedom without God and religion would be a barren posession.

"Well I must be off" said Saddler after a short pause.

"Hannah you will go with me?"

His voice was really kind.

"I suppose, Sir, that I must" I answered.

"But don't you go willingly, don't you want to go. Why you don't know what good fortune may be in store for you. Some of my girls have done first rate. I bought one up here last season, took her to New Orleans, put her in the market, and sold her to a rich man, who became so much pleased with her person and accomplishments that he has since given her freedom and made her his wife. What's happened once may happen again, and I shouldn't at all wonder if some such good thing was to fall in your way."

"Is that the way you flatter your gals?" said Trappe.

"I always coax and flatter first, if that don't answer I resort to harsher measures."

"And does it answer?"

["]For the most part it does; admirably too I have no difficulty, except when there's a child in the case. Hannah will be docile as a lamb I know."

"You'd better put on the cuffs" suggested Trappe. "Make her safe first, comfortable afterwards."

"No, Trappe I shan't do it. I never put irons on women unless they prove refractory. You are going to be good a[i]n't you Hannah?"

"Yes Sir" I sobbed. ~~"I know you will~~

"There's no knowing" interposed Trappe.

"Yes there is" answered Saddler. "I believe that Hannah can be trusted. I almost know she can. I see it in her countenance, and I've got eyes that ~~most ofte~~ are seldom deceived in the human face.["]

CHAPTER 9

The Slave-trader

"Remember, Oh Lord, what is come upon us; consider, and behold our reproach."

JEREMIAH

My new master I followed him to the little wagon. Just outside the yard, we got in, and he drove off. My mind was too busily occupied, and my thoughts too confused and agitated for any close observation of what we passed, or whither we went. I remember, however that it had been raining for the roads were very slippery, and little ponds of water, and sometimes quite large ones, were gathered in all the holes and shallow places. But the air was fresh and bracing, and had a fragrant smell of buds and early flowers.

I remember too that I was quite surprised that spring had so far advanced, and that even my anxiety or sorrow gave way before a sensation of pleasure awakened by the vernal influences of nature. The lambs were skipping beside the dams, the trees were alive with the harmony of birds busily engaged in building their nests. We could see them passing and repassing with feathers, horse-hair and small sticks in their little bills, and it almost brought tears into my eyes to think how free they were, and how happy they must be. Then I remembered the words of our Saviour that God even noticed the fall of a sparrow, and that the least of his disciples was of more value than many of them. Soothed by his comforting assurance my mind became composed, and I fell into a sort of reverie in which the past, present, and future seemed indistinctly blended. I thought of the stately mansion of Lindendale, its master and mine, the portrait of Sir Clifford, the Linden tree with its ominous creak; then of my mistress beautiful, young, and beloved, ~~after that of her affection~~ as she appeared on her bridal night; as she looked afterwards worn, weary, and half dead with apprehension, of all we felt and suffered together in the wilderness, and in prison, of her sudden death, and then I wept, not that she had escaped ~~from~~ the tormentor, but that I did not know the place of her burial. It would have been so comforting to associate the idea of her last resting place with some green spot overswept by soft shadows and adorned with wild flowers. Then by a sudden transition I thought of the place to which I was going, of the people I should see and serve, what they would say and whether I should like them and they me. I was recalled to passing events by a sudden start of the horse, and the voice of Saddler calling "to take care." I came near falling over at which he laughed and then inquired of what I was thinking.

"I was thinking of many things connected with my past life" I answered.

"It was almost too bad to disturb such a fine train of meditation" he replied. "Had you been long in the service of Mr Trappe?"

I told him that I had not.

"I thought so" he answered. "Trappe never keeps a servant long. He buys only for speculation. He is one of the strangest, most mysterious, and unfathomable of old gentlemen. I never saw such a man before, tho' I have seen many hard cases. Why he has no more feeling than a bit of iron. A tortoise has quite as much sentiment."

"Have you been acquainted with him?" I asked.

"Why yes for a considerable time I have, though we never had any intimacy except in the line of our trade. I believe my society is somewhat repulsive to his aristocratic notions, but I think that my business is quite as respectable as his."

"I don't understand you I said "very likely."

"I am called a slave-trader—I am one—I know that it is not considered reputable, but I don't care. I try to deal honest, and act honorably. I would rather be cheated myself than cheat another. Public opinion is arbitrary and unjust, so I don't care for it. Very respectable people, honorable gentlemen, grave Senators, and even the republican Presidents buy slaves; are they better than I am, who sells them?["]

"I should suppose not, yet what has that to do with Mr Trappe."

Without noticing my inquiry he proceeded.

["]Now strictly speaking Trappe cannot be considered a slave-trader, yet he is quite his business is quite essential to trade. Then going around the country as he does, prying into secrets, and watching his chance, he has all the opportunity in the world to make great bargains. Many a likely wench whom he had bought or obtained in a private manner and for a mere trifle, I have purchased of him for a good round sum, and sold again, making money by the operation. Yet few know him for what he is a slave speculator, and still fewer are aware of his true character as a hard uncompromising grinding man.["]

"Well, I am beyond his power now" I remarked in the a manner of thinking aloud.

"And you needn't be sorry for it neither" said Saddler. ["]Worse hands, that is more selfish and unfeeling you can scarcely fall into. But you are getting hungry I should think; at any rate you ought to be, and see here I have got something good.["]

Saying this he thrust his hand deep into the capacious pocket of his outer garment and drew thence a paper parcel, which he threw in my lap.

Opening it I found some very nice cake, iced over with sugar, and highly delicious.

"It's very good, eat" he said again.

Though not hungry, rather than appear insensible to his kindness I ate a small ~~quantity~~.

"Very good isn't it?" he inquired.

I answered that it was.

"Well now" he continued "do try just to oblige me to look glad and cheery. You will feel better, and I shall feel better. Don't you never smile?"

I shook my head and said "not lately."

"That's rather bad news" he answered. "I always like to hear my people sing, to have them laugh, and see them jovial and merry."

At this juncture of the conversation another ~~carriage~~ wagon approached and attempted to pass ours. This aroused the temper of Dan, ~~as Saddler~~ Saddler's horse, and throwing his head around, a habit he had, he set off at full speed ~~Saddler called to him~~ utterly regardless of the rein or voice of his master. I was surprised and then frightened at his velocity. Trees, houses, fences seemed to fly past us with the speed of the wind. I heard the ringing of bells, the shouts of people, and the barking of dogs. Sometimes men came running out, or we obtained a glimpse of women and children standing with uplifted hands before doors and windows. The people, the voices, and the noise seemed still more to frighten the horse, and though flecked with foam from flank to nostril, his limbs apparently acquired new vigor with every moment. Up hill and down, along hedges, over bridges on, on, we flew. At first the horse kept the road admirably; then as we neared a bridge with a high embankment some of the fastenings broke and he began to plunge and rear. I have an indistinct remembrance of boards flying about in every direction, of a loud noise, a spinning whirling motion, and then all was darkness. When I came to myself the scene was changed, and I almost doubted my identity. I was in a warm pleasant little bed, in a darkened room, and several persons whom I had no remembrance of ever having seen before were passing in and out. There was one lady with so benevolent a countenance that my heart warmed towards her as if she were my own mother, my mother whom I had never seen. She was sitting beside me, and seeing that I partly recovered she approached her sweet face to mine and whispered "Lie still, dear, very still, you have been badly injured, but are among friends."

I attempted to reply, but became aware of an overpowering weakness that benumbed all my senses. A mountain seemed seated on my breast, and I could not stir.

"There, dear" she whispered again "don't worry or exert yourself. You shall know all in time."

Presently I ascertained that my arm was bandaged as if some one had been drawing blood. I discovered also that my limbs were securely ~~fastened down~~ splintered and fastened down as in cases of broken bones. The benevolent lady went out, but soon returned with a nourishing cordial, of which I partook sparingly, and felt greatly revived. I soon became aware that several persons were collected in an adjoining apartment and I ~~thought~~ fancied they spoke of me, of my master, and our horse that ran away. Hearing myself thus spoken of brought back the past, and I shuddered and grew faint with the remembrance.

Again the benevolent-looking woman was at my side.

"Fear nothing, dear" she said in her pleasant way, and then added suiting the action to the word "Have a little more drink."

The beverage was cool and refreshing. I would have thanked her, but ~~my lips refused to give utterance to~~ the words died on my lips.

I wanted to ask for my master, as the last I remembered was seeing him white as a sheet, holding to the reins, while the horse was kicking and plunging and the boards flying just on the brink of a precipice. Again I strove to speak, ~~but could not~~ and this time articulated "Master, where?"

The benevolent Lady, whose name I subsequently ascertained to be Mrs. Henry, looked rather surprised and coming close to the bed again cautioned me to be silent. But I had sufficiently recovered to experience the most intense anxiety, and would not be put off so.

"Master, where" I cried again and this time in a louder tone.

The attendants whispered among themselves. They were all colored with the exception of Mrs Henry, and one of them going to that Lady whispered something in her ear, to which she nodded affirmatively.

I knew very well that some dreadful casuality had befallen us, and I asked to know the particulars the very worst.

Just then a door was suddenly opened, and naturally turning my eyes in that direction I caught a glimpse of something white and stiff. I knew what it resembled—a dead man laid out. I looked for an explanation to Mrs. Henry. She understood my mute appealing glance.

"Do you inquire for the gentleman with whom you were riding?" she said approaching the bed.

I assented.

"Was he a near relative?"

I replied in the negative.

"Only a dear friend?"

It now occurred to me that she was ignorant of our true characters, as master and slave. Should I perpetuate the delusion, or acknowledge frankly my humble condition. I was sorely tempted, but only for a moment. My better nature prevailed.

"Only a friend" she repeated.

"My master, Madam" I faltered.

"Your master" she reiterated slowly "were you then—"

"A slave" I answered. "I am one of that miserable class."

"Your master, then is dead" she said. "The horse it seems ran away."

"I know that."

["]And you were precipitated down a precipice. The gentleman struck with his head on a rock, or so it appears. Appearances indicate that he died instantly."

"And the horse?"

"Was dying when found. Your escape seems almost a miracle. You were lying insensible, buried beneath the rubbish of the broken wagon. I was passing in my carriage, and saw when they drew you out. You were a woman, and a stranger, and I gave them directions to bring you to my house."

"We found papers on the gentleman" continued Mrs Henry ["]that informed us of his name and place of residence, but nothing further. And now, my dear" she went on ["]since I have gratified your curiosity try to be composed, and go to sleep if you can, remembering that a merciful Providence watches over the humblest as the greatest. Do you ever pray."

"I try to, Madam. A prayer was on my lips, and in my heart at the moment of that fearful fall."

["]And it was doubtless heard, and answered, too" she replied. "What a blessed thing is prayer?—and the duty of thanksgiving should not be forgotten.["]

I felt the rebuke implied in her words, and lifted ~~up my~~ my heart to God.

I had feared for a moment that Mrs Henry, when she discovered my abject condition, would withdraw the smiles of her loving-kindness. I even watched her countenance to see if I could detect in it any change. But all honor to the Spirit of Christ within her—there was none—though I sometimes fancied that her looks were more tender and compassionate, that her voice had a softer, perchance a more pitying tone. It was evident that she neither hated nor despised me for a misfortune that I could not help.

I shall say little of these sick experiences lest I prove tedious or unintelligible. I was not unhappy though the path before me was all dark. It might have been owing to the utter prostration of my nervous system that rendered me unable to experience any intensity of emotion, or it might be that the Redeemer was leading me in spirit through the green pastures and beside the still waters of Gospel truth and peace, but a long repose succeeded to my recent trials and distresses—repose of body and mind—so calm so placid, so undeviating, that ~~even more after the vicissitudes of years~~ had they told me I was dying, or was to be exposed in the market on the next day, it would only have awakened a sensation of deeper trust, a firmer reliance on the Mighty hand.

My injuries, too, though precluding exercise or motion were not of a painful kind. I enjoyed long long hours of the sweetest sleep rendered luxurious by pleasant dreams. I had no care for myself, but I could see them watching over and caring for me. I could see Mrs Henry, so tender and careful, superintending the servants who were setting the room in order, or speaking softly to her children who were playing beneath the window, ~~and~~ requesting them to make less noise. I could understand the deep quietude that pervaded the house, and it spoke so much of their thoughtfulness and solicitude that it nearly affected me to tears. What was I?—a slave yet no one seemed to know it, or to treat me on that account with any less tenderness. What had I ever done to merit so much kindness? Nothing. Nothing. I could only recognise in it the hand of my Father. By and by my strength began to be restored, and my bruised and shattered limbs became capable of motion. At first of very little, then gradually and by degrees of more and much more, untill I could set [sit] upright, and instead of lying all day watching with a strange calmness the motions of the nurse, and quietly submitting to what she thought proper to do for me, I began to be useful to myself, and interested in attending to my own wants.

How well I remember the pleasant evening when I left my room for the first time to enjoy the social conviviality of a wedding party. Mrs Henry who seemed sent into the world to dispense good-feeling and happiness loved to indulge her servants in all innocent pleasures not inconsistent with their duties. Her favorite slave, a beautiful Quadroon was to be married that night to a young man belonging to a neighboring estate, and the amiable mistress determined to make the nuptials of one the occasion of a holiday for the whole establishment. The woods and fields had been ransacked for early spring flowers and violets to adorn the drawing room. Cakes, confectionary and wine had been abundantly provided, and all the servants old and young big and little were invited to be present. Queer looking old men, whose black faces withered and puckered contrasted strangely with their white beards and hair; fat portly dames whose ebony complexions were set off by turbans of flaming red, boys, girls and an abundance of babies, were there—all flaunting in finery and gay clothes of rainbow colors, and all doing their utmost to appear to the best advantage. The bride and bridegroom with their attendants were elegantly dressed; Mr Henry, the master and a clergyman, pronounced the nuptial benediction. ~~Then there was feasting and~~ Then there was exchanging of compliments, and so much feasting, and laughing, and talking, and rejoicing that I was quite confused and hardly knew what to do with myself. Mrs Henry entered with all her heart into the spirit of the scene. She really seemed to exult in the happiness around her. Her countenance beaming with smiles and her eyes sparkling with animation she passed around the room, caressing the children, greeting the mothers, and bestowing little attentions here and there on the aged or infirm. All eyes followed her and I am sure that all hearts blest her.

As the evening advanced the party seperated, but there was a great noise of fiddling and dancing till late at night. From the window of my little apartment which opened on the lawn I could see the gay groups collected on the smooth green, and chasing each other through the flying dance, or laughing and chatting in a great state of mirthful enjoyment. I gazed at them and wondered if they were really so happy—wondered if no dark shadows of coming evil never haunted their minds. Then I thought of the young couple, who had so recently taken the vows and incurred the responsibilities of marriage—vows and responsibilities strangely fearful when taken in connection with their servile condition. Did the future spread before them bright and cloudless? Did they anticipate domestic felicity, and long years of wedded love: when their lives, their limbs, their very souls were subject to the control of another's will; when the husband could not be at liberty to provide a home for his wife, nor the wife be permitted to attend to the wants of her husband, and when living apart in a state of separate bondage they could only meet occasionally at best, and then might be decreed without a moment's warning to never meet again.

The night had been beautiful and balmy, and the fine moonlight lay like a mantle of soft resplendence over the scene, but a cloud had suddenly risen, and just as the bride, conspicuous in her snowy robes joined the group of dancers, it swept over the moon extinguishing her light, and a burst of thunder announced the approaching tempest. Suddenly and without further warning the winds arose, clouds obscured the firmament, and there was darkness, and lightning, and rain, where only a few minutes before had been youth, and beauty, and love, and light, and joyousness.

Did this change prefigure the destiny of the wedding pair.

CHAPTER 10

The Henry Family

Favor is deceitful, and beauty is vain; but a woman that feareth the Lord: she shall be praised.

SOLOMON

It was in May I think; at least I remember that the first roses were blowing, when I recovered my accustomed strength, and became able to pass in and out as I pleased, and to form an acquaintance with the many interesting objects surrounding the house, and connected in various ways with this amiable family.

Every house with its surroundings possesses an air of individuality. In some it is more strongly developed than in others, yet it appertains to all in a greater or less degree. "Forget me not" as this dwelling had been beautifully and not inappropriately named was one of those dear old houses rich in panel work and fresco, and whose construction from first to last bespeaks an association with the past. Who does not find a charm about these ancient houses, with their delightfully irregular apartments, embellished with quaint carvings and mouldings, brown with age, and awaking in the mind a thousand reminiscen[c]es of olden times and fashions. Such houses were built rather for solid utility than for show, consequently the materials are durable and the timbers massy, but there is likewise a great deal of variety, taste, and elaborate ornamenting. You cannot take them in at a glance, or understand their design at first sight as in those of modern style. But you pass from one room into another, and go up and down steps, and note a bountiful supply of little halls, entries, and passages leading you cannot tell where. Then every room seems a wonder in itself, with its old-fashioned fire place, and little windows, surrounded by lattice work with the luxuriant growth of honey-suckle and jasmine pressing through it; to say nothing of the great numbers of small doors concealed behind panels, and opening into closets, wardrobes, and beaufats [buffets] abundantly provided with shelves and hooks for storing away or hanging up things, with other little contrivances for convenience and usefulness that it might be tedious to mention.

Such a house as this was "Forget me not." And then ~~the furniture coincided exactly with the style of the building~~ it was furnished in a style and manner that corresponded exactly with itself. The furniture was not old, but rather old-fashioned, various, and pleasantly irregular. One room really seemed a parterre of flowers—flowers natural and artificial—flowers of wax, of paper, of needle-work, and embroidery—flowers of chintz, of velvet and of brocade. Yet there was no sameness about it; for these beauties of the fields and gardens, whatever might [be] their substance, were so varied in shape and color, and arranged with so much taste that they had a happy and surprising effect. The furniture of this room was light airy and fantastic after the fashion of garden chairs and benches, with a small table deeply carved with the design of a wreath, turning around the legs, along the sides, and gathered into a ~~bunch~~ bunch of leaves on the top.

Another room was adorned with shells, another with pictures of birds, all various yet so beautiful and true to nature that I never wearied in looking at them. Here were birds of Paradise just dropping into the balmy recesses of some cinnamon grove; and there were flocks of splendid macaws hovering over the magnificent palms of the tropics. The great white owl of the North ~~was not forgotten; indeed all the countries of the earth were represented in the portraits of the~~ with the surrounding deserts of snow was not forgotten; indeed all the countries of the earth were represented in the portraits of their birds.

In other rooms there was a mingling of unique and singular objects in tasteful confusion. Pictures of men, angels and domestic animals side by side with landscapes wrought in needle-work, or sketches in crayons of rocks, crags, and rivers.

In these rooms the tables and chairs were of great variety and pattern. No two were alike. There were great chairs stuffed and covered with courtly brocade and little chairs in chintz, some had high backs and some had low, some were turned, others carved, while some were provided with rockers, others with castors [casters], and others again had neither.

The same quaint variety prevailed everywhere and in every thing. It ~~the carpets, hangings, glasses~~ was displayed in the carpets, the hangings, and the glasses, and even in the scent-bottles and pincushions on the toilet tables. They agreed in nothing, but perfect neatness and good taste.

In the lodges of the servants, and every thing pertaining to the establishment the same variety was observable. There was a garden for flowers, another for vegetables, and a third for fruit. There was a spring in one place, a well in another, and a fountain in a third. I could never sufficiently admire the order and harmony of the arrangements, which blent [blended] so many parts into a perfect whole.

Method and regularity likewise prevailed over the estate. The overseer was gentle and kind, and the slaves were industrious and obedient, not through fear of punishment, but because they ~~felt it to be their duty~~ loved and respected a master and mistress so amiable and good. Of these, especially the master, I have hitherto said little, and even now it is not my intention to draw their portraits. I could not do so if I wished. I might, indeed, describe their size and figure, might enlarge on the color of ~~their~~ their eyes and hair, but after all what language could portray the ineffable expression of a countenance beaming with soul and intelligence? how should I convey in words an adequate idea of a manner refined by education, polished by mingling in good society, and perfected by that true Christian politeness which springs from kindness of heart?

Mr Henry was a clergyman, and his naturally mild and genial disposition had been softened and tempered by the benignacy of religion. Early in life he found a partner like himself wise, pious, and gentle, and the fruit of their union was two docile children, a girl and a boy, named respectively Charley and Anna.

It would be a difficult matter to tell what station I filled in this lovely family. I was not considered a servant, neither was I treated exactly as a guest, though with quite as much kindness and consideration. There was a pleasant familiarity in their manner towards me that a visitor could scarcely have expected, mingled with a sort of reserve that continually reminded me I was not one of them. How much I desired to be so it would be impossible to tell.

Mrs Henry one day desired to speak with me in the parlor. I felt a strange misgiving that some unpleasant communication awaited me, and I was still more convinced of this when I saw the compassionate expression of her countenance. Tears spring to my eyes unbidden.

"Hannah, my dear, be seated, and don't weep" said Mrs Henry. "I have important news for you. The gentleman to whom we communicated the fact of your late master's death, and who it appears was his next of kin, and consequently his heir, states in this letter" and she drew one from her pocket "that he shall be here next week to establish his claim to you. He supposes that there will be no difficulty in that, or in your removal hence."

Much as I had feared and anticipated all this, the dread reality shocked me like a thunderbolt. I stood silent for a moment, and then threw myself at her feet.

"Mrs Henry" I said "you can save me from this. I have an inexpressible desire to stay with you. You are so good, accomplished, and Christian-like, could I only have the happiness to be your slave, your servant, or—"

"Hannah, dear" she said interrupting me "you must not talk in that way, neither should you kneel to mortal woman; now rise and let us discuss this matter calmly.

She held out her hand so white and soft and beautiful.

"No; Mrs Henry" I continued "here let me kneel at your feet till you promise to pity and save me. My sphere is so humble, and I am so forlorn and destitute, and you are by nature and position so far above me that you may not think how I feel in view of this dreadful doom, but Oh: my dear good madam be mindful of what I have suffered, and of what I still must suffer, thus transferred from one to another, and save me; for you can.["]

"No; Hannah, I cannot" she said stifling the emotion that was choking her.

"Do not decide so soon" I replied. "Let me hope a moment. I do not ask you to buy me and then set me free. I do not require any extra favors or advantages. Let me perform the menial service of your household—Let me go to the fields and labor there—let me be a drudge, a scallion I care not—nay I would accept the situation with the greatest thankfulness—all I ask is to feel, and know of a certainty that I have a home, that some one cares for me, and that I am beyond the gripe [grip] of these merciless slave-traders and speculators.["]

"Hannah: Hannah, tempt me not."

"And why not, my dear Madam. Why not tempt you to accept the service of one who would be so faithful devoted, and zealous to serve you every day—who would do her utmost in all possible things. You would never repent it, you could not repent it, because we should both be happier."

There was so much sympathy and such an affectionate tenderness in her looks that I was encouraged to press myself upon her. I felt that everything which could render life valuable to me was at stake, no wonder then that I spoke with ardor, or forgot the rules of good breeding in my earnestness to gain my point.

"You do not imagine" I continued. "You have no idea how good I will be, or how exactly I will conform myself to all your wishes."

She lifted me from the floor, she embraced me, and compassionated over me. She wept, and our tears were mingled together.

"I must tell you my history, Hannah" she said "and then you will see how utterly impossible it is for me to do as you desire, unless, indeed, I perjure my own soul. This house, this estate and these servants were all the property of my father. He was a worldly-minded man, and a man of the world, but during the long lingering and painful illness of which he died his views of property were materially changed. I was an only child, and consequently an heiress. I had married Mr Henry contrary to his will, but face to face with death and eternity his anger relaxed, and he summoned me to his dying bed, to receive his forgiveness, and last solemn counsel and benediction. He could only converse at intervals of great agony. Oh: it was a mournful death-bed, a mournful death-bed.["]

She paused overcome by strong emotion.

"I would not describe the scene if I could, and I could not if I would" she continued recovering herself by a strong effort of self-control "but his last moments were embittered by remorse. He had been a trafficker in human flesh and blood, in the lives and souls of men, and conscience arrayed them all against him. Like the accusing spirit of Cesar summoning Brutus to Philippi they charged him to meet and answer them at the bar of God.

"In those awful moments he exacted from me a solemn promise never on any occasion to sell or buy a servant, as then with the realities of a judgement and eternity before him it appeared the greatest crime, he said, of which a human being could be capable. He conjured me if I desired a death-bed of peace, and an immortality of blessedness to avoid the hedious traffic in every form."

"And you promised?"

"I promised, Hannah, promised by [a] dear dying parent in the presence of the ministers of religion, and with the awful solemnities of the hour and scene pressing upon my soul. That oath I never can violate. My right hand may forget her cunning, or my tongue cleave to the roof of my mouth, but such an engagement, made too at such time is of too sacred and solemn an import ever to be broken."

"Even so."

"My father to show his sincerity, and right as far as possible the wrong he had practiced as much as possible, set apart a certain portion of his estate to lie with the interest accumulating during my natural life, and then to be equally apportioned among the servants, who are all to be emancipated. And now dear Hannah, do you wish me to break that vow?" she asked.

I could not say that I did, and yet my heart rose against the man, who in a slave-holding country could exact such a promise. Since in a multitude of cases the greatest favor that a mild kind-hearted man or woman can bestow on ~~the out cast servile race~~ members of the outcast servile race is to buy them. I almost felt that he had done me as a personal injury, an irreparable wrong.

Perhaps she divined my thoughts. With a countenance sympathising, yet half-reproachful she inquired if there was no other way in which she could assist me, and thereby prove how much interest she felt in my forlorn condition.

I answered that I did not know.

"I have a friend and distant relative in North Carolina" she continued. "Their names are Wheeler, and they are considered very kind and humane to their slaves. They are coming here this summer, and Mrs Wheeler informs me that she wishes to purchase a maid-servant, providing she can find one whose capabilities and acquirements meet her approbation. If your prospective master is a lenient man, and has no other views in regard to you I should think that you might probably be transferred to her.["]

She looked towards me, and I saw that she waited for an answer. Just at that moment I felt that it mattered little where I went, or what became of me. I was disheartened and disappointed, without hope in this world, and half-forgetful of my trust in the next. I replied not with the patient, meek, and thankful spirit that I ought, but as my feelings for the time being dictated, that I was hopeless, helpless and friendless, and that I had no further choice.

"Hannah" the word was uttered in such a sorrowful tone of reproach that I looked involuntarily towards the speaker. If her voice had expressed much, more a great deal more of forbearing sympathy was shown in her countenance. I perceived in a moment the injustice and unkindness of my remarks. I remembered her patient care of me, a stranger and a slave. Again I knelt at her feet, and poured out in ~~long bitter language my feeling dictated all the~~

~~fondness of my gratitude~~ language, rendered impassioned and burning by my strong feelings, all the ful[l]ness of my gratitude to her, my sensibility to the kindnesses of her family, and my perfect conviction that I had no reason to expect any more.

"But you may expect more, Hannah" she replied. "You may expect any favor or kindness of me, with that one exception. And after all that is not much. You may be happier with some one else than you could have been with me. You know not the good things Providence may have in store for you. You must not forget him, and His abounding grace."

And thus she soothed, and comforted, and consoled me, and through her blessed influence I came to experience a better state of mind.

In the passage leading to my room I met little Anna. As usual I was a great favorite with the children, and stretching out her white beautiful arms towards me she clamed a kiss. My cheeks were wet with tears, which the affectionate child was not slow in perceiving.

"I don't see what makes everybody so unhappy" she said in her artless manner.

"Why, are they?" I replied.

"I guess so, you weep, and so does Lotty, and I can't tell how many more."

"Lotty weeps" I repeated.

She was the new-made bride, and should have been happy.

"To be sure she does" answered the simple child. "And then don't you think she refuses to tell me what ails her, and when I ask her, and coax her, and kiss her she only cries the more."

"Have you told your mamma?" I inquired.

"No: Lotty said that I must not, that it would only make Mamma unhappy to hear it, and I don't want to make her unhappy, you know."

It struck me that probably Charlotte had some other reason for wishing to conceal her tears from her mistress, though why she should be so unhappy I could not divine. She was young, well-educated, and possessed of many advantages. Her mistress was kind and indulgent, she was not required to do any menial service, but only to attend on the children. What multitudes of people, white and black, might have envied the situation in which she was miserable.

Alas; those that view slavery only as it relates to physical sufferings or the wants of nature, can have no conception of its greatest evils.

CHAPTER 11

An Elopement

Deliver me, Oh Lord.

DAVID

And hurry, hurry, off they rode
As fast as fast can be;
G. A. BÜRGER

I have always thought that in a state of servitude marriage must be at best of doubtful advantage. It necessarily complicates and involves the relation of master and slave, adds new ties to those already formed, and is at the bottom of many troubles and afflictions that might otherwise be escaped. The slave, if he or she desires to be content, should ~~never think of~~ always remain in celibacy. If it was my purpose I could bring many reasons to substantiate this view, but plain, practical common sense must teach every observer of mankind that any situation involving such responsibilities as marriage can only be filled with profit, and honor, and advantage by the free.

The information conveyed by little Anna, light and trivial as it might have appeared to another, had real weight and importance with me. Not that it is anything remarkable for the best-conditioned women to weep occasionally, but such frequent bursts of sorrow attended with attempted concealment, at a time too, considered to be the happiest in a woman's life, had an air of mystery sufficient to excite the conjectures of even a more curious person than myself.

I now recollected that I had observed something singular in the manner of Charlotte, especially for the few last days. On several occasions I had caught her eyes lifted to my face with an intense expression of inquiry, and many times I had fancied that she wished yet feared to ask me for a private interview. Then, too, I was aware that she generally spent the night in some mysterious employment. I had seen lights gleaming ~~from the~~ through the windows of her apartment at unusual hours, I had remarked shadows passing and repassing by the moonlight in concealed places. Simultaneously with this the servants became alarmed, and strange reports of an unearthly visitant were put in circulation. Some averred that they had seen him breathing fire and smoke as he crept stealthily along the halls and through the passages. Others declared that there were two, instead of one, and others again were of the opinion that the spirit had the power of appearing single or double either.

At first Mr and Mrs Henry were disposed to treat the whole matter with silent contempt, but it soon became an affair of serious difficulty. Not a servant could be persuaded to leave the house after dark on any emergency. Lights must be kept burning all night in their various apartments lest "de ghost" should steal on them unaware, and an infant that had been sick a long time actually died very sudden one night, and its mother preferred to lie with the cold stiff corpse ~~there~~ untill morning, to getting up and alarming the house.

For my own part, however, I seldom ~~never~~ gave way to imaginary terror. I found enough in the stern realities of life to disquiet and perplex, without going beyond the boundaries of time to meet new sources of apprehension, and so I rested calmly in the assurance that whether spirit or man, angel or devil, or neither, it was nothing that could change my destiny, or affect in the least degree my happiness or misery. I was accustomed to set [sit] up late; of that probably every person in the house was aware. Harassing anxiety is not a friend to sleep. Then I preferred the still quiet of night for meditation. Two weeks had elapsed since my prospective master was expected, and he came not. This rather contributed to increase than alleviate my uneasiness, as the worst reality is always preferable to suspense.

The bell had just chimed the midnight hour when I was startled one night by a slight noise in an adjoining apartment. Very slight, indeed, and had there been nothing unusual in the sound, scarcely sufficient to have attracted attention. Night is certainly the time for mysterious noises. Window shutters will rattle, when apparently there is no wind. Sounds like heavy objects falling to the floor will break your slumbers, and then the rats and mice in their antics and gambols will create a thousand startling echoes, but this was not like either. It resembled, in fact a suppressed human cough. I listened. There was certainly the sound of muffled footsteps, and then the suppressed creaking of a door stealthily opened. My heart beat audi[b]ly. Should I rise, open my own door, and attempt to penetrate the mystery. There might be a robber in the house, or some one bent on an evil purpose. But instantaneously, and before I had time to decide old Jo, a negro, who loved above all things to indulge in strong potations of brandy, burst into my apartment in the most ludicrous state of terror conceivable. His eyes, large and glaring, seemed actually starting from their sockets, his teeth chattered and his whole frame trembled as with the ague. Before I could rebuke his very unceremonious ingress, he cried out

"Oh: Missus, de ghost, de ghost, sabe me from de ghost."

"The ghost" I replied "where is it?"

The old fellow, however was to[o] badly frightened to give anything like a coherent statement, but putting this and that together as the adage runs I was enabled to make out that Jo as usual was drunk and asleep in one of the entries leading to Charlotte's room. That he was suddenly awakened by the gleam of light, and a sensation of pain, for the ghost, to employ his own expression tread on his toes, and was plaguey heavy.

"And, Missus" continued Joe, "he looked so orful."

"How did he look, Jo?"

["]I cant 'scribe it, but orful, so orful, that I jumped up quicker dan dese old bones hab moved afore dis menny a day. He guv fist [gave first] one spring arter [after] me as I shot by, and den he vanished."

"I am not so sure of that, Jo."

Waiting till Jo partly recovered from his fright I persuaded the old fellow to leave me, and go to bed, as I wished to be alone.

We had that day heard that Charlotte's husband, ~~having~~ after being severely, and as he thought unjustly punished by his master had run away, ~~and that he had been~~ that he had been gone several days, and that all efforts to discover his place of concealment had signally failed. It occurred to me at once that some connection existed between his elopement and the appearance of this ghost, or was the man and the ghost identical? The conjecture was wild, though not beyond the bounds of probability. I determined at once to fathom the mystery without reflecting whether honor or justice strictly considered required such exertion on my part. Neither did I pause to ask myself by what right I presumed to interfere with the secrets of a house where I was myself admitted only by tolerance, but settling in my mind the best manner of proceeding I drew on my cloak and bonnet, and passed without noise from my room, and thence by a narrow entry reached the outer door. This I opened and shut silently, and passing around the house in its broad shadow paused immediately beneath the windows of Charlotte's room. These were usually shaded by white curtains so delicate and thin, that the light could be readily discerned shining through them, but it seemed to me that in order to court security, if her runaway husband were really concealed within, some deeper and darker drapery would probably be considered necessary. Neither was I disappointed. Paper hangings were suspended over the white curtains, though at the bottom of one, which slightly rolled up, the gleam of a lamp within could be distinctly seen. This rather stimulated than gratified my curiosity. For what purpose was he there; did Mr Henry know of it; would he approve of Charlotte's concealing him, and ~~were~~ would not serious consequences ensue if the matter became known. Such and similar questions arose to my mind at once, and I determined to acquaint Mr Henry of my suspicions in the morning.

Then I recollected that I had no certain proof; that it [was] mere belief, founded on impressions I could scarcely analyze, and certainly could not transmit to any one else, and that silence after all would probably be the wisest course.

From my post of observation I could discover nothing more, but I knew very well that her room had only one door, and that her visitor must make his exit as he had entered; for certain detection would follow any attempt to remain in that apartment during the day, it being one of those appropriated to the children. Re-entering the house without noise I was just in time to discover two persons softly gliding out by another door. I felt certain that they had not discovered me, and I quickly perceived that one was a man, the other a woman, and it was no difficult matter to decide their identity. I hesitated a moment, and then decided to follow them though not sufficiently near to excite observation.

Gliding directly down the graveled walks, they paused for an instant only before the small gate that communicated with a narrow lane, or bye-road shaded on either side by forest and fruit trees. The gate opened and shut mechanically, and I lost sight of them in the broad deep shadows. The night had been beautifully bright and starlight [sic], but a cloud was rising and the heavens became blacker and darker every moment. The wind soughed wildly among the branches, and the gleam of lightning accompanied at intervals by the low distant mutter of thunder betokened an approaching shower. I felt my resolution giving way, not that night, or darkness, or tempest were the occasion of terror. I could have braved them all in a good cause, but I began to question the use, or necessity, or even the expediency of my instituting an espionage on the actions of one every way my equal, perhaps my superior. Wherefore should I attempt to unravel a mystery that did not concern me, or to interfere in affairs, of which I should only be an observer. Then would not ignorance be more consistent with my own peace? How could I acquit my conscience of cruelty and wrong if through discoveries made and information given by me the happiness of Charlotte and her husband should be destroyed, by his subjection for the second time into servitude.

Full of these thoughts I retreated into the house, and to my room, half ashamed that I had suffered my curiosity to overstep the bounds of strict propriety.

It was near morning when Charlotte returned, though I had not yet been asleep.

The next morning the old house-keeper sought Mrs Henry with a great complaint. The rats, she said, had devoured her pies, and made sad havoc with the cakes. Charlotte was present, and her cheeks burned, and her eyes fell beneath the gaze of mine. Jo declared that the ghost had doubtless eaten them, but several others well versed in such matters assured him that ghosts did not eat. From this difference a quarrel arose, that finally terminated in heavy blows, and Mr Henry was oblidged to settle the difficulty by refusing any further allusion to the subject.

Sometime that day Charlotte contrived to slip a note privately into my hands. I thrust it into my pocket and made an excuse for retiring that I might read it. It ran thus

"Will you have the goodness to favor an unfortunate woman with a private interview to[-]night in the bower at the bottom of the garden; the hour of meeting midnight."
Charlotte

With a penetrating glance of inquiry she looked towards me, when I came again into her presence. I slightly nodded when her countenance brightened up with pleasure, and she soon after left the apartment.

I spent the time in vain conjectures of what could be the purport of Charlotte's errand with me. That it was something connected with her husband I doubted not, but if she required assistance why not make a confidant of Mrs Henry, or of some one less helpless than myself. Of what use could I be to them, or why should they burden me with a secret that I began to think must be onerous? At last it occurred to me that I was attaching to[o] much importance to the whole affair, that it might be nothing of importance consequence, and that it would be much the wisest course to dismiss the subject from my mind.

It was the Sabbath, and Mr Henry was accustomed to instruct his servants in the great truths of the Gospel on that day. His labors, however, occupied only the morning hours, and were confined to catechetical instruction, while during the afternoon they held ~~prayer meetings among themselve~~ meetings for prayer and exhortation in which any one who wished to was permitted to hold forth.

In attending these religious exercises I found an agre[e]able diversion for my thoughts. The appeals to heaven though not characterised by much grace or elegance of diction were nevertheless earnest and fervid, and I doubt not that they found a place in the vial of odours which the angel in the apocalypse offered before the Throne of God.

After the evening repast I attended Mrs Henry in a very pleasant walk among the ~~various~~ negro lodges, and in looking over their little truck patches and gardens, all of which gave evidence of being neatly attended in the absence of weeds and the appearances of thrifty growth in the various plants, vegetables, and flowers, designed for use and ornament. Various groups of persons, young and old, all of whom seemed impressed with a ~~feeling of reverence of the day~~ reverential feeling of the sanctity of the day, and of regard for their mistress, were seated on little low benches at their doors, quiet[l]y enjoying the beauty of the evening. They all rose with courteous reverence to salute us as we passed, and invited us to walk over their grounds, and gather such flowers as we liked. I shall not soon forget the pleasing intimation of a devotional character impressed on each little party, by some perhaps formally assumed, but sincerely characterising the greater number, hushing the cheerful gayety of the young into a more quiet, though no less interesting exchange of sentiments, and suppressing the vehement arguments of those in more advanced age.

Sauntering along by one of the lodges, which stood a little apart from the others in a picturesque spot beneath the shade of some trees we were surprised to hear the sharp and unmusical voice of Jo detailing to a group of wondering listeners an account of his ~~last~~ night's ghostly visitant. Of course the story lost nothing of the strange or marvellous by the recital, and the ludicrous countenances of the auditors, as they were variously excited by fear, wonder and apprehension were enough to have provoked a smile on the lip of Heraclitus. Their remarks were no less comical, as no one thought of attributing the appearance to natural causes.

"Lord help de poor gose" said one old woman, with a withered smoke-dried face, black as ebony. "Doh say somebody hab been kilt, though I don't see no use of haunting ebery body 'cause dat."

Others delivered themselves with equal effect; while an expression of deep concern and anxiety was manifested in the countenance of Mrs Henry.

"It is really strange," she remarked, as we returned towards the house. "My servants were never indulged in superstitious tendencies, ~~I am not aware that previous to this time there was cherished any such fears and apprehensions~~ I have always striven to instruct them better than to put any confidence in such wild and unfounded reports. Jo was certainly drunk, and as all the servants are acquainted with his peculiar failing how absurd it is in them to encourage him to tell such stories.["] ~~by listen~~

"And yet, Mrs Henry, there may be something in it after all" I answered.

"Why, Hannah, superstitious, too" she said looking into my face with peculiar archness.

"Not a particle of it, Madam" I replied. "And yet I know of a certainty that this house is visited."

"By whom—a spirit?"

"Not a spirit seperated from the flesh," and then I told her in as brief and concise a manner as possible of all that I had observed and witnessed.

With a painful expression of curiosity she heard me to the end without saying a word. When I ceased to speak she remarked that admitting all I supposed it was a very delicate case, and something that neither of us had better meddle with. In fact that having eyes we had better not see, and having ears we should not hear. That she hoped and trusted Charlotte's good sense would prevent her taking any rash or precipitate step likely to embarrass either, and that she should make it in her way to give the former a few words of caution and advice.

"Now" I asked.

["]No: not immediately. It is only natural that she should wish to protect and assist her husband. She can do so, and not be cognisant as breaking the law of the land. The same action by us would be construed to infringe it. Therefore he must not come here. I must and do pity them both, but I cannot harbor him."

We had music and family prayers at bed-time. All the servants, those, I mean, belonging to the house, were present with the exception of Charlotte. She excused herself on a plea that I thought trivial at the time but as it was optional with the servants to attend these services or not, her absence elicited no remarks. Mr Henry's family were distinguished for early hours and the bell was just chiming twelve, though a dead silence had reigned for some time in the house, when putting on my bonnet and drawing a small shawl over my shoulders as a protection from the dew, I passed hastily from the house, descended the garden alley, and paused beside the bower that had been specified in the letter as the meeting place.

Perfect silence reigned, but passing round to the entrance I ~~discerned through the thick gloom that the form of~~ perceived that some one was within. My approach was not unnoticed. A low voice whispered "Hannah."

"The same."

The figure rose, and through the thick gloom I discerned the form and lineaments of a man. The next moment I was joined by Charlotte.

"Be not afraid" she whispered "it is only William."

"And what is William doing here?" I inquired.

"Oh, Hannah: you must hear him tell his story, and all that he has suffered; you will pity him then I know, you cannot help it.["]
~~and will be ready~~

"Very likely, and yet my pity would not be available to any useful purpose."

We had entered the arbor and all three were seated.

"You must not talk so" said Charlotte. "We require your assistance, and more, your company. Hannah wouldn't you like to be free?"

"Oh I should, I should, but then—"

"What?"

"The dangers, the difficulties, the obstructions in the way.["]

"Yet these will all vanish before resolution and perseverance" said William.

"There you are mistaken" I replied. "I have tried elopement once. I know what it is. I know what hunger, and thirst and exposure of every kind means. I know what it is to fear the face of man, to seek hiding places in woods, and caverns, and God helping me I never wish to endure the like again.["]

"But we want you to go with us" said Charlotte.

"With you; are you going, too."

"I am," she replied courageously. "I am going with my dear husband, but Hannah I wanted a female friend to go with us, a good stout-hearted woman, who can look danger in the face unblenched [undaunted], whose counsel could guide us in emergencies, who would be true, and zealous, and faithful; my heart turned to you as the one."

"And you are the one" continued William. ["]Virtually you are free. Your old Master is dead. He met just the fate he deserved. As yet no other has claimed you, and no one has the right, even according to the laws of this accursed country, to prevent your going wherever you will. I told Charlotte to ask this interview, and now we urge, we insist that you should go with us. We have friends only a few miles hence. Once with them we shall be safe and can defy our enemies."

That I was greatly surprised, and altogether unprepared to answer such a proposal in the most proper manner no one can for a moment doubt, but I did not hesitate to tell them that their scheme looked wild and unpromising, and that I feared the result would be unfortunate.

Charlotte sighed.

"There; Hannah, now don't dishearten my dear wife" he said, drawing her affectionately to his bosom. "Our minds are fixed; they cannot be changed, because we have no alternative. We must either be seperated or runaway, and which, think you, that an affectionate wife would choose? My master sold me to a southern trader, through sheer cruelty, I believe, and because he said that I was proud of my marriage. I happened to overhear the bargain. I cared nothing for the exchange of masters, because I had no fears of falling into the clutches of a worse one, but the idea of such premature seperation from Charlotte nearly drove me wild. That night I came here and told her all, and she proposed that we should fly together to a land of freedom. How my heart bounded at the blessed name."

During this long speech I had time to collect my thoughts, and

I answered plainly that however just, or right, or expedient it might be in them to escape my accompanying their flight would be directly the reverse, that I could not lightly sacrifise the good opinion of Mrs Henry and her family, who had been so very kind to me, nor seem to participate in a scheme, of which the consummation must be an injury to them no less than a source of disquiet and anxiety. Duty, gratitude and honor forbid it.

"And so to a strained sense of honor you willingly sacrifise a prospect of freedom" said William. "Well, you can hug the chain if you please. With me it is liberty or death."

"You refuse to go with us, then" said Charlotte.

"I must."

"But you will not betray us. We have placed our secret in your hands."

["]And it shall be well kept, but don't tell me anything more. Let me remain in utter ignorance of all the circumstances you have connected with your flight, ~~the way that you are going~~ give me no clue to the time, the course, the means, or the way."

"Why not?" said William.

"Because it will be better for all that I should know nothing."

Thus our brief interview ended.

The next morning Charlotte was missing. She did not appear to assist Mrs Henry at her toilet. A child was sent to summon her, who returned with the information that she could not be found. Her room was in the neatest order, her bed nicely made, and the drawers of her bureau closely shut. Then there was a great opening and shutting of doors, a calling through the rooms, and around the house. Mr Henry was the first to suggest that possibly she had gone off with her husband, and inquired whether her clothes remained in their accustomed places. But her wardrobe when examined was found nearly empty; all the valuables having been removed.

Mrs Henry wept. Charlotte had been to her as a daughter, ~~and even now it was not her own so much as the wan~~ and more, much more than her own loss she regretted the misery, want, and exposure, which the infatuated woman was bringing on herself.

"And yet I cannot find it in my heart to blame her" remarked the amiable woman. "I ought to have foreseen all this, and yet I did not. The language of Scripture is just as true to[-]day as it was six thousand years ago. 'Thy desire shall be thy husband.' For him Charlotte could abandon her home, and long-tried friends. Heaven grant, that he prove worthy of the trust, and that they may reach in safety the land of freedom."

That day we were somewhat surprised by the appearance of William's master, a Mr Cropp. He came attended by a party of Negroes, several blood-hounds, and the before-mentioned trader. He was evidently a hard stern man in whose soul pity never found refuge. The trader looked at me inquiringly. He had heard my story and asked if I was for sale. Mr Henry replied that he guessed not, at which the fellow expressed his sorrow. Mr Cropp expressed very plainly and firmly the object of his visit. The servants, he said, had reported that the house of Mr Henry was visited at night, as they supposed by a spirit, but being himself a matter-of-fact man and having little faith in supernatural visitants he thought it much more probable that his runaway slave sought in this manner to enjoy the society of Charlotte, and perhaps obtain assistance and provision from her. He further stated that William had actually been seen only the evening previous on Mr Henry's premises, and; finally ended by inquiring for Charlotte. Mrs Henry's countenance turned pale as death.

He repeated the question with something of sternness in his tone.

"In fact, Sir" said Mr Henry, coming forward. "We can tell you tell you [sic] nothing about Charlotte. She was here yesterday, to[-]day she is not."

"Then she went off last night, eh" said the trader.

"And they went together" answered Cropp. "This is better than I hoped, we can now put the dogs on the fresh track, and they can hardly fail to run them down."

The dogs were long, gaunt, and lean, inexpressibly fierce with a cannibal look that made me tremble.

Mr Henry inquired of Cropp if the dogs belonged to him.

"No such good news as that" he answered. "They belong to my brother-in-law fifty miles from here."

"And you sent for them?"

"I did, thinking Bill's recovery well worth the trouble and expense. He was well worth fifteen hundred of any man's money, to say nothing of the example. If one of these fellows gets off safe, another will soon follow, and then another untill all the best hands have gone. But they hate mortally to be overtaken, and brought back, and with these hounds real Cuban, and the best in the country I think we can catch them."

"Do let them go" said Mrs Henry imploringly.

"Let 'em go, indeed" said Cropp, and he exchanged glances with the trader.

"Do you really sympathise with them so much, madam?["] inquired the latter.

Mr Henry ~~caught the eyes of his wife before she had time to answer and shook his head significantly~~ feared the consequences of his wife's imprudence.

"Let me reply for her" he said. "It is her nature to sympathise with everything weak and unprotected, and I believe most women are alike in this respect.["]

"Far from it" said Cropp. "Why my wife is dev'lish hard on the slaves, worse than I be. She actually killed two or three of the best gals I ever had. Just worked them to death. I told her 'twasn't right, and money out of pocket, too."

"Very well, Cropp" said the trader. "Your wife is sharp no doubt, and keen for her own interests which is right, but in one thing I don't agree with you. I don't believe there ever was a negro that would hurt himself at work. However I think we had better be off."

The two arose, went out on the piazza, and stood a few minutes conversing in a low tone. Then Mr Cropp came back, put his head in at the door, and asked if ~~William had been to the~~ Mr Henry would object to letting the dogs into Charlotte's room.

"They are undoubtedly together" said Cropp "and if Tiger, there, can get the scent of both on a fresh track their chances of escape a[i]n't worth a farthing."

Mrs Henry involuntarily raised her eyes to heaven; while her husband rose and himself led the way to the room they sought.

The dogs ran round and round snuffing and smelling at the carpet. At length Tiger uttered a fierce bay.

"He has found the scent" said Cropp. "Hunt: seek 'em find 'em Tiger, that's a good dog."

Thus encouraged the dog leaped furiously against the outer door. It was opened. He rushed out, tore down the garden alley, and entered the bower baying madly. We had no desire to look after them, but an hour later I heard their wild voices ringing through the forest.

That night the prayer of Mr Henry was characterised by unusual solemnity, and he especially asked the blessing and protection of Heaven for such wanderers as had not where [sic] to lay their heads.

CHAPTER 12

A New Mistress

I am poor, and sorrowful.

DAVID

Two days elapsed without our hearing any news of Charlotte, or her husband. During all this time Mrs Henry was in the greatest state of alarm and anxiety, her appetite failed, sleep nearly fled her eyelids, and her feverish imagination conjured up many pictures of direful misery. She thought of her beautiful favorite hunted like a wild beast from place to place, without food or shelter; and strong only in her love, or even yet more fearful painted her torn by dogs, and expiring without a friend to wipe the death-damps from her brow, or point her parting soul to the Cross of Calvary.

But on the third day Mr Henry ~~at her earnest so~~ in compliance with her earnest solicitation, rode over to Cropp's farm to learn the result of the hunt. To our great delight he returned with information that the fugitives had escaped. By some mysterious process they had baffled the dogs, outwitted their pursuers, and were probably on the high road to freedom and happiness. The trader, however had gone forward thinking to intercept them in crossing a river; while Cropp returned to his estate his temper soured by disappointment, and fully prepared to wreak vengeance for his loss on the innocent and helpless.

It was now ~~June, the laboriest month~~ summer, and Nature wore her gayest robes, but my expected Master had not arrived. Indeed he had written another letter stating that sickness in his family detained him, and commanding me to abide where I was for the present. Events are usually crowded, and the same day we received this letter Mrs Wheeler came on her summer visit. Mrs Henry received her with gracious politeness, and led her to the apartments appropriated for her use. It would be a difficult undertaking to describe all the costly and elegant and beautiful things they contained. The dainty drawers, the exquisite little cases and boxes for jewelry and fancy things. Then the tables set off with flowers and damask, the chairs in velvet and brocade, and the bed so white, and fresh and sweet that it resembled an Alpine snow-drift. I remember thinking at the time what a blessed thing it must be, not only to have friends, but to [be] able to treat them so luxuriously.

Mrs Wheeler complained of feeble health, and required the most incessant attendance. Her two waiting maids had ran [sic] off to the North, and she had been thus far unable to suit herself with another. Now that Charlotte was absent Mrs Henry could not supply her wants, unless I consented to perform the ~~service~~ service. This I readily engaged to do, wishing not only to oblige the lady, but to show my gratitude to Mrs Henry. The next morning Mrs Wheeler sent for me to her room. She was languidly reclining in a large chamber chair deeply cushioned, loosely enveloped in a light morning wrapper. She made an effort to smile as I advanced, and inquired in a particularly bland, soft, insinuating voice if I could perform the duties of Lady's maid.

"I can try, madam" I answered.

"But trying will not suit me, unless you succeed" she answered quickly. "Can you dress hair?"

"I have done something at it."

"Did you do it well and as it should be done?"

"There was no fault found."

"Well, that I may be enabled to judge of your skill in that fashionable art I wish you to dress my hair this morning."

"But Madam."

"What?"

"There are many styles of dressing hair."

"Certainly, put mine in the most graceful style of morning costume you know."

"Yes, Madam." And I went to work with combs, brushes and pomatum [pomade].

"Be careful" she exclaimed. "My hair, I expect, is excessively tangled, as it hasn't been combed for more than a week."

"Indeed, Madam."

~~It's more than a week I think, yes I know it is~~

"I was too feeble to think of attempting it myself, and since Jane ran off, there has been no one to whom I could think of entrusting my head, till Mrs Henry so warmly recommended you."

"I am much obliged to Mrs Henry I am sure.["]

"Jane was very handy at almost everything" she continued. "You will seldom find a slave so handy, but she grew discontented and dissatisfied with her condition, thought she could do better in a land of freedom, and such like I watched her closely you may depend; there, there, how you pull."

The comb had caught in a snarl of hair.

"Forgive me, madam, but I could not help it; the hair is actually matted."

"Oh dear, this is what I have to endure from losing Jane, but she'll have to suffer more, probably. I didn't much like the idea of bringing her to Washington. It was all Mr Wheeler's fault. He wanted me to come, and I couldn't think of doing without her in my feeble health. Are you getting the tangles most out?"

"I believe so."

"My husband, you are aware, occupies a high official position in the Federal City, which gives us access to the best society the Capital affords. While there my time was chiefly occupied in giving and receiving visits, attending parties, and going to places of amusement. As I knew that Washington was swarming with the enemies of our domestic institution I told Catharine, my second maid, to keep a sharp eye on Jane, and if strangers called on her during my absence, or she received messages from them to inform me. Hannah Hannah, why I can't stand such rough usage.["]

"I do my best, madam, but your hair is in a dreadful state."

"I know that, but do be careful" and she continued the rehearsal of Jane's conduct.

Those who suppose that southern ladies keep their attendants at a distance, scarcely speaking to them, or only to give commands have a very erroneous impression. Between the mistress and her slave a freedom exists probably not to be found elsewhere. A northern woman would have recoiled at the idea of communicating a private history to one of my race, and in my condition, whereas such a thought never occurred to Mrs Wheeler. I was near her. She was not fond of silence when there was a listener, and I was pleased with her apparent sociality.

"Catharine, however" she went on "was false to her trust, but I had a little page, or errand boy, who discovered that something was not right, and so came to me one day, with the information that both Jane and Catharine had received a letter from somebody. [']And who were they from?['] I inquired.

"[']Can't tell for certain, but I think['] he answered, scratching his head."

"[']And what do you think?[']"

"[']Why Missus, to tell you all about it. The 'Hio man's servant has been here good many times, and Jane said he was her brother, but I knowed better and told her so; then she wanted me not to tell you, but I told her that I should. And to[-]day he was skulking round here and then they both had letters, and that's just what I know.[']"

"Who did he mean by the 'Hio man?"

"The Senator from Ohio, whose name I forget, but who professed a great regard for slaves and negroes, I don't know why, unless because he was so black himself, his mulatto servant being much the whitest, and best looking man of the two. This fellow was thought to have his master's concurrence in persuading servants to abandon their masters; it was even suspected that the grave senator assisted in spiriting them away."

"Did many go?"

"I should think so. Nearly every family lost two or more, and these generally speaking the most valuable ones they possessed. I told my husband that there was something in the wind, but he only laughed at me, said there was no danger of our servants going, that they were too well off, and knew it, and so one night when I was attending a party at the Russian Minister's they took themselves away off.["]"

"Did you try to recover them?["]"

"Oh, no: Mr Wheeler said that it would be of no use, and then he disliked making a hue and cry about a slave at the Federal Capital, so we said little as possible about it."

"Well Madam, your hair is completed; will you tell me how you like it?" said I, bringing forward a mirror. "To me it looks well."

"So it does, why Hannah I must retain you in my service."

I bowed, but said nothing. Notwithstanding her sociality and freedom of conversation there was something in her manner that I did not like. Her voice ~~had that low~~ was soft and low, but the tone was rather artificial than natural. Her manner was exceedingly pleasant and kind, though I could not help fearing that it was affected. Then there was a sparkle in her eye, and a tremor in her frame when she became agitated that indicated an effort to keep down strong passion.

While assisting at her toilet I was greatly amused with the gossip and titbits of Washington scandal she related, yet my heart did not yearn towards her as it [did] to Mrs Henry, and I felt a certain presentiment that ~~by acquaintance with her~~ she must be less good.

Her toilet preperations being finished she retired to her breakfast room, a dainty little boudoir, with a great bow window, completely trellised by climbing rose vines. Here she was joined by Mrs Henry, and they partook together the~~ir~~ morning meal.

"You find Hannah right handy, don't you?" inquired Mrs Henry.

"Oh, very, I have serious thoughts of dictating a letter to that gentleman this day, if you will give me his name and address. I must endeavor to secure her. She could fill the place of Jane so exactly."

"She would do more" said Mrs Henry. "Hannah is a good girl; she has good principles, and is I believe a consistent Christian. I don't think your Jane was either."

"Oh, as to that" said Mrs Wheeler ["]it makes little difference. I never trouble myself about the principles of my girls; so they are obedient is all I require."

After breakfast Mrs Henry went out to give the servants their orders for the day, while Mrs ~~Wheeler se~~ Wheeler requested me to read for her. I had not gone over two pages, when she called for pillows, which were to be disposed about her person to facilitate slumber; then she inquired if I was musical, adding that Jane used to soothe her to sleep with the guitar. I had played a little on the harp, and so I told her. She bade me get it, and play softly, very softly on account of her nerves. Then settling her person among the pillows, but in such a manner as not to derange her hair she prepared to take a nap. My music, however, did not suit her. It was sharp, or flat, or dull, or insipid anything but what she wished.

I was sorry at my inability to please her, and apologised of course in the best language I was able to command.

It was singular, indeed, but there was something imperative in her manner. Her requests, though made in the softest voice, implied command. You were not forced, but awed to obedience.

That afternoon she dictated a letter for me to write. It was to my prospective master, and the subject was myself. It opened as business letters usually do, very brief and concise. Then it stated that she, (Mrs Wheeler) was visiting Mrs Henry, that she had seen me, that I was very homely, and what was worse a bigot in religion; that I wept and shuddered at the idea of being transferred to his family, though I was very fond of her, and that my earnest solicitations had induced her to offer to purchase me, though she could not give anything like a great price, as she had many doubts of my ability to serve her properly, and thought from my previous character that I would be likely to run away the first opportunity.

No one can doubt that I hesitated to pen such a libel on myself. She perceived my feelings.

"All in the way of a bargain, my dear" she said smiling in her blandest manner. "I think you quite beautiful but of course others might not; then you are doubtless very good, yet some might consider your notions of religion and truth as highly improper for one in your station, and of course you prefer the service of a lady to that of a gentleman, in which probably you would be compelled to sacrifise [sic] honor and virtue. Upon the whole my dear, that letter is destined to do you a great kindness, greater in all probability than you can imagine. Don't you think so?"

I said like enough.

"Again" she continued "though you have not solicitated me to become your purchaser Mrs Henry has, which is just the same thing in substance, and as to my last remark of not being perfectly satisfied with your ways, as no one can pretend to perfection in this world it is nothing. Don't you see it so?"

"I cannot say that I do" I answered faintly.

Her eyes sparkled, her frame trembled, but her voice retained the same soft persuasive tone.

["]Now Hannah, don't be foolish, you know that I have great need of your services. Do you wish me to write that you are very beautiful and good?"

"Oh, Madam, you know I do not."

"Then why not remain satisfied with it as it is?"

"I am satisfied."

"Very well, that is all. Now seal the letter."

The letter was sealed, and despatched by the errand boy to the Post Office. Mrs Henry came in, and Mrs Wheeler informed her that I had written a beautiful letter at her dictation, being myself perfectly ~~suited and~~ satisfied with the contents. Mrs Henry congratulated me on my improved prospects, and I saw how her open and guileless nature had been duped.

Days passed away and still I was the attendant of Mrs Wheeler, though it is impossible to say how irksome the duty had become. There seemed no end to her vanities, and whims, and caprices. She reminded me exactly of a spoiled child that never cares for what it has, but is always wanting something new. She would call for a pomegranite, just taste, and then order it away, and ask for a nutmeg or citron. These obtained were not prized, and something else was wanted. Yet I observed that such exhibitions of disquiet and discontent were never made in the presence of Mrs Henry. Everything, then, was nice, beautiful, and excellent. It seemed never to occur to her that a person could be ill or weary, though all the time complaining of feebleness herself. Sometimes in the dead hours of night she would call me out of bed to get her some kind of candy or confectionary. Then she would call for water to take away the saccharine taste; and then again for more candy. Sometimes it would be for salt, and at others vinegar; there was no telling. She used always to ~~charge me~~ order me not to let Mrs Henry know how foolish she was, and I was silly enough to obey her.

In due time a letter arrived from my master, and it seemed that he had heard a different report of me, and and [sic] my qualifications from that given by Mrs Wheeler, and he rather dissented from her opinion in other particulars. However he expressed his readiness to dispose of me on reasonable terms, leaving to Mr Henry the arbitration of the sale. I was not pleased, yet what could I do? Should I expose the inconsistencies ~~revealed in my~~ in Mrs Wheeler's character that my intimacy with her had discovered? Should I accuse her of deception, and almost open falsehood? Could I expect to be believed when I said she was a hard mistress, and a woman unworthy of confidence? What would her friends and mine say to such a proceeding? All these considerations I weighed deliberately, and finally concluded to let them consummate the bargain without objection or difficulty. But I never felt so poor, so weak, so utterly subjected to the authority of another, as when that woman with her soft voice and sauvity of manner, yet withal so stern and inflexible told me that I was hers body and soul, and that she did and would exact obedience in all cases and under all circumstances. "And yet" I thought "Mrs Henry told me how kind you were."

But the best and wisest may be deceived.

~~service This I readily engaged to do, wishing not only to oblige the lady, but to show my gratitude to Mrs Henry The next morning I was duly installed~~

CHAPTER 13

A Turn of The Wheel

~~Thou but my hiding place~~

Now Ninevah was a great ~~Psalms~~ city and full of people.

JONAH

Washington, the Federal City. Christmas holidays recently over. The implacable winter weather. The great President of the Great Republic looks perhaps from the windows of his drawing room, and wonders at the mud and slush precisely as an ordinary mortal would. Perhaps he remarks to the nearest secretary that the roads are dreadful; and the secretary bound to see with the same eyes and hear with the same ears echoes "dreadful." What inconsistency, and what a pity it is that great men should care about roads or such common things.

But perhaps his excellency wished to take a drive, for Presidents generally admire splendid equipages and are fond of display. No wonder, then, that he notices the mud—mud so deep and dark that you half fancy the waters of the deluge have but newly retired from the earth, and that perhaps a Python might be caught by another Apollo floundering in the neighborhood of the Capitol. Carriages dragging through mire; horses splashed to their manes. Congress men jostling each other at the street crossings, or perhaps losing their foothold, where a negro slave was seen slipping and sliding but a moment before. Alas; that mud and wet weather should have so little respect for aristocracy.

Gloom everywhere. Gloom up the Potomac; where it rolls among meadows no longer green, and by splendid country seats. Gloom down the Potomac where it washes the sides of huge warships. Gloom on the marshes, the fields, and heights. Gloom settling steadily down over the sumptuous habitations of the rich, and creeping through the cellars of the poor. Gloom arresting the steps of chance office-seekers, and bewildering the heads of grave and reverend Senators; for with fog, and drizzle, and a sleety driving mist the night has come at least two hours before its time.

~~Gas is lighted in divers~~ The lamps are lighted in divers[e] places, but rather serve to render the gloom visible than to dispel it. The shops are lighted too, and soon, very soon there is a gleaming of lights from little windows and great windows that seems to betoken warmth and comfort within.

Just where the gloom was densest, and the muddy street the muddiest there was I, wrapped in a very thin shawl and carrying a very small box in my hand. I had been to a shop in Pennsylvania Avenue, much frequented by the slaves of fashionable Ladies, who sought to add artificial to natural charms. Paints and cosmetics in every variety, perfumes from China and India, hair of every color in curls or braids, teeth, washes, powders magnetic or otherwise, filters, love-tokens, and similar articles of great perfection and infinite variety were to be exchanged for gold.

Mrs Wheeler conceived her beauty to be on the wane. She had been a belle in youth, and the thought of her fading charms was unendurable. That very day an antiquated lady, with a large mouth filled with false teeth, a head covered with false hair, and a thin scrawny neck, beneath which swelled out a false bust, had called on my mistress with what she designated very highly important information. I supposed at first that the President's wife was dead, or the secretary's daughter about to be married, but it was something more interesting to fashionable ladies than even that. Some great Italian chemist, a Signor with an unpronounceable name had discovered or rather invented an impalpable powder, fine, highly scented, and luxurious, that applied to the hands and face was said to produce the most marvellous effect. The skin, however sallow and unbeautiful, would immediately acquire the softness and delicacy of childhood. Tan, or freckless [freckles], or wrinkles, or other unseemly blotches would simultaneously disappear, and to render the article still more attractive it was said that only two or three boxes of it yet remained. Of course Mrs Wheeler was all impatience to obtain one of them, and her visitor was scarcely out of hearing when I was summoned, and directed to go at once to the Chemist's, and get a box of the Italian Medicated Powder. No hesitancy on account of mud or bad weather was allowable. I went, purchased the last box, and when returning passed two gentlemen, standing in a somewhat sheltered place apparently conversing on some subject of deep interest. There was something in the coat of seedy black, and the general bearing and manner of one of them, which instantly arrested my attention, but the driving mist and sleet was full in my face, with the gloom momentarily thickening, so that I failed to obtain a perfect view of his features. It was certainly very ill-mannered, but stimulated by curiosity I even turned back to look at them, and not minding my footing through pre-occupation of mind I slipped very suddenly and came down with all my weight on the rough paving stones. The two gentlemen immediately came forward, and one of them assisting me to rise, kindly inquired if I was hurt. I looked into the face of the other I knew. ~~I knew him on the instant~~ Oh then I knew him on the instant, I could have remembered his eyes and countenance among a thousand. It was Mr Trapp[e].

Whether or not the recognition was mutual I had no means of ascertaining, but his presence to me seemed ominous of evil, and hastily murmuring my thanks I hastened home.

Mr Wheeler was in the apartment of his wife when I entered it. He was a little dapper man, very quick in his motions, and with little round piercing black eyes set far back in his head. He had the exact air and manner of a Frenchman, but was reputed to be very obstinate in his way, and to have little respect for constituted authorities in his moments of passion. Report said that he had actually quarreled with the President, and challenged a senator to fight a duel, besides laying a cowhide on a certain occasion over the broad shoulders of a member of Congress. At any rate he had been turned out of office, and now was busily engaged in hunting another. Consequently he was seldom at home, being usually to be found haunting the bureau of some department or other, and striving to engage attention by talking in sharp shrill voice, accompanied with violent gesticulation of what should be done in one place, or had been left undone in another. He knows exactly where a screw is loose, and he understands perfectly to tighten it again. On many matters he is better informed than the President. He could give instructions to the secretaries of the army and navy, but they are old, obstinate, and headstrong, and won't listen to his advice.

Of course Mrs Wheeler was particularly interested in these schemes of her husband, and when he came home occasionally they had a little familiar talk on the affairs of the nation generally, and the chances for office in particular, where a vacancy has occurred and where another is likely to occur, and similar interesting matters.

"How are you getting along, any chance yet?" was the spousal salutation repeated perhaps for the thousandth time in the same soft voice, with the same languid air.

"Well" replies Mr Wheeler, crossing his legs and rubbing the topmost up and down "I am not discouraged. It takes a great deal to discourage me, you know, besides I have a promise"

"A promise" the languid air is dropped for a moment, then taken up and put on again, as though it were a mantle.

"A veritable promise" repeats the husband. "You know Riggs of the Naval Department is almost dead. His physician, who has been consulted, says he can't live over a week; Trotter expects to succeed him, and if Trotter does succeed him, I'm in for it."

"In for it, how vulgar you are" says the lady.

Riggs, however, contrary to the expectations of his physician, and notwithstanding the pills, powders, and doses of which he had taken enough to have killed two or three common men actually recovered, and so both Trotter and Mr Wheeler had to turn their attention to some other quarter. I occupied a little room, communicating by a single door with that of my mistress. She wanted me always near and handy, she said, so that when summoned I could come on the instant. A little bell stood on a table by her side, and its ting a ring ding reminded me of my servitude a hundred times a day. In this room I could hear every word of conversation repeated in the other.

"I don't see what old people must live forever for" said Mrs. Wheeler to her husband, when the astounding news that Riggs was actually abroad reached her ears. "But that's just the way, and thus younger and better ones are kept out of their legitimate sphere.["]

"Well I don't know" replied Mr Wheeler "but it's an old saying that some people will live as long as they can see anybody alive, and I verily believe that Riggs must be of that sort. However there's another vacancy. A clerk connected with the Treasury Department after lining his pocket well with the funds has suddenly decamped. If I could only obtain that situation."

"Why can't you, is there opposition?" inquired the lady.

"Opposition" repeats her husband "why there were two hundred applicants there to[-]day, crowding and jamming each other, and each one intriguing to set forth his claims to the best advantage. There was one, a blacksmith's son from New York, who actually had the insolence to smile when I recommended myself as being the most proper person from my extensive acquaintance with political business."

"A blacksmith's son" repeated the lady, with ~~a sparkling~~ a sparkle of the eyes and agitation of manner. "A blacksmith's son, indeed; an Abolitionist I dare say, who would reverse the order of nature, and place Negroes at the top instead of at the bottom of society. Really smiled at you, the wretch."

The next day it was ascertained that the blacksmith's son had obtained the appointment.

On the present occasion Mr Wheeler came to ask a favor of his wife. Another vacancy had occurred, but the gift was in the power of a gentleman, with whom at some time or another of his life Mr Wheeler had some disturbance, and much as he desired the office he dreaded still more the humiliation of asking for it. Could not his wife be induced to make the request? He thought with a little well-timed flattery she might. Ladies of great consideration not unfrequently petitioned for their husbands. The President had been importuned by them till he almost feared the sight of a woman. The Secretaries had fared little better; indeed all who had offices to bestow had been coaxed, and flattered, and addled by female tongues untill they scarcely knew what they were about. They said, too, that female petitioners were likeliest to succeed. Perhaps that was the reason of his frequent failure. Had he brought his wife sooner into the field, in all probability he would have secured a prize with far less trouble. The experiment is worth trying at any rate, though he is not positive that the lady will concur.

"My dear" says Mr Wheeler, discreetly eyeing his wife. "My dear."

"What?" inquires the lady in a very soft voice, and with a very languid air.

"I have been thinking that ~~if your galaxy~~ you are not quite in your usual spirits to[-]day, yet I never saw you looking better."

"Well, I don't know" says the lady brightening a little.

For say what you will of lovers there's nothing so flattering to female vanity as the praise of a husband, because it is universally considered a more difficult matter to retain affection than to win it.

"And faith, nor do I know" reiterates the husband. "A woman of your fine presence has no right to be out of spirits. That isn't a countenance to be sad or meloncholly. Then you haven't no care, no public or private burdens on your mind. You never ask for offices without expectations of gaining them. You never ask for offices, my dear."

He dwells rather longer on this phrase than is strictly necessary, considering the extent and variety of his conversational abilities. Twice or thrice he repeats it with his peculiarly listening face, as if expecting an answer. "You never ask for offices, my dear"

~~"And I don't know why I should" she answers "Since~~

At last the answer is elicited with a sort of vague smile. "I never have indeed, I don't know why I should, since my husband is fully capable of doing his own business."

The little man runs his fingers thoughtfully through his hair, and replies

"But his abilities, my dear, are not rightly appreciated. It takes time to convince people that you possess abilities. Then abilities are so very common; they are possessed by every man. Lord bless you, Mrs Wheeler, men of abilities are as thick all over Washington as are cherries in June."

The lady looks at him and wonders what he is driving at. He continues.

"With female beauty, my dear, it is very different. Any one having the use of his eyes can readily discover that. Then, too, beauty is rarer. It's only once in awhile that a beautiful woman crosses your path, and when such is the case, why, Lord, the men run nearly stark mad. ~~Any she wishes, must be complied with~~ Her slightest wish is obeyed, and they are proud and happy to do her a service. That is the reason I suppose why so many women have succeeded in obtaining offices for their husbands, when the husbands themselves failed to do so. There was Mrs. Perkins, you know."

"Mrs Perkins" retorted the lady scornfully "you don't call her beautiful, I hope."

["]Rather good-looking, that is all, and nothing comparable with you. I was thinking, however, that as her good looks accomplished much, perhaps your beauty might do more."

A gleam of intelligence flitted over her countenance, mingled I thought with an expression of slight displeasure, and she inquired in a voice raised somewhat above the common key.

"Is it possible that you wish me to do as Mrs Perkins did? Is it possible that you desire me to hang around some haughty official till I weary him ~~by my constant~~ with continual coming, that you ask me to weep before him, and kneel at his feet with importunities that will not be answered in the negative?—is it possible Mr Wheeler, I say—?"

"No, my dear, it is not possible," said the gentleman deprecatingly. "I require you to do no such thing. Of course I don't, but my love could you feel willing to lend your influence in the affair. I am certain it would go a great way. No mind. I don't require this of you. Indeed, it would be too much to expect from any other woman of your admirable presence and beauty, but you have always been so kind to me, and so considerate of our interests, and I am under so many obligations to you already that I shouldn't be at all surprised if another still greater was to be added to them."

What this prospective obligation might be he did not think proper to specify, but his finishing of the sentence restores him to favor, and the lady's looks imply, tho she does not say "what a sensible man this husband of mine is. Surely if the public understood its interests he would have been laden with offices before this time."

"I regret to say, my dear" continued Mr Wheeler "that I am the object of continued opposition. Men of attainment in a high position of society always have their enemies of course. I have mine. Not so with you. You, I am proud to say it, are universally admired. Then no gentleman would think for a moment of opposing a lady. Certainly not. Now a vacancy has just occurred, and Mrs Piper is intriguing to have it filled by her husband. It is a very important office, worth about two thousand a year."

"Then she expects to get it, does she?—and a failure would mortify her exceedingly. She is so haughty, vain, and conceited. Wouldn't it be pleasant to disappoint her?"

"It would, indeed."

"Who makes the appointment?"

Mr Wheeler gave the desired information.

The lady sate [sat] a few moments in profound silence, then she spoke though rather as talking to herself than any one else. "Mrs Piper, indeed, going to obtain a situation for her husband when mine has none. But I'll disappoint her, that I will. Mr Wheeler you shall have this office. I'll see to it that you do."

Mr Wheeler bowed complacently. Nothing could suit his purpose better.

"I'll go now, this very evening" continued the lady. "The weather is so bad that probably the gentleman will be at home. And then he will be more likely to be disengaged. Hannah you can prepare my toilet."

"Certainly."

"My rich antique moire, and purple velvent [velvet] mantilla. Mr Wheeler be so good as to order the carriage."

Two bows, and a two expressions of "certainly Madam" were the response to this.

Mrs Wheeler did not forget her beautifying powder.

"How lucky" she exclaimed ["]that I sent for it just when I did. Don't be sparing of it Hannah, dear, as I wish to look particularly well."

The powder was very fine, soft, and white, and certainly did add much to the beauty of her appearance. I had never seen her look better. Mr Wheeler complimented her, hoped that she would be careful of herself and not take cold, and actually kissed her hand as he assisted her into the carriage, observing to me as he stepped back on the pavement "She is a dear, good, noble woman."

The next moment I heard my voice called, and turning round beheld Mrs Wheeler leaning from the carriage window and beckoning.

"Hannah, dear" she cried on my approach. "I forgot my smelling-bottle, go and bring it, that new one I ~~obtained~~ purchased yesterday."

"Yes Madam" and back I went to the house, procured the smelling-bottle, Mr Wheeler advanced to meet me, took the little delicate supporter of weak nerves, and handing it to his wife, the carriage drove off.

In two hours a carriage stopped at the door; the bell was rung with a hasty jerk, and the servant admitted a lady, who came directly to Mrs Wheeler's apartment. I was greatly surprised; for though the vail, the bonnet, and the dress were those of that lady, or exactly similar, the face was black.

I stood gazing in mute amazement, when a voice not in the least languid called out "What are you gazing at me in that manner for? Am I to be insulted by my own slaves?"

Mr Wheeler just that moment stepped in. She turned towards him, and the mixture of surprise and curiosity with which he regarded her was most ludicrous.

"Are you all gone mad?" inquired the not now languid voice. "Or what is the matter?"

"You may well ask that question" exclaimed Mr Wheeler, sobbing with suppressed laughter. "Why, Madam, I didn't know you. Your face is black as Tophet.["]

"Black?" said the lady, the expression of astonishment on his countenance transferred to hers.

"Hannah bring the mirror."

I complied.

She gazed a moment, and then her mingled emotions of grief, rage, and shame were truly awful. To all Mr Wheeler's inquiries of "how did it happen, my dear?["] and ["]how came your face to turn black, my dear?" she only answered that she did not know, had no idea, and then she wept and moaned, and finally went into a fit of strong hysterics. Mr Wheeler and myself quickly flew to her assistance. To tell the truth he was now more concerned about his wife than the office ~~now~~.

"Heaven help me" he said bending over her. "I fear that her

beauty has gone forever. What a dreadful thing it is. I never heard of the like."

"It must have been the powder."

"The powder was white I thought."

"The powder certainly is white, and yet it may posses such chemical properties as occasion blackness. Indeed I recently saw in the newspapers some accounts of a chemist who having been jilted by a lady very liberal in the application of powder to her face had invented as a method of revenge a certain kind of smelling bottles, of which the fumes would suddenly blacken the whitest skin provided the said cosmetic had been previously applied."

"You wretch" exclaimed the lady suddenly opening her eyes. "Why didn't you tell me of this before?"

"I—I—didn't think of it, didn't know it was necessary" I stammered in extenuation.

"Oh no: you didn't think of it, you never think of anything that you ought to, and I must be insulted on account of your thoughtlessness, right before Mrs Piper, too. Get out of my sight this instant. I never want to see you again."

"My dear Madam" I said, kneeling at her feet, and attempting to kiss her hand "how should I know that those mentioned in the papers were identical with those you purchased."

Here Mr Wheeler interposed and told her that he did not see how I could be to blame.

"Of course, you don't" she replied mockingly eager to vent her spleen on somebody "of course, you don't. No: no: what husband ever could agree with his wife Slaves generally are far preferable to wives in husbands' eyes."

Mr Wheeler's face flushed with anger. The allusion was most uncalled for, and ungenerous. However recovering his serenity in a moment he inquired who had insulted her.

"Why everybody" she replied, making another demonstration of hysterics.

"Don't have another fit, pray" said the husband, applying the camphor to her nose. "Hannah bring some water and wash off this hedious stuff."

I procured the water, brought a basin, soap, napkin, and cloth, and went to work. Gradually and by little and little the skin resumed its natural color.

"Now, my dear" said Mr Wheeler ["]you look like my own sweet wife again, fresh and rosy as the morning, and if you are not too nervous and agitated I should be glad to hear who has presumed to insult you."

"Why Cattell, and his clerks, with Mrs Piper, too."

" 'Tis strange" muttered Wheeler half inaudibly.

"Mrs Piper, how I hate her" ejaculated the lady. ["]How absurd she dresses. False teeth much too large which have the effect of thrusting out her lips; ~~complexion highly rouged~~ a face on fire with rouge and a ringletty wig. Then she was pinched in and swelled out, and puffed up, and strapped down in a way I never saw. I can't say that she knew me. I can't say that she didn't, but she gave me no sign or token of recognition."

"It's lucky if she didn't," said Mr Wheeler, with a look of extreme mortification.

"At any rate I gave your name as that of my husband, and when Mr Cattell said [']by courtesy perhaps['] I said [']No, by law['] when they all burst into a titter."

"Then you really asked Cattell for the office?" said Mr Wheeler, hoping to reach indirectly the information he desired.

"Certainly I did."

"And what did he say?"

"That it was not customary to bestow offices on colored people, at which Mrs Piper blustered and said that [']would be very ~~ungentlemanly~~ unconstitutionally indeed.['] [']Then you positively refuse this office to my husband.['] I said going down on my knees."

["]Positively, and if either you or him had possessed a particle of common sense, you would not have asked for it.["]

"I recollected your old disturbance, and supposing that was the occasion of his harsh language, I bade him farewell and came away, determining as that was my first, it should be my last attempt at office seeking."

"Confound all smelling-bottles, I say" exclaimed Mr Wheeler. "Here I have probably lost the appointment to a valuable office, and you, my wife, have been rendered ridiculous by a dam—d little smelling bottle. Was ever anything so provoking?"

A day or two only elapsed before Mrs Wheeler's face was the topic of the city. Who was it? What was it? How was it? For the fashionable intelligence had not succeeded in obtaining the full particulars. Some viewed it in the light of a little masquerade; and thus taken it became extremely funny. Others considered it to have originated in a wager, and thought the lady rather debased herself. Very few regarded it as it really was, the deserved punishment of an act of vanity.

Mrs Wheeler like Byron woke up in the morning and found herself famous. An eminent divine in a fashionable sermon held forth for two whole hours on the sin and wickedness of wantonly disguising the form or features, and suggested it was a wonder of mercy that the presumptuous lady had not been turned irrecoverably black. A philosophic M.D. discoursed learnedly of the cuticle and color and pigments, and it was even broached among milliners that black for the time being should be fashionable style.

A bit of scandal, so fresh and original, and entirely new how the fashionable world loved it? How they handed it round and round their circle like some dainty morsel? How it was discussed at the President's levees, and retailed at the Russian minister's. How dull old ladies carry it about with them from one place to another and thereby render their morning calls less irksome. How antiquated spinsters, who affect to be young chat and giggle over it.

In the circle where Mrs Wheeler has been most popular she is discussed with the most perfect freedom, and the phrase of "town talk" becomes a significant fact ~~in her use~~. The rumor flies from sphere to sphere, from circle to circle. People who never heard of her before, and who positively know nothing about her relate many little items of scandal and anecdote with which her name is connected. Even kitchens and cellars grew merry and chatty over it. Faces black by nature were ~~excessively pleased~~ puckered with excessive exultation that one had become so by artificial means. It even extended to the slave market, but the miserable victims of that dreadful traffic found little in it to ameliorate their woes.

Mrs Wheeler's notoriety extended to her husband, and even to me. His affairs were sagely discussed in financial circles. Speculators talked of stocks, and bonds and martgages Even the price of his last year's cotton crop, the value of this estate in North Carolina, and the number of his slaves was retailed by bar-tenders and post-boys with great satisfaction. Some went so far as to think that political capital might be made of it, and even the nomination of the next President influenced thereby.

Finding themselves the subjects of such unwelcome notoreity they concluded to forsake the capital and remove to their estate. The splendid mansion they occupied having been taken only temporarily could be abandoned at any time. Suddenly and without any previous intimation a certain circle was astounded with the intelligence that the Wheeler's [sic] had gone.

But the day before we went I was out on some errand for Mrs

Wheeler when I was surprised by the voice of some one calling ~~me~~ behind me. I turned around and instantly recognised Lizzy. She had many things to tell me concerning Mr Vincent, our old master and Mr Trappe, which would scarcely bear repeating here but I was deeply interested in what she told me of Mr Cosgrove, her present master and the owner of Lindendale, as well as the changes she reported to have occurred to the dear old place. Then she said that the children now grown to be great boys and girls remembered me with affection, and often mentioned my name, and told how kind I ~~was to them~~ used to be to them, how I taught them to pray, and love one another; that Mr Cosgrove once in her hearing inquired of Mr Trappe for me, and said that he thought I must be worth having.

"Is your master kind, Lizzy dear?" I inquired.

"Sometimes very, and sometimes not, just as it happens" she replied. "At times he is so moody and morose that I fear him greatly; at others he will laugh so loud and long that I think he is getting crazy, but he didn't use to be so, it all comes of." She lowered her voice, gazed around her to see that no one was near.

"Of what, Lizzy?" I inquired.

"Of his being haunted."

"Haunted."

"Yes. It's a long story, and a fearful one, but I want you to hear it. So come in here, and I will tell you."

She led me behind some piles of ~~timber~~ lumber where we could be effectually screened from observation, and seating ourselves she began.

CHAPTER 14

Lizzy's Story

The dark places of the earth are the habitations of cruelty.

BIBLE

"You see" began Lizzy "there has been strange doings at the old place, as you call it, stranger than you can imagine. Our master, whose beautiful wife had gone to Europe to attend the dying bed of some near and dear relatives, took a great fancy to beautiful females slaves. He preferred those who were accomplished in music and dancing, and no Turk in his haram ever luxuriated in deeper sensual enjoyments than did the master of Lindendale. More than one of these favorites gave birth to children and the little ones were caressed and petted by their father with all imaginable fondness, but I used sometimes to wonder how his lady would bear it if she knew. She was an English woman of aristocratic family and connections, and very high. How would she bear it? We soon found out.

The lady arrived at her mansion in the evening. She was of stately presence, and no Empress could have been more dignified and commanding. She took little notice of the house or its appointments, and still less of the servants. Indeed had we been the most loathsome and degraded reptiles she could not have treated us with greater hauteur and contempt. But she had the good taste to perceive and appreciate beauty. You recollect Lilly, that sweet child who was so fond of you."

"I have not forgotten her."

"Well our mistress took a great fancy to her at the first sight, I believe, she actually called the girl to her side and caressed and praised her, to the infinite astonishment of her maid who had always been kept at a distance. Henceforth when she descended to dinner or tea her eyes instinctively sought that beautiful face and the child conscious of the notice she inspired would drop her head and blush, which made her look all the lovelier.

At length Mrs Cosgrove dismissed her maid. It was a cruel act; for the girl had accompanied her from beyond the seas and had neither friends nor relatives in this country, but who might question her imperious will: and greatly I pitied Lilly when the haughty English woman promoted her to the rank of ~~waiting maid~~ attendant.

Hitherto the lady had known nothing of her husband's favorites. The mansion, you know, was large and irregular in its dimensions, besides being built in a kind of rambling style, that precluded the occupant of one part from knowing anything of the other. In obedience to his orders they had kept themselves ~~seclu~~ secluded and out of her sight, and the servants were forbidden ~~under pain of the severest punishment~~ to mention them in her presence under the penalty of the severest punishment.

But one morning when Lilly was dressing her hair as she sate [sat] in her apartment beneath the windows that overlooked the garden, ~~when suddenly~~ two or three beautiful and well dressed women appeared in an arbor plainly in view and each one led or carried a young child. Mrs Cosgrove beheld them with speechless amazement, and turning to Lilly she inquired "Who are these Ladies. I was not aware that Mr Cosgrove entertained guests?"

"Guests" repeated Lilly in great confusion.

"Certainly, those ladies do not belong to the house, how well they are dressed, and what beautiful children."

Lilly made no reply.

"Do you know anything about them?"

"Master said I mustn't tell you" she replied, falteringly.

"Mustn't tell me, why not pray?"

"I can't tell you, only he said so."

"But I will know" she replied. "I will know what ladies are entertained in this house, and that immediately. Ring for the waiter."

The page appeared.

"Go, and request those ladies in the arbor to come to me."

"Ladies" echoed the page with a broad grin "why they're slaves."

"Slaves are they, well no matter bid them come here directly."

Pale with suppressed passion the lady awaited their arrival in silence, but the boy soon returned with information that they would not come.

"Won't come, eh, are they slaves and do they dare to disobey?"

"But master has told them to keep out of your sight."

"Well they haven't done that, but is your master at home?"

["]He is in the Library.["]

["]Request him to walk up here.["]

The servant disappeared, and in a few moments the steps of the husband and master echoed in the passage. He came in smiling, advanced to his wife, and attempted to take her hand, saying "what would my sweet wife [want] with me this morning?"

She repulsed him rudely, and pointing from the window inquired "what women are those? the servants say you have forbidden them to tell me."

The utterly blank and amazed expression of his countenance Lilly would not attempt to describe.

"Who be they, I say?" she demanded.

Still he answered not.

"Mr Cosgrove" she said, in a tone of great bitterness tho her manner was perfectly cool "I understand it all. I am perfectly well aware in what relation you stand to those hussies and they to you. I have heard that in this detestable country such things are common. I heard so before I came here, I know it now."

"You really think you have found out something then" he said with a scornful laugh.

The lady did not foam at the mouth; she was too well bred for that, but she looks as if a little more might make her do it.

"And if you had heard such pleasant tidings of our country before hand, why did you consent to come here?" he inquired taking advantage of her silence.

"Because I was a fool" she replied.

He bowed with perfect composure.

"You are a brute" said the lady, and her emotions getting the mastery she burst into a passion of tears.

Mr Cosgrove was moved by her sorrow. He would have loved his wife had not her haughtiness so cruelly repulsed him. He approached and attempted to embrace her, but she shrunk from him as she would from a toad or viper. Rage, jealousy, hate, revenge all burned in her bosom. To think that she had been rivaled by slaves. She, with English and aristocrat blood in her veins. It was too much to be endured, but she had great self-command; her tears soon dried, and she said in a voice perfectly calm.

"Knowing these women as I do, knowing them to be what they are I do not request, that were beneath me, but as your wife I command that they be dismissed. Their presence in this house I will not endure. They shall tramp and their children with them."

Irritated by her tone and manner be commenced whistling, and walking up before the mirror adjusted his neck-tie.

"Do you hear me? I say they shall tramp and their children with them."

["]Certainly I hear you" he replied with the most perfect indifference. "Did you take me to be deaf?"

"Well, what do you say?"

"I say that you can threaten much easier than execute."

"But I will not stay in the house if they do."

"You are at perfect liberty to go."

["]That may be, and yet I will not go. No Sir, I am your wife, you can't shake me off so easily, but I say that they shall go, if they are carried out in their coffins."

"And I say" he returned eyeing her closely "that there is law in this country for the slave as well as the free, and if you attempt to injur[e] them you will find it so to your sorrow. Proud as you are, and rich as you think you be, the key of the prison door has been turned on richer and nobler people times without number. You know so much, you should know that."

"That would be a great thing certainly. It would be an honor to yourself wouldn't it—a great honor to have your wife the inmate of a prison, because she resented the presence of your favorites. I'll speak of that."

Mr. Cosgrove's manner had somewhat softened. Perhaps he thought on deliberation that the lady had some ground for complaint, or perhaps he considered it best to temporise. Be that as it may he suddenly exclaimed "you shall have your will, madam, they shall be sent away."

Her countenance brightened and her eyes sparkled exultingly. She had triumphed. He had felt and acknowledged her power, he should feel and acknowledge it more, and she went on.

["]They must not only be sent away, they must be sold far off—into another state—them and their children both. What do you say to that?"

"That you are very severe, but your wishes must be obeyed."

"Immediately."

"I suppose so."

"And to whom will you sell them?"

["]Oh; there are plenty of traders, who will be glad enough to get them."

And thus they continued conversing untill Lilly having finished her toilet duties was dismissed for an hour. She told me of what had happened, and how Mr Cosgrove had promised to dismiss his favorites. Which promise he will never keep I replied. And then we had quite a little dispute about it.

Before many days elapsed a slave trader called. The beautiful girls were summoned to meet him, and came leading or bearing their lovely children. They wept bitterly and implored their master to kill rather than sell them. One of the children, a beautiful boy of three or four years run {ran} to Mr Cosgrove exclaiming "Why, pa you won't sell, will you? you said that I was your darling and little man."

"Go to your mother, child" said the cruel father.

At length one of the youngest and most beautiful, with an infant at her breast hastily dried her tears. Her eyes had a wild phrenzied look, and with a motion so sudden that no one could prevent it, she snatched a sharp knife which a servant had carelessly left after cutting butcher's meat, and stabbing the infant threw it with one toss into the arms of its father. Before he had time to recover from his astonishment she had run the knife into her own body, and fell at his feet bathing them in her blood. She lived only long enough to say that she prayed God to forgive her for an act dictated by the wildest despair. Mr Cosgrove bent over her fondly and asked if she could forgive him? She smiled faintly, turned her eyes to the child which had breathed its last. A slight spasm, a convulsive shudder and she was dead. Dead, your Excellency, the President of this Republic. Dead, grave senators who grow eloquent over pensions and army wrongs. Dead ministers of religion, who prate because poor men without a moment[']s leisure on other days presume to read the newspapers on Sunday, yet who wink at, or approve of laws that occasion such scenes as this.["]

CHAPTER 15

Lizzy's Story Continued

["]The sale was completed, the gold paid, and Mrs Cosgrove from her windows beheld their departure. But even then the lady was not satisfied. She was rather disposed to watch her husband, and he was not pleased with the espionage. Her jealousy construed the minutest act of kindness, even a word or smile bestowed on a slave as something criminal. She could not bear that he should speak in terms of approval of the oldest and most faithful domestic. Especially was she disgusted that his notice of their children should extend to a caress or small presents of fruit and candy. All of a sudden to [she] took a notion to explore the house in its remotest corners. She might have expected the presence of a rival, or might have been stimulated by simple curiosity, but in company with Lilly she threaded the long galleries and winding passages, traversed the various suit[e]s of apartments, and came at last to a door that seemed to be fastened within. This only increased her anxiety, but there was neither crack nor crevice, nor key hole that could reveal its secrets. But it occurred to her that the rooms ~~being in~~ from their situation in the wing must be lighted by windows in the wall, and that ingress might be thus obtained, if in no other way. She was not a woman to be balked. Indeed her perseverance seemed sharpened by difficulties. She must and would know who or what that apartment contained. Did her husband then think to keep secrets from her? Was she to be excluded from certain parts of the house? She would teach him a lesson different from that. She had not come to America to be placed quietly under any man's feet. Far from it. She would assert her rights, that she would; and it was her right to go all over the mansion, and into every chamber as she pleased. ~~Perhaps a lurking idea that a rival might be concealed there stimulated her curiosity But whatever might~~ Accordingly the servants were ordered to procure a ladder and place it against the windowsill she pointed out. They obeyed reluctantly, and she ascended, bidding Lilly follow her.

"Take care my dear mistress you will fall" said the child. And she came near it, never having been on a ladder before.

Looking in at the window she saw a well-furnished apartment, with chairs, a sofa, mirror work stand, and conspicuous in the midst a cradle, in which from the appearance two babies had been lying, as a pillow was placed at the head and another at the foot each bearing the impress, of a tiny form. Then there was a small cup in which ~~a quain~~ a quantity of arrow root had been prepared, besides linen and other baby necessaries. No one was within yet the room had apparently been recently occupied. There was a low fire on the hearth, and Mrs Cosgrove turning to Lilly inquired if she knew who inhabited the room. The child replied that she did not, and the mistress considering the mystery not half cleared up decided to enter and ascertain. The servants to their infinite surprise beheld her disappear through the window, but they saw not what followed. They saw not how bent on investigation she rushed into another chamber communicating with the first. They saw not what she saw there, a beautiful woman, so young and innocent, and dove-like that she seemed only a large child, with two children, twins, and as near alike as two cherries at her breast. In an instant Mrs Cosgrove comprehended the scene and the extent of her injury. Her husband, then, to his other crimes had united that of wil[l]ful falsehood, but with the strange inconsistency of human nature, her anger and revenge turned not so much against her husband as the helpless victims of his sensuality. Pale, and in an attitude of the profoundest sorrow and humiliation the young mother lifted her eyes to the face of her visitor, whom she recognised at once by her queenly bearing, and then with a mute glance at her children seemed to implore pity. Mrs Cosgrove had never been a mother. To jealousy in her bosom the fiercest feeling of envy united. All her well-bred politeness and courteous bearing vanished in a moment, and she more resembled a Fury of Orestes than a Christian woman.

Seizing the young mother by the hair she dragged her to the floor, demanding "who and what are you, and why are you here?" To which the terrified creature replied "A slave, a slave, nothing more."

"That is a lie" she almost screamed. "A lie, and I know it. You are the favorite the minion of my husband. Are you not? Say: say."

Mrs Cosgrove listened, shall we say she hoped to hear the slave answer in the negative. It would have been an infinite relief to her pride and inordinate self-esteem; for though ~~caring little for him~~ she had never loved him, her vanity was enlisted to secure his love. She felt outraged, scandalized and humiliated by his manifest preference for another, and had that other been her nearest and best friend she would have trampled and spit upon her, what favor then could a slave under such circumstances expect?

"It is true" said the wretched creature sobbing. "It is true that

I have received favors from my master, but I couldn't help it, indeed I couldn't."

"Oh you couldn't, did you try, say did you try, and these children whose are they?"

The children were almost beneath her feet, kicking and screaming.

"Whose can they be, but mine" replied the tearful mother.

They were two boys, with round fat cheeks, great blue eyes and plump little hands, quite as beautiful and fresh and healthy as if the most favored lady in the land had been their mother.

Mrs Cosgrove had released her hold of the mother, and now sate [sat] in a chair the very picture of contending passions. That she had made up her mind to some stern resolve was evident, though the nature of this it might be difficult to determine. She was a woman after all, and the heart of the proudest and sternest woman has a touch of weakness, if that which moves to compassion can be so termed. The female mind, likewise, though capable of the strongest passions and most violent emotions cannot long maintain their force and energies. They sink overcome by their own violence, and rising rapidly they as rapidly culminate. It was so with Mrs Cosgrove. She had lashed herself into a perfect fury, and now she felt almost to wonder at her own rashness. Then, too, the pale creature kneeling so meek and supplicant before her, her low pleading tones, her mute glances towards her children, and the infants themselves, helpless in their tiny helplessness appealing to every feeling and sentiment of generosity in a manner not to be entirely withstood by any heart retaining a vestige of humanity. All these had their effect though she would scarcely have acknowledged it to herself.

"If these children are yours, as you say, take them up, get their clothes and prepare to leave this house instantly" she said but in a manner calm and deliberate compared with her former violence.

"This roof" she continued "shall not shelter a minion of my husband, when I am beneath it, and if I know it."

"But where shall I go?" inquired the mother taking up her babes. "Where shall I go? we shall perish along the road."

"Anywhere, I care not" replied Mrs. Cosgrove. "I am not going to sell you, you can have liberty, freedom only go."

"But my master."

["]Never mind your master, I am mistress of this house, and will be. No one, not even him, of whom you speak, shall thwart or interfere with my will. Get yourself and your children ready and be off. Steer right for the North, and never stop short of Canada. You will be safe then, and your infants will not inherit the curse of their mother's slavery."

And thus with an infant on each arm and a bundle of clothes at her back was this frail and delicate woman thrust from her home, and so inconsistent is the human heart that Mrs Cosgrove actually congratulated herself on having done a good action, and setting [sitting] in her sumptuous parlor and watching the poor creature toiling up the hill in the distance she observed to Lilly who was in attendance "Well I shall have the consolation of having once performed my duty in giving freedom to a poor slave. No one can say that I have not the English spirit and blood in me."

Did it not occur to her that night when laying down on ~~her splendid bed~~ her splendid bed with snowy counterpanes and downy pillows that the poor freed slave with her tender infants had not where to lay her head? Did she think waking up the next morning ~~that the one~~ and preparing to breakfast daintily on soft rich cakes and golden butter, with luscious honey, strawberries melting in cream and the richest beverage that the one she had so unfeelingly dismissed had not a morsel wherewith to satisfy the cravings of nature, or support her strength under the most onerous maternal duty—that of providing nourishment for her offspring. Did she remember when the dinner hour with its bright sun drew near that one whom she had driven out to be a wanderer might be fainting wearied and toil-worn beneath the roadside hedge? Far from it, she only thought, as she expressed it, that "the coast was clear" and exulted over the idea of her husband's surprise and indignation when he ascertained the fact. Mr Cosgrove was absent, and had been for several days. On returning he went directly to the chamber of his ~~mistress~~ favorite. To his great astonishment it was deserted, and turned into a store-room. What could it mean? He ordered the overseer of his household and estate into his presence immediately, and inquired what had become of Evelyn and her babes.

"I shouldn't wonder" replied the man "if they had furnished food for the vultures before now."

"What do you mean?" inquired the anxious lover and parent. "No one has killed them certainly." And his mind reverted to the threatening language employed by his wife.

"No one that I know of" replied the overseer "but mistress, you must know, drove them away from here, and I don't see how such a frail and delicate creature as Evelyn could bear such heavy children far, or—"

The man paused. He had just that moment discovered that his conversation had become a monologue. Cosgrove, long before the ending of the sentence, had sprung from the room and mounted hastily to the chamber of his wife. To seek, to upbraid her, and even to inflict some summary punishment upon her was evidently his first thought conceived in a moment of fierce anger. His fancy depicted Evelyn and her babes, those dear beautiful little boys, slowly dying through famine or exposure in some lane or ditch, with the vultures hovering over them, eager to begin their horrible banquet.

"Madam" he cried bursting wildly into her presence. "By what authority do you presume to interfere in my absence with my slaves? Who gave you the power to dismiss them so unceremoniously from my dwelling?"

"Indeed, Mr Cosgrove" exclaimed the lady, with a ~~scornful~~ scornful expression disfiguring her countenance "you present the model of an affectionate husband after a long absence whose first greetings of his wife is to demand by what authority she exercises her rights."

"But you have no right to make away with my property, or conduct yourself contrary to my interests."

"Pray, be seated, Mr Cosgrove" said the lady coolly who in her perfect self-satisfaction determined to keep down her temper. "Pray be seated. You are rich enough yet, and have plenty of these human cattle. Of what possible use could Evelyn be mewed up like a nun in that close chamber, and more than that Mr Cosgrove I tell you again as I told you before I will not suffer these creatures about the house, and no woman with the least particle of pride, or honor, or womanly feeling would."

["]And so you talk of pride, and honor and womanly feeling, do you? Heaven knows you have enough of the first, but was it womanly feeling that led you to thrust out a frail delicate female and her babes to certain exposure and famine, and almost certain death?"

"I gave them freedom it is true. If freedom implies starvation or death, it is not my fault, but their misfortune."

"Madam, it is your fault. Evelyn did not desire freedom, and least of all the freedom you gave her."

"No matter" answered the Lady "it was my will that she should have it, and so she has got it, and what necessity is there for your fuming and fretting about it. Did you really suppose that you could keep her here without my knowledge? that you could have such a secret about the house without my ascertaining and resenting its presence. If you did, Mr. Cosgrove, you know little of woman."

And thus they bickered and quarreled without any hope or prospect of reconciliation. Their happiness ruined, their domestic peace a wreck.

Mr Cosgrove left the presence of his wife, and without speaking to any one, mounted a fleet charger, and rode away. He was absent two days, and returned as he went, without giving any information of his business, or where he had been. The servants said that he had been searching for Evelyn; they said, too, that he had found her; for he looked so pleased and gratified. Mrs Cosgrove probably expected as much, and she received him with the most chilling indifference, seeking rather to awe than win him to virtue. After that the absences of our master were many and prolonged. But he left disquietude at home in the heart of his wife. Her days and nights were blackened with the foulest suspicion. She had cleared the house of his favorites it is true, but she could not clear them from her imagination. They do come, they will come. She knows of a certainty that he has a secret now. She sees it in his countenance, in his eyes, in every crease of his garments. Even his bearing is less frank than formerly. His tread seems stealthy as if fearing to reveal something. She even thinks that he fears to meet her eye, ~~and those suspicions~~ and these various signs and tokens prompt her to dishonorable acts. She takes a strange fancy to nocturnal examinations of his letters to private researches in all manner of places, to listening behind doors, and watching at windows, to questioning slaves and even visitors. The haughty woman descends all at once from her high position, and condescends to converse with any one, and every one, condescends to go to church, but the worshippers remark that she is restless and uneasy, and pays much more attention to the congregation than to the minister.

But untiring vigilance had its reward, and a mere accident discovered the secret, when all her plans had failed. The overseer mentioned to Mr Cosgrove in her hearing the name of "Rock Glen." "Hush" replied her husband "never mention that place again, as the very walls have ears."

"Rock Glen" the name was romantic, the place was doubtless picturesque. Where could it be? And why should the walls have ears especially to hear the mention of that? Too well her suspicions told her, but she summoned Lilly.

"Lilly do you think that I am your friend?"

"I hope so" said the beautiful girl.

"And do you perceive that I treat you differently from any one else?"

"You seem much gentler, and not so lofty."

"It is my purpose, Lilly."

"Your purpose."

"I have a purpose for every thing I do. As a general thing I care little for kindness, but now I want a service, a small service that must be won from affection and for which money will not pay. Can you love me Lilly? Can you do this thing for me?"

"I can try" said Lilly. "If you can trust me."

"I can, and do trust you" replied the Lady.

"And what would you have me do?" inquired Lilly whose curiosity began to be awakened.

"Find out for me where is the place called Rock Glen."

"Is that all?[''] inquired the child simply.

"Not quite. You must be very nice and cunning about it. You must not for the world let any one know that I have sent you, or that I wish to know. Especially observe never to mention my name in connection with that, but find out and I will give you this."

So saying she held up a beautiful bracelet of turquoise and emerald.

"But how shall I find out?" inquired Lilly, charmed with the magnificence of the gift.

"You can ask the slaves, ask everybody. Some of them will know."

"Think so?"

"I know it. The overseer knows, and he cannot be wiser than any one else."

"But why?" began Lilly.

"Not a word" said the lady with a gesture kind yet imperious. ["]Ask me no questions. Don't care to know my motive or purpose. The knowledge could do you no good, and might be a snare. Only find out and come to me with the information."

"Indeed, I will do my best." And so she did.

We all wondered why the name of Rock Glen should be forever on her lips. True, the name was pleasant, and pretty, and interesting yet nothing so very extraordinary after all. Why then should Lilly take such a fancy to tease and torment everybody with it? What had we done that Rock Glen must be forever ringing in our ears?

"Who knows anything about Rock Glen?" she would exclaim bounding down the steps, gay and blithe as a butterfly. Some of the slaves were ignorant, others had their commands, and the question was likely to remain unanswered when an old beggar woman came to the house one day.

"Why, I do" she answered to Lilly's playful sally.

"And where is it, good mother" inquired Lilly, with an earnestness we could not but notice.

"Why it isn't far from here, I can't tell just how far, though I can direct you how to go to get there."

"That will do quite as well" said Lilly.

The old woman then directed her what road to follow, where to turn to the right, and where to the left, where there was a brook to ~~cross, a meadow to pass over~~ pass over, a meadow to cross, and a fence to leap, where there was a tavern and a store a blacksmith's shop, and an undertaker, where we might see negroes working in a field of tobacco, and just catch the glimpse of a habitation nestled beneath an overhanging crag, that looked as if it would fall every moment, though the wear and tear of centuries had failed to displace it. "And that crag" she continued ["] and that little habitation beneath it is called Rock Glen."

Lilly hastened to Mrs Cosgrove with the information she had obtained.

"Well done Lilly" said the Lady "But bid this old woman into my presence, perhaps she can tell me more."

And that old woman bent and decrepid with age, coarse, repulsive, clothed in rags, and hobbling along with the most awkward unseemly gait, ascended the broad staircase, pressed the magnificent carpets, and half blinded and overwhelmed with the sumptuousness of all she saw, was introduced to the presence of the Lady, who, robed in satins and glistening in jewelry was no happier than herself.

Mrs Cosgrove would have shrunk from the embodiment of squalid poverty presented before her, but her strong purpose restrained her and she received the old beggar almost courteously.

'Twas a strange contrast these two women. The one so elegant and refined, so lofty in manner and luxurious in appointment, with such magnificent eyes, such splendid hair such a beautiful countenance; and the other a hedious old mummy, toothless, with blear eyes, driveling lips. Nothing elegant or tasteful about her. And yet that one so adorned so accomplished, so enviable in every worldly consideration, forgets herself, her aristocratic name, and high connexions, forgets that in exposing the honor of her husband she compromises her own, forgets everything else in her anxiety to ascertain who is the inhabitant of Rock Glen.

To her questioning on this point the old woman responded that for a long time it had been uninhabited, but that a gentleman had recently purchased the estate and she believed had put somebody in the house, because going near there one day in her wanderings to get berries, she heard a sweet voice singing a cradle song

"But you saw no one?"

"No one, the doors and windows were carefully shut."

No further information of any importance could be elicited from the old woman, and Mrs Cosgrove dismissed her with a very handsome present.

"Heaven help me" she exclaimed to Lilly when the old woman departed "I verily believe that sale was a sham after all. Who knows. Ten chances to one he has them all there. Singing a cradle song. That was doubtless Evelyn, but I will know—that I will. It's plain enough now why he spends so much time from home. Go tell the servants to saddle our horses.["]

"You are not going now" said Lilly in great surprise.

"Yes, now, immediately, but don't tell them of my purpose."

Lilly bowed, a "Yes Missus" and departed on her errand.

Mrs Cosgrove was an accomplished horsewoman, and her fine figure and rich complexion never showed to better advantage than when she was engaged in this graceful and exhilerating exercise.

Lilly usually rode by her side with a man servant following in attendance. However his services were not required or admitted on the present occasion.

The breeze was fresh, the sky clear, the scene beautiful, but it is certainly questionable whether the lady in her eagerness would have been aware if it had they been quite the reverse.

Putting her horse in to a brisk canter they rode off. In ~~about~~ two or three hours Mrs Cosgrove was brought back insensible, with Lilly weeping at her side. She was carried to her rooms, which she never left again.

As Lilly related the story they came near Rock Glen when they encountered Mr Cosgrove returning thence. Reining in his horse he inquired "where they were going?" to which the Lady replied that he would probably know soon enough for his satisfaction, and attempted to pass on, when he seized the bridle of her horse. She requested him to let go, which he refused to do, unless she ~~told him~~ would promise to return with him. Both became angry, and high words passed between them. What occurred next Lilly could not say for she was looking in the opposite direction. But her mistress screamed, and looking round she beheld the horse loose and running, the Lady hanging suspended by his side, her foot apparently fast in the saddle. Mr Cosgrove sate [sat] motionless a moment on his horse like one thunderstruck and then called loudly for assistance. Assistance came, but too late to prevent her receiving dreadful injuries.["]

"Did she fall from the horse?" I inquired interrupting Lizzy's long story.

"To be sure she fell from the horse, but why? Lilly said that she should always believe master struck her."

"And he did not return?"

["]He came soon after, but he didn't go to her room, nor inquire after her, nor seem to know that such a person was in existence. Her back and hips had been injured so severely that she could not leave her bed, and it was a pitiful sight to behold [sic] that woman once so matchless and queenly in bearing, now painfully reclining day after day in the same posture, her face ever turned towards the window, in a watching listening attitude as if she waited the coming of some one, or the occurrence of some event. But her thoughts flew homeward, and she would murmur of those beautiful lands beyond the seas where she had dwelt so happily, and wonder why she ever came away, and what her dear, dear friends out there would think should they hear of her misfortune.

["]Then she used frequently to ask of her husband, whether he was at home, whether he spoke of her, and whether or not he looked contented and happy. These questions we answered according to the circumstances, when she would close her eyes and sigh bitterly. How a long continued illness humiliates the proudest, and brings home to the mind the thought of death and eternity and a judgement to come; while in view of these considerations we become disposed to forgive even as we would be forgiven. Mrs Cosgrove was no longer the haughty self-conceited woman, but a gentle, humble lamb-like follower of Christ. This change was not wrought suddenly. It came only after nights and days of tearless mental agony, after deep humiliation of spirit, and bitter supplications. Then gradually and beautifully and calmly as the moon breaking over stormy seas came the light of hope to her mind. It was accompanied by peace and love and gentle chi child-like trust, and though lame and weary and fast losing her hold of time she became happier than ever she had been in the days of her pride, and beauty, and prosperity. And then she requested to see her husband. He came walking proudly at first and with an air of affected indifference, but beholding the divine light of her countenance, and the soft expressive beam of her eyes his whole manner changed. He came prepared for an expression of contempt and hatred he beheld a manifestation of love. Instead of meeting reproaches he was greeted with smiles, and a voice of unwonted softness breathed in his ear. [']My husband can you forgive me?['] The words, the tone, the manner, the scene before him, the past that to his conscience must be forever the present rose up before him. He melted into tears beside her, exclaiming [']I have nothing in the world to forgive, but you Oh: how deeply, have I injured you. I cannot ask your forgiveness, I only ask that you will not curse me.[']

["]Then followed a scene of mutual explanations and regrets. For the first time during their married lives the husband and wife began to understand each other, now that the grave was closing between them. They began to perceive that a little more forbearance, and sympathy, and love on one side, with a little more respect and consideration on the other would have rendered them happy and prevented at least to one the bitterness of unending remorse.

["]At length to a painful and restless night succeeded a a [sic] day of comparative comfort and repose. Since their reconciliation Mr Cosgrove had ceaselessly attended her bedside, supported her drooping fainting head on his bosom, and administered the soothing cordial with his own hand. But that day worn out with fatigue and watching he had been persuaded by Lilly to retire and take some rest, while Mrs Cosgrove slept. ~~Hour after hour confiding in the gentle care of Lilly~~ Alone and unaccustomed to scenes of sickness and death, the gentle girl felt sad and lonely. She noticed, too, that a deep mysterious shadow was slowly falling over the countenance of her mistress, that her breathing grew labored and difficult, and that her brow was bathed with a cold and clammy sweat. Noiselessly she stole down and asked me to return with her. I did so, and just as we entered the room, the last flutter expired on her sinking lip. She was dead.["]

Lizzy then told me of many other things connected with her master and his family, and how that from the hour of his wife's death he had never seemed like himself, probably in consequence of grief, more probably in consequence of remorse. That Mrs Bry, the old housekeeper had removed to another state and lived in the family of her son; that the Linden with its creaking branches had bowed to the axe, and that great changes had been wrought inside the house as well as out; that some of the ancient rooms, whose walls ceiled with oak were brown with age, had been newly renovated, and now shone in all the glory of fresh paint and plaster. Above all that Sir Clifford's portrait and its companions of both sexes, had been publicly exposed in the market ~~to the highest~~ and knocked down to the highest bidder. "Sic transit gloria mundi."

CHAPTER 16

In North Carolina

We are sold for nought, I and my people.

ESTHER

I had waited long with Lizzy, to[o] long. Of course it wasn't right in me, and I received a sound rating for it.

"Hannah you are a bad girl, very bad, if you don't mind your P's and Q's a little better, I shall sell you that is certain. I can't have such work as this. You go out on an errand that shouldn't occupy more than ten minutes and stay all day. I never heard the like."

It was not for me to reply. The lady would have took it in high dudgeon had I opened my lips to make the most reasonable excuse, and one unreasonable would have been a still greater insult.

"And mind, too" she continued "when you get to my place in North Carolina that you don't dare to mention that—that—that—" she hesitated and stammered.

"I understand, I will not mention it."

"And you needn't make a merit of that neither" she said in a voice, whence every bit of languor had departed. "You needn't make a merit of that as much as to say Mrs Wheeler has a secret I am keeping it for her, and she is much obliged, and bound to be thankful, indulgent, and what not."

"Of course that would be very foolish" I said.

"Why don't you just bow and keep your mouth shut" she inquired angrily.

I thought her temper becoming worse and worse every day, but it was not so, I was getting better acquainted with her.

And yet she had her good spells and these generally came when she fancied herself ill. Langour of voice and feebleness of motion were sure to be attended with conversational displays of neighborhood gossip, family history or the like, and when no one else was near I was obliged to listen to her.

As we rode down to the boat designed to convey us to Mrs Wheeler's "place in North Carolina" I was admiring the splendid show made by the President's House and the Capitol; the quantity of Congress men, Senators, navy and Army officers going to and fro; the number of vehicles containing fine Ladies the wives and daughters of foreign Ministers and distinguished strangers. I say I was admiring these no less than ~~at the extraordinary contract to their pre~~ wondering at the extraordinary contrast to them presented by some wretches in rags, who appeared to be searching ~~the rubbish for bones, pins, or rather refuse~~ for bones, pins, or other refuse among the rubbish which had accumulated in several places when an incident occurred which affected me greatly. A negro designed for sale had broken away from his master and the assistants, and taken refuge beneath the equestrian statue of Jackson, that lover of freedom; and thence he was dragged, though shrieking and praying, and struggling, manacles placed on his limbs, and borne back to the market.

Mrs Wheeler had her state room on the boat. She was very languid and feeble, and as usual at such times very talkative. It was really astonishing what a bad opinion she entertained of the Capital, how heartily she detested office-seekers, and how much she pitied that poor man, the President, who was dunned and worried by them till almost ready to break his neck to escape their importunities.

"Why they tell me" she continued, "that there is scarcely a man in Washington who has not been an office seeker at some time or another of his life, and the women are quite as desperate as the man [sic]. ~~and those who are the~~ Those especially who ~~cannot manage their own private affairs~~ are too weak and silly, and negligent to manage their own private affairs have uniformly an itching fancy to dabble in the public business."

It being obligatory on me to give my assent I said "very likely."

"To be sure" she responded. "It really appears that some of them must pass their whole lives looking and intriguing for an office, and it matters very little how it is what it is, or what principle it involves. It matters still less what duties are attached to it; for all these gentlemen consider themselves competent for any station under the sun. They want a secretaryship, they want a clerkship, they want to be foreign ministers, they want to be consuls, they want to be Governors of Territories, they want a Custom house appointment and if nothing better offers they will gladly accept even a commission to keep Lights, or attend the mail."

"And what would they do if they had these offices?" I inquired.

["]To hear their account of it they would do extraordinary things. They would build new ships and hire new steamers, they would go to war and make peace they would take Cuba, or Canada, or Dominica, they would have a rail-road to the Pacific, and a ship Canal across the Isthmus, they would quell the Indians and oust the Mormons, in short their [there] is nothing of possible or impossible that they would not do or try."

I thought it very funny that Mrs Wheeler should inveigh so loudly against office-seekers when [she] herself and [her] husband had both tried their hands at the same game but it would not ~~have done to~~ do to say so, and she went on.

"Then, too, these fellows, office-hunters I mean, are utterly insensible to anyone's feelings. They are always excited about nominations, candidates, and elections. They are always discussing votes and voters. How this one would run and that one wouldn't. You find them in all sorts of places, from the President's levee to a pot-house broil. In stores, in low taverns, in great hotels, in unmentionable out-of-the-way places, at the corners of streets, and beneath awnings, in fact wherever a political squabble can be discussed or commented on."

Again I said "Very likely" and again she continued.

"It is really disgusting to think of the associations they form, the low company they patronise, the degrading and vulgar connexions they affect not to despise. How they will shake hands with loafers and drunkards, bow to the half crazy and idiotic, and hand over small bribes of half-dollars and bad rum to vagabond Irishmen. Then they are never satisfied. Success only makes them more ravenous and rapacious."

How far the lady would [have] gone on, or how extravagant she might have become in her description of this unfortunately too large class of men it is impossible to say, had not Mr Wheeler, luckily for me, come into the room, and made some remarks which for the time being changed the tenor of her conversation.

In due time we reached North Carolina without the occurrence of any incident worthy of notice. Mr Wheeler's fine plantation was situated near Wilmington the principal port of the state and was altogether one of the most beautiful places I had ever seen. Yet the house had none of that stately majesty characteristic of Lindendale; neither had it that home-bred air of genial quiet and ropose, which gave Forget-me-not its chief attractions, but there was a luxurious abundance of vines, and fruits, and flowers, and song-birds, and every thing wore such an aspect of maturity and ripeness that I was fairly charmed. The lime-tree walks were like green arcades, the very shadows of the orange trees seemed dropping with fruit, the peach trees were so laden that their branches bent nearly to the earth and were supported by stout props, and the purple clusters of grapes hung tempting from the trellis work of I don't know how many arbors. Tumbled about among the wide frames and the spread nets there were great heaps of marrows, glowing pods, and lucious ~~cucumbers~~ melons, with the greatest profusion of green leaves sparkling and glistening in the sun. As every foot of ground seemed occupied with some rich vegetable treasuse [treasure], the whole atmosphere was redolent with fragrance like one great bo[u]quet. Then there was sweet smelling and savory herbs, and a wondrous flush of roses, and such a world of pinks that I never grew tired of admiring them.

In the distance was a cotton field with the snowy fleece bursting richly from the pod, and sweeping down to the river's edge was a large plantation of rice. Of course the labor of many slaves was required to keep such a large estate in thrifty order. The huts of these people were ranged on the back-side of the place, and as far from the habitation of their master as possible. They were built with far less reference to neatness and convenience than those in Virginia. They had not the little garden patch, the tiny yard with its bright flowers, or the comfortable home aspect of white-~~was~~ washed walls. Then they were more crowded. There was not that division of families I had been accustomed to see, but they all lived promiscuously anyhow and every how; at least they did not die, which was a wonder. Is it a stretch of imagination to say that by night they contained a swarm of misery, that crowds of foul existence crawled in out of gaps in walls and boards, or coiled themselves to sleep on ~~nauseous~~ nauseous heaps of straw fetid with human perspiration and where the rain drips in, ~~and the midnight dew imparts some~~ and the damp airs of midnight fatch [fetch] and carry malignant fevers.

They said that many of these huts were old and ruinous with decay, that occasionally a crash, and a crowd of dust would be perceived among them, and that each time it was occasioned by the fall of one. But lodgings are found among the rubbish, and all goes on as before. Since if a head gets bruised or a limb broken, head and limbs are so plentiful that they seem of small account. So true it is that if a great man sneezes the world rings with it, but if a poor man dies no one notices or cares. Perhaps a fond wife and tender children shed a few natural tears, and then the one dries her eyes and begins to look around for another lord, while the others in the busy whirl of life would forget his name were it not their own. This is all the result of that false system which bestows on position, wealth, or power the consideration only due to a man. And this system is not confined to any one place, or country, or condition. It extends through all grades and classes of society from the highest to the lowest. It bans poor but honest people with the contemptuous appellation of "vulgar." It subjects others under certain circumstances to a lower link in the chain of being than that occupied by a horse.

Many of these huts ~~now very ancient They~~ were even older than the nation, and had been occupied by successive generations of slaves. The greatest curse of slavery is it's [sic] heriditary character. The father leaves to his son an inheritance of toil and misery, and his place on the fetid straw in the miserable corner, with no hope or possibility of anything better. And the son in his turn transmits the same to his offspring and thus forever.

If the huts were bad, the inhabitants it seemed were still worse.

Degradation, neglect, and ill treatment had wrought on them its legitimate effects. All day they toil beneath the burning sun, scarcely conscious that any link exists between themselves and other portions of the human race. Their mental condition is briefly summed up in the phrase that they know nothing. ~~care for nothing, and hope for nothing~~ They know indeed that it is hard to toil unceasingly for a scanty pittance of food, and coarse garments; nature instructed them thus far.

What do you think of it? Doctors of Divinity Isn't it a strange state to be like them. To shuffle up and down the lanes unfamiliar with the flowers, and in utter darkness as to the meaning of Nature's various hieroglyphical symbols, so abundant on the trees, the skies, in the leaves of grass, and everywhere. To see people ride in carriages, to hear such names as freedom, heaven, hope and happiness and not to have the least idea how it must seem to ride, any more than what the experience of these blessed names would be. It must be a strange state to be prized just according to the firmness of your joints, the strength of your sinews, and your capability of endurance. To be made to feel that you have no business here, there, or anywhere except just to work—work—work—And yet to know that you are here somehow, with once in a great while like a straggling ray in a dark place a faint aspiration for something better, ~~or gli~~ with a glimpse, a mere glimpse of something beyond. It must be a strange state to feel that in the judgement of those above you you are scarcely human, and to fear that their opinion is more than half right, that you really are assimilated to the brutes, that the horses, dogs and cattle have quite as many priveledges, and are probably your equals or it may be your superiors in knowledge, that even your shape is questionable as belonging to that order of superior beings whose delicacy you offend.

It must be strange to live in a world of civilisation and, elegance, and refinement, and yet know nothing about either, yet that is the way with multitudes and with none more than the slaves. The Constitution that asserts the right of freedom and equality to all mankind is a sealed book to them, and so is the Bible, that tells how Christ died for all; the bond as well as the free.

Mr Wheeler had neglected his plantation as well as his slaves for several reasons. In the first place he didn't think it worth while to take much pains with such brutalised specimens of humanity. They could work just as well, and it might be even better to leave them alone in their degradation. ~~than to~~ He expected nothing of them but toil. He wanted nothing else. Their ideas were not a whit above their condition which might be, were a reformation in their manners to be attempted. So the steward only received an injunction to keep the mater's residence in a manner comporting with the family dignity, to see that the vines were properly trained, the flowers tended and especially to look after the figs and pomegranates. Alas that fruits and flowers should claim more consideration than human souls.

In the second place an office was his hobby. He preferred to live at the public expense. Life in the Federal Capital ~~and an office~~ was the most he cared for, and while intriguing and speculating and striving to get a moiety of the public business into his hands his private affairs were suffered to run to waste. Of course the family residence was stocked with slaves of a higher and nobler order than those belonging to the fields. They were better dressed, better provided for and better looking. It was necessary that those surrounding the person of the Mistress should have nothing offensive or disgusting about them. It was necessary, not for him but her, that the coachman should be cleanly and well kept, that the cook should be neat, with well washed hands and a snowy apron, and that all her attendants should well understand their part and preserve appearances. Yet I thought they exhibited little pleasure on the return of their master and mistress. Their [there] was no hardy demonstrations of delight, but merely a cold formal welcome scarcely removed from positive indifference or something worse.

There was one however, a girl named Maria, who having been a favorite of Mrs Wheeler in other days greatly resented my advancement to the situation of waiting maid, and I saw at once that I had to deal with a wary, powerful, and unscrupulous enemy. She was a dark mulatto, very quick motioned with black snaky eyes, and hair of the same color. Yet she was an adept in the art of dissembling and her countenance would be the smoothest and her words the fairest when she contemplated the greatest injury. For a long time I strove by every means in my power, by kindness, attention, and good-will to soften her animosity, but she turned from me with hatred and bitterness, and even mocked my efforts at reconciliation, and a good understanding.

I soon ascertained that gradually yet surely she was supplanting me in Mrs Wheeler's favor. When the lady desired some personal service she no longer summoned me, but Maria. Her conversations were all with Maria; her presents were all to Maria. She scarcely noticed me at all, while I vainly wondered in what I had offended.

One day Mrs Wheeler called me to her apartment. I perceived at the first glimpse of her countenance that she was very angry.

"Hannah" she said "there can be no use of any preamble between me and you. You have disobeyed my positive commands, exposed me to the derision of my slaves, and made my name the subject of neighborhood scandal. Fool that I was to have ever retained such a viper in my family."

There was nothing languid in her manner now. Her voice was loud and agitated, and her frame trembled with excessive passion.

"My dear Mistress" I began. "You greatly surprise me. How have I done all this?"

"Don't ask me how? You know well enough. Oh; you needn't put on that aggrieved and innocent look. I've seen hypocrites before."

"Very likely, and will again I presume. But the child unborn knows quite as well to what you allude as I do."

"You don't pretend to say that you haven't told to all the servants in this house the misfortune that happened to me at Washington."

Her allusion to that ludicrous circumstance actually forced me to smile. Had the penalty been some dreadful punishment I could not have helped it. This roused her to a perfect fury. She broke out in language unsuitable for any lady, and snatching a chair hurled it with all her force at my head. I stooped to escape the blow when it passed over me, and shivered to pieces against the door. I rose and attempted to retire.

"Stay" she cried. "I have not done with you yet, base ungrateful wretch that you are. What punishment do you think ought to be awarded you?"

"I have deserved no punishment" I replied calmly.

"No punishment, eh, for basely betraying the confidence of your Mistress."

"I have not betrayed your confidence, having never mentioned to a solitary soul the incident of which you speak."

"Now don't tell lies, Hannah. I thought you to be a very good Christian" she said tantalizingly.

"However that may be I have told you no lies."

"Now Hannah there is no ~~use~~ sense in your denial of this fact. You have told it, and I know it, else how did Maria, and the other servants hear of it?"

"That I cannot tell, though probably they might."

"They have told, they accuse you."

["]Well, I am innocent, in the face of heaven and earth I am innocent. I am the victim of a conspiracy. Maria does not certainly say that I told her when we have scarcely spoken together for months. I saw from the first that she hated me" and I burst into tears.

"You can weep now" said Mrs Wheeler "now that your baseness has been discovered, but it will do you no good, my resolution is unalterably fixed. You shall depart from the house, and go into the fields to work. Those brutalized creatures in the cabins are fit companions for one so vile. You can herd with them. Bill, who comes here sometimes has seen and admires you. In fact he asked you of Mr Wheeler for his wife, and his wife you shall be."

"Never" I exclaimed rashly and hastily, and without thought of the consequences. "Never."

"Do you dare to disobey" she almost shrieked. "With all your pretty airs and your white face, you are nothing but a slave after all, and no better than the blackest wench. Your pride shall be broke, your haughty spirit brought down, and now get you gone, and prepare to change your lodgings and employment."

"What preparation shall I make?"

"Why, bundle up some of your coarsest clothes. The best and finest I have given to Maria. Then go to the overseer and he will place you."

"Mistress" I began and fell on my knees.

She spurned me contemptuously with her foot. "Begone, I want none of your blarney."

I arose silently, and left the room.

Retreating to the loneliest garret in the house I sate [sat] down to weep, and pray, and meditate. I had never felt so lonely and utterly desolate. Accused of a crime of which I was innocent, my reputation with my Mistress blackened, and most horrible of all doomed to association with the vile, foul, filthy inhabitants of the huts, and condemned to receive one of them for my husband my soul actually revolted with horror unspeakable. I had ever regarded marriage as a holy ordinance, and felt that its responsibilities could only be suitably discharged when ~~they were~~ voluntarily assumed.

CHAPTER 17

Escape

In Thee is my trust.
PSALMS

I hear a voice you cannot hear
Which says I must not stay
I see a hand you cannot see
Which beckons me away
TICKELL

Had Mrs Wheeler condemned me to the severest corporeal punishment, or exposed me to be sold in the public slave market in Wilmington I should probably have resigned myself with apparent composure to her cruel behests. But when she sought to force me into a compulsory union with a man whom I could only hate and despise it seemed that rebellion would be a virtue, that duty to myself and my God actually required it, and that whatever accidents or misfortunes might attend my flight nothing could be worse than what threatened my stay.

Marriage like many other blessings I considered to be especially designed for the free, and something that all the victims of slavery should avoid as tending essentially to perpetuate that system. Hence to all overtures of that kind from whatever quarter they might come I had invariably turned a deaf ear. I had spurned domestic ties not because my heart was hard, but because it was my unalterable resolution never to entail slavery on any human being. And now when I had voluntarily renounced the society of those I might have learned to love should I be compelled to accept one, whose person, and speech, and manner could not fail to be ever regarded by me with loathing and disgust. Then to be driven in to the fields beneath the eye and lash of the brutal overseer, and those miserable huts, with their promiscuous crowds of dirty, obscene and degraded objects, for my home I could not, I would not bear it.

Yet I feared haste or rashness. I wished to do right and determined to be guided by the Holy book of God. I had a little Bible, one that Aunt Hetty had given me, a plain simple common book, with leather binding, and leaves brown with age. It was well worn and thumbed, too, with neither margin, nor notes, nor quotations, but the precious word itself was their [there] and that was enough.

I opened it as chance directed but immediately at the place where Jacob fled from his brother Esau. The sceptic may smile, but to me it had a deep and peculiar meaning. "Yes" I mentally exclaimed. "Trusting in the God that guided and protected him I will abandon this house, and the Mistress who would force me into a crime against nature." As I have observed before nothing but this would have impelled me to flight. Dear as freedom is to every human being, and bitter as servitude must be to all who experience it I knew too much of the dangers and difficulties to be apprehended from running away ever to have attempted such a thing through ordinary motives.

Shutting my precious Bible and placing it in my bosom I meditated a plan of escape. I had no friends in whom I could confide. I was surrounded by watchful prying eyes. The blood-hounds would doubtless be set on my track. I confess the way looked dark, the scheme almost hopeless, but I remembered the Hebrew Children and Daniel in the Lion's den, and felt that God could protect and preserve me through all.

Determining, however, to feign submission at first I went the next morning and placed myself under the command of the overseer. It was toilsome and weary work. My fingers unused to such employment blistered and bled, and towards night I grew faint with the unwonted exertion. But there was no one to pity or assist me. Bill, indeed, who had sought the favor of becoming my husband came towards me with a hedious grin, meant for a smile, and inquired what he could do for me. I hastily repulsed him with "Nothing, nothing, only leave me. I shall be better directly."

The overseer came up. He was a short thick-set big-headed man, with a countenance grossly sensual and repulsive. His little eyes set far back in his head, gleamed beneath shaggy overhanging brows, like glow-worms beneath the jutting buttress of a rock, his thick lips were always parted over teeth yellow and dirty with tobacco, and his person was extremely offensive and indelicate from want of cleanliness.

"A[i]n't much used to such as this" he said taking my bleeding fingers in his coarse hands. "But will be after awhile. I've seen many a gal likely as you put into the fields to work, though she had never done a hand's turn before. We must all come to it sooner or later."

Bill kept hanging around, and would occasionally stop working to look at me. The overseer observed this, and beckoned him to approach. "You seem interested in Hannah" he remarked. "Now take her to your cabin, she has, I believe, finished her task.["] Bill's eyes sparkled with delight, and I was too weak and weary, too dispirited and overcome to offer resistance.

Bill's cabin was in the midst of the range of huts, tenanted by the workers in the fields. In front was a large pool of black mud and corrupt water, around which myriads of flies and insects were whirling and buzzing. I went in, but such sights and smells as met me I cannot describe them. It was reeking with filth and impurity of every kind, and already occupied by near a dozen women and children, who were sitting on the ground, or coiled on piles of rags and straw in the corner. They regarded me curiously as I entered, grinned with malicious satisfaction that I had been brought down to their level, and made some remarks at my expense; while the children kicked, and yelled, and clawed each other, scratching each other's faces, and pulling each other's hair I stumbled to a bench I supposed designed for a seat, when one of the woman [sic] arose, seized me by the hair, and without ceremony dragged me to the ground, gave me a furious kick and made use of highly improper and indecent language. Bill, who had retired to the outside of the hut, hearing the noise of the fray came hastily in. It was his turn then. He commenced beating her with a hearty good-will, and she scratched and bit him, furiously. In the rough and tumble they knocked over two or three of the children, besides treading on the toes of some of the women, who irritated by the pain started up and joined the contest which soon became general.

Frightened, and anxious to escape such a scene I whispered to one of the women that I was going to the house, and left the hut unnoticed by the others. It was sometime after sunset, and I soon encountered the slaves coming in from the fields. I told them all I was going to the house and passed on.

Before I reached the mansion, however, the lamps were lit for the night, and as I chiefly wished to avoid observation I concealed myself in a thicket of roses. I had now matured my plan, and nothing remained but to put it in operation. To do this I must get into the house, but time was precious very precious. A moment was a step, and every step would lead me further from danger and detection. I could not wait till the family retired, and as the night was fortunately dark, and the front door ajar, having been left so by the carelessness of the servants, I contrived to slip in unperceived, and ascended with a noiseless tread to the garret. Here was a suit of male apparel exactly corresponding to my size and figure. To whom it had belonged or who had worn it was alike a mystery to me. Neither did I care; it would answer my purpose admirably, and that was sufficient. I had previously and in anticipation of this event secreted a candle, some matches, scissors and other necessary utensils in this same chamber. I found them all in their places, and they wonderfully facilitated my transformation of myself. This done, I quenched the light, cautiously descended as I went up, let myself out by a back door, stood a moment to collect my thoughts and then starting ran for my life.

CHAPTER 18

~~The Wandering~~
~~Trials And Difficulties~~

Strange Company

The foxes have holes, and the birds of the air have nests. I stopped not till overcome with fatigue and complete exhaustion. I had traversed fields, leaped fences, and passed for some distance the boundaries of Mr Wheeler's estate, when I was greatly startled by the baying of a dog. There was nothing singular or portentous in the sound. It was just such a bark as you will hear at all times of the night, and probably with unconcern, but mental anxiety and apprehension was one of the greatest miseries of my fugitive condition. In every shadow I beheld, as in every voice I heard a pursuer. Sometimes I paused to listen, when even the ordinary voices of the night filled me indefinite alarm. And then I rushed on heedless of obstacles and anxious only to place as great a distance as possible between me and my enemies.

It was near morning when I sate [sat] down to rest, and cogitate my plans. I trusted that my escape would be unnoticed probably for some time, as those in the house would naturally conclude that I was living at the huts, and those at the huts might be deceived in the same manner with the expectation of my being at the house. But even I must be careful of my strength, as on that depended all my hopes of ever seeing a land of freedom. I had neither map, nor chart, nor compass, but I could be guided at night by the North Star, and keep the sun to my back through the day. Then God would be with me, Christ would be with me, good angels I hoped would ever be near me and with these comforting assurances I fell asleep.

When I awoke the morning was far advanced. The birds were singing sweetly, and everything wore an aspect of life and joy. I felt refreshed, but hungry, and while debating with myself how to obtain a breakfast, a cow approached. Her udder was distended with the precious fluid. I thought of Elijah and ravens, and when she came still nearer, and stopped before me with a gentle low as if inviting me to partake. I hesitated no longer, but on her milk and a few simple berries I made a really luxurious meal. I cannot describe my journey; the details would be dry, tedious, uninteresting. My course was due North but I made slow progress. Occasionally I found ~~friends~~ friends, and this my disguise greatly facilitated. The people had no idea of my being a fugitive slave, and they were generally kind and hospitable.

I told them I was an orphan who had been left in destitute circumstances, and that I was endeavoring to make my way on foot to join the relatives of my mother who lived at the North. This account, so true and simple, greatly won the sympathies of all especially the women. They would press gifts of food and clothing on me, or condole the cruel fate which deprived me of friends and property at one blow.

One day I stopped at a house and asked for dinner. It was generously bestowed, and during my repast the mistress of the mansion, a plain well-spoken woman, inquired if I had met a woman in my wanderings answering that description, and she held up a paper on which was delineated my exact size and figure, in female apparel. I commanded my countenance and voice sufficiently to answer in a natural manner that I had not.

"Some men were here to[-]day in search of such a one" she continued. "They thought she could not be far off."

The speaker turned to the closet, as she spoke, to bring thence a pie, or it is probable that she would have discovered my alarm. Were they then so near me? I trembled in every limb, and declining the dessert provided by my hostess hastily thanked her, and taking up my hat departed.

I always made it a point to call at the houses at such times as I thought the men would probably be absent in the fields or on business; for I was not long in discovering that the females were far less inquisitive and curious about my affairs, besides being more gentle and considerate than the sterner sex. Indeed had no males belonged to the house I should not have hesitated a moment to throw myself on the compassion and generosity of the noble woman whom I had just left.

On gaining the public road I heard some hounds in full cry a short distance behind me. I doubted not they were on my track, and commending myself to God I took refuge in the shelter of a friendly wood. Presently I heard the murmur of water, and soon beheld at a little distance the sparkling waves of a rivulet. It w[as] broad but shallow. I entered it, waded down the current for probably half a mile, crossed over, and was in safety. That night, fearing to approach the habitations of men I slept in a cave, on a bed of dry leaves, but resumed my journey with the morning light.

In consequence, however, of incessant walking my feet became excessively sore. My shoes were worn off, and my sufferings most intense. In this state I came one day by a heap of garments, which some boys had lain aside ~~while~~ to bathe. With my blistered, swollen and inflamed feet I could not resist the temptation to appropriate a pair of boots. It was doubtless wrong, and great necessity must be my excuse.

During all these wanderings I managed to keep the time. I carried a small cord, and tied in it a knot for every day. This amused my loneliness, and seemed a sort of connecting link between me and the other portions of mankind. Perhaps you might have smiled, perhaps you would have wept to hear me running over the names of the days on my cord, as the Catholic devotee calls over the names of his favorite saints while counting his beads.

According to this record I had been two weeks a wanderer, and must have passed the borders of North Carolina when I became suddenly aware of the proximity of human beings. I was in the midst of a deep thick wood, nocturnal shadows surrounded me, and from appearances there was not a human habitation for many miles. Yet I had become so accustomed to darkness and solitude that it occasioned an agre[e]able feeling rather than otherwise. My only fears were of man. Thus far I had been mercifully preserved from the attacks of wild beasts, and my strength had been supported in an almost miraculous manner. Trusting to him likewise, who hears and feeds the young ravens, nature had supplied to my wants an abundance of wholesome food. And now calmly and confidingly with a grateful heart and undiminished faith, I composed myself to sleep in the friendly shelter of a small thicket, and felt almost happy in the consciousness of perfect security.

I cannot tell how long I had slumbered, as I had no means of knowing, but it must have been for some time, when I was unaccountably wakened by a noise of an unusual kind. Raising myself on my elbow I looked around and listened. The moon had risen, partially dispelling the darkness, and casting long bright streaks of light amid the thick mass of shadows. Near by was a little opening in the branches, through which streamed a large patch of radience, and to that my eyes instinctively turned. Directly crossing this were the figures of two people. They were speaking, and the voices were those of a man and a woman.

"We will rest here" said the man. "I think we can do so in perfect safety, and you are so ill and weary."

His companion heaved a deep sigh. "This will be my last resting place. This dreadful fever is consuming me, I feel weaker and weaker every moment, and before morning I shall be unable to rise."

"Oh no: dearest, say not so. You must not be discouraged. We have distanced our pursuers, and—"

"I know, I know" said the invalid sinking heavily to the earth with a bitter groan.

Her companion said no more, but busied himself as I could see by the moonlight in making her bed of dry leaves as comfortable and soft as possible. Then he sate [sat] down to wait and watch over her. Her sleep was accompanied with delirium. She would moan and call for water, and talk of home, and rest, and heaven in the most plaintive tones.

Towards morning, however, the paroxysm of her fever subsided, and she sunk into a gentle slumber. Her companion folded her garments closely around her, and then stretching himself by her side seemed to prepare for repose. Presently my thoughts became confused, with that pleasing bewilderment which precedes slumber. I began to lose the consciousness of my identity, and the recollection of where I was. Now it seemed that Lindendale rose before me, then it was the jail, and anon the white towers of Washington, and—but the scene all faded; for I slept.

The scarcely awakened morn was feebly peering through a curtaining of clouds, when I opened my eyes to encounter those of a black man fixed on me with the most intense expression of wonder, apprehension, and curiosity. A few words, however, sufficed to inform him that my circumstances were quite as deplorable as his, when he gave me his hand, and expressed a wish that I would see his companion.

Cheerfully, and without the least apprehension I complied with his request. She was in a fever, delirious, her face flushed, her hands burning to the touch. She called for water incessantly, and I proposed that as we had no means of conveying it to her he should take her in his arms and bear her to the margin of the stream. He did so, and thus we had the satisfaction of being able to slake her thirst.

It soon commenced raining and Seated beneath the shelter of a huge tree we made a breakfast on some wild fruits, which my newly discovered friend had gathered the day before. His name was Jacob. The female was his sister, and together they had traveled from the frontiers of South Carolina. He told me the history of their many wrongs, their master's cruelty and oppression, and the hardships which had occa occasioned their flight. Then he described their sufferings, and long wanderings in the woods, with the constant exposure and want they had undergone. How his sister's strength had gradually failed, and how often and often when she had given out, he had borne her on his back for miles. And then with the strongest manifestation of fraternal affection he took her burning hand, pressed it to his lips, and declared that he should only be to[o] happy to do the same again. I could only admire his fraternal piety and hope that it would meet with its proper reward.

He dashed a tear from his eye. "She was my only relative" he said. "We played together before our mother's door. I could not bear to leave her to be sold into Texas, but much I fear that she will never see a free land." This he said in broken incoherent expressions to which I have given suitable language.

"Yes" he continued "I fear that she will never see a free land."

"Have you, then" I inquired "no faith in God, no hope in heaven? Are you not a believer in that free land where the spirits of just men made perfect eternally abide?"

He shook his head unmeaningly.

I could only regard him with compassion that in his trials, and difficulties he was unaware of the greatest source of abiding comfort.

Meanwhile it began raining. The morning had been unusually dull and cloudy, and then a sort of misty drizzle commenced falling, that soon changed to incessant rain. The woods became one great shower bath. Dripping with excessive humidity the long branches of the still trees were like water spouts. The mosses and leaves were a mass of wet. The rain dripped in the face and on the bosom of the poor sufferer; it ran and stood in little pools beneath her, and we could not hinder it.

At my suggestion Jacob started out to look [for] a better shelter for her. Fortunately he succeeded in finding one, and thither dripping with the humidity we removed her. It was a rude little hut formed by strips of bark and branches of trees resting over and against the projecting buttress of a huge rock that jutted out from the side of the hill and overlooked the stream. It had been used as a dwelling place before, perhaps by hunters or woodmen; possibly by fugitives like ourselves. With grateful hearts we took possession, and were far more comfortable than we anticipated.

But our patient was unconscious of the change. Night and morning, rain and sunshine were henceforth to be alike to her. She is in a stupor, and bending over her I looked down on her wasted form. Her brother sate [sat] beside her on the ground, holding her hand in his, while tears that were no shame to his manhood streamed down his face. We saw that her time had come, that her struggle with the last great enemy had commenced. I touched her chest and heart. The pitcher was ~~near~~ broken at the fountain.

'Twas a moment of deep interest, and death at all times so solemn became doubly so under such circumstances. It often happens that the ceremonial attendant on the dying hour burdens it with unmeaning pomp, and that the hush and sanctity of the ~~sanctiety~~ occasion give way before the elaborate and commonplace manifestations of condolence and sympathy. The heartless throng who press around the bed, through curiosity or even a worse motive, the glare of lights, the attendance of the physician, watching with strange professional interest the peculiar circumstances of the case, and more than all the minister, not of religion but sectarianism, striving to elicit something of which to make capital for his next sermon, all intrude themselves in the chamber and on the hour which should be sacred to grief, and the highest and holiest emotions of the human nature.

Where is the tender and susceptible heart that has bled at finding the places around a dying bed which should be occupied only be [by] the nearest and dearest relatives, rudely filled by gossiping neighbors ready to count the tears of the wife or daughter, to descant on her words if she speaks, on her silence if she says nothing, and really anxious to discover something that will bear comment and afford discussion for a week or two.

The world even exacts something of death. It says in effect to the grim monarch, "You will have us, that is certain, but it shall only be on our own terms. A certain formality must be observed before we bow to you. We must have a due course of physic and religious attendance. There must be the throng of visitors, and the ceaseless inquiry [']How do you find yourself to[-]day[']" And when the last conflict is passed another ceremonial as dull, as cold, and even more heartless must be conformed to, before the wasting clay can be peacefully consigned to its last resting place. Public opinion says to the grave "Here is one of our species, an individual of Adam's race, whom death has overcome, but what of that? You shall not take him to your embrace till he has lain in state a day or two, attired in just so many yards of satin or flannel. And then a coffin just so rich, and with just such adornments must be provided, and this and that must be managed in exactly such a manner. Don't think to get him on any other terms, or if you do there will be gossip, and scandal, and small talk, and who can imagine what?["]

Of course we had none of this. The dull light looked in at our doorway; the rain dripped and pattered monotonously. Occasionally some little bird or insect would glance by ~~momentarily~~ and disappear.

"What is it, dear?"

She had started up with wild eyes and a frightened look.

"I thought I was back in South Car'lina. I a[i]n't there am I?["]

"No" says the brother.

"Who is that?" she inquired for the first time noticing me.

"A friend, who is assisting me to watch over and take care of you" he answered.

Falling back she closed her eyes, bowed her head, and murmured "I'm very glad."

I watched her closely a little while. I could not bear that she should die ~~that she she~~ thus like a brute with no mention of his name, who had died that we might live. Putting my mouth closely to her ear, I asked "did you ever pray?"

She was sensible, and murmured

"When I was a child."

["]Do you know it now?["]

She shook her head.

"But you have heard people pray?"

She nodded her head affirmatively, and said though with a very great effort

["]I have heard them, when they called it praying, and when it seemed to me they were talking to themselves, or master, or some one else. Ministers used to come among us and pray, but I never minded them. They mostly prayed that we the slaves might be good and obedient, and feel grateful for all our blessings, which I know was fudge. It hardened my heart, I could not bear it."

She says this slowly and studiously, and occupies a long time in doing it. How I pitied the poor benighted soul to whom the sweetest influences of religion had become gall and wormwood. Again she relapsed into a sort of stupor, and then suddenly made a strong effort to rise.

"What now? What now?["] I said soothingly.

"I hear them calling me. They say, come: come" she answered. "I think one of them is my mother. It's time for me to go to her. Oh, I want to go to her. She looks happy and blessed."

"Presently you shall go."

"Her mind wanders" whispered Jacob.

I bowed.

"There are no slaves there" she murmured.

"Neither is there sorrow or sighing there, nor parting of friends."

"Shall I go soon?"

"I think so, yes."

"Speak louder, I cannot hear you. It's growing very dark, and I am cold. Oh: so cold. Is there a fire acoming?"

"There is a warmth, a rising of the sun."

Jacob knelt impressively. I followed his example.

"My dear sister" he said bending his mouth to her ear.

"I hear, but I can't see you. Is the sun arisin?"

"It is, it is."

"It see it now; it is comin, a light, a very bright light."

The light came, the sun arose, the sun of righteousness.

Dead.

We could weep in silence and privacy. Public opinion came not to dictate the outward expressions of our grief. We were not required to mourn discreetly or in fashion. No ceremonial was dictated by officious friends, but tenderly and delicately we disposed the fragile limbs, crossed the meek hands quietly over the frozen bosom, and closed the blank expressionless eyes, and doing this we discovered, what had hitherto escaped us, the unmistakeable tokens of an infectious disease, at once malignant and dangerous. Jacob said she must have caught it in an old deserted house where they had remained a day or two, and in which they discovered and appropriated a bundle of old garments.

Towards night Jacob went out to pick some berries for our supper, ~~Hitherto all this day~~ leaving me alone with the dead. I had not eaten since morning, and even now was insensible to hunger. But I felt that was in consequence of the agitation of my mind, and that food was really necessary.

His stay was prolonged, but I thought little of it, untill night set in; the wild dark night, with the trees shuddering in the wind. The rain, so thick and heavy all day, had ceased falling, and though the sky had partly cleared and a few dim stars might be seen overhead it was exceedingly gloomy. Once or twice I went out to look and listen. The heavens wore a fearful an[d] awful aspect. In the north, and northwest, where the sunset had faded three hours before, there was a rich red arch of beautiful light, whence ascended what fancy might easily have pictured as sheets of waving flame.

As I gazed long lines of clouds, came sweeping on before the wind, the glowing arch with its fiery banners gave way before them, and all was darkness. I retreated to my hut in which the sad wreck of mortality lay stark, stiff, and immovable. Was it the presence of death, or that my nerves were weak and agitated, but a great and unaccountable terror seized me. I shuddered in every limb, great drops of sweat started to my forehead, and I cowered down in the corner like a guilty thing. My apprehensions were increased tenfold by the mysterious voices of the night. Mutterings, chatterings, and sounds of fearful import echoed through the gloom. Owls shrieked hediously to which was added the dismal howling of wolves. Then the corpse seemed to leer horridly, to gibe and beckon and point its long skinny fingers towards me, and though I knew that this was all fancy, though I had sense enough left to perceive even then the absurdity of my fears I could not overcome them, I could not pray for the protection of Heaven; Heaven seemed to have turned its face against me.

I was tortured moreover with the anxieties of suspense. Was it possible that Jacob could have deserted me in such a place? Could he purposely have left me alone with the dead without the intention of returning? Or had he perished by the wolves, which to judge from their noise were out in great numbers, or had some other accident overtaken him? Had he become lost and bewildered and unable to find his way back? These and a thousand other questions of a similar nature rushed into my brain, to be solved only by conjecture. It was the longest night of my existence, and I shall never forget its horrors. I, who had learned to sleep as calmly and composedly on a bed of leaves as in a palace chamber, was thus alarmed and terrified by ~~the immediate presence of the dead~~ I know not what.

Towards morning I fell into an unquiet slumber, slumber that brought visions more horrible than even those of my waking hours. The corpse seemed to rise and stand over me, and press with its cold leaden hand against my heart. In vain I struggled to free myself, by that perversity common to dreams I was unable to move. I could not shriek, but remained spell-bound under the hedious benumbing influence of a present embodied death. Then it seemed that some one was calling me. I knew the ~~voice~~ voice to be Jacob's, and strove to answer, but my tongue seemed palsied and my lips immovable. Then concentrating all my energies in one great effort I suddenly awoke. The dream was thus for real; some one was calling. I roused myself ~~it was~~ and listened, it was and listened, it was a human voice, and the shout or hallo was such as a person lost from his companions generally makes to discover their locality. My previous fears were for the moment forgotten. I crept to the door way of the hut and answered. The sound reverberated in a thousand echoes through the woods. It was still very dark, but the day-star was just rising; and the sky was almost clear. The shout was repeated again and again; each time I answered it and each time it came nearer and nearer. Soon I heard hurrying footsteps, a crackling in the bushes and under wood, and shortly discerned the figure of a man. It was Jacob. He had strayed farther than he designed to, while looking for food, night and darkness came on; he was bewildered and could not find his way back.

That day we busied ourselves in carrying brush and stones to fill up the entrance of the hut in which she lay, and the next morning resumed our tramp.

CHAPTER 19

An Old Friend

I have never seen the righteous forsaken.

Jacob and myself traveled many days together, but strange to say he had not penetrated my disguise. He learned to love me, however, as a younger brother, and his society and gentle care greatly relieved the difficulties of our toilsome journey. When we encamped for the night he would insist on my setting down to rest, while he went off to look for food, though when compelled by necessity to approach the habitations of men it devolved on me as his color made him obnoxious to suspicion. To avoid observation we sometimes traveled all night, ~~but rested through the day~~ and then concealed ourselves in dens, and hollows, and caverns through the day. We scaled mountains, and crossed rivers. The latter was easily accomplished. We lingered near some small village, or fisherman's hut till night-fall, and then when all was silent and the "wee small hours" had commenced their march, a boat could readily be found. Ferrying ourselves over we set it adrift and proceeded on our way. An adventure of this kind, however, proved fatal to my companion, and ~~had~~ well nigh to me.

It was near night when we reached the borders of a narrow

stream, that ran among rocks with a very strong current. Jacob, as usual remained concealed in the friendly shelter of a thick pine grove, while I went out to reconnoitre, and select some place for crossing, besides ascertaining where a boat could be procured. As there were no signs of a human habitation, we ~~went~~ traveled much farther down in the hope of finding one, as with that contingency was associated a certainty of obtaining a boat.

It was near midnight to judge from the aspect of the stars, when we discovered a dark object looming in the distance. As we approached a light was seen gleaming for a moment apparently from ~~one of the~~ a window, and we heard the cries of a child. Fearing to alarm the inmates of the cabin, it was some time before we ventured to look for a boat. There was a dim star-light, and the trees along the bank afforded an admirable shelter. At length we found the boat half-hidden in a little clump of willows, and Jacob proceeded to loosen it. Just then the light flared brightly up, the cries of the child were redoubled, and a fierce dog roused from his slumbers by the noise rushed upon us with a deep yell. As we sprang into the boat we heard the quick opening and shutting of the cabin door, and the voice of a man encouraging the mastiff. Then followed a rapid volley of firearms. Jacob gave one groan, dropped his oar and fell down in the bottom of the boat, which instantly swung around, became unmanageable, and drifted down the stream. The man ran along the bank, shouting and halloing, calling us boat stealers and all manner of villainous epithets, till exhausting his passion he struck off into the woods and disappeared.

To depict my consternation and alarm would be impossible. I called the name of my companion; he answered not. I touched his hand and cheek; they were icy cold. I laid my hand on his bosom; there was no pulsation. The stunning the dreadful truth rushed upon me with all its force. He was dead, and I, whither was I being carried? I strained my eyes in every direction, but could see ~~nothing~~ only the turgid mass of water slowly heaving and swelling, with now and then a foundered tree or granite boulder, jutting far out and breaking its dark bosom into foaming billows. Recommending myself to God I saw ~~with less anxiety than might be suffered~~ my boat approaching one of these dangerous spots with less anxiety than might be supposed. It rolled and rocked terribly whirled around in a foaming eddy, dashed against a rock, and upset. I felt the motion, and knew myself precipitated into the water, but nothing more. My first sensations of returning consciousness were those of intense pain, and more than mortal weakness. It was more like the nightmare of sleep than any thing else to which I can compare it. A noise of rushing waters was in my ears, a dreadful sense of suffocation oppressed me, and I struggled wildly and fiercely struggled to shake it off.

Gradually and by degrees I became sensible of my condition, and that the water was still dashing over my lower extremities. The instinct of self[-]preservation prompted me to crawl up higher on the bank, where the sun shone brightly, and I remember experiencing a vague impression that the generous warmth of his beams would restore my torpid and benum[b]ed limbs to their natural exercise. I was soon recovered sufficiently to look around, when I ascertained that the branches of a fallen tree, into which I had been washed by the eddying waves had saved me under Providence from a violent death. While breathing out my gratitude to Him, who holds the waters in the hollow of his Hand, and wondering for what wise purpose I had been preserved I heard the sound of approaching footsteps and presently a woman bending with age and infirmity drew near. Her benignant countenance inspired me with hope, and when she was passing without discovering me I called to her.

"Mother, good mother."

She stopped, turned around in great surprise, and with something of alarm, saying "Who calls me?"

I knew the voice, though I had not recognised the countenance. It was that of my old friend, Aunt Hetty. ~~Of course she failed to recognise me through my singular disguise~~ Tears of joy ran down my cheeks, while I revealed my name and circumstances to the venerable dame, and when she learned that I was really the Hannah whom she had taught to read, and instructed in the truths of Christianity at Lindendale, her happiness fully equaled mine.

"But where have you come from, dear? and what is the meaning of this disguise?" she inquired. "But stop" she continued when I opened my lips to speak. "Don't tell me a word till you are properly cared for. How came your garments so wet? and why are you so weak?" and then she laughed at herself for asking ~~me~~ questions when she had forbidden my answering them.

"I will tell you all, dear Aunt Hetty; everything, but not now" I whispered, for a strange sensation of faintness overpowered me. She observed it.

"You have suffered, dear" she said tenderly, drawing my head to her bosom, as she sate [sat] beside me.

But the sickness passed off, and I did not faint.

"You must go home with me" she continued. "You can rest there and recruit your strength. I have nothing grand or elegant to offer you yet better is a dinner of herbs where love is, than a stalled ox, and hatred therewith."

"Dear Aunt Hetty, you have suffered much for my sake already, I fear to be the means of your suffering more."

"We will see to that" she answered tenderly "can you walk?"

I attempted to rise, but fell back, again overpowered by a mortal faintness.

"I see how it is" she said encouragingly. "You require nourishment. Have you eaten lately."

"Not since yesterday morning, and then only a few berries."

"Heaven help the child, no wonder you are weak; indeed it would be a wonder if you wasn't. And now" she continued ["]I will leave you here for awhile, and go to get you some food, and procure a conveyance to take you to my house, but of one thing I must warn you. Be careful not to betray to these people our former acquaintance, or to let them into the secret of your former life."

"No Aunt Hetty" I replied. "Your scheme does not appear to me a feasible one. Let me say or do as I will their suspicions will be excited, because doubt and suspicion is natural to man. Procure me the food you think I require, but mention to no one the fact of my existence, rather assist me to remove to some place of concealment, where I can wait to recover my strength, unnoticed and alone. It will probably be but a few hours."

"Perhaps that would be best" she answered thoughtfully. ["]My home is but a little way hence. I can soon go there and return.["] I watched her disappearing figure with the liveliest emotions, and felt that I could never be sufficiently grateful to that over ruling Providence, who by such eventful and devious ways had led me to the bosom of my old friend.

The old lady soon returned with such food as she thought most proper for my exhausted state. I ate only a little, yet felt strengthened and revived.

"My dear Aunt Hetty, what do I not owe you?" I said kissing her hand, and bathing it with my tears.

"Nothing to me; everything to the Lord Jesus" she replied solemnly.

I soon felt comfortable, and began to be strong more like my former self. Then I sate [sat] up, and we talked about many things.

I must give her the history of my life, and she must relate to me all that befell her and Uncle Siah. How Mr Vincent's overseer caused them to be conveyed to jail for violation of the statute that forbade the instruction of slaves. How they remained there several weeks, and found like Paul and Silas of old that bonds and imprisonment when unjustly suffered might even be the means of spiritual consolation and improvement. How an old friend and distant relative passing through the village heard of their detention, and by long earnest solicitation of the proper authorities combined with the liberal use of money succeeded in liberating them removed them to his estate, where he appropriated a small house and regular monthly stipend of money and provisions to their necessities. Uncle Siah she told me had recently departed to that good land where the just receive their reward and consequently she dwelt alone with the companionship of one little girl. Her habitation was situated near a small village of miners, but she could not tolerate their rude and profane habits, and so had neither connection nor association with them. One woman only, a widow like herself, distinguished for piety and good works ever came to her house or received her visits in return, excepting of course the family of her friend and relative.

That night after dark when the village ~~had become silent~~ became silent she led me to her home. It was a neat little cottage, tidy and comfortable, with a bright fire glowing on the hearth near which was placed for my especial benefit a large well-cushioned rocking chair. Anna, the little girl was bustling about in all the dignity and importance of incipient womanhood preparing tea. She was much older than she seemed; her petite figure and round rosy face giving her a look of childishness not often seen in one of her years. Like small people generally she was very active, very straight, and very impulsive, and I could scarcely help smiling to see the flush that mounted instantaneously to her face, when Aunt Hetty persisted in addressing her as "little girl."

I remained with this good venerable friend several weeks and then the flight of time admonished me that it was necessary to be moving again, as my journey was not yet accomplished, and it was impossible to feel anything like a sense of security while remaining in a slave-state. Greatly as I feared discovery on my own account, I feared it no less on that of my friend. I well knew that the charge of concealing and feeding a fugitive slave would be a serious one, and involve her in great difficulties. Agre[e]ably to her advice, moreover, I determined to somewhat change my plan. She insisted that I should resume female attire, and travel by public conveyances, as she conceived so much time had elapsed and I was so far from the scene of my escape that I could do so with perfect safety. She said that she never would consent for me to leave her on any other terms, that she should never enjoy another moment's peace if she permitted me to go forth again a wanderer, to seek shelter in dens and caves of the earth. She likewise proposed that I should find refuge among the colored inhabitants of New Jersey, as thereby my journey would be proportionately shortened, and I would escape the extreme cold of Canadian winters. In order to facilitate acquaintance, and assist me in getting employment, she prepared letters of introduction to various persons whom she had known in former times as friends of the slave, though she expressed apprehension that they were removed or dead.

Yeilding my plans to ~~hers~~ what seemed the superior feasibility of hers the good old woman supplied me with female apparel, and also with the means of prosecuting my journey in an expeditious manner. At first I declined taking her silver, but she pressed it upon me saying that she had been saving it little by little for a long time, purposely to bestow it on some one in poorer circumstances than herself, that it would give her great pain if I persisted in refusing her bounty, ~~and~~ as it would comparatively increase her happiness if I accepted it. I could refuse no longer, but with emotions of gratitude I should vainly attempt to express I took the proffered gift.

CHAPTER 20

Retribution

Say to the wicked it shall be ill with him, for he shall eat the fruit of his doings.

BIBLE

With many tears I bade adieu to Aunt Hetty—tears of gratitude and sorrow and reverential affection. Farther down the river was a steamboat landing and my preparations being complete she accompanied me thither, and saw me safe on board. Our farewell was a mute impassioned silence deeper and more expressive to the heart than any words could have been. I gazed long and earnestly, my eyes blinded with tears, at her retreating figure, and then at then [sic] at the spot where she disappeared till the ringing of the bell, the puffing of the steam, and the rocking motion of the boat gave warning that ~~we were underweigh~~ we were passing down the river. I felt very lonely and desolate, and there is no desolation so deep as that you feel when surrounded by a crowd with whom you have no sympathies in common. There was conviviality and laughter among the passengers, there was eating, drinking and talking, there was [sic] babies crying, mothers coaxing, and fathers smoking. I endeavored to interest myself in what was passing around me, but could not till a couple of gentlemen who were sitting near me, mentioned a name that thrilled through ever nerve of my body. In an instant I was all attention, and when they spoke of a violent death and assassination I felt how true it is that "even-handed justice returns the ingredients of the poisoned chalice to our own lips."

"From first to last, the circumstances were most singular" said one of the gentlemen, a tall good-looking man dressed in black.

"Very much so, indeed, very much so" answered his companion, speaking with a quick nervous accent, and reiterating his expressions over and over again. "Very much so, indeed, I should say."

"I only heard the particulars yesterday" continued the tall man.

"Did you ever see the old gentleman?" inquired the other.

"Oh yes frequently, he was a noted character, a great trav[e]ller, and almost everybody knew him, though it is doubtful if all his aristocrat associates were aware of ~~how he had obtained his great wealth~~ the means by which he had obtained his great wealth, or how hard and unfeeling he could be when it suited his purposes. He was a man of no principle."

"He had neither feeling, nor sympathy in common with other people. Love of gold had blunted all the finer sensibilities of his heart, and he would not have hesitated a moment to sell his own mother into slavery could the case have been made clear that she had African blood in her veins. No blood-hound was ever keener in scenting out the African taint than that old man."

"And one of his victims slew him?"

["]It is so supposed. He had a country house in a lonesome and retired place to which he generally caused the girls whom he purchased to be removed, and where he kept them concealed till some trader came around to whom he could sell them at an advanced price. His recent speculations in that line involved a peculiar and complicated affair. A wealthy planter with whom he had associated on terms of the closest intimacy had a family of beautiful children both boys and girls, but the mother was, or had been a slave, though she enjoyed all the perquisites and priveledges of a wife. Indeed her master had told her times without number that he had made out and signed the bill of her emancipation, besides making herself and her children his heirs in the event of his death. Of course the poor woman saw no reason to dispute his truth or honesty and so the matter rested. The children were well educated for stations of honor and usefulness, and little dreamed of the terrible blow that awaited them. At length the father, who had been long ailing, died. He had brothers, ~~and these so~~ who were extremely angry at the tenor of his will, and who employed Mr Trappe to ~~endeavor~~ invalidate it, while to the infinite surprise of all no bill of emancipation for either the mother or her children could be discovered. It was more than hinted that Mr Trappe, who had ~~access to the planter's papers during his illness~~ visited the sick man, and had access to all parts of the house, had found and destroyed it. But this was mere conjecture, as no positive proof could be adduced that such an article had ever been in existence.["]

"How unfortunate."

"The distress of the family may be imagined; it certainly never can be described. Prostrated at once from happiness and wealth to the lowest depth of degradation and misery they spent the days in tears and the nights in bitter lamentations over the past.

["]The sons, however, were not so easily disconcerted as the mother and daughter. It seems they worried the old man dreadfully, followed him about, went to his chambers and openly accused him of destroying or secreting their father's papers."

"This was during the course of the litigation, I suppose."

"Certainly, during the litigation which lasted a long time, and finally ended by consigning mother and children to the slave-market. Mr Trappe, who always took opportunity by the forelock had foreseen the end, and accordingly purchased the females at a risk, previous to the final settlement of the business, at a very reduced price. The sons and brothers had disappeared and no one knew where. Many supposed they had ran [run] off to the North, and wondered why their dear and near relatives did not accompany them.["]

"It certainly was singular."

"Not at all; they had other plans in view I suppose. One of them was heard to observe that if Trappe succeeded in trapping his mother and sisters he would never entrap anyone else, that he thought the old fellow had been the occasion of enough misery already, and that whoever put him out of the way would deserve the thanks of the community for ridding the world of a villain.["]

"Plain spoken indeed."

"Very, plain spoken, and it has been ascertained that Mr Trappe considered himself so much in danger from these fellows that he took the precaution of making oath against them, and nothing in the world hindered their arrest only the simple fact that they could not be found."

"A very good reason truly" laughed the little man. "An admirable reason."

["]But they could not have been as far off as was at first supposed. Mr Trappe's man-servant caught a glimpse once or twice of fellows answering their description, who seemed to be lurking, as he thought and as it proved, for evil purposes around the habitation of the former. He informed his master of the circumstances, and the old man manifested considerable agitation.["]

"Were these females at Mr Trappe's county seat?"

"They were; and by some unknown ways and means they must have kept up a constant communication with their relatives."

"Well, they fled."

"Certainly, they fled, and their absence in the morning was the first intimation the old man received that mischief had been done, or that strangers had been there during the night.["]

"He can tell a straight story, then."

"Oh yes. He says that he shut and barred the doors as usual and went to look at the ladies; it being his duty to see them at least three times a day, that the mother was weeping while the girls were endeavoring to comfort her and that he left them thus pleasantly engaged."

"Pleasantly engaged" said the little man. "Does he call weeping a pleasant engagement?"

"He seemed to think it was for women. However on going to their apartments next morning he was greatly surprised to find the doors and windows fastened as ~~usual~~ he had left them, though the birds were flown, while neither sign nor trace of where they had gone, or how they had escaped could be discovered. Deprecating his master's anger which he knew would be fierce, and striving to frame some vindication of his own conduct he ascended to the chamber the lawyer occupied. The door was shut; he knocked loudly, there was no response. Somewhat astonished he opened it and walked in. Mr. Trappe was lying with his face downward to the floor.

"Master" said the servant.

All silent.

"The girls have escaped."

No answer.

He advanced, touched his hand, turned him over. There was a hole in his forehead, a bullet had penetrated his brain. His schemes of wealth and ambition had suddenly terminated, ~~He was dead~~ and he had gone to that fearful and final reckoning which none can escape."

"And nothing further is known?"

"Nothing, except that a lady who was watching over her sick child in the night heard a carriage driven furiously by, apparently towards the north."

"And so the miscreants escaped."

"They did, and thus far no claim to their farther progress has been obtained."

'Twas pitiful, 'twas mournful to think of that old man sent to his long account with all his imperfections on his head, and without a moment's time for shrift or prayer. 'Twas a dreadful thing, I shuddered ~~with the lone idea~~ and could have wept, though what better could one so heartless and unfeeling expect? "Since he that sows the wind, must reap the whirlwind."

CHAPTER 21

In Freedom

"*He leadeth me through the green pastures, and by the still waters.*"

DAVID

There is a hush on my spirit in these days, a deep repose a blest and holy quietude. I found a life of freedom all my fancy had pictured it to be. I found the friends of the slave in the free state just as good as kind and hospitable as I had always heard they were. I dwell now in a neat little Cottage, and keep a school for colored children. It is well attended, and I enjoy myself almost as well ~~in~~ imparting knowledge to others, as I did in obtaining it when a child myself. Can you guess who lives with me? You never could—my own dear mother, aged and venerable, yet so smart and lively and active, and Oh: so fond of me. There was a hand of Providence in our meeting as we did. I am sure of it. Her history is most affecting and eventful. During my infancy she was transferred from Lindendale to the owner of a plantation in Mississippi, yet she never forgot me nor certain marks on my body, by which I might be identified in after years. She found a hard master, but he soon died, and she became the property of his daughter who dwelt in Maryland, and thither she was removed. Here she became acquainted with a free mulatto from New Jersey, who persuaded her to escape to his native state with him, where they might be married and live in freedom and happiness. She consented. Their plan of escape proved successful, and they lived together very happyly many years when the husband died.

She said it had been her incessant prayer by day and by night for many long years, that her child left in slavery might be given to freedom and her arms. She had no means of bringing about this great desire of her heart, but trusted all to the power and mercy of heaven. So strong was her faith that whenever she beheld a stranger she half-expected to behold her child. We met accidentally, where or how it matters not. I thought it strange, but my heart yearned towards her with a deep intense feeling it had never known before. And when we became better acquainted, and fonder of each other's society, and interested in each other's history, I was not half so surprised as pleased and overwhelmed with emotions for which I could find no name, when she suddenly rose one day, came to me, clasped me in her arms, and sobbed out in rapturous joy "child, I am your mother." And then I—but I cannot tell what I did, I was nearly crazy with delight. I was then resting for the first time on my mother's bosom—my mother for whom my heart had yearned, and my spirit gone out in intense longing many, many times. And we had been brought together by such strange and devious ways. With our arms clasped around each other, our heads bowed together, and our tears mingling we went down on our knees, and returned thanks to Him, who had watched over us for good, and whose merciful power we recognised in this the greatest blessing of our lives.

I have yet another companion quite as dear—a fond and affectionate husband. He sits by my side even as I write and sometimes, shakes his head, and sometimes laughs saying "there, there my dear. I fear you grow prosy, you cannot expect the public to take the same interest in me that you do" when I answer "of course not, I should be jealous if it did." He is, and has always been a free man, is a regularly ordained preacher of the Methodist persuasion, and I believe and hope that many through his means, under Providence, have been led into wisdom's ways, which are those of pleasantness.

I must not omit telling who are my neighbors. You could scarcely believe it, it seems so singular, yet is none the less true. Charlotte, Mrs Henry's favorite, and her husband. From the window where I sit, a tiny white cottage half-shaded in summer by rose-vines and honeysuckle appears at the foot of a sloping green. ~~Before it is now~~ In front there is such an exquisite flower-garden, and behind such a dainty orchard of choice fruits that it does one good to think of it. It is theirs. He has learned the carpenter's trade, and gets plenty of work, while she takes in sewing. Need I describe the little church where we all go to meeting, and the happiness we experience in listening to the words of Gospel truth; and as I could not, if I tried, sufficiently set forth the goodness of those about me, the tenderness and love with which my children of the school regard me, and the undeviating happiness I find in the society of my mother, my husband, and my friends. I will let the reader picture it all to his imagination and say farewell.

TEXTUAL ANNOTATIONS

∞

There is convincing textual evidence that the writer of *The Bondwoman's Narrative* had recourse to the library of John Hill Wheeler (see introductory material to this volume). In the first case, several of the source texts for many of the obvious literary echoes in Hannah Crafts's novel were owned by Wheeler, including Horace Walpole's *Castle of Otranto,* Walter Scott's *Rob Roy,* and Charlotte Brontë's *Jane Eyre.* In the second case, many of the short phrases and individual lines that she quotes (seemingly from memory) can be found in various volumes owned by Wheeler. (Of course, several, such as lines from Shakespeare, were very popular.) In the third case, a number of contemporary political allusions (to Indians, Mormons, railroads, the Panama Canal) point to Wheeler's particular political interests. (The first page of the catalogue of the sale of his library refers to "American History and Biography, Slavery, Civil War and Confederate Publications, Indians, Mormons, Quakers, Masonry.") These allusions may be a function of her knowledge and experience in the Wheeler household, as well as a function of concern with identifying him by name.

Clearly, Crafts wanted her novel to point to Wheeler—the persistent repetition of her predecessor Jane (mentioning her name ten times between pp. 153 and 157) is evidence of that. Perhaps while she was grappling with naming him she allowed herself to drop such textual clues. Although there is no "smoking gun" that proves without a doubt that his library provided these works, the pattern of her allusions—from national policy to women poets—corresponds to the compass of his library. The majority of these allusions can be characterized as echoes or brief quotes; that is, she most likely read these works months or years before she began writing.

But it is also the case that the text Crafts draws on most extensively, Charles Dickens's *Bleak House* (1852–53), is not in the 1882 catalogue. In some ways this is not surprising: the borrowing is so thorough and thematic that she must have had a copy in front of her while she was writing her own novel in the latter half of the 1850s. It is possible that she took his copy or that she discovered the book after she left. Much more interesting is the possibility that Crafts read *Bleak House* in *Frederick Douglass' Paper* from April 1852 through December 1853, in which Douglass chose to serialize Dickens's work in its entirety. "We wish we could induce everyone to read *Bleak House*," Douglass wrote in the June 3, 1853, edition:

> Charles Dickens has ever been the faithful friend of the poor—God bless him for that!—and in the portraitures that he, ever and anon, weaves into his books of fiction, we see the touch of a master hand. His delineations are true, to the life; and his being able to give them evinces his being intimately acquainted with the dense ignorance, squallid misery, and pressing wants of "the London poor."...Tis true that "the story is long," but time spent upon its perusal is not ill bestowed.

In Douglass's paper, as well as in the pages of other abolitionist periodicals such as the *National Era*, characters and themes from *Bleak House* functioned as a rich source of comic and ironic allusions for the community of anti-slavery readers, columnists, and letter writers. Douglass's decision to serialize the novel was controversial (many readers thought the space and ink could be used more productively), but readers responded to the story's humor and satire.

The following annotations are the combined work of Henry Louis Gates Jr., Hollis Robbins, and Gregg Hecimovich.

Preface

Crafts prefaces her novel with a traditional apologia, modestly questioning the very possibility of successfully achieving her goal of "portraying any of the peculiar features of that institution whose curse rests over the fairest land the sun shines upon," because her background as a slave is "a sphere so humble." Slavery, well before the 1850s, was commonly referred to as "the peculiar institution," a phrase that she echoes here. Her rhetorical strategy claims that slavery "blights the happiness of the white as well as the black race," southerners as well as northerners. This argument was common among authors of slave narratives, such as Frederick Douglass, whose bestselling slave narrative was published in 1845, and abolitionist novelists, such as Harriet Beecher Stowe, whose *Uncle Tom's Cabin* was published in 1852.

In addition, it was also traditional to assert, as Crafts does, the factual nature of fictional narrative. Despite the fact that her text is so pervaded with gothic themes, Crafts claims that the work "makes no pretensions to romance." Throughout her text, Crafts shows an easy familiarity with fictional literary genres, such as the gothic and sentimental novels, both exceedingly popular forms in the 1850s. Referring to George Gordon, Lord Byron (1788–1824), Crafts writes that truth is "stranger than fiction." Ironically, Byron wrote that "truth is always strange—stranger than fiction" in his major work of fiction, *Don Juan* (canto 14, stanza 101).

Chapter 1

p. 5: "It may be that... I was dull and stupid." The opening lines of Crafts's novel are a clear echo of the opening lines of chapter 3 of Charles Dickens's *Bleak House,* in which the young orphan Esther Summerson is introduced. (The epigraph to chapter 1 of *The Bondwoman's Narrative,* "Look not upon me because I am black; because the sun hath looked upon me," from Song of Solomon, perhaps comments upon Esther Summerson's name.) Here is the opening of Esther's narrative:

> I have a great deal of difficulty in beginning to write my portion of these pages, for I know I am not clever. I always knew that. I can remember, when I was a very little girl indeed, I used to say to my doll, when we were alone together, "Now Dolly, I am not clever, you know very well, and you must be patient with me, like a dear!"

Crafts's careful use and transformation of these introductory lines not only signals a clear interest in creating a kinship between Hannah and Esther but also evinces a clear understanding of the differences between them. The breadth and extent of such borrowings suggest that Crafts had the text of *Bleak House* (either in volume form or in back issues of *Frederick Douglass' Paper*) in front of her while she was writing her narrative. Her borrowings come from throughout the novel. But the copied passages are not plagiarism. In the first place, her status as so-called "property" (or fugitive property) complicates and perhaps mitigates her act of violating intellectual property rights, and, in the second, her craft in transforming and transmuting these borrowed passages suggests that the more appropriate term for her act is what Henry Louis Gates Jr., calls "double-voiced discourse": a narrative voice characterized by a hybrid character, a character who is neither the novel's protagonist nor the text's disembodied narrator, but a blend of both, an emergent and merging moment of consciousness. The value of a hybrid or polyvocal character to Crafts is that it complicates the idea of a speaking subject. It is not necessarily Hannah's voice that is telling her story.

p. 5: The narrator's claim to have been reared without parents is a common theme in slave narratives. As in *Narrative of Frederick Douglass, an American Slave* (1845), Crafts's childhood as a slave is marked by "no training, no cultivation." Similarly, her reference to animals such as the "birds of the air" and "beasts of the feild [sic]" as comparisons for the status of a slave was a common feature of the slave narratives, again as in Douglass. Distinctly unlike the slave narratives, however, Crafts's text rarely uses verisimilitude—specific names, places, or dates—to authenticate her text, signaling early on that *The Bondwoman's Narrative* is a fictionalized text, even if based on a slave's actual experiences. See the Introduction to this volume for details about Hannah Bond's real-life family members and personal history.

p. 6: Crafts refers to her African heritage ironically as "the obnoxious descent," parodying commonly held racist views of black ancestry. Despite the protagonist's light complexion and European features, she is influenced by her "obnoxious descent" to prefer "flaming colors." Throughout the text, this supposed preference for bright colors by African Americans is a source of fascination for the narrator. Her claim that her black genetic heritage was also responsible for "a rotundity to my person, a wave and curl to my hair," and "fancy pictorial illustrations" as well as a fondness for "flaming colors" reflects commonly held pseudoscientific beliefs about the dominant role of genetics in both physical and metaphysical characteristics, and preferences of taste.

p. 6: The phrase "my lot and portion" may allude to a line in the famous sermon titled "A Peculiar People," preached by Reverend J. C. Philpot (1802–69) in 1841 and circulated widely.

p. 6: The phrase "I felt the immortal longings in me" echoes a line (282) in Shakespeare's *Antony and Cleopatra,* act V, scene 2 ("I have / Immortal longings in me"). The volume *Beauties of Shakespeare* (1827) is included in the 1850 catalogue of John Hill Wheeler's library.

p. 6: Crafts's observation that her master felt that education made slaves "less subservient to their superiors" echoes Douglass's claim that his master said that "learning would *spoil* the best nigger in the world.... It would forever unfree him to be a slave."

p. 6: Crafts's reference to her master's opinion of the status of slaves as similar to that of "horses or other domestic animals" reflects Douglass's use of the same comparison.

p. 6: Echoing the passionate desire for literacy that is a structural principle in many slave narratives, Crafts yearns for "knowledge and the means of mental improvement" despite fear of punishment from her master. Although she concedes that her owner was "generally easy and good-tempered," he insists upon ignorance and subservience rather than literacy training among his slaves. Like Douglass, Crafts decides to teach herself by examining old books or newspapers.

How a slave learned to read and write—and hence eventually gained the wherewithal to write his or her own narrative—is a standard feature of several slave narratives, the signal scene of instruction that sets the text's plot "from slavery to freedom" in motion.

p. 7: The narrator's plan for literacy is aided when she meets a kindly, old northern woman. In explaining why she intends to defy the ban on teaching slaves to read, the pious woman answers that she was thinking of Christ's admonition to Peter to "feed my lambs" (John 21:15).

p. 8: Hannah's description of herself during this first encounter with literacy as "a being to whom a new world with all its mysteries and marvels was opening" again echoes Douglass's observation that literacy was "the pathway from slavery to freedom."

p. 8: Describing her desire to share her feelings, Crafts writes, "I had no mother, no friend." Douglass says, in his 1845 *Narrative,* that he saw his mother only "four or five times," and only "at night." He "received the tidings of her death with much the same emotions [as] I should have probably felt at the death of a stranger."

p. 9: In what appears to be an appeal for abolitionist support, the narrator states that in the North "the colored race had so many and such true friends." On p. 10, she idealizes northern whites as those who implicitly feel "keenly on the subject of slavery and the degradation and ignorance it imposes on one portion of the human race." The claim that slaves were members of "the human race" was meant to counter pro-slavery claims that they were not, that they were subhuman.

p. 9: Crafts's description of the kindly, virtuous old herb-gathering couple in the cottage, Uncle Siah and Aunt Hetty, appears to draw upon the description of Baucis and Philemon from Thomas Bulfinch's *Age of Fable* (1855). In classical mythology, Baucis and Philemon were a virtuous old couple who shared their humble cottage and simple dinner of herbs with Jupiter (who was in disguise) and were transformed, after they died, into a linden and an oak, standing forever intertwined. Craft's emphasis on their expertise on "salves and ointments" (p. 7), "simple herbs," and "salves and unguents" (p. 10) adds to their magical, mythological aspect.

p. 10: Describing her trips to Aunt Hetty and Uncle Siah, Hannah says that she would "steal away" to learn about Christianity. This invocation of the spiritual titled "Steal Away" is one of the few references to the African American musical tradition in this text. Hannah's admirable piety is underscored by the smugness of the contrast between her evening activities and the other slaves' enjoyment of "the banjo and the dance."

p. 11: "I had formed a resolution...to win some love if I could." Crafts continues drawing upon and transforming Esther Summerson's narrative:

> I often thought of the resolution I had made on my birthday, to try to be industrious, contented, and true-hearted, and to do some good to some one and win some love if I could.

The passage "the little slave children were almost entirely confided to my care. I hope that I was good and gentle to them; for I pitied their hard and cruel fate very much" is also taken from chapter 3 of *Bleak House:*

> At last, whenever a new pupil came who was a little downcast and unhappy, she was so sure—indeed I don't know why—to make a friend of me, that all new-comers were confided to my care. They said I was so gentle; but I am sure *they* were!

Crafts changes Esther's words in important ways: Esther worries that the task is too difficult; Hannah worries that she assumes too much responsibility. Esther seeks to be content, Hannah to be cheerful. These two changes alone speak volumes about the author's understanding of Hannah's difference from Esther: Hannah will never be content as long as slavery continues, and she has a responsibility to the cause of ending it.

p. 13: Aunt Hetty's banishment is a restatement of the text's valorization of white abolitionists and their willingness to be punished for their defiance of unjust laws on behalf of the slave.

p. 13: "Oh the difference to me" is the last line of William Wordsworth's famous poem "She Dwelt Among the Untrodden Ways" (1799).

p. 13: Lindendale is based on Willow Hall, the Bertie County plantation where Crafts was born and where she spent her early years.

p. 13: "Hitherto our master had been a bachelor." North of Milton, in Westmoreland County, is a large home called Linden, which is close to a Lee Hall, home to the "famous bachelor" and party-giver, Squire Richard Lee. The Squire remained a bachelor until he was about sixty years of age, then married his cousin, Sally Poythress, and had three daughters—Mary, Lettice, and Richarda. After his death, Sally Poythress married Willoughby Newton, who built Linden.

In 1773, according to a letter quoted in Paul C. Nagel's *The Lees of Virginia*, a cousin wrote that Squire Lee "looks fresh and hearty; and is, I am afraid, as lewdly indulgent as ever, from the appearance of his waiting maids, Bab and Henny.... If ever he marries, you may depend on it (as I told him the other day), it will be with some mop-squeezer who can satiate his filthy amours in his own way" (p. 53). Perhaps Squire Lee serves as a model for the later owner of Lindendale, Mr. Cosgrove (see chapters 14 and 15, "Lizzy's Story").

In May 1774, a Princeton student and tutor named Philip Fithian wrote of a ball here "attended by over seventy persons, of whom forty-one were ladies." With occasional intermissions for sleep, the party continued for three days. The music "was from a French horn and two violins. The Ladies were Dressed Gay and splendid, and when dancing their Skirts and Brocades rustled and trailed behind them.... There were parties in Rooms made up, some at Cards; some drinking for Pleasure; some toasting the Sons of America; some singing 'Liberty Songs,' as they call them, in which six, eight, ten or more would put their heads near together and roar."

p. 13: "it was whispered" Douglass uses *whispered* in this sense, describing the slaves' rumors of their master's secrets, and more especially of his own paternity.

p. 14: "Then our preparations were quite wonderful...up and down the staircases, along the galleries and passages, and through the rooms where floors were undergoing the process of being rubbed bright, carpets were being spread, curtains shaken out, beds puffed and covered... and the fastidious taste of its expected mistress." The language describing preparations undertaken by Mrs. Bry and the slaves at Lindendale follows closely the language that Dickens uses to narrate arrangements undertaken by Mrs. Rouncewell at Chesney Wold in chapter 40 of *Bleak House*:

> And hence the stately old dame, taking Time by the forelock, leads him up and down the staircases, and along the galleries and passages and through the rooms, to witness before he grows any

older that everything is ready; that floors are rubbed bright, carpets spread, curtains shaken out, beds puffed and patted, still-room and kitchen cleared for action, all things prepared as beseems the Dedlock dignity.

p. 14: "whose sweat and blood and unpaid labor had contributed to produce it" Crafts here echoes the economic-justice argument from abolitionist propaganda for the abolition of slavery.

pp. 15–16: The description of the long galleries filled with portentous portraits of the family of Sir Clifford De Vincent, the current master's ancestor, is reminiscent of the central role played by portraiture in Horace Walpole's *Castle of Otranto* (1765). Walpole's novel is considered to begin the gothic novel tradition. In American literature of the nineteenth century, Edgar Allan Poe is the most important practitioner of this genre, which often involves ancient houses, forlorn brides, and supernatural occurrences. Even for Virginia (the Old Dominion), Lindendale seems to be exceedingly aristocratic and antique for a New World setting.

pp. 16–17: Crafts is citing a longtime practice of portrait hanging by the family of the enslavers who first brought her family to the United States, the Pugh family of Virginia and North Carolina. See Hecimovich, *Life and Times*, 112–13.

pp. 17–18: "I was not a slave with these pictured memorials of the past.... In their presence my mind seemed to run riotous and exult in its freedom as a rational being, and one destined for something higher and better than this world can afford." Crafts here argues for the transformative powers of the higher arts—in this case, the visual arts—on even a humble slave. While virtually all the slave narrators used the mastering of literacy in this way, few slave narrators, if any, used an appreciation of painting to show the common humanity of the slave and his white masters. Crafts's mistress's true identity as the daughter of a slave mother will be authenticated by a portrait. See p. 48.

p. 17: "Involuntarily I gazed as the fire of the sun died out, even untill [sic] the floor became dusky, and the shadows of the linden falling broader and deeper wrapped all in gloom." Here Crafts conflates two echoes from *Bleak House* (chapters 40 and 36, respectively):

> But the fire of the sun is dying. Even now the floor is dusky, and shadow slowly mounts the walls, bringing the Dedlocks down like age and death.
>
> The perspective was so long, and so darkened by leaves, and the shadows of the branches on the ground made it so much more intricate to the eye, that at first I could not discern what figure it was.

pp. 17–18: The phrases "freedom as a rational being" and "immortal mind" (as well as the philosophy of the entire passage) evoke Immanuel Kant's *Foundations of the Metaphysics of Morals* (1785).

Chapter 2

p. 19: In addition to the author's modernization of "speaketh" to "speaks," she changes Proverbs' seven abominations to "severe" abominations. Proverbs 26:25:

> When he speaketh fair, believe him not: for there are seven abominations in his heart.

p. 19: This opening passage draws upon two minor moments more than thirty chapters apart in *Bleak House,* the first of which (chapter 7) suggests that Mrs. Bry shares something with Mrs. Rouncewell, and the second of which (chapter 45) notes the loss of an Indian ship.

> It has rained so hard and rained so long, down in Lincolnshire that Mrs. Rouncewell the old housekeeper at Chesney Wold, has several times taken off her spectacles and cleaned them, to make certain that the drops were not upon the glasses. Mrs. Rouncewell might have been sufficiently assured by hearing the rain, but that she is rather deaf, which nothing will induce her to believe.

p. 20: "The clear cold sunshine glancing down the long avenue of elms" Crafts, in passages such as these, reveals exceptional powers of description. See pp. 125–127, and 197–198. The Linden tree is based on the Gospel Oaks in Indian Woods, North Carolina. See Hecimovich, *Life and Times*, 28–29, 50–51, 53–54, 117, 156.

p. 20: Stormy weather and the creaking of the old linden tree trigger the narration of the legend of the linden and its "wild and weird influence." In much of this text, storms, particularly at night, foreshadow crises, particularly for African Americans.

p. 21: The curse on the house is earned by a series of cruelties by its first owner, culminating in the torture and death of a trusted old nurse and a lovable, shaggy, white dog. In the South, it is only the "direst act of cruelty" that could distinguish this master from other slave owners. Of course, the reason that a tree symbolizes extreme cruelty is partly historical, the very real use of trees for lynching. Its other connection is to crucifixion imagery, the use of a "tree" during the Passion.

p. 22: "Sir Clifford made it a boast...that his commands and decisions like the laws of the Medes and Persians were unalterable." This passage resembles Scott's use of the same reference in chapter 22 of *Rob Roy*:

> The dictates of my father were to MacVittie and MacFin the laws of the Medes and Persians, not to be altered, innovated, or even discussed; and the punctilios exacted by Owen in their business transactions, for he was a great lover of form.

This classical reference is to Media, an ancient country of West Asia that extended its rule over Persia circa 700 B.C. This dynasty was not overthrown until 550 B.C.

p. 26: "Lanterns were lighted and rooms illuminated; doors flung open and chambers hastily surveyed. The stately mansion is no longer a darkening mass of front, but looks most imposing to the brilliant circle as they descend from their carriages and move on towards it." This passage describing the arrival of the wedding party to Lindendale resembles the arrival of Sir Leicester and Lady Dedlock to Chesney Wold in chapter 12 of *Bleak House.*

> [T]he travelling chariot rolls on to the house; where fires gleam warmly through some of the windows, though not through so many as to give an inhabited expression to the darkening mass of front. But the brilliant and distinguished circle will soon do that.

p. 26: The "Madras handkerchiefs" that are worn by many of the slaves for the celebration of their master's wedding was a term used from approximately 1833 to 1881 to describe the slaves' silk-and-cotton kerchiefs used as headdresses.

p. 27: "opened and shut bureau-drawers, or plunged into caskets and jewel-cases" This scene of rifling through drawers is taken almost verbatim from chapter 56 of *Bleak House,* suggesting that Crafts wanted to make clear that such scenes weren't taken from real life.

> Opening and shutting table-drawers, and looking into caskets and jewel-cases, he sees the reflection of himself in various mirrors, and moralizes thereon.... Ever looking about, he has opened a dainty little chest in an inner drawer.

Crafts's literary imagination is also manifested in the turrets and drawing rooms, cloaks and embroidery that color her text. These are poetic and imaginative places and things; Crafts uses them to create set pieces of betrayal, concealment, forgiveness, and revenge.

p. 27: The true identity of Hannah's mistress is implied upon her introduction in the text. Physically, she is "small" and "brown" with a profusion of wavy, curly hair. Although those might be neutral descriptions, her lips, which are "too large," signal a warning about hidden ancestry, particularly in the racially charged South. Although the narrator owns to being "superstitious"—"people of my race and color usually are," she writes—her fear of her mistress being "haunted by a shadow or phantom" foreshadows coming disclosures.

p. 27: "There were jeweled ladies and gallant gentlemen." Once again, Crafts borrows descriptions of wealthy visitors from Dickens: "All the mirrors in the house are brought into action now: many of them after a long blank. They reflect handsome faces, simpering faces, youthful faces, faces of threescore-and-ten that will not submit to be old" (chapter 12, *Bleak House*).

p. 28: "Instead of books I studied faces and characters" Crafts here is reinforcing her authority as a narrator who, though a slave and uneducated formally, nevertheless possesses "the unerring certainty of animal instinct."

p. 28: "He was a rusty seedy old-fashioned gentleman" The character of Mr. Trappe is obviously taken from Dickens's Mr. Tulkinghorn, who is also described as an "old-fashioned old gentleman...rusty to look at" (chapter 2, *Bleak House*).

p. 28: "Yet it was not his singular features...what the old man knew." Here, the transformation of a scene from chapter 12 of *Bleak House* is much more complex. Crafts clearly knows the following passage, but adapts it for her own purposes:

> Mr. Tulkinghorn is always the same speechless repository of noble confidences: so oddly but of place, and yet so perfectly at home. They appear to take as little note of one another, as any two people, enclosed within the same walls, could. But whether each evermore watches an suspects the other, evermore mistrustful of some great reservation; whether each is evermore prepared at all points for the other, and never to be taken unawares; what each would give to know how much the other knows—all this is hidden, for the time, in their own hearts.

p. 29: " 'And we will have music and dancing there' said the host. 'Twill be such a novelty' and thither he conducted the glittering train across the hall, and along the passages, and through the rooms, and up the staircase to the illustrious presence of ancestral greatness." The passage owes a debt to Dickens's description of Mr. Tulkinghorn being conducted into the presence of Lady Dedlock in chapter 2 of *Bleak House*:

Across the hall, and up the stairs, and along the passages, and through the rooms, which are very brilliant in the season and very dismal out of it—Fairy-land to visit, but a desert to live in—the old gentleman is conducted, by a Mercury in powder, to my Lady's presence.

pp. 29–30: During the wedding party, the groaning of the linden tree signals the invocation of Rose's curse upon the house's descendants. In apparent protest, Sir Clifford's portrait falls from the wall as the new bride enters the portrait gallery. While this is not as dramatic as Walpole's *Castle of Otranto,* in which a ghost steps out of his portrait, gothic echoes can be heard.

Chapter 3

p. 31: To begin this chapter, Crafts offers a portion of Psalm 39:6:

> Surely every man walketh in a vain show: surely they are disquieted in vain: he heapeth up riches, and knoweth not who shall gather them.

Immediately following is a line of verse from "Lochiel's Warning" by Thomas Campbell (1777–1844). This warning, heavy with supernatural language, is issued by a wizard. The setting and the language of this citation underscore the gothic nature of the text:

> Tis the sunset of life gives me mystical lore And coming events cast their shadows before [55–56]

A volume of both *The Life and Letters of Thomas Campbell* (1849) and Walter Scott's *The Legend of Montrose,* in which these lines also serve as the epigraph to chapter 6 (*Collected Works,* 1824), are included in the 1850 catalogue of John Hill Wheeler's library.

p. 32: "He never mingled" Crafts continues drawing upon Dickens for her description of Mr. Trappe: "He never converses, when not professionally consulted. He is found sometimes speechless but quite at home, at corners of dinner-tables in great country houses, and near doors of drawing-rooms, concerning which the fashionable intelligence is eloquent" (chapter 2, *Bleak House*). The passage "a plainly furnished chamber...old-fashioned...and having a quiet impassive air" comes from much later (chapter 12) in Dickens's novel: "Only one room is empty. It is a turret chamber of the third order of merit, plainly but comfortably furnished, and having an old-fashioned business air."

p. 33: "the old man of the name of Trappe" Crafts follows Dickens's phrase "an old man of the name of Tulkinghorn" (chapter 33, *Bleak House*).

p. 33: Lizzy's, a quadroon, pride in the fact that her white ancestors came from "a good family" and her contention "that good blood was an inheritance," even to the slave, is a common theme in the African American literary tradition.

p. 34: "suffered the extremes of a master's fondness, a mistress's jealousy and their daughter's hate" Crafts is unusually open about discussing sexual relations between masters and their female slaves. See below, p. 177.

p. 37: "My mistress was very kind, and...she indulged me in reading whenever I desired." Compare this indulgence with that of Douglass's mistress, Sophia Auld. A mistress flouting her husband's strict prohibitions about literacy training for a slave is extraordinarily rare in the slave narratives. But so, too, of course, is a mistress who turns out to be black.

p. 37: "The next morning...I was entirely concealed." This passage echoes the following scene in the first chapter of Charlotte Brontë's *Jane Eyre* (1847):

> A small breakfast-room adjoined the drawing room: I slipped in there. It contained a book-case: I soon possessed myself of a volume, taking care that it should be one stored with pictures. I mounted into the window-seat: gathering up my feet, I sat cross-legged, like a Turk; and, having drawn the red moreen curtain nearly close, I was shrined in double retirement."

The novel is included in the 1850 catalogue of John Hill Wheeler's library.

pp. 37–38: "I am very much surprised that you should.... It is not your secret, but mine." Here, Crafts borrows her dialogue overtly from a scene between Mr. Tulkinghorn and Lady Dedlock (chapter 48, *Bleak House*), perhaps to suggest that she is guilty of neither eavesdropping nor presuming to ventriloquize the private conversation of wealthy slaveholders.

> "I am rather surprised by the course you have taken."
> "Indeed!"
> "Yes, decidedly. I was not prepared for it. I consider it a departure from our agreement and your promise. It puts us in a new position.... It is a violation of our agreement.... Why, bless my soul, Lady Dedlock.... It is no longer your secret.... It is my secret...."

p. 38: "the bank which contained my property broke" There are several volumes in both the 1850 and 1882 catalogues of John Hill Wheeler's library that deal with bank failures in the 1830s, including Michael Chevalier, *Society, Manners, and Politics in the United States* (1839).

p. 38: "You say... that you do not approve of the course" Crafts continues the conversation between Hannah's mistress and Mr. Trappe by drawing upon a much earlier dialogue between Mr. Tulkinghorn and Lady Dedlock: "'Lady Dedlock, I have not yet been able to come to a decision satisfactory to myself, on the course before me. I am not clear what to do, or how to act next. I must request you, in the mean time, to keep your secret as you have kept it so long, and not to wonder that I keep it too (chapter 41, *Bleak House*).'"

p. 40: "Finding that she remains silent...with reference to the past." Again, Crafts draws from Dickens to finish her own scene: "She is not the first to speak; appearing indeed so unlikely to be so, though he stood there until midnight, that even he is driven upon breaking silence" (chapter 48, *Bleak House*). On p. 41, the passage "She said nothing...he replied" comes from this earlier scene in chapter 41:

"Sir," she returns.... "I had better have gone. It would have been far better not to have detained me. I have no more to say."
"Excuse me, Lady Dedlock, if I add, a little more to hear."

pp. 41–42: "He pauses, and she inquires.... She breathes quickly and heavily, but answers not." The scene continues to parallel the interview between Lady Dedlock and Mr. Tulkinghorn from Dickens's *Bleak House*, chapter 41, closing with nearly the same language.

"Then why," she asks in a low voice, and without removing her gloomy look from those distant stars, "do you detain me in his house?"
"Because he *is* the consideration. Lady Dedlock, I have no occasion to tell you that Sir Leicester is a very proud man; that his reliance upon you is implicit; that the fall of that moon out of the sky, would not amaze him more than your fall from your high position as his wife."
She breathes quickly and heavily, but she stands as unflinchingly as ever he has seen her in the midst of her grandest company."

Chapter 4

p. 44: "The sins of the fathers shall be visited on the children." This phrase also appears in chapter 17 of *Bleak House:*

"I think," said my guardian, thoughtfully regarding her, "I think it must be somewhere written that the virtues of the mothers shall, occasionally, be visited on the children, as well as the sins of the fathers."

p. 50: There is an old plantation in Charles City County, Virginia, called Milton, near Tyler's Mill. It is close to the James River, and there are several steamboat landings within walking distance (a mile or so). One reader has also suggested similarities between Crafts's description of the rocks and small rapids of the river with Midlothian, Virginia, where there was another steamboat landing (Rockett's Landing), from which boats sailed to the Chesapeake and parts beyond. The area of the boating mishap fits a description of the James River near Midlothian, fifteen miles south of the James in Chesterfield County and about fifty miles west of Milton.

p. 51: "The still still night on the dusty roads, and over the quiet woods over the gardens and the feilds [sic] I lifted the window and looked out with a feeling akin to regret." The passage echoes Dickens's description of the silence before Mr. Tulkinghorn's murder in chapter 48 of *Bleak House*:

> A very quiet night. When the moon shines very brilliantly, a solitude and stillness seem to proceed from her, that influence even crowded places full of life. Not only is it a still night on dusty high roads and on hill-summits, whence a wide expanse of country may be seen in repose, quieter and quieter as it spreads away into a fringe of trees against the sky, with the grey ghost of a bloom upon them.

pp. 52–56: The scene of Hannah and her mistress hurrying away from home and spending the night in the wild with moss and cloaks as pillows echoes the scene of Jane Eyre's harrowing flight from Mr. Rochester.

Chapter 5

p. 53: In this verse, Saint Paul warns of the danger of spiritual complacency and preaches of the need to prepare for the coming of the Lord. From I Thessalonians 5:3:

> For when they shall say, Peace and safety; then sudden destruction cometh upon them, as travail upon a woman with child; and they shall not escape.

p. 53: "We took the road leading to the river, and walked hastily forward. It was not time to loiter or linger...and stumps and hillocks were strangely transferred into blood-hounds crouching to spring on their prey." The description of Hannah and her mistress's escape transforms a similar description of Mr. Jarndyce, Ada Clare, and Ellen Summerson fleeing a thunderstorm in chapter 18 of *Bleak House*:

> As it was not a time for standing among trees, we ran out of the wood, and up and down the moss-grown steps which crossed the plantation-fence like two broad-staved ladders placed back to back, and made for a keeper's lodge which was close at hand. We had often noticed the dark beauty of this lodge standing in a deep twilight of trees, and how the ivy clustered over it, and how there was a steep hollow near, where we had once seen the keeper's dog dive down into the fern as if it were water.

p. 55: When lost in the forest, Hannah comforts her frightened mistress by reciting the Holy Scriptures. Crafts chooses Psalm 46:1–2 and quotes it almost verbatim. The exact King James verse follows:

> God is our refuge and strength, a very present help in trouble.
> Therefore will not we fear, though the earth be removed, and though the mountains be carried into the midst of the sea.

p. 57: "She quietly acquiesced in my proposal" This exact line appears in Walter Scott's *Rob Roy* (1817), a volume of which appears in the 1850 catalogue of Wheeler's library. The Linden tree is based on the Gospel Oaks in Indian Woods, North Carolina. See Hecimovich, *Life and Times*, 28–29, 50–51, 53–54, 117, 156.

p. 58: Unlike slave narratives, sentimental and gothic novels rarely use the names of actual people for their characters. Place names, too, can be fictionalized. However, Milton, Virginia, is in Charles City County on the James River. Crafts's use of an actual locale in Virginia, where this section of the novel is set, made it possible to locate several individuals whose surnames are identical to several characters whom Crafts places in residence near Milton. Milton is upriver from Jamestown and downriver from Richmond.

p. 59: Frederick Hawkins is one of the novel's few characters identified with a first and last name. According to the U.S. federal census, in 1810 and 1820, Frederick Hawkins was living in Dinwiddie County, Virginia;

the distance between Milton and the closest northwestern boundary of Dinwiddie County is approximately thirty kilometers.

p. 61: Hannah and her mistress take refuge in a "sanctuary of sweet home influences." This simple, clean house with its wholesome food, pious inhabitants, and the absence of slaves is reminiscent of northern, Quaker homes in *Uncle Tom's Cabin*. However, this domicile is in Virginia and is pervaded by the influence of slavery, as is revealed when the travelers learn that Mr. Trappe lives there.

p. 62: "revolving these things in my mind" This exact phrase appears in Walter Scott's *Redgauntlet* (1824), a volume of which appears in the 1850 catalogue of Wheeler's library.

p. 64: "'We are discovered' she said with a suppressed cry of utter despair." Hannah's mistress's words follow almost exactly Lady Dedlock's expression when she confesses her sins to her daughter, Esther Summerson, after disclosing her identity to her abandoned daughter in chapter 36 of *Bleak House*:

> These words she uttered with a suppressed cry of despair, more terrible in its sound than any shriek. Covering her face with her hands, she shrunk down in my embrace as if she were unwilling that I should touch her; nor could I, by my utmost persuasions, or by any endearments I could use, prevail upon her to rise.

p. 67: The only safe place that Hannah and her mistress can find in Virginia is a deserted cabin made in the fashion of a Native American wigwam. However, it was made by "some forester," presumably white, and the description of the hut emphasizes its filth and abandonment rather than the connection to Native Americans.

p. 68: The degraded nature of the wigwam is revealed when dried blood and a hatchet with hair on the heft are found on the premises. Nearby, in the woods, skeletal remains prove that they are living at the scene of a murder. Hannah's high-strung mistress becomes further unbalanced by fear of being haunted. Instead of a pastoral resting place, they have found another cursed, gothic domicile.

p. 69: When Hannah's mistress's paranoia extends to accusations against her servant, Crafts echoes Jesus in the Garden of Gethsemane when he asks God to spare him from the Passion. From Matthew 26:39 (and in slightly different forms in Mark and Luke):

> O my Father, if it be possible, let this cup pass from me: nevertheless not as I will, but as thou wilt.

p. 72: "'I do not ask you to consider all this, well knowing that were I not dumb you would be deaf...whatever that may be." Hannah's entreaty to her captors echoes Lady Dedlock's response to Mr. Tulkinghorn when she becomes ensnared by his designs in chapter 41 of *Bleak House*:

> "Of repentance or remorse, or any feeling of mine," Lady Dedlock presently proceeds, "I say not a word. If I were not dumb, you would be deaf. Let that go by. It is not for your ears."

p. 72: Horace (65–8 B.C.) was one of the most outstanding Latin lyric poets within the Augustan circle. His work is characterized by the themes of love and friendship.

p. 75: The directive "go to him" famously appears in Charles Dickens's *Old Curiosity Shop* (1841), a copy of which appears in the 1850 catalogue of Wheeler's library.

Chapter 6

p. 77: This verse is Psalm 11:2:

> For, lo, the wicked bend their bow, they make ready their arrow upon the string, that they may privily shoot at the upright in heart.

p. 78: The description of the prison is taken almost word for word from chapter 4 of Scott's *Rob Roy*, with the important substitution of a bowie knife for a partisan, a seventeenth-century broadsword, suggesting that Crafts was aware of the differences between American and British weaponry:

> A few words were exchanged between my conductor and the turnkey in a language to which I was an absolute stranger. The bolts revolved, but with a caution which marked the apprehension that the noise might be overheard, and we stood within the vestibule of the prison of Glasgow,—a small, but strong guardroom, from which a narrow staircase led upwards, and one or two low entrances conducted to apartments on the same level with the outward gate, all secured with the jealous strength of wickets, bolts, and bars. The walls, otherwise naked, were not unsuitably garnished with iron fetters, and other uncouth implements, which might be designed for purposes still more inhuman, interspersed with partisans, guns, pistols of antique manufacture, and other weapons of defence and offence.

p. 79: "At our first entrance I turned an eager glance towards my mistress, and our conductors, but the lamp in the vestibule was too low in flame to afford my curiosity any satisfaction. Had her countenance expressed all the horror...by the dim uncertain rays." The description continues to borrow directly from Scott's *Rob Roy*, chapter 5, with the focus squarely placed on the effect produced on Hannah's mistress:

> At my first entrance I turned an eager glance towards my conductor; but the lamp in the vestibule was too low in flame to give my curiosity any satisfaction by affording a distinct perusal of his features. As the turnkey held the light in his hand, the beams fell more full on his own scarce less interesting figure.

p. 80: Crafts describes the darkness of the prison cell as Egyptian; later, the word "Stygian" was substituted. Stygian is a reference to the Greek myth of the river Styx in Hades, across which the souls of the dead are ferried.

p. 81: After Hannah is bitten by a rat in prison, she begins "to conjure strange fancies. I had heard of rats in prisons and ancient charnel-houses."

Any number of gothic stories use the horror of vermin feeding on living flesh, although this passage seems to invoke Edgar Allan Poe.

p. 82: When left alone in the dark with the rats, Hannah feels peace when she remembers parts of Scripture. In one line, Crafts writes, "The hairs of your heads are numbered your tears are in his bottle." This sentence conflates two verses, one from the Hebrew Bible and the other from the New Testament. The gospel states in Luke 12:7, "But even the very hairs of your head are all numbered. Fear not therefore: ye are of more value than many sparrows." And the Psalmist sings in Psalm 56:8, "Thou tellest my wanderings: put thou my tears into thy bottle: are they not in thy book?"

pp. 84–85: Mrs. Wright, a woman driven insane by her imprisonment, is a white woman guilty of defying slavery and attempting to save her beautiful servant, Ellen, from being sold into sexual bondage in New Orleans. In response, Mrs. Wright had cut Ellen's hair, dressed her as a boy, and tried to escape with her. This cross-dressing disguise foreshadows Hannah's own—successful—escape in masculine attire. Ellen's mode of escape—disguised initially as a white boy—mimics that used by Ellen Craft, who escaped from slavery with her husband, William, in December 1848. Their dramatic escape was widely reported in the abolitionist press in 1849 and 1850. William Wells Brown's novel, *Clotel* (1853), employs this device, and two other female slaves, Clarissa Davis and Anna Maria Weems (alias Joe Wright), used this form of cross-dressing to escape enslavement in 1854 and 1855, respectively.

Chapter 7

p. 88: From the long Psalm 119, verse 121:

> I have done judgment and justice: leave me not to mine oppressors.

p. 88: "An accumulation of misfortune...contrary operation." In this passage, Crafts follows Scott's *Rob Roy*, chapter 18:

There is one advantage in an accumulation of evils differing in cause and character, that the distraction which they afford by their contradictory operation prevents the patient from being overwhelmed under either.

p. 93: Crafts quotes Job 3:25 to indicate her despair:

For the thing which I greatly feared is come upon me, and that which I was afraid of is come unto me.

p. 94: "Then, too, the country through which we passed had such a cheerful appearance with rickyards, milestones, farm houses, wagons, swinging signs, horse troughs, trees, fields, fences, and the thousand other things that make a country landscape." Hannah and her mistress's passage in the custody of Hayes parallels the language Dickens uses to describe a journey through the countryside by Esther Summerson, Ada Claire, and Richard Carstone at the beginning of chapter 6 in *Bleak House*:

By-and-by we began to leave the wonderful city, and to proceed through suburbs which, of themselves, would have made a pretty large town, in my eyes; and at last we got into a real country road again, with windmills, rickyards, milestones, farmers' waggons, scents of old hay, swinging signs, and horse troughs: trees, fields, and hedgerows. It was delightful to see the green landscape before us, and the immense metropolis behind.

pp. 94–95: "The sun was probably an hour high when we caught the glimpse of a white house...on the top of a hill....Our conductor pointed to it with his whip, and said 'There's your journey's end.' Then putting his horses into a canter he took us forward at a great rate, though it was up-hill....Presently we lost the house, presently saw it, lost it again and again saw it; then turned into an avenue of cedar, and drew up before a fine cottage residence." The arrival of Hannah and her mistress at the cottage residence of Mr. Trappe follows almost exactly Dickens's depiction of Esther, Ada, and Richard's arrival at Mr. Jarndyce's home, in chapter 6 of *Bleak House*:

There was a light sparkling on the top of a hill before us, and the driver, pointing to it with his whip and crying, 'That's Bleak House!' put his horses into a canter, and took us forward at such a rate, up-hill though it was, that the wheels sent the road-drift flying about our heads like spray from a water-mill. Presently we lost the light, presently saw it, presently lost it, presently saw it, and turned into an avenue of trees, and cantered up towards where it was beaming brightly. It was in a window of what seemed to be an old-fashioned house, with three peaks in the roof in front, and a circular sweep leading to the porch.

p. 99: "He was sitting…an expression in his face at once complacent and self-satisfied…strictly too severely self-repressed to exhibit much feeling of any kind." In this passage, Crafts takes descriptions of Mr. Tulkinghorn from two passages twenty chapters apart (chapters 22, 41, *Bleak House*), indicating a careful sifting of the text to put together her own.

Mr. Tulkinghorn sits at one of the open windows, enjoying a bottle of old port.
There is an expression on his face as if he had discharged his mind of some grave matter, and were, in his close way, satisfied. To say of a man so severely and strictly self-repressed that he is triumphant, would be to do him as great an injustice as to suppose him troubled with love or sentiment, or any romantic weakness. He is sedately satisfied.

p. 100: "I led her to an old-fashioned sofa that stood in a little recess. She sunk down upon it, and buried her face in the cushions." Hannah's mistress is described once more in language that directly invokes Lady Dedlock in Dickens's *Bleak House*, chapter 55:

She has thrown herself upon the floor, and lies with her hair all wildly scattered, and her face buried in the cushions of a couch.

p. 101: "We are all slaves to something or somebody." Trappe seems to be familiar with common Christian phrases; this one is perhaps meant ironically. "Dash the cup of pleasure from your lips" is another popular saying, perhaps quoting Calvin's reading of Psalm 49. The line "[t]hey are mere shadows the very reverse of realities," seems to be an allusion to Plato's *Republic*, Book 9.

p. 101: "Indeed I had my suspicions for a long time—for days, weeks, months, and years."

> "I have suspected it a long while—fully known it, a little while."
> "Months?"
> "Days."
> (chapter 41, *Bleak House*)

p. 101: "You are not the first fair dame whose descent I have traced back—far back to a sable son of Africa" The scholar Werner Sollors has traced the history of novels of passing in his masterful study, *Neither Black Nor White Yet Both*.

p. 103: "Her excessive agitation had ruptured a blood-vessel, and she was fast approaching that bourne where the wicked cease from troubling and the weary are at rest." In citing the Book of Job (3:17), Crafts again follows language from chapter 19 of Scott's *Rob Roy*:

> There is therefore no room for the long rank grass, which, in most cases, partially clothes the surface of those retreats where the wicked cease from troubling, and the weary are at rest.

Chapter 8

p. 104: Crafts uses Psalm 10:12 to begin this chapter:

> Arise, O Lord; O God, lift up thine hand: forget not the humble.

p. 104: The idea for this opening scene also seems to have come from Dickens (chapter 16, *Bleak House*):

> "Is this place of abomination, consecrated ground?"
> "I don't know nothink of consequential ground," says Jo, still staring.
> "Is it blessed?" "WHICH?" says Jo, in the last degree amazed.
> "Is it blessed?" "I'm blest if I know," says Jo, staring more than ever; "but I shouldn't think it warn't. Blest?" repeats Jo, something troubled in his mind. "It an't done it much good if it is. Blest? I should think it was t'othered myself. But I don't know nothink!"

p. 107: According to the historian John W. Blassingame, suicide, such as that which Saddler reports of a slave named Louise, was not entirely uncommon within the slave community. Saddler also reports that he "lost six in one season" to suicide. See John W. Blassingame's *Slave Testimony: Two Centuries of Letters, Speeches, Interviews and Autobiographies* (Baton Rouge: Louisiana State University Press, 1977).

p. 108: "religion is so apt to make people stubborn" Throughout her text, Crafts argues implicitly that truly devout Christians will inevitably be anti-slavery.

p. 110: "'What the devil are you crying for?' he asked... 'No sir, I am not' I faltered." The scene reworks Esther Summerson's first encounter with John Jarndyce in chapter 3 of Dickens's *Bleak House*:

> It said, "What the de-vil are you crying for?"
> I was so frightened that I lost my voice, and could only answer in a whisper. "Me, sir?" For of course I knew it must have been the gentleman in the quantity of wrappings, though he was still looking out of his window.
> "Yes, you," he said, turning round.
> "I didn't know I was crying, sir," I faltered.
> "But you are!" said the gentleman. "Look here!" He came quite opposite to me from the other corner of the coach, brushed one of his large furry cuffs across my eyes (but without hurting me), and showed me that it was wet.
> "There! Now you know you are," he said. "Don't you?"
> "Yes, sir," I said.

"And what are you crying for?" said the gentleman. "Don't you want to go there?"
"Where, sir?"

p. 111: Trappe's lecture to Hannah on how to deport herself as a slave enables Crafts to expose one of the processes of objectification of a slave. Trappe admonishes her that as a slave, she "must have no mind, no desire, no purpose of your own."

p. 111: "the Alpha and Omega" "I am the Alpha and the Omega, the first and the last, the beginning and the end" (Revelation 22:13).

p. 112: "took her to New Orleans…and made her his wife" New Orleans was thought to be a site of unusual ethnic hybridity and miscegenation in antebellum America.

Chapter 9

p. 114: Although Crafts identifies her citation as from the Book of Jeremiah, this verse is actually Lamentations 5:1:

> Remember, O Lord, what is come upon us: consider, and behold our reproach.

p. 114: Seeing the freedom of birds, Hannah despairs of her enslavement until she remembers God's concern for all living creatures, but especially for his people. She paraphrases Luke 12:6–7, whose text is quoted below:

> Are not five sparrows sold for two farthings, and not one of them is forgotten before God?
> But even the very hairs of your head are all numbered. Fear not therefore: ye are of more value than many sparrows.

p. 115: "Then by a sudden transition I thought of the place to which I was going, of the people I should see and serve, what they would say and whether I should like them and they me. I was recalled to passing events by a sudden start of the horse and the voice of Saddler calling 'to take care.'"

Once again Crafts appears to be transforming a scene from Dickens's *Bleak House* (chapter 3). Hannah's thoughts parallel exactly Esther Summerson's reflections on her first journey following the death of her godmother.

> I thought of my dead godmother; of the night when I read to her; of her frowning so fixedly and sternly in her bed; of the strange place I was going to; of the people I should find there, and what they would be like, and what they would say to me; when a voice in the coach gave me a terrible start.

p. 116: "Very respectable people...; are they better than I am, who sells them?" Crafts is at pains to weave the blanket of guilt shared by slave catcher and slaveholder alike.

p. 117: "he thrust his hand deep into the capacious pocket... 'It's very good, eat'" This passage echoes a famously kind moment in Esther Summerson's life (in chapter 3, *Bleak House*), which either curiously suggests that Crafts does not want us to dislike Saddler, the slave trader, or suggests that Esther's guardian is a kind of slave trader himself.

> After a little while, he opened his outer wrapper, which appeared to me large enough to wrap up the whole coach, and put his arm down into a deep pocket in the side.
> "Now, look here!" he said. "In this paper," which was nicely folded, "is a piece of the best plum-cake that can be got for money—sugar on the outside an inch thick, like fat on mutton chops. Here's a little pie (a gem this is, both for size and quality), made in France. And what do you suppose it's made of? Livers of fat geese. There's a pie! Now let's see you eat 'em."

p. 117: "to hear my people sing, to have them laugh, and see them jovial and merry" Frederick Douglass makes the point that "slaves sing most when they are most unhappy. The songs of the slave represent the sorrows of his heart; and he is relieved by them, only as an aching heart is relieved by its tears."

p. 119: "They were all colored" Harriet Wilson, author of the novel *Our Nig* (1859), employs the word *colored* in the same effortless manner as

Crafts does here. In the preface to her novel, Wilson appeals to her "colored brethren universally" to purchase her book.

p. 120: "I am one of that miserable class" Crafts's refusal to pass for white—except to escape—is a leitmotif of her novel, culminating in her decision to live in a free colored community in New Jersey when she finally manages to reach the North.

p. 121: While recovering from the wreck that kills Saddler, Hannah is strangely calm. She speculates that "it might be that the Redeemer was leading me in spirit through the green pastures and beside the still waters of Gospel truth and peace." She is paraphrasing Psalm 23:2: "He maketh me to lie down in green pastures: he leadeth me beside the still waters."

pp. 121–122: "I shall say little of these sick experiences . . . How well I remember the . . . wedding party." Once again, Crafts has modeled Hannah's thoughts on Esther Summerson's:

> Perhaps the less I say of these sick experiences, the less tedious and the more intelligible I shall be. . . . By and by, my strength began to be restored. Instead of lying, with so strange a calmness, watching what was done for me, as if it were done for some one else whom I was quietly sorry for, I helped it a little, and so on to a little more and much more, until I became useful to myself, and interested and attached to life again.
>
> How well I remember the pleasant afternoon when I was raised in bed with pillows for the first time, to enjoy a great tea-drinking with Charley! (chapter 35, *Bleak House*)

p. 123: "vows and responsibilities strangely fearful when taken in connection with their servile condition" The slave narratives frequently draw attention to the perilous nature of "marriage" among slaves. No one is more eloquent about the fragility of marriage within the slave community than Harriet Jacobs. See her slave narrative, *Incidents in the Life of a Slave Girl* (1861), edited by Jean Fagan Yellin (Cambridge: Harvard University Press, 1987).

p. 124: "the winds arose, clouds obscured the firmament, and there was darkness, and lightning, and rain" Crafts often indicates a reversal in fortune for her characters by a rapid weather change. This is a standard convention of gothic novels.

Chapter 10

p. 125: The author attributes this verse to King Solomon. The King James version of Proverbs 31:30 reads as follows:

> Favour is deceitful, and beauty is vain: but a woman that feareth the Lord, she shall be praised.

pp. 125–127: Nearly the entire description of Forget Me Not (perhaps taken from an Amelia Opie poem of the same name) comes from chapter 6 of *Bleak House*.

p. 128: "and even now it is not my intention to draw their portraits" Crafts, in this passage, substitutes what we might think of as a metaphysical verisimilitude—a portrait of inner attributes and characteristics—for the physical verisimilitude common to the slave narratives. John H. Henry, a Presbyterian clergyman, was living in Stafford County, Virginia, in 1850. Stafford County is eighty miles from Milton. Henry was born in New York.

p. 129: "'Mrs Henry' I said . . . 'I have an inexpressible desire to stay with you. You are so good, accomplished, and Christian-like, could I only have the happiness to be your slave, your servant.'" Hannah echoes directly Mademoiselle Hortense, Lady Dedlock's servant, when she applies to Esther Summerson to become her domestic maid in chapter 23 of *Bleak House*:

> "Assuredly; mademoiselle, I am thankful for your politeness. Mademoiselle, I have an inexpressible desire to find service with a young lady who is good, accomplished, beautiful. You are good, accomplished, and beautiful as an angel. Ah, could I have the honour of being your domestic!"

p. 129: "'My sphere is so humble, and I am so forlorn and destitute, and you are by nature and position so far above me that you may not think . . . and save me; for you can.'" One of the most fascinating aspects of Hannah Crafts's borrowings is how varied she is in using passages while reworking them. After drawing on the language of Dickens's Hortense in chapter 23 of *Bleak House* to depict Hannah's plea to Mrs. Henry to buy her, Crafts immediately draws on the language of Mrs. Rouncewell seeking Lady Dedlock's assistance from chapter 55:

> "My Lady, my good Lady," the old housekeeper pleads with genuine simplicity, "I am so humble in my place, and you are by nature so high and distant, that you may not think what I feel for my child; but I feel so much, that I have come here to make so bold as to beg and pray you not to be scornful of us, if you can do us any right or justice at this fearful time!"

And then she switches right back to echoing Mademoiselle Hortense in chapter 23. Crafts writes, "Let me hope a moment. I do not ask you to buy me and then set me free"—echoing directly Hortense: "Let me hope, a moment! Mademoiselle, I know this service would be more retired than that which I have quitted."

p. 129: "a scallion"   Crafts meant "scullion," a kitchen helper.

p. 130: "And why not, my dear Madam. . . . one . . . who would do her utmost in all possible things . . . we should both be happier" parallels Hortense again in chapter 23, "Mademoiselle, I will—no matter, I will do my utmost possible, in all things. If you accept my service, you will not repent it. Mademoiselle, you will not repent it, and I will serve you well. You don't know how well!"

p. 130: "Compassionated" means "sympathize with or pity."

p. 131: "the accusing spirit of Cesar summoning Brutus to Philippi" Marcus Junius Brutus (78?–42 B.C.) was made governor and then praetor of Cispaline Gaul by Julius Caesar in 46 and 44 B.C., respectively. He famously took part in the assassination of Caesar. Mark Anthony and Octavian, the first of the Roman emperors, fought Brutus and Cassius at Philippi in 42 B.C. Brutus committed suicide after his forces were defeated. Shakespeare immortalized Brutus in his tragedy *Julius Caesar*, which is most probably Crafts's source for this reference. Crafts, like Harriet Wilson, enjoyed a broad, if not deep, exposure to literature through the sort of texts or "classics" commonly found in a small library in a middle-class household in America in the mid-nineteenth century. See Appendix C for books in Wheeler's library.

pp. 131–132: "and yet my heart rose against the man. . . . I almost felt that he had done me a personal injury, an irreparable wrong." While Crafts demonstrates remarkable self-control throughout her text, this reaction of anger, disgust, and disbelief seems quite genuine and human, unlike the unbelievable Christian tolerance and forgiveness of some of the black characters in *Uncle Tom's Cabin*. Crafts's attitude here, if rendered in contemporary terms, would be "Are you serious? You must be joking!"

p. 132: "a friend and distant relative in North Carolina" Mrs. Henry is referring to John Hill Wheeler.

p. 132: "Their names are Wheeler" The passage refers to John Hill Wheeler, a native of North Carolina, and his second wife, Ellen. In Washington, D.C., Mr. Wheeler served in a number of government positions during the Pierce and Buchanan administrations. See notes to chapter 12.

p. 134: "Alas; those that view slavery only as it relates to physical sufferings or the wants of nature, can have no conception of its greatest evils." Crafts, like Douglass, makes several perceptive counterintuitive claims about the nature of slavery and its effects on the slaves, seemingly from inside of the slave community.

Chapter 11

p. 135: This is one of the three chapters in which Crafts uses a poetic as well as a biblical citation. The first quotation is Psalm 140:1:

> Deliver me, O Lord, from the evil man: preserve me from the violent man.

The second citation is translated from the German poet G. A. Bürger, "The Ballad of William and Helen."

p. 135: "I have always thought that in a state of servitude marriage . . . is at the bottom of many troubles and afflictions that might otherwise be escaped." Hannah's refutation of slave marriages echoes Mr. Tulkinghorn's baiting denunciation of marriage in general to Lady Dedlock in chapter 41 of *Bleak House*:

> "My experience teaches me," says Mr. Tulkinghorn, who has by this time got his hands in his pockets, and is going on in his business consideration of the matter, like a machine. "My experience teaches me, Lady Dedlock, that most of the people I know would do far better to leave marriage alone. It is at the bottom of three-fourths of their troubles. So I thought when Sir Leicester married, and so I always have thought since."

p. 135: "The slave, if he or she desires to be content, should always remain in celibacy" The slave narratives are replete with observations of this sort about the evils that slavery can inflict, capriciously, on those slaves who think that they are "married." Slavery recognized no legal institutions such as marriage among slaves.

p. 136: "lest 'de ghost' should steal on them unaware" Crafts, like Douglass and Harriet Jacobs, uses black dialect to distinguish between house and field servants, educated and uneducated, rational and superstitious slaves. Crafts does not romanticize the members of the slave community, drawing distinctions among the slaves as an insider would rather than reducing their differences and distinctions to a blanket, common identity, consciousness, or culture predetermined by their race or ethnicity. The more distinctions between blacks that an author draws, in other words, the more likely it is that he or she has observed slavery from inside the institution. Here, Crafts distances herself from the Henrys' other house servants by dismissing them as slaves to superstition, unlike herself. All the slave narrators, in one form or another, draw distinctions between the "representative," intelligent, questing narrator and the bulk of the slaves demeaned by slavery whom the narrator will ultimately leave behind. In a sense, this class of slaves will become the progenitor of W. E. B. Du Bois's (1868–1963) famous concept of "The Talented Tenth."

p. 137: "the most ludicrous state of terror conceivable" This hilarious scene, at the servant Jo's expense, is designed to reinforce Hannah's status as a superior, rational person, one capable, of course, of writing her own narrative. This is a common rhetorical strategy found in the slave narratives. The ex-slave author William Wells Brown (1814–84) used dialect and humor brilliantly, especially in his novel, *Clotel*. Parody of the sort that Crafts uses here is dependent for its effect on intimate knowledge of the original. See also Jo's argument with the other servants about whether ghosts can eat! Not all of the slaves speak in black vernacular English. See pp. 145–147 for Charlotte's and William's discourse about escape.

p. 138: "[B]ut putting this and that together as the adage runs . . . " resembles "and a general putting of this and that together by the wrong end" in chapter 25 of *Bleak House*.

pp. 138–140: "Neither did I pause to ask myself by what right I presumed to interfere with the secrets of a house where I was myself admitted only by tolerance. . . . Wherefore should I attempt to unravel a mystery that did not concern me, or to interfere in affairs, of which I should only be an observer." This passage was borrowed from the following interior dialogue from chapter 17 of Scott's *Rob Roy*:

> I was led to question the right I had to interfere with Miss Vernon's secrets, or with those of my uncle's family. What was it to me whom my uncle might choose to conceal in his house, where I was

myself a guest only by tolerance? And what title had I to pry into the affairs of Miss Vernon, fraught, as she had avowed them to be, with mystery, into which she desired no scrutiny?

p. 140: "How could I acquit my conscience of cruelty and wrong"   Hannah, seemingly obsessed with conformity to duty, here chooses loyalty to her fellow slave Charlotte over an inner obligation to be a consistently truthful person.

p. 142: "In attending these religious exercises"   The religious practices of the slaves, "earnest and fervid," as Crafts puts it, were frequently commented upon in slave narratives. Though obviously conservative in her manners, beliefs, and practices, Crafts nevertheless found these services "an agre[e]able diversion for my thoughts."

p. 142: "a very pleasant walk among the negro lodges"   Crafts is demonstrating in this paragraph the inherent love of beauty, order, and industry among slaves who are respected, nourished, and well cared for.

p. 142: "Various groups of persons, young and old, all of whom seemed impressed with a . . . reverential feeling of the sanctity of the day. . . . I shall not soon forget the pleasing intimation of a devotional character impressed on each little party, by some perhaps formally assumed, but sincerely characterising the greater number, hushing the cheerful gayety of the young into a more quiet, though no less interesting exchange of sentiments, and suppressing the vehement arguments of those in more advanced age." Crafts describes a Sunday evening visit among the slave huts on the Henrys' plantation by following, but significantly altering, similar lines describing a Sunday walk outside Glasgow just beyond the banks of the Clyde by Scott's protagonist Frank Osbaldistone in chapter 21 of *Rob Roy*:

> Various groups of persons, all of whom, young and old, seemed impressed with a reverential feeling of the sanctity of the day, passed along the large open meadow which lies on the northern bank of the Clyde, and serves at once as a bleaching-field and pleasure-walk for the inhabitants, or paced with slow steps the

long bridge which communicates with the southern district of the county. All that I remember of them was the general, yet not unpleasing, intimation of a devotional character impressed on each little party, formally assumed perhaps by some, but sincerely characterising the greater number, which hushed the petulant gaiety of the young into a tone of more quiet, yet more interesting, interchange of sentiments, and suppressed the vehement argument and protracted disputes of those of more advanced age.

p. 143: Crafts states that the "ludicrous countenances" of the fearful slaves could have "provoked a smile on the lip of Heraclitus." The author consistently distances herself from other slaves by her lack of fear and superstition. The Greek philosopher Heraclitus (535–475 B.C.) was often contrasted with "the laughing philosopher," Democritus, because of his "melancholy philosophy."

p. 143: "a withered smoke-dried face, black as ebony"   Black authors in the nineteenth century often strove to differentiate among the variety of colors of the slaves, both to chart their individuality and to testify to the master's or overseer's penchant for sexual relations with female slaves, leading to the birth of mulattos. Over subsequent generations, the colors of members of the black community became quite variegated.

pp. 143–144: Despite her initial decision to remain discreet, Hannah here shares Charlotte's secret with Mrs. Henry. She seems to have done so to enlist Mrs. Henry as Charlotte's ally rather than to betray her, judging from Mrs. Henry's calm and circumspect reaction. The entire scene, as it unfolds over the next four pages, is designed to specify the cruelties of slavery through the severing of the marriage bond, one of the holiest institutions of Christianity.

p. 144: "That she hoped and trusted Charlotte's good sense would prevent her taking any rash or precipitate step . . . to give the former a few words of caution and advice." The scene resembles in language and structure a scene from chapter 14 of *Bleak House*:

> As I trusted that I might have sufficient influence with Miss Jellyby to prevent her taking any very rash step, if I fully accepted the confidence she was so willing to place in me, poor girl, I proposed that she and I and Peepy should go to the Academy, and afterwards meet my guardian and Ada at Miss Flite's—whose name I now learnt for the first time.

pp. 145–146: "I am going with my dear husband, but Hannah I wanted a female friend to go with us . . . who can look danger in the face . . . whose counsel could guide us in emergencies, who would be true, and zealous, and faithful; my heart turned to you as the one." Charlotte's attempt to enlist Hannah in her escape to the north matches language Mademoiselle Hortense uses in chapter 23 of *Bleak House* when seeking service to Esther Summerson:

> "Why not, when you can have one so devoted to you? Who would be enchanted to serve you; who would be so true, so zealous, and so faithful, every day! Mademoiselle, I wish with all my heart to serve you."

p. 147: "Duty, gratitude and honor forbid it." Throughout her text, Crafts seeks to chart her inner nobility of spirit in such a way as to justify—at last—her own inevitable need to flee slavery, ultimately, to protect her virtue and virginity, contrary to stereotypes of black women as licentious and hypersexualized. This was a clever rhetorical and, implicitly, ideological strategy, but one not without its risks. Crafts often comes across as the metaphorical grandmother—a prototype—of the tragic mulatto commonly found in black fiction at the turn of the century who renders herself noble against the ignobility of lower-class, or darker, African Americans. She can also be taken as an antecedent of the light-complexioned members of the middle class whose aristocratic pretensions are bitterly critiqued in E. Franklin Frazier's *Black Bourgeoisie* (Glencoe, Ill.: Free Press, 1957). While often masked or muted, in other words, class divisions in the black community have a long and consistent history, and arose within the institution of slavery.

p. 147: "Well, you can hug the chain if you please. With me it is liberty or death." The phrase "hug the chain" has as its source a short, sardonic poem by Byron called "Stanzas": "Could Love for ever / Run like a river, / And Time's endeavour / Be tried in vain— / No other pleasure / With this could measure; / And like a treasure / We'd hug the chain." Furthermore, William Wirt's popular *Life of Patrick Henry* (1831) is listed in the 1882 catalogue of John Hill Wheeler's library.

p. 148: "Thy desire shall be thy husband"   In Genesis 3:16, God rules that because of Eve's involvement in eating the fruit of the tree of knowledge, women shall desire and be ruled by their husbands. Moreover, God says, "I will greatly multiply thy sorrow and thy conception; in sorrow thou shall bring forth children." The actual quotation from Genesis is "thy desire shall be to thy husband."

p. 149: "and with these hounds real Cuban"   Bloodhounds were used to track fugitive slaves. The three principal breeds of bloodhound are English, Cuban, and African. Cuban bloodhounds are thought to be a variety of the mastiff.

Chapter 12

p. 151: From Psalm 69, verse 29:

> But I am poor and sorrowful: let thy salvation, O God, set me up on high.

p. 151: "wipe the death-damps from her brow"   This line echoes a passage from Felicia Hemans's poem "Gertrude, or Fidelity Til Death" (1828) ("She wiped the death damps from his brow / With her pale hands and soft") and prefigures a similar scene from chapter 3 of *The Adventures of Tom Sawyer* (1876): "And thus he would die—out in the cold world, with no shelter over his homeless head, no friendly hand to wipe the death-damps from his brow, no loving face to bend pityingly over him when the great agony came."

p. 152: "Mrs Wheeler came on her summer visit"   At this point in the text, Crafts is drawing upon an actual historical event—the escape of a female slave named Jane Johnson from John Hill Wheeler in 1855—to develop her plot. Her decision to do so and to use the real names of Jane and the Wheelers greatly facilitated the authentication of her narrative. The most likely time of Mrs. Ellen Wheeler's visit to the Henrys, as suggested by a scrutiny of Mr. Wheeler's diary, was mid-1856. She was in Nicaragua when Jane escaped, having moved there with her husband in 1854. At this date he still held the post of Resident Minister to Nicaragua and was therefore absent from the United States. The latter half of Wheeler's diary for 1856 is lost (last entry: May 23), but his return in November 1857 is recorded in his diary for the following year. If Mrs. Wheeler visited the Henrys in summer 1856, then she must have returned to the United States from Nicaragua some time between late 1855 and early 1856.

> John Hill Wheeler diary, 1857 [p. 97]:
> Sunday, November 15
> This day a year ago I landed at New York from Central America in bad health and spirits. Today I am well and contented, thanks to kind Providence.

p. 152: "Her two waiting maids had ran [sic] off to the North"   Crafts is fictionalizing Jane Johnson's escape with her two sons, Daniel and Isaiah, from Wheeler in July 1855, on a trip from Washington to New York. Jane escaped in Philadelphia. Wheeler's diary entry on the escape reads as follows:

> Wed, 18 [July 1855]
> Left Washington City at 6 o'clock with Jane Daniel and Isaiah (my servants) for New York. D. Webster Esq. 6th Street Phila. in Co. Reached Phila. [a]t 1 1/2—went to Mr. Sully's to get Ellen's [i.e., Wheeler's wife] things—and hurried to the Warf [sic]. The Boat had just left—so we remained until 5 o'clock—took dinner at Bloodgood's Hotel foot of Walnut Street. At 4 1/2 went on board of the Steamer Washington, and a few minutes before the boat started a gang of Negroes led on by Passmore Williamson an Abolitionist came up to us, and told Jane that [i]f she would go ashore she was free—On my remonstrating they seized me by the collar, threatened to cut my throat if I resisted, took the servants by force, they remonstrating and crying *murder*. Hurried them on

Textual Annotations 287

shore—to a carriage which was waiting, and drove [stricken: "off"] them off.

p. 153: "Jane was very handy at almost everything." Mrs. Wheeler is referring to Jane Johnson.

p. 154: "He wanted me to come, and I couldn't think of doing without her in my feeble health." Crafts is fictionalizing an actual event here: Wheeler was bringing Jane from Washington to Nicaragua, to serve his wife, Ellen. When Mrs. Wheeler remarks that "I didn't much like the idea of bringing her to Washington," Crafts is echoing warnings that Wheeler had received about attempting to transport a slave from Washington through Philadelphia—a hotbed of anti-slavery sentiment. Slavery was legal in Washington. It was in Philadelphia that Jane Johnson escaped.

p. 154: "My husband . . . occupies a high official position in the Federal City" Wheeler held a number of government jobs.

Wheeler's diary for 1854 [p. 19] reads as follows:

> Wed. 2 Aug. [1854]
> My Birthday—48 years of age—This day I received a commission from the President [Pierce] appointing me by and with the advice and consent of the Senate Minister Resident of the U.S. near the Republic of Nicaragua, Central America.

> Thurs. 10th [August 1854]
> Resigned my commission as Assistant Sec[retar]y to the President and Henry E. Baldwin of New Hampshire appointed my successor.

p. 154: "swarming with the enemies of our domestic institution": slavery.

p. 154: "and if strangers called on her during my absence, or she received messages from them" Crafts here echoes Wheeler's command to Jane Johnson not to speak with abolitionists or free colored people while they visited Philadelphia.

p. 154: "Those who suppose that southern ladies keep their attendants at a distance, scarcely speaking to them" This is one of the several keen observations about slavery that Crafts makes throughout her text, reflecting her experience of slavery—and especially of the master- or mistress-slave relationship—from the inside, that is, as a slave. As William Andrews observes, Elizabeth Keckley, in her slave narrative, *Behind the Scenes or Thirty Years a Slave, and Four Years in the White House* (1868), states that such scenes between mistress and slave are not uncommon. Andrews, author of the definitive study of the slave narratives, finds this passage convincing proof of Crafts's authenticity as an African American woman and a former slave. I quote Andrews's argument at length:

> In chapter 14 of *Behind the Scenes* Keckley notes that soon after the war is over, her former mistress, Ann Garland, asks her to come back to see the family in Virginia. The idea that such a reunion would appeal to her former owners is incredible to Keckley's northern friends, who think that since Keckley was a slave she couldn't possibly care about the Garlands or they about her. Keckley goes on to recount her reunion with the Garlands to show that they think very highly of her even after the war.
>
> Of course, Mrs. Wheeler doesn't think highly of Hannah, but the fact that the narrator of that story is at pains to point out to her reader that female slaveholders treat their female slaves with a great deal more intimacy than standard abolitionist propaganda acknowledges allies the Crafts narrative to that of Keckley, who also insists to her northern white friends, equally convinced by antislavery propaganda that black women and white women couldn't possibly have any basis for communication after the war, that there was an intimate connection between her and her former mistress. In Keckley that intimacy is based on genuine mutual concern—at least that's the way she portrays it—whereas in Crafts's, Mrs. Wheeler cares nothing for Hannah as a person. The key similarity, however, is that in both texts, a black woman is trying to get her white readers to realize that the relationship between white and black women in slavery was not one of mere dictation, white to black, or mere subjugation of the black woman by the white woman. A white woman in the North in the antebellum era who wanted to preserve her antislavery credentials would have found it hard to make such a characterization of intimacy between women slaveholders and their female slaves. A white south-

ern woman sympathetic to slavery might make such a claim, but she wouldn't suggest that Mrs. Wheeler is as shallow and self-interested in cultivating Hannah as Crafts makes her out to be. Thus only a black woman who had herself been a slave would be in a position of authority to make such a claim about this kind of intimacy between white and black women in slavery.

(Letter to Henry Louis Gates Jr., October 26, 2001)

p. 155: "Did you try to recover them? . . . he disliked making a hue and cry." As is clear from Wheeler's diary entries, a protracted attempt was made during the next few years to secure Jane Johnson's return; failing in this, Wheeler attempted without success to obtain an indemnity for her value from the state of Pennsylvania. These overtures were made through legal channels, "making a hue and cry" of enormous proportions. Crafts here is mocking the Wheelers for their desperate efforts to retrieve Jane Johnson.

> Wed. 18 [July 1855]
> I went to the Marshal's [sic] Office and with his Deputy, Mr. Mulloy, went to Judge Kane, who ordered a Habeas Corpus—returned to town about 10 o'clock, to Mr. J. C. Hazlitt the Dep[uty] Cl[er]k—took out the writ, then we went to the House of Williamson who had absconded. At 1 o'clock I left Phila. and arrived at New York at 6—and put up at the Washington House.

p. 155: "The Senator from Ohio" is a thinly veiled reference to Passmore Williamson, the head of the Pennsylvania Anti-Slavery Society, who facilitated Jane Johnson's escape.

pp. 156–157: "while Mrs Wheeler requested me to read for her" Crafts is demonstrating her mastery of literacy at this point in her life, implicitly establishing her credentials as an author. This reversal of the topos of a white person reading to an illiterate slave is a very powerful rhetorical gesture, underscoring Crafts's intellectual superiority over other slaves and her equality—or superiority—of intellect with her white mistress. Similarly, on p. 157, Crafts writes of how "that afternoon she [Mrs. Wheeler] dictated a letter for me to write." Frederick Douglass equates learning to read and write with the desire to be free, to run away.

p. 158: "you prefer the service of a lady to that of a gentleman, in which probably you would be compelled to sacrifise [sic] honor and virtue" Crafts foreshadows the event that will force her to escape—the sacrifice of her virginity to rape sanctioned by her master and mistress.

Chapter 13

p. 161: Although Ninevah is mentioned four times as a "great city" in the short Book of Jonah, it is never described as "full of people" in the Bible. However, in Jonah 4:11, Ninevah is said to have "sixscore thousand persons." Crafts's reliance on the oral tradition, while inaccurate, certainly conveys the meaning.

p. 161: This description of Washington is an obvious transformation of the opening lines of *Bleak House:*

> London. Michaelmas Term lately over, and the Lord Chancellor sitting in Lincoln's Inn Hall. Implacable November weather. As much mud in the streets, as if the waters had but newly retired from the face of the earth, and it would not be wonderful to meet a Megalosaurus, forty feet long or so, waddling like an elephantine lizard up Holborn Hill.

The description also seems to draw once again on Bulfinch's *Age of Fable:*

> The slime with which the earth was covered by the waters of the flood produced an excessive fertility, which called forth every variety of production, both bad and good. Among the rest, Python, an enormous serpent, crept forth, the terror of the people, and lurked in the caves of Mount Parnassus. Apollo slew him with his arrows—weapons which he had not before used against any but feeble animals, hares, wild goats, and such game [Chapter 3].

p. 161: "perhaps a Python might be caught by another Apollo" According to legend, Delphi, home of the famous Greek oracle, was protected by a dragon or serpent (Python) in the pre-Hellenic period.

Greek mythology states that the god Apollo slew the Python, ousted the deity (Mother Earth) it was guarding, and founded his oracle there.

pp. 161–162: "where a negro slave was seen slipping and sliding but a moment before Alas; that mud and wet weather should have so little respect for aristocracy" Crafts is parodying the snobbery of white governmental officials in this passage.

p. 162: "Gloom everywhere." This passage also echoes and transforms Dickens (chapter 1, *Bleak House*):

> Fog everywhere. Fog up the river, where it flows among green aits and meadows; fog down the river, where it rolls defiled among the tiers of shipping, and the waterside pollutions of a great (and dirty) city. Fog on the Essex marshes, fog on the Kentish heights. At the time that Crafts served the Wheelers in D.C., the Stabler-Leadbetter Apothecary was a popular cosmetics retailer with a location near the capital that served the District's leading families. The scene of fetching the beautifying powder from "a shop on Pennsylvania Avenue, much frequented by the slaves of fashionable Ladies," matches the author's likely experiences. See Hecimovich, *Life and Times*, 230–32.

p. 163: "great Italian chemist, a Signor with an unpronounceable name" A February 22, 1851, article in *Scientific American* (an issue owned by Crafts's master, John Hill Wheeler) asserts that pomades made from silver nitrate powder will turn hair black. A June 11, 1853, article, "Fulminating Substances," in *Scientific American* (also in Wheeler's collection) discusses the work of French chemist Claude-Louis Berthollet and Italian chemist Luigi Brugnatelli, who in 1798 made a fine white powder from silver nitrate with tremendous detonating power:

> Fulminating silver may be made by precipitating a solution of nitrate of silver by lime water, drying the precipitate by exposure to the air for two or three days, and pouring on it liquid ammonia. When it is thus converted into a black powder, the liquid must be poured off, and the powder left to dry in the air. It detonates with

the gentlest heat, or even with the slightest friction, so that it must not be removed from the vessel in which it is made. If a drop of water fall upon it, the percussion will cause it to explode.

p. 163: "Tan, or freckless [freckles], or wrinkles, or other unseemly blotches would simultaneously disappear" The description seems to echo a passage from John Gauden's *Discourse on Artificial Beauty* (1662), which was included in the 1882 catalogue of John Hill Wheeler's library:

> [women who] contend against the Defects, Deformities and Decayes of Nature and Age, as may be, by Washings, Anointings, and Plasterings, by many Secret Medicaments, and Close Recipes, which may either fill and plump their skins, if flat and wrinkled, or smooth and polish them, if rugged and chapt, or clear and brighten them, if tann'd and freckled...

p. 164: "Report said that he [Mr. Wheeler] had actually quarreled with the President, and challenged a senator to fight a duel, besides laying a cowhide... over the broad shoulders of a member of Congress." Wheeler states his difficulties in office at this time in entirely circumscribed terms, ignoring his indiscreet support of the self-styled General Walker's exploits in Central America, which led to his dismissal from his position in Nicaragua.

> Diary for 1857 [p. 10]:
> Monday, March 2, [printed "February," struck out, replaced by hand printed "March"]
> Went to President's, heard him reply to a com[mittee?] from Texas—had a conference as to Nic[aragu]a. He resolved to have no diplomatic relations with Nic.a and of course no use for me—[I] resigned on this ground alone.

Later in 1857, after the Wheelers' visit to North Carolina and Hannah's escape from the plantation there, Wheeler's political fortunes changed for the better. At some point after his return, he was appointed clerk of the Department of the Interior. Later, he was selected for another post, as appears below, but he apparently did not accept it.

Diary for 1857 [p. 109]:
Tuesday, December 22
Met Mr. Craig who informed me that I had been selected by the Com.[mittee] for For.[eign] Affairs as their Clerk—

There are references in this diary to Mr. Wheeler's own pugnacious nature, as remarked by Crafts, but notices of other attacks occur later in his diary for 1860. Crafts is most probably referring to the attack of Preston Brooks of South Carolina with a cane on Charles Sumner of Massachusetts in the Senate on May 22, 1856. This event is not recorded by Wheeler, though as it occurred a day before the last surviving entry in his diary of 1856, it may have been reported by him in a later, now lost, entry. Wheeler's diary reports two other incidents of violence following Hannah's escape:

Diary for 1860 [p. 55]:
Friday 13th [April]
Went to Capitol; Pryor of Va. Challenged Potter of Missouri; accepted to fight with bowie knives—declined by Pryor as unseemly & so the matters end—Friends of both claim for each the triumph—which will produce other difficulties.
Diary for 1860 [p. 102]:
Sunday 8th [July]
Lovely day but very cool for the time of year. Bathed and called to Gen[era]l Bowman, my opposite neighbour, who was attacked on yesterday morning by E. B. Schnabel, with a cane, and severely wounded. He made a speech at a Douglass [sic] meeting on Tuesday evening last, which the Constitution (Genl. Bowman's paper) spoke of, and of Schnabel—hence [?] the attack.

p. 165: Crafts could be referring to George Washington Riggs (1813–81), a prominent banker and co-owner of the Corcoran and Riggs Bank in Washington, D.C., between 1837 and 1848, when Riggs resigned his partnership. In 1854 Riggs took over the bank, renaming it Riggs and Co., and expanded it considerably. Riggs, in other words, was a prominent name in Washington when Hannah Crafts lived there.

p. 167: "'And faith, nor do I know' reiterates the husband. 'A woman of your fine presence has no right to be out of spirits. That isn't a countenance to be sad or meloncholly [sic]. Then you haven't no care, no public or private burdens on your mind. You never ask for offices without expectations of gaining them. You never ask for offices, my dear.'" The passage reworks Mr. Bucket's interrogation of George Rouncewell in chapter 49 of Dickens's *Bleak House*, altering gender and circumstance to match the Wheeler household.

> "That's your sort!" says Mr Bucket. "Why should you ever have been otherwise? A man of your fine figure and constitution has no right to be out of spirits. That ain't a chest to be out of spirits, is it, ma am? And you haven't got anything on your mind, you know, George; what could you have on your mind!"

The parallel continues in the next paragraph. In *The Bondwoman's Narrative*, Crafts writes, "He [Mr. Wheeler] dwells rather longer on this phrase ['You never ask for offices'] than is strictly necessary, considering the extent and variety of his conversational abilities. Twice or thrice he repeats it with his peculiar listening face, as if expecting an answer." Dickens's original presentation features Mr. Bucket: "Somewhat harping on this phrase ['what could you have on your mind!'], considering the extent and variety of his conversational powers, Mr. Bucket twice or thrice repeats it to the pipe he lights, and with a listening face that is particularly his own."

p. 169: "What this prospective obligation might be he did not think proper to specify, but his finishing of the sentence restores him to favor, and the lady's look imply, tho she does not say 'what a sensible man this husband of mine is. Surely if the public understood its interests he would have been laden with offices before this time.'" The passage directly echoes and reworks Sir Leicester Dedlock's conversation with Volumnia in chapter 40 of *Bleak House*:

> Volumnia's finishing the sentence restores her to favour. Sir Leicester, with a gracious inclination of his head, seems to say to himself, "A sensible woman this, on the whole, though occasionally precipitate."

p. 171: Mr. Wheeler points out that Mrs. Wheeler's face is "black as Tophet." Tophet is the Hebrew Bible's name for hell, and Tophet is mentioned nine times in the Book of Jeremiah. In Isaiah 30:33, Tophet's history is explained as follows:

> For Tophet is ordained of old; yea, for the king it is prepared; he hath made it deep and large: the pile thereof is fire and much wood; the breath of the Lord, like a stream of brimstone, doth kindle it.

Obviously, Tophet's "blackness" relates to the ash and burned wood present in large amounts.

p. 173: "'Now, my dear' said Mr Wheeler {'}you look like my own sweet wife again, fresh and rosy as the morning.'" The passage resembles Mr. Bucket's banter with Mrs. Bagnet in chapter 49 of Dickens's *Bleak House*: "'I generally am near,' returns Mr. Bucket, 'being so fond of children. A friend of mine has had nineteen of 'em, ma'am, all by one mother, and she's still as fresh and rosy as the morning.'"

p. 173: "Why Cattell, and his clerks" "Cattell," as spelled by Hannah Crafts, probably refers to Mr. Cotrell, a government officeholder and associate of John Hill Wheeler's.

> Diary for 1855 [p. 106]:
> Thurs. 19 [July 1855]
> Friend Cotrell aided me with all his power.
> [p. 116]:
> Sat. 1 Sept. 1855
> Cotrell was selected as consul [to San Juan del Norte] and his commission ordered—
> [p. 117]:
> Wed. 5 [1855]
> Packing up and preparing to leave [for Nicaragua]—At 3 1/2 left New York in the steamer Star of the West, Capt. Turner in company with Dr. & Mrs. Van Dy[ke] Thos. V. Dandy—Cotrell.

p. 173: "Then she was pinched in and swelled out, and puffed up, and strapped down in a way I never saw." Mrs. Wheeler's description of Mrs. Piper echoes Dickens's description of Mr. Turveydrop, the dancing master in *Bleak House,* chapter 14: "He was pinched in, and swelled out, and got up, and strapped down, as much as he could possibly bear."

p. 174: "Mrs Wheeler like Byron"   George Gordon, Lord Byron, the great Romantic poet, author of *Don Juan.* See note to Preface.

p. 175: "the phrase of 'town talk' . . . flies . . . circle to circle."   This passage also appears to echo lines from Dickens: "'You know what you related. Is it true? Do her friends know my story also? Is it the town-talk yet? Is it chalked upon the walls and cried in the streets?'" (chapter 41, *Bleak House*)

p. 175: The Wheelers owned a substantial home in Washington at this time. In the first entry in the "Memoranda" section of his diary for 1857 (dated 1st January 1857), Wheeler lists a "Town House & Lot in Washington City," valued at $6,000. Later, Wheeler owned at least two residential properties in the city, one of which was located on I Street and provided rental income.

p. 176: "Mr Vincent"   Several Vincents are listed as living in Dinwiddie County and Henrico County, Virginia, in the U.S. federal census between 1830 and 1850. Henrico County is twenty kilometers from Milton, while Dinwiddie County is thirty kilometers from Milton.

p. 176: "Mr Cosgrove"   The Cosgrove family lived in Henrico County from 1840 to 1860.

Chapter 14

p. 177: The passage used below is located rather generally as from the "Bible." The citation is Psalm 74:20:

> Have respect unto the covenant: for the dark places of the earth are full of the habitations of cruelty.

p. 177: "Our master . . . took a great fancy to beautiful female slaves" Lizzy's tale of Mr. Cosgrove's infidelity is an unusually explicit account of master-slave sexual relations on the plantation. In the slave narratives, these relations are usually referred to in veiled, or metaphoric, language.

p. 178: "Well our mistress . . . called the girl to her side and caressed and praised her" This scene evokes a similar one between Lady Dedlock and her servant Rosa in chapter 12 of *Bleak House*.

p. 180: "The lady did not foam at the mouth; she was too well bred for that, but she looks as if a little more might make her do it." This description of Mrs. Cosgrove aligns her directly with Mademoiselle Hortense in chapter 42 of *Bleak House*: "It would be contradictory for one in Mademoiselle's state of agreeable jocularity to foam at the mouth, otherwise a tigerish expansion thereabouts might look as if a very little more would make her do it."

p. 180: "To think that she had been rivaled by slaves" Here, Crafts seems to be speaking as a person who had directly experienced or witnessed this tension over sexual rivalry.

p. 182: "her eyes had a wild phrenzied look" This line and its unorthodox spelling echoes a phrase from Matthew Lewis's 1796 gothic thriller, *The Monk* ("his eyes wild and phrenzied").

pp. 182–183: "and with a motion so sudden that no one could prevent it, she snatched a sharp knife which a servant had carelessly left after cutting butcher's meat, and stabbing the infant . . . she had run the knife into her own body" The most famous case of slave infanticide—the murdering of one's child to prevent its sale as a slave—was that of Margaret Garner on January 28, 1856. Garner's case became the basis of the plot of Toni Morrison's magnificent novel *Beloved* (1987).

 Garner; her husband, Robert; their two children, Mary—age two—and Cilla, an infant; and Robert's parents were escaping to freedom from a plantation in Kentucky. Pursued by her master, Archibald Gaines, Garner chose to slit her daughter Mary's throat with a butcher knife rather than allow her to be returned to slavery. Gaines was thought to be the child's father. Garner was returned to slavery and sold to another slave owner. She died in Mississippi in 1858. This story was widely discussed because of its sensational aspect and because of its implications in light of the Fugitive Slave Act of 1850. Crafts most probably knew this story. Garner's actions, of course, echo those of Medea, in the tragedy of Euripides. It is quite possible that Crafts knew both sources.

p. 183: "Dead, your Excellency" This apostrophe is borrowed overtly from Dickens: "Dead! Dead, your Majesty. Dead, my lords and gentlemen. Dead, right reverends and wrong reverends of every order. Dead, men and women, born with heavenly compassion in your hearts. And dying thus around us every day" (chapter 47, *Bleak House*)

Chapter 15

p. 184: This chapter continues the story related by Lizzy; Crafts omits a heading presumably to aid the flow of Lizzy's narrative.

p. 186: "she more resembled a Fury of Orestes" The Furies, or Eumenides, were the avengers of crimes against kinship bonds in Greek mythology. The Furies play an important role in the classical tragedy of Euripedes titled *Orestes*.

p. 190: "plenty of these human cattle" Slaves were frequently referred to as chattel, and their status compared to that of cattle.

pp. 191–192: "She knows . . . he has a secret . . . listening behind doors, and watching at windows" Once again, Crafts borrows from a scene in *Bleak House* (chapter 25):

> To know that he is always keeping a secret from her . . . and will look anywhere rather than meet his eye.
> These various signs and tokens, marked by the little woman, are not lost upon her. . . . prompting her to nocturnal examinations of Mr. Snagsby's pockets; to secret perusals of Mr. Snagsby's letters; to private researches in the Day Book and Ledger, till, cash-box and

iron safe; to watchings at windows, listenings behind doors, and a general putting of this and that together by the wrong end.

The difference is, of course, that Mr. Snagsby is innocent whereas Mr. Cosgrove is not. His sexual relations with his slaves lead to murder, suicide, battery, and death. What is comic marital suspicion in Dickens is brutal reality in the slave narrative.

p. 192: Rock Glen was a geographic name in Walter Scott's *Lady of the Lake*, which was included in the 1850 catalogue of Wheeler's library and which is the poem from which Frederick Douglass took his last name. When Hannah Crafts was in Wheeler's possession between 1856 and 1857, Wheeler, like Mr. Cosgrove in the story, maintained and visited a property near Washington, D.C., where he enslaved at least one woman. It is wholly possible that he kept these details from his wife. In the novel, the location is identified as "Rock Glen." The property Wheeler maintained in Prince George's County, Maryland, was situated on Rock Creek, quite possibly known as Rock Glen, although there is no record of Wheeler referring to the property by that term in the few diary records where this property is traceable. See Hecimovich, *Life and Times*, 160–61.

p. 194: "negroes working in a field of tobacco" North Carolina was a center of the tobacco industry in antebellum America.

p. 199: "Sic transit gloria mundi" Well-known Latin phrase meaning "so passes away the glory of the world." Crafts probably encountered the phrase through *The Imitation of Christ*, by Sir Thomas à Kempis (1370–1471).

Chapter 16

p. 200: This introductory quote appears to be drawn from Esther 7:4, although it is a very loose and incomplete variation. Crafts leaves out the rest of the verse, in which Esther mentions the possibility of the Hebrews being sold into slavery as "bondmen and bondwomen" as a more attractive possibility than the total destruction that Haman has planned. Considering the novel's title, this biblical quotation is obviously very important. In chapters 16 and 17, Crafts, who had fled slavery previously only to help her mistress, finally rebels when she is given to a male slave as his "wife." As she says on p. 212, being forced into a "compulsory union" makes her see that "rebellion would be a virtue." The full verse from Esther that inspires these sentiments is as follows:

> For we are sold, I and my people, to be destroyed, to be slain, and to perish. But if we had been sold for bondmen and bondwomen, I had held my tongue, although the enemy could not countervail the king's damage.

pp. 200–201: "'You needn't make a merit of that as much as to say Mrs[.] Wheeler has a secret.'... 'Of course that would be very foolish' I said." Hannah's exchange with Mrs. Wheeler echoes Esther Summerson's much more benevolent exchange with Caddy Jellyby in chapter 4 of *Bleak House*, beginning with "'You needn't make a merit of that,' said she" and ending with "Her bosom was heaving in a distressful manner that I greatly pitied; but I thought it better not to speak."

p. 201: "As we rode down to the boat designed to convey us to Mrs[.] Wheeler's 'place in North Carolina' I was admiring...navy and Army officers going to and fro; the number of vehicles containing fine Ladies....I say I was admiring these no less than...wondering at the extraordinary contrast to them presented by some wretches in rags, who appeared to be searching...for bones, pins, or other refuse among the rubbish which had accumulated in several places." John and Ellen Wheeler and their servants sailed from Baltimore to North Carolina on the steamer *Georgia* on Saturday, March 21, 1857. This is the sort of detail that attests to Crafts's accuracy and veracity in reporting and to her firsthand experience as a slave of the Wheelers and as a member of their traveling party. The 1857 date is consistent with the internal sequence of events that transpires in the novel, commencing with Jane Johnson's escape in 1855.

Overall, the passage echoes Esther Summerson's description of London while on an excursion with Mrs. Jellyby in chapter 5 of *Bleak House*:

> Thus interrupted, Miss Jellyby became silent, and walked moodily on at my side; while I admired the long successions and

varieties of streets, the quantity of people already going to and fro, the number of vehicles passing and repassing, the busy preparations in the setting forth of shop windows and the sweeping out of shops, and the extraordinary creatures in rags, secretly groping among the swept-out rubbish for pins and other refuse.

p. 201: "and taken refuge beneath the equestrian statue of Jackson" John Wheeler's diary refers to the equestrian statue of Andrew Jackson in reference to a monument to Washington of this type commissioned to the same sculptor, Clark Mills (1810 or 1815–83). The statue of Jackson, the first equestrian monument made in America, is considered Mills's masterpiece and was completed in 1853. His statue of Washington was erected in 1860.

> Diary for 1857 [p. 65]:
> Saturday, August 15
> Day hot as blazes. Went to Interior Department, Patent Office about Genl. Jackson's portrait—
> [p. 101]:
> Saturday, November 28
> Visited Clark Mills, saw his equestrian Statue of Washington—on which he is at work and by which he will be immortalized—as it is equal or superior to his Jackson.

pp. 202–203: "'It really appears that some of them must pass their whole lives looking and intriguing for an office, and it matters very little how it is what it is, or what principle it involves.... They want a secretaryship, they want a clerkship, they want to be foreign ministers.... To hear their account of it they would do extraordinary things. They would build new ships and hire new steamers, they would go to war and make peace they would take Cuba, or Canada, or Dominica.... Then, too, these fellows, office-hunters I mean, are utterly insensible to anyone's feelings.... They are always discussing votes and voters.'" This litany clearly situates the novel in the 1850s. Several books in Wheeler's library, including *The Isthmus of Darien in 1852, Donophan's Campaign against the Navajos* (1847), and *The Mormons: A History of the Rise and Progress* (1852), may also have been available to Crafts.

Mrs. Wheeler's extended declaration against "office-hunters" borrows language and rhetorical structure from Dickens's critical depiction of benevolent associations in chapter 8 of *Bleak House*:

> They threw themselves into committees in the most impassioned manner, and collected subscriptions with a vehemence quite extraordinary. It appeared to us that some of them must pass their whole lives in dealing out subscription-cards to the whole Post-office Directory— shilling cards, half-crown cards, half-sovereign cards, penny cards. They wanted everything. They wanted wearing apparel, they wanted linen rags, they wanted money, they wanted coals, they wanted soup, they wanted interest, they wanted autographs, they wanted flannel, they wanted whatever Mr. Jarndyce had — or had not. Their objects were as various as their demands. They were going to raise new buildings, they were going to pay off debts on old buildings, they were going to establish in a picturesque building (engraving of proposed West Elevation attached) the Sisterhood of Mediaeval Marys; they were going to give a testimonial to Mrs. Jellyby; they were going to have their Secretary's portrait painted, and presented to his mother-in-law, whose deep devotion to him was well known; they were going to get up everything, I really believe, from five hundred thousand tracts to an annuity, and from a marble monument to a silver tea-pot. They took a multitude of titles. They were the Women of England, the Daughters of Britain, the Sisters of all the Cardinal Virtues separately, the Females of America, the Ladies of a hundred denominations. They appeared to be always excited about canvassing and electing. They seemed to our poor wits, and according to their own accounts, to be constantly polling people by tens of thousands, yet never bringing their candidates in for anything.

p. 203: The introduction to this edition matches the location of the Wheeler family plantation near Murfreesboro, North Carolina, with its literary portrayal in this chapter.

The Wheelers' 1857 trip to North Carolina lasted six weeks, from March 21 to May 4, as detailed in John Hill Wheeler's diary, including the following entries:

Diary for 1857 [p. 16]:

At 3 1/2 left for North Carolina in cars via [?] Baltimore. At 6 left Balt. On steamer *Georgia*...
[p. 20]:
Thursday 2 [April]
Wrote to Sully and Woodbury [Wheeler's sons]
Weather very cool.
Went to Cousin Mollie Mebane's
Bertie County - Ellen in company
Also Esther and John & James
Mr. Ferguson and Williams Allan hauling the seine [herring fishing on the Meherrin River]
Thomas Ganet & others there.
[p. 30]:
Sunday, May 3
Visited with my dear Brother, the grave of our Father and Mother.
[p. 31]:
Monday, May 4
At 12 left and reached Boykin's [Landing] at 2
At 3 1/2 left Boykin's and reached Ports.o [Portsmouth, Va.]
At 7—left in steamer *Herald* for Balt.

pp. 203–204: "Yet the house had none of that stately majesty characteristic of Lindendale... but there was a luxurious abundance of vines, and fruits, and flowers... and every thing wore such an aspect of maturity and ripeness that I was fairly charmed. The lime-tree walks were like green arcades, the very shadows of the orange trees seemed dropping with fruit, the peach trees were so laden that their branches bent nearly to the earth and were supported by stout props, and the purple clusters of grapes hung tempting from the trellis work of I don't know how many arbors. Tumbled about among the wide frames and the spread nets there were great heaps of marrows, glowing pods, and lucious... melons, with the greatest profusion of green leaves sparkling and glistening in the sun. As every foot of ground seemed occupied with some rich vegetable treasuse [treasure], the whole atmosphere was redolent with fragrance like one great bo[u]quet." This extended description of the Wheelers' plantation reworks in interesting ways Dickens's depiction of the grounds of Mr. Boythorn's home, formerly the Parsonage-house in chapter 18 of *Bleak House*:

> He lived in a pretty house, formerly the Parsonage-house, with a lawn in front, a bright flower-garden at the side, and a well-stocked orchard and kitchen-garden in the rear, enclosed with a venerable wall that had of itself a ripened ruddy look. But, indeed, everything about the place wore an aspect of maturity and abundance. The old lime-tree walk was like green cloisters, the very shadows of the cherry-trees and apple-trees were heavy with fruit, the gooseberry-bushes were so laden that their branches arched and rested on the earth, the strawberries and raspberries grew in like profusion, and the peaches basked by the hundred on the wall. Tumbled about among the spread nets and the glass frames sparkling and winking in the sun, there were such heaps of drooping pods, and marrows, and cucumbers, that every foot of ground appeared a vegetable treasury, while the smell of sweet herbs and all kinds of wholesome growth (to say nothing of the neighbouring meadows where the hay was carrying) made the whole air a great nosegay.

Writing her narrative ostensibly from the safe haven of New Jersey, Crafts is recollecting the types of fruits that she saw growing in North Carolina. Figs, peaches, and grapes flourished there; pomegranates could be cultivated privately, within the homes of wealthy plantation owners. Although limes and oranges did not thrive there—efforts to introduce citrus fruits to North Carolina in the colonial period proved unsuccessful—linden trees, commonly nicknamed "limes," and osage oranges did. Crafts is most probably using a shorthand for these two plants. The linden tree is a leitmotif throughout the novel. Cherries, apricots, pears, plums, pecans, quinces, damsons, and nectarines also flourished in North Carolina. I am indebted to Sharon Adams, a garden designer in Cambridge, Massachusetts, and Brian Sinche, for this information. See also Cornelius Oliver Cathey's *Agricultural Developments in North Carolina* (Chapel Hill: University of North Carolina Press, 1956).

pp. 204–205: "Is it a stretch of imagination to say that by night they...fatch [fetch] and carry malignant fevers" It is curious that Crafts also turns to Dickens (chapter 16, *Bleak House*) for her description of the slave quarters:

Now, these tumbling tenements contain, by night, a swarm of misery. As, on the ruined human wretch, vermin parasites appear, so, these ruined shelters have bred a crowd of foul existence that crawls in and out of gaps in walls and boards; and coils itself to sleep, in maggot numbers, where the rain drips in; and comes and goes, fetching and carrying fever....

p. 205: "that false system which bestows on position, wealth, or power the consideration only due to a man" Crafts's critique of the social system of the antebellum South is quite consistent with abolitionist and Protestant Christian rhetoric of the period.

p. 205: "to a lower link in the chain of being than that occupied by a horse" Crafts is referring to the slaves, held to be subhuman by many pro-slavery advocates, and therefore occupying a lower order on the Great Chain of Being.

pp. 205–206: "If the huts were bad, the inhabitants it seemed were still worse.... they know nothing." The philosophizing about squalor is also borrowed from chapter 16 of *Bleak House:*

> What connexion can there be, between the place in Lincolnshire, the house in town, the Mercury in powder, and the whereabout of Jo the outlaw with the broom, who had that distant ray of light upon him when he swept the churchyard-step? What connexion can there have been between many people in the innumberable histories of this world, who, from opposite sides of great gulfs, have, nevertheless, been very curiously brought together!
>
> Jo sweeps his crossing all day long, unconscious of the link, if any link there be. He sums up his mental condition, when asked a question, by replying that he "don't know nothing."

What connection can there be between the very poor and the very rich (and their servants), even if there is a link? Dickens asks. The link exists, Crafts suggests, but the slaves are not conscious of it. Jo speaks his ignorance directly, while in free, indirect discourse, Crafts puts the phrase in the minds—not the mouths—of her slaves.

p. 206: "To be made to feel that you have no business here . . . you are scarcely human"   Crafts in this passage moves—in a series of rhetorical questions asked of "Doctors of Divinity"—back and forth between referring to herself as a member of the class of slaves ("you have no business here") and the third person "It must be . . . strange," a phrase she repeats for effect. James Baldwin often used a similar rhetorical device, identifying himself for effect with the "us" or "we" of the non-black American population.

p. 206: "to fear that their opinion is more than half right"   Crafts's catalogue of the degrading effects of slavery upon the slave is astonishingly honest and frank. Rarely do we find in the slave narratives a more compelling statement of slavery's debilitating effects upon the sense of self-worth that slaves struggled to maintain. By framing her questions in the form of "it must be," Crafts is also distinguishing herself from her fellow slaves who ostensibly have been crushed by the system of slavery. Both Douglass and Jacobs also draw distinctions of class and individual merit, intelligence, and worth between themselves and other slaves.

p. 207: "Of course the family residence was stocked with slaves of a higher and nobler order than those belonging to the fields."   The traditional class (and often color) distinctions between house slaves and field slaves was commonly remarked upon by slave narrators and white writers alike, but Crafts's descriptions are especially stark.

p. 208: "I had to deal with a wary, powerful, and unscrupulous enemy. She was a dark mulatto, very quick motioned with black snaky eyes"   One of Crafts's tendencies as a narrator is to draw distinctions—to individuate—effortlessly between black characters rather than treating them in a blanket or an undifferentiated manner. When the librarian and bibliophile Dorothy Porter refers to the natural manner in which Crafts treats black characters, it is this sort of description of the slave Maria that I believe she had in mind, as well as her frank account of the degrading living conditions of life in the slave quarters.

p. 210: "Retreating to the loneliest garret in the house"   Harriet Jacobs hides in a garret in her grandmother's home in North Carolina for seven years. See *Incidents in the Life of a Slave Girl,* especially the chapter "The Loop Hole of Retreat."

p. 211: "and most horrible of all doomed to association with the vile, foul, filthy inhabitants of the huts, and condemned to receive one of them for my husband my soul actually revolted with horror unspeakable" Crafts's "horror" is based in part upon her perception of the extreme gap in class—breeding, education, sensibility, and cleanliness—between herself as a mulatto house servant and the lack of these virtues and characteristics among the "degraded" field hands. The severity of her characterizations here are unusually extreme, compared with similar distinctions drawn in the slave narratives. A large part of her revulsion arises from being forced to marry someone not "voluntarily assumed," as she writes in her next sentence. Protecting herself from rape is Crafts's motivation for fleeing. See the first paragraph in chapter 17. In comparison, Stowe, in *Uncle Tom's Cabin,* describes Legree's slave huts as being "mere rude shells, destitute of any species of furniture, except a heap of straw, foul with dirt, spread confusedly over the floor, which was merely the bare ground, trodden hard by the tramping of innumerable feet."

Chapter 17

p. 212: The Psalm cited here is 141, verse 8. The full biblical quotation is as follows:

> But mine eyes are unto thee, O God the Lord: in thee is my trust; leave not my soul destitute.

The four lines of poetry are from Thomas Tickell's (1685–1740) "Colin and Lucy." In this part of Tickell's poem, a brokenhearted maiden is being called to her death.

The same lines were used by Scott in *Rob Roy* as the epigraph to chapter 17.

p. 212: "a man whom I could only hate and despise" See note for p. 208 above. When Crafts writes that "it seemed that rebellion would be a virtue, that duty to myself and my God actually required it," she is referring to the protection of her virginity as a moral principle worth risking her life for. Crafts goes on to repeat her belief that "marriage" was "something that all the victims of slavery should avoid as tending essentially to perpetuate that system." "[N]othing but this," she writes on p. 213, "would have impelled me to flight."

p. 213: "where Jacob fled from his brother Esau" The narrator opens the Bible and finds the passage in Genesis, chapter 28, where Jacob flees his brother's wrath after cheating Esau out of his birthright and Isaac's blessing. Crafts is invoking divine authority for her own flight.

p. 214: "but I remembered the Hebrew Children and Daniel in the Lion's den, and felt that God could protect and preserve me through all" In the sixth chapter of the Book of Daniel, King Darius's exaltation of Daniel leads to jealousy from the other, non-Hebrew ministers. Daniel must choose between prayer to his God and avoiding the den of lions. Choosing God, Daniel survives the lions with God's help and lives to see his accusers devoured.

p. 214: "The overseer came up" Crafts's description of the overseer seems quite realistic, as is her description of Bill's hut "reeking with filth and impurity." Crafts is especially gifted at evoking the physicality of the field slaves and their habitations.

p. 215: "Bill's cabin was in the midst of the range of huts, tenanted by the workers in the fields. In front was a large pool of black mud and corrupt water, around which myriads of flies and insects were whirling and buzzing. I went in, but such sights and smells as met me I cannot describe them." Crafts's description of the slave Bill's cabin continues the earlier parallels she developed in chapter 16, with Dickens's depiction of Tom-All-Alone's from chapter 22 of *Bleak House*.

> When they come at last to Tom-all-Alone's, Mr. Bucket stops for a moment at the corner. . . . Between his two conductors, Mr. Snagsby passes along the middle of a villainous street, undrained, unventilated, deep in black mud and corrupt water—though the

roads are dry elsewhere—and reeking with such smells and sights that he, who has lived in London all his life, can scarce believe his senses. Branching from this street and its heaps of ruins, are other streets and courts so infamous that Mr. Snagsby sickens in body and mind, and feels as if he were going, every moment deeper down, into the infernal gulf.

p. 216: "Here was a suit of male apparel exactly corresponding to my size and figure" This sort of coincidence is commonly found in sentimental novels. Hannah's use of a disguise as a male echoes that of Ellen Craft in 1848, Clarissa Davis in 1854, Anna Maria Weems (alias Joe Wright) in 1855. Crafts escaped as a white male; John Wesley Gibson also escaped as a white male. (See William Still's *The Underground Railroad* for accounts of these cases of cross-dressing.) John Wheeler, the nephew of John Hill Wheeler, held a record of antislavery sympathies. As Gregg Hecimovich suggests, the nephew may have provided the "suit of male apparel" that assisted Hannah Crafts with her escape, if the scene in the novel reflects the author's escape. Significantly, in Wheeler's diary, John calls on his uncle on July 26, 1856, and receives an order to purchase clothes at Lahter and Walls, in the District, with Wheeler noting the expense as $5.50. It is conjecture, but this acquisition of "male apparel" by the nephew may have been arranged to purchase clothing with which Hannah Crafts could disguise herself. The nephew's presence in Crafts's life at both Wheeler House (1852–56) and then in Washington, D.C. (1856–57), and upon the Wheeler family's return to Murfreesboro in March–May 1857, just before the author's escape, may signal a relationship or friendship no longer recoverable in the historical record. See Hecimovich, *Life and Times*, 146, 286, 293–94, 317–18, 322.

Chapter 18

p. 217: In both Matthew 8:20 and Luke 9:58, Jesus warns a potential follower:

> The foxes have holes, and the birds of the air have nests; but the Son of man hath not where to lay his head.

That Crafts wished to emphasize her own homelessness during her flight from slavery is reflected in the fact that she considered giving this chapter three titles: "The Wandering," "Trials and Difficulties," and "Strange Company." The first two titles were rejected for the third, "Strange Company."

p. 217: The "window of opportunity" for Hannah's escape from the Wheeler plantation near Murfreesboro, North Carolina, is established in John Hill Wheeler's diary by the earlier escape of Jane in July 1855, referred to in her first meeting with Mrs. Wheeler, and the onset of the Civil War in 1861. Judging from the relevant information contained in Wheeler's diary, Hannah's escape would most likely have occurred between March 21 and May 4, 1857. This period corresponds not only with the Wheelers' recorded trip to the plantation from Washington but with several other unique circumstances in their lives during this time, such as Wheeler's recent dismissal from his government post. Negative evidence supporting the year 1857 for the escape is provided by the lack of known visits by the Wheelers to the plantation during the years 1855, 1856 (only the first half of the diary is extant, but Mr. Wheeler was still in Nicaragua until November of that year), and 1858 (only the last half of this diary survives). Trips were made by the Wheelers to North Carolina in 1859 (with President Buchanan in early June), 1860 (in the latter half of December), and 1861 (about July, from which point Wheeler stayed in North Carolina), but Mr. Wheeler's continual employment as clerk of the Interior Department in Washington from 1857 would not have occasioned Hannah's reference to his recent dismissal from office during any of these years. Furthermore, the relative proximity in time between the departure of Jane, a much-valued personal servant of Mrs. Wheeler, and the acquisition of Hannah as a competent replacement (less than two years) logically supports the year 1856 as the date of Hannah's involvement with the Wheelers and her subsequent escape in early 1857.

p. 218: "guided at night by the North Star" The use of the North Star by fugitive slaves as a natural compass was a common feature of the slave narratives.

p. 218: "I thought of Elijah and ravens" Crafts here recalls 1 Kings 17:6, in which the prophet Elijah is fed "bread and flesh" by ravens in the morning and evening while following God's command to live in the wilderness.

p. 218: "I cannot describe my journey" Despite their dogged use of verisimilitude—of listing in painstaking detail the who, what, and where of their experiences as slaves—it was a common feature of most slave narrators to remain silent or sketchy about their mode of escape, in order to protect the secrecy of their routes and methods from slave catchers. This was especially the case after the passage of the Fugitive Slave Act of 1850. Frederick Douglass severely criticized Henry "Box" Brown for publishing a book in which he detailed his unusual mode of escape: he was shipped in a crate from Richmond to freedom in Philadelphia. Douglass argued that other slaves could have utilized this method of escape had Brown only kept it a secret.

p. 220: "as the Catholic devotee calls over the names of his favorite saints while counting his beads" Crafts is referring to the rosary. Roman Catholicism was a relatively rare form of Christianity in North Carolina and Virginia in the nineteenth century.

p. 221: "This will be my last resting place" Crafts uses standard English for some slaves, especially house servants, to distinguish them from uneducated field slaves, who usually she depicts speaking dialect. Crafts writes, "This he said in broken incoherent expressions to which I have given suitable language." (p. 223)

pp. 221–222: "I began to lose the consciousness of my identity, and the recollection of where I was. Now it seemed that Lindendale rose before me, then it was the jail, and anon the white towers of Washington, and— but the scene all faded; for I slept. The scarcely awakened morn was feebly peering through a curtaining of clouds, when I opened my eyes to encounter those of a black man fixed on me with the most intense expression of wonder, apprehension, and curiosity." Crafts significantly reworks Esther Summerson's description of her broken sleep while comforting Caddy Jellyby at the close of chapter 4 in *Bleak House*. Again, Crafts appears to borrow language and rhetorical structuring but to tell a very different story, this time Hannah's escape north.

> I began to lose the identity of the sleeper resting on me. Now, it was Ada; now, one of my old Reading friends from whom I could not believe I had so recently parted. Now, it was the little mad woman

worn out with curtseying and smiling; now, some one in authority at Bleak House. Lastly, it was no one, and I was no one. The purblind day was feebly struggling with the fog, when I opened my eyes to encounter those of a dirty-faced little spectre fixed upon me.

p. 224: "and more than all the minister...striving to elicit something of which to make capital for his next sermon" Crafts's critique of organized religion is somewhat reminiscent of Frederick Douglass's critique of the hypocrisy of Christianity vis-à-vis slavery. For a person so expressly devout, Crafts's critique of the funeral practices of her time is quite refreshing and perceptive.

p. 224: "grim monarch" This phrase in combination with the phrase "immortal mind" (p. 18) suggests an allusion to Phillis Wheatley's "To a lady on the death of her husband." A volume of Wheatley's work *Memoir and Poems* (1838) appears in the 1882 catalogue of Wheeler's library.

p. 226: "They mostly prayed that we the slaves might be good and obedient" See note above.

p. 227: "His stay was prolonged, but I thought little of it, untill [sic] night set in; the wild dark night, with the trees shuddering in the wind. The rain, so thick and heavy all day, had ceased falling, and though the sky had partly cleared and a few dim stars might be seen overhead it was exceedingly gloomy. Once or twice I went out to look and listen. The heavens wore a fearful an[d] awful aspect. In the north, and northwest, where the sunset had faded three hours before, there was a rich red arch of beautiful light, whence ascended what fancy might easily have pictured as sheets of waving flame." Crafts's description of the night following Jacob's sister's death follows the language and rhetorical forms that Dickens uses to describe the night sky when Esther Summerson is summoned to Jo's sickbed at a brick-maker's house at St. Albans in chapter 31 of *Bleak House*:

> It was a cold, wild night, and the trees shuddered in the wind. The rain had been thick and heavy all day, and with little intermission for many days. None was falling just then, however. The sky had partly cleared, but was very gloomy—even above us, where a few stars were shining. In the north and north-west, where the

sun had set three hours before, there was a pale dead light both beautiful and awful; and into it long sullen lines of cloud waved up, like a sea stricken immoveable as it was heaving.

Chapter 19

p. 230: The full text of this verse, Psalm 37:25, is as follows:

I have been young, and now am old; yet have I not seen the righteous forsaken, nor his seed begging bread.

p. 230: "but strange to say he had not penetrated my disguise. He learned to love me, however, as a younger brother" Crafts is reassuring her readers that her virtue remained intact, despite her intimacy with Jacob as they fled the South.

p. 230: "though when compelled by necessity to approach the habitations of men it devolved on me as his color made him obnoxious to suspicion" *Obnoxious* was commonly used to mean "subject, liable, exposed, or open to," as *Webster's* reports. Crafts's use of a disguise as a white man traveling with a black man replicates the method of escape used by Ellen and William Craft in 1848. (See note to pp. 84–85 above)

pp. 230–231: Despite her confessed reticence to divulge details of this escape route, Crafts provides fascinating details about how Hannah and Jacob traveled together.

p. 233: "I knew the voice, though I had not recognised the countenance. It was that of my old friend, Aunt Hetty." Coincidences such as this were a common feature of sentimental novels. Crafts reminds us of the source of her literacy training by describing herself as "the Hannah whom she had taught to read."

p. 235: "the statute that forbade the instruction of slaves" It was illegal in most antebellum southern states to teach slaves to read and write.

p. 235: "like Paul and Silas of old" Both Paul and Silas escaped from prison while evangelizing the new faith of Christianity, in Philippi. See Acts, Chapter 16.

p. 235: "a small village of miners" Crafts could be referring to a village in the coal fields of western Virginia, or the state of West Virginia today. West Virginia became a state in 1863.

p. 236: "I should find refuge among the colored inhabitants of New Jersey" Crafts's manuscript was recovered from New Jersey by a "book scout" in 1948. New Jersey "became a haven for slaves escaping the South," according to Giles R. Wright's *Afro-Americans in New Jersey* (Trenton: New Jersey Historical Commission, 1988), p. 39.

p. 236: "the good old woman supplied me with female apparel" Crafts is now traveling disguised as a white woman.

Chapter 20

p. 238: In the book of Isaiah, the prophet warns:

> Woe unto the wicked! It shall be ill with him: for the reward of his hands shall be given him.

Crafts gives her chapter of "just rewards" the title "Retribution."

p. 238: "Farther down the river was a steamboat landing" Several navigable rivers flowed through, or near, coal fields in West and western Virginia, including the Kanawha, the Guyandotte, the Shenandoah, and the Ohio.

p. 239: "even-handed justice returns the ingredients of the poisoned chalice to our own lips"

> From *Macbeth*:
> If it were done when 'tis done, then 'twere well
> It were done quickly: if the assassination

> Could trammel up the consequence, and catch
> With his surcease success; that but this blow
> Might be the be-all and the end-all here,
> But here, upon this bank and shoal of time,
> We'd jump the life to come. But in these cases
> We still have judgment here; that we but teach
> Bloody instructions, which, being taught, return
> To plague the inventor: this even-handed justice
> Commends the ingredients of our poison'd chalice
> To our own lips.

p. 240: "but the mother was, or had been a slave, though she enjoyed all the perquisites and priveledges of a wife" Examples of romantic intimacy and faithfulness between masters and slaves were to be found even in the antebellum South. Perhaps the most famous is that of Thomas Jefferson and Sally Hemmings. Trappe's death—the demise of the villain, hoist with his own petard—was a common feature of sentimental novels.

p. 243: Crafts comments on Mr. Trappe's demise with the well-known passage from Hosea. The full verse is Hosea 8:7:

> For they have sown the wind, and they shall reap the whirlwind: it hath no stalk: the bud shall yield no meal: if so be it yield, the strangers shall swallow it up.

Chapter 21

p. 244: Crafts prefaces her final chapter with the second verse of Psalm 23, one of the most popular of all the Psalms:

> He maketh me to lie down in green pastures: he leadeth me beside the still waters.

p. 244: "I dwell now in a neat little Cottage, and keep a school for colored children" A fairly large free black community thrived in New Jersey before the Civil War, founding several all-black communities. As Giles R. Wright puts it, "By the Civil War, black New Jerseyans numbered nearly 26,000 and had structured a vibrant institutional life that included churches, schools, literary societies, fraternal lodges, and benevolent associations. They had also organized to protest racial injustice, in 1849 holding a statewide convention for restoring the franchise lost in 1807." As Wright concludes, reinforcing Crafts's claim to be living there at the end of her novel: "Both free southern blacks and Fugitive Slave participants in the Underground Railroad settled in New Jersey, dating from the antebellum period,... they helped create or expand all-black settlements such as Lawnside, which was incorporated in 1926, as a municipality, the state's first and only all-black community to achieve such a status." Giles R. Wright, "New Jersey," *Encyclopedia of African-American Culture and History,* edited by Jack Salzman, David Lionel Smith, and Cornel West (New York: Macmillan, 1996), p. 1989.

p. 244: When Crafts writes that "There was a hand of Providence in our meeting"—referring to meeting her long-lost mother—she is putting the matter mildly. And when she writes, on p. 246, that "[y]ou could scarcely believe it," that "Charlotte, Mrs Henry's favorite" slave, lives near her as well, we know that we are deep within the realm of the sentimental novel, which tends to end "happily ever after." What is curious about this coincidence, however, is that Crafts's level of detail here—"a free mulatto from New Jersey," "the property of his daughter who dwelt in Maryland," her "school for colored children"—offers promising leads for ascertaining eventually more particulars about the life and times of Hannah Crafts.

p. 245: "So strong was her faith that whenever she beheld a stranger she half-expected to behold her child.... I thought it strange, but my heart yearned towards her with a deep intense feeling it had never known before.... I was not half so surprised as pleased and overwhelmed with emotions for which I could find no name, when she suddenly rose one day... clasped me in her arms, and sobbed out in rapturous joy "child, I am your mother." And then I—but I cannot tell what I did, I was nearly crazy with delight. I was then resting for the first time on my mother's bosom—my mother for whom my heart had yearned, and my spirit gone out in intense longing many, many times.... With our arms clasped around each other, our heads bowed together, and our tears mingling we went down on our knees, and returned thanks to Him." Crafts provides a powerful rewriting of the doleful reunion scene between Esther Summerson and her mother Lady Dedlock in chapter 36 of *Bleak House*:

> I looked at her; but I could not see her, I could not hear her, I could not draw my breath. The beating of my heart was so violent and wild, that I felt as if my life were breaking from me. But when she caught me to her breast, kissed me, wept over me, compassionated me, and called me back to myself; when she fell down on her knees and cried to me, "O my child, my child, I am your wicked and unhappy mother! O try to forgive me!"—when I saw her at my feet on the bare earth in her great agony of mind, I felt, through all my tumult of emotion, a burst of gratitude to the providence of God that I was so changed as that I never could disgrace her by any trace of likeness; as that nobody could ever now look at me, and look at her, and remotely think of any near tie between us.
>
> I raised my mother up, praying and beseeching her not to stoop before me in such affliction and humiliation. I did so, in broken, incoherent words; for, besides the trouble I was in, it frightened me to see her at *my* feet. I told her—or I tried to tell her—that if it were for me, her child, under any circumstances to take upon me to forgive her, I did it, and had done it, many, many years. I told her that my heart overflowed with love for her; that it was natural love, which nothing in the past had changed, or could change. That it was not for me, then resting for the first time on my mother's bosom, to take her to account for having given me life; but that my duty was to bless her and receive her, though the whole world turned from her, and that I only asked her leave to do it. I held my mother in my embrace, and she held me in hers; and among the still woods in the silence of the summer day, there seemed to be nothing but our two troubled minds that was not at peace.

p. 246: "He is, and has always been a free man, is a regularly ordained preacher of the Methodist persuasion" The African Methodist Episcopal Church was well established in New Jersey by the 1850s. The Mount Pisgah African Methodist Episcopal Church was founded in 1800 in Salem.

APPENDIX A

Authentication Report:
The Bondwoman's Narrative

Prepared for:　　Laurence J. Kirshbaum, Chairman
　　　　　　　　Time Warner Trade Publishing

　　　　　　　　and

　　　　　　　　Henry Louis Gates Jr.
　　　　　　　　Harvard University

Prepared by:　　Joe Nickell, Ph.D.

　　　　　　　　June 12, 2001

NOTE: Page numbers in the Authentication Report refer to pages in the actual holograph, not this edition.

JOE NICKELL, Ph.D., is an investigator and historical-document examiner. He is author of 17 books including *Pen, Ink and Evidence: A Study of Writing and Writing Materials for the Penman, Collector, and Document Detective* (1990) and *Detecting Forgery: Forensic Investigation of Documents* (1996).

He has been a private investigator, an investigative writer, and teacher of technical writing and literature at the University of Kentucky. He is now Senior Research Fellow at the Center for Inquiry—International at Amherst, New York, where he investigates fringe-science claims. He has appeared on numerous television shows as an expert on myths and mysteries, frauds, forgeries, and hoaxes.

CONTENTS

ABSTRACT 322
1. INTRODUCTION 322
   Assignment 322
   Description 323
   Examination 323
2. PROVENANCE 324
3. PAPER 326
   Folios 326
   Embossments 327
   Rag content 327
   Paper manufacture 328
   Writing paper 328
4. INK 329
   Infrared examination 329
   Ultraviolet examination 329
   Chemical tests 330
5. PEN 331
6. HANDWRITING 332
7. ERASURES AND CORRECTIONS 333
   Wipe erasures 334
   Crossouts and insertions 334
   Knife erasures 335
   Pasteovers 336
   Revised folios 337
8. BINDING 338
   Pre-cover "binding" 338
   Professional binding 340
9. TEXTUAL MATTERS 341
   Vocabulary and spelling 341
   Readability level 342
   Fictionalization 343
   Date indications 344
   Authorial indications 346
SUMMARY 347
CONCLUSIONS 348
RECOMMENDATIONS 350
APPENDIX 351
REFERENCES 352

ABSTRACT

A handwritten manuscript, *The Bondwoman's Narrative*, was examined as to paper, ink, and other writing materials, as well as internal evidence, in order to authenticate and date its composition.

It was determined to be an authentic writing of the mid-nineteenth century, and to date between circa 1853 and 1861. It was probably written by a woman, and her insights as a young female, an African-American, and a Christian seem consistent and credible. She has apparently struggled to achieve a significant level of education.

It was rendered in modified round hand (a style of American handwriting ca. 1840–1865) with a quill pen and iron-gall ink. One of the types of stationery she used is known from examples in 1856 and 1860. All of the other accoutrements (vermilion wafers, writing sand, etc.) are consistent with the 1850s.

1. INTRODUCTION

This report presents the results of an examination of a manuscript, *The Bondwoman's Narrative, by Hannah Crafts a Fugitive Slave Recently Escaped from North Carolina*.

Assignment

At the recommendation of manuscript expert Kenneth Rendell, I was commissioned to conduct this examination by Laurence J. Kirshbaum, Chairman, Time Warner Trade Publishing, which is planning to publish an edition of the narrative. In a letter dated April 24, 2001, Kirshbaum referred to the preliminary finding of Harvard professor Henry Louis Gates Jr., who acquired the manuscript and determined that it appeared to date to ca. 1855. "We need your investigative expertise to authenticate this date," wrote Kirshbaum. In discussions with him, Gates, and Rendell, I determined to make a detailed examination of the manuscript that would include a study of the writing materials used to produce it as well as the "internal evidence" of the text that would bear on its authorship and date. Attempts to verify the existence of Hannah Crafts were being conducted by Professor Gates and researchers under his direction.

Description

The manuscript is a 301-page, cloth-bound volume measuring about 20 x 25 cm high overall. The binding is broken, but no numbered pages are missing. The title page bears the handwritten title: "The / Bondwoman's Narrative / By Hannah Crafts / A Fugitive Slave / Recently Escaped from North Carolina."

Examination

The investigation included visual, spectral, chemical, microscopic, and textual examinations.

This report discusses the following aspects: Provenance, Paper, Ink, Pen, Handwriting, Erasures and Corrections, Binding, and Textual Matters. A Summary, Conclusions, and Recommendations are presented along with illustrative photographs and photomacrographs, an Appendix and References.

2. PROVENANCE

A paragraph on *The Bondwoman's Narrative* appears in an article on recent African-Americana manuscript sales by various dealers, notably the Sixth Annual Auction of Printed and Manuscript African-Americana at Swann Galleries (104 East 25th Street, New York, N.Y. 10010). The Swann auction consisted of 394 lots—including *The Bondwoman's Narrative*—offered by Wyatt Houston Day, an African-American cataloguer and dealer in rare books. The article, in *The Manuscript Society News*, referred to the manuscript as a "fictionalized slave narrative" that was "Of highest note, and one of the true crown jewels of the [Swann] auction" (Feigen 2001).

Professor Gates provided some letters and papers relating to the manuscript's known provenance. A letter to him from Wyatt Houston Day, dated April 6, 2001, states that Day first saw the narrative while conducting an appraisal of the Dorothy Porter Wesley papers in Fort Lauderdale, Florida. He continued:

> The Hannah Crafts Narrative was in a large manilla folder along with a 1948 catalog from Emily Driscoll (a New York based book and autograph dealer) offering the manuscript narrative. This was together with some correspondence between Dorothy Porter and Driscoll. The correspondence was from 1948 through 1951. Ms. Driscoll was convinced that the narrative was written by a "Negro," and had catalogued it as such. Apparently Dorothy Porter thought so too because she acquired the manuscript for $80.00 sometime soon after. A pencilled precis is all that accompanied the ms.

Professor Gates also sent me a copy of a letter written September 27, 1951, by Emily Driscoll (from her Fifth Avenue autograph and manuscript business in New York City) to Mrs.

Dorothy Porter (of Howard University, Washington, D.C.). Driscoll notes that Mrs. Porter has decided to keep the manuscript (which she obviously had on approval), adding: "I bought it from a scout in the trade" (a man who wanders around with consignment goods from other dealers) but that all she could learn of its prior history "was that he came upon it in Jersey!"

Accompanying the copy of the Driscoll letter was a typed record (under Howard University letterhead) describing the narrative as a "Manuscript Novel" and a "fictionalized personal narrative" that was "Written in a worn copy book." The purchase price was noted as "85.00."

The manuscript contains some penciled notations that may be by Mrs. Porter. Notably, on the verso of the inside front flyleaf (facing the title page) is hand printed "MSS61" which suggests the record of a small archive (i.e., "manuscripts no. 61").

Being on the flyleaf, this writing was necessarily done after the present binding was affixed. There are also penciled parentheses on page 64 (beginning line 15, ending line 19), and above the penned word "Egyptian" (in "Egyptian darkness") someone has penciled "Stygian?"

Written large on the back page of the original manuscript (facing the end flyleaf) is "C A Alma" (with a final flourishing or paraph or possibly "Jr.") also in pencil. The handwriting suggests it may have been done earlier than the other pencil markings. Also black and white striations in the graphite lines are consistent with soft and hard spots in the "lead," possibly indicating natural graphite sawed into square sticks rather than the more homogeneous leads made from a mix of powdered graphite and clay, extruded into strands, and kiln fired. The former type was used for some American pencils of about the 1860s (see Nickell 1990, pp. 25–27).

3. PAPER

The statement in Mrs. Porter's record that the narrative was "Written in a worn copy book" is not really correct. It was actually penned on stationery and subsequently bound. (The binding will be described in more detail presently.)

Folios

The stationery is in a form common to the eighteenth and nineteenth centuries: folio sheets, i.e. sheets of paper folded in half and thus having two leaves and four pages. By the late 1830s, such folios were often embossed (a group at a time) with a stationer's crest or design in the upper-left corner. *The Bondwoman's Narrative* consists of at least four different types of stationery folios:

1. Folios embossed "SOUTHWORTH / MFG. / CO." in a horizontally elongated octagon. This type of paper was utilized through page 78, and also for pages 105–126, 129–144, and 217–301 (the last page of the manuscript).
2. Folios embossed "SOUTHWORTH / [indistinct emblem] / SUPERFINE" in a shield-like crest. This was used for pages 79–104 and for 127–128 (a single leaf).
3. Folios that are unembossed, pages 145–208 and 213–216.
4. One unembossed folio that is shorter and lighter toned than the ones it separates; this four-page folder was used for pages 209–212.

Embossments

The wording of the first embossment, "SOUTHWORTH / MFG. / CO.," represents the name of the company (which still exists in West Springfield, Massachusetts) as it was used from 1839 to 1873, according to a representative (Kennedy 2001). More specific dating information comes from the second type of embossment, the "SOUTHWORTH / SUPERFINE" crest. This type is known from documents dated 1856 and 1860 (Nickell 1993). Although the exact beginning and ending dates for the manufacture are unknown, it is apparent that it was produced during the second half of the decade of the 1850s. This paper measures about 19.4 by 24.7 cm, the approximate size of the other folios (except, as mentioned, the slightly shorter type 4).

Rag content

Stereomicroscopic examination of the surface of the various pages reveals the presence of bits of thread, occasionally still colored red, blue, etc., indicating the paper pulp was not bleached but was made largely of white cloth. I obtained some small slivers of paper from frayed outer edges (slivers that were about to become dislodged in any case), moistened a sliver with distilled water and teased it apart on a microscope slide, stained it with Herzberg stain and observed the fibers microscopically. I identified rag—linen and cotton—fibers (the latter with their characteristic twist) but found no evidence of ground wood pulp (first successfully commercially produced in North America in 1867).

Paper manufacture

Transmitted light shows the paper to be unwatermarked except for a type of "accidental watermark" indicative of the paper-making process. This is the appearance of stitch marks running across the sheet of paper (across two leaves as folded) produced by the seam of the wire belt of the early paper machine. This is seen in several places (near the top of leaves pp. 11–12, 105–108, 119–122; at the top edge of pp. 61–64 [scarcely visible on 63–64]; and near the bottom of pp. 191–194).

Because the paper was machine-made, it is necessarily of the "wove"—as opposed to "laid"—pattern. (Some machine-made paper, after 1825, was impressed with a pseudo-laid pattern by means of a device called a dandy roll, which also was employed when a watermark was desired. For a discussion see Nickell 1990, pp. 74–79.)

The smoothness of the paper indicates it was calendered, that is, pressed between a series of rollers after the continuous web of paper was newly formed. ("Calender" is a corruption of the Latin word *cylindrus*, "cylinder.")

Writing paper

All of the paper was specifically produced as writing paper, having been sized to retard the absorbance of writing ink. Testing a paper fragment for starch (with iodine reagent) was negative, but stereomicroscopic examination of the surface shows the typical appearance of gelatine sizing (i.e., of having been dipped in a hot solution of natural collagen made by boiling animal scraps).

The paper was also given blue guidelines (machine ruling of lines on paper dating back to ca. 1770 in England).

4. INK

The appearance of the ink in ordinary light is brown, consistent with a typical iron-gall ink that has oxidized over time. The ink was examined with ultraviolet light and infrared radiation, then tested chemically.

Infrared examination

Infrared radiation (observed through a special viewing scope) offers a nondestructive means of differentiating between certain types of ink (some absorbing the infrared radiation and thus darkening, others reflecting the rays and consequently lightening, still others transmitting the infrared and so disappearing—see Nickell 1996, 163). The appearance of the ink throughout *The Bondwoman's Narrative* was unremarkable, merely consistent with the possibility of an iron-gallotannate variety.

Ultraviolet examination

The examination with ultraviolet (UV) light was more productive. Under UV, the ink tended to darken, a characteristic consistent with iron-gall ink. More significantly, there were everywhere instances of "ghost writing"—mirror-imaged, fluorescing traces of writing from the facing page. Such fluorescence results from cellulose degradation, caused in turn by the acidic nature of the ink (iron-gall being highly acidic), and it is normally a sign of genuine age in a document (Nickell 1996, 157–158).

Chemical tests

Tests were conducted to chemically identify the ink, to determine whether it was indeed an iron-gall type and if so whether it contained a provisional colorant. (When first written with, iron-gall ink was often dark gray rather than black—although it later darkened on the page before eventually turning to its rusty brown appearance over time, an effect of the iron oxidizing. To make the ink darker at the outset, various coloring agents were added, including such dyes as logwood and indigo. See Nickell 1990, 37.)

The tests were done using a technique that I developed with forensic analyst John F. Fischer. Whereas some examiners make tests directly on the document, or remove pinhead-size samples with a scalpel, or punch out tiny discs of ink-impregnated paper, our technique is much, much less destructive and more suitable for historical documents.

In this procedure, a small piece of chromatography paper is moistened with distilled water, placed over a heavy ink stroke, and rubbed with a blunt instrument using moderate pressure, by which means a small trace of ink is lifted onto the paper. Such samples were taken randomly from several locations throughout the manuscript. The chemical tests were then conducted on the chromatography paper.

Two reagents were used. First, hydrochloric acid was applied, which produced a light yellow color typical of an iron-gall ink that lacks a provisional colorant. (A blue reaction would have indicated a colorant such as indigo; red would have indicated logwood). This was followed by potassium ferrocyanide which yielded a prussian-blue color, thus proving the presence of iron and indicating an iron-gallotannate ink. This type of ink was the most common in use during the middle of the nineteenth century.

5. PEN

The text of *The Bondwoman's Narrative* is characterized by sequences of writing in which the ink becomes progressively lighter before abruptly becoming darker again. This dark-to-light progression is a feature of a "dip" pen, whereby less and less ink is deposited until the writer recharges the pen by dipping it once again into the inkwell.

Also, pen strokes in the narrative are sometimes much finer than others. Note that the writing at the top of page 259 (the four lines that end Chapter 16) is noticeably more heavily stroked than the heading and opening lines of Chapter 17. This indicates a sharper pen being used for the latter, and such variance—moving from a blunt to sharp nib—is a characteristic of the quill pen. The more hairline appearance of the latter results from the quill having been sharpened (a special quill-pen knife was used for the purpose) or from the pen having been put aside for a sharp one. (Inkstands of the period often had a series of "quill holes" around the inkwell into which quills could be stood ready for use. Boxes of machine-built quill pen nibs, for use on a holder, were also sold [Nickell 1990, 3–8].)

Stereomicroscopic examination confirmed that the narrative was indeed written with quill pens. There are no nib tracks (furrows caused by metal pens or by "dutched," i.e. fire-hardened, quills) in the paper. Quill pens began to be supplanted by steel pens in the 1840s and 1850s, and—by the end of the Civil War (during which quills were used by the impoverished Confederates)—the quill was almost completely abandoned (Nickell 1996, 108).

The writing in the narrative is consistent with that produced by the standard goose quill rather than by the crow quill. (The latter was used for the minuscule script that was sometimes affected by Victorian ladies as an expression of femininity. See Nickell 1990, pp. 3–4.)

6. HANDWRITING

The handwriting of the manuscript is of a class succeeding that of the American round-hand system (ca. 1700–1840). That earlier penmanship style was characterized by uniformly hairline upstrokes and heavy ("shaded") downstrokes, flourishes, and such now-archaic forms as the long *s* and superscript abbreviations (i.e. the use of raised letters in such contracted forms as "W<u>m</u>" for "William"). The manuscript handwriting is rather of the transitional form called modified round-hand (ca. 1840–1865), lacking the features of the later "Spencerian" system (1865–1890) that had more angular connecting strokes and was relatively devoid of shading on the small letters.

Of course it is difficult to precisely date a handwriting from its style, especially since people tended to continue writing the way they had been taught, into their old age. Given that the writing materials indicate composition in the 1850s, the absence of archaic forms like the long *s* suggests to me that the writer was relatively young when the pages were penned.

The author's handwriting may best be described as serviceable. It is neither an untutored hand nor an example of elegant penmanship, and it lacks the diminutive size sometimes affected by ladies (referred to earlier in the discussion of quills). It is not possible to determine on the basis of the script alone whether such a handwriting was produced by a man or woman, although there are indications (to be discussed later) that it was the latter. It is consistent with the writing of a woman.

The script was produced with relative slowness rather than swiftness, but it is a natural, genuine handwriting (unlike, say, the bogus script of the alleged Jack the Ripper Diary [Nickell 1996, 45–48].) The author apparently desired to make the writing legible. It is generally unadorned, although one interesting feature is an extra little stroke—a deliberate fillip (comparable to a comma)—that is found as a final stroke of lower-case *s* but only when it is at the end of a word. This feature does not seem to have precise date significance. I find examples in my reference collection dating from 1821 to 1878.

The punctuation is eccentric. Periods are absent, although semicolons are sometimes used. Hyphens used for word breaks typically appear not at the end of the line but at the beginning of the next (although occasionally—including three instances on page 18—there is a hyphen at both places). Most curiously, apostrophes and quotation marks appear not as they should, raised (at the top of the lettering), but rather at the baseline (like commas). These characteristics differ even from the conventions of the period (see Cahoon et al. 1977) and seem explicable only as a measure of unsophistication on the part of the writer. (One possibility is that the placement of quotation marks somehow derived from European romance-language [French, Italian, Spanish, etc.] *guillemets,* small angled marks used for quotations and "placed on the lower part of the type body" [*Chicago Manual* 1993].)

7. ERASURES AND CORRECTIONS

The author of the manuscript has utilized a wide variety of methods for correcting and revising the text. Kenneth Rendell (2001) is quite justified in having suggested "that the manuscript is a composing copy, and it is not a fair copy."

Wipe erasures

Many changes were made in progress, quite often utilizing a common method of the quill-pen era: wipe erasures. This method (mentioned by Charles Dickens in *The Pickwick Papers*, 1837) involved the writer "smearing out wrong letters with his little finger, and putting in new ones which required going over very often to render them visible through the old blots." This method is employed frequently in *The Bondwoman's Narrative*, one instance being page 132, line 9, where "with" was wiped off—while the ink had remained wet on the page—and "in" was written over the spot. The process is facilitated in the manuscript by the "calendered" (smooth) surface of the paper. The direction of the wipe indicates that the author is using the little finger of the right hand and is thus almost certainly right-handed (as the script also indicates). Wipe erasures declined with the advent of the steel pen which dug into the paper and left furrowed nib tracks that filled with ink and were not so readily removed (Nickell 1991).

Crossouts and insertions

The writer also used the techniques of striking out words (utilizing a series of slashes or multiple long lines) and making insertions using a caret (inverted v) to indicate the exact placement of added words. Some of these corrections were made in the process of writing, others as later changes.

Knife erasures

Where the author wished to erase a small portion of text after the ink had thoroughly dried, the offending portion was scraped off with an ink-eraser knife. (See Nickell 1990, 64–66.) An example is found on page 41, line 17, when a word was scraped off and the word "salver" was written over. (If a special ink-eraser knife was unavailable, the writer might have used the available penknife for the erasure.) Note the rough appearance of the overwriting and the scrape marks (visible by transmitted light).

It is with the knife erasures that I found the only evidence of blotting in the manuscript. I searched in vain for any use of blotting paper, instead discovering a few instances of the use of writing sand. For example on page 67 is a blot of ink that has a speckled appearance. When one turns the leaf there is a corresponding blob. What happened is that the author penned a sentence that included the word "oblidged" (misspelled). Later deciding to correct this, the writer used a knife to scrape off the last half of the word (all but "obli"), then wrote "ged" to complete the word. However, the knife had removed the sizing, roughened the paper, and left thin places in it. As a consequence, the ink was drawn out of the quill by capillary attraction, making a heavy blob that soaked through to the other side. Quickly, the writer grabbed for her sand-box or sander (similar to a small confectionary shaker only with a recessed top) and dusted sand over the blob on each side of the leaf. In the writer's subsequent brushing off of the particles—which has left a speckled appearance—a few still ink-wet grains were carried down and to the right, leaving a little trail in the form of a smear with more speckles.

Writing sand was used on some other ink blobs that resulted from knife erasures. On page 225, line 17, there are tiny indentations in the letter "A" of "Accordingly" that I attribute to sand. At the left side of that letter is embedded a single speck of clear crystalline material that suggests the sand was a quartz variety (not the presumably more expensive "black writing sand"—powdered biotite—that was often preferred; see Nickell 1990, 59–60).

Pasteovers

When more extensive revisions were necessary, involving a few lines, the writer used a slip of paper attached to the page to cover the old text. The new text was written on the slip before it was attached. (The paper used is, in most instances, recycled from rejected manuscript pages, utilizing a blank side but leaving old text on the underside. The recovered text of one such slip is given in Appendix.)

The slips have been cut with small scissors (possibly sewing scissors) and attached by affixing halves of moistened paste wafers. (A wafer was a disc of flour paste usually colored—like those in the manuscript—with vermilion.) To make the paste bond better to the paper, it was common to impress the paper over the wafer with a small seal-like device having a pattern like a waffle iron. Sometimes a writer improvised, for example using a knife to score the paper (Nickell 1990, 97).

In the narrative the writer appears to have used a thimble. (This would not be surprising because a thimble was sometimes employed, as was the top of a key, as an improvised seal for pressing into sealing wax [Nickell 1990, 91].) Unlike the typical squarish grid pattern, that of the manuscript shows rows of raised dots that are quite like those I produced experimentally using old thimbles. (The tiny hemispheres are convex, corresponding to the concave indentations of thimbles.) If this evidence is correct, it is a further indication (not proof of course) that the author was a woman.

In any event, the use of wafers is instructive. With the advent of adhesive envelopes in the 1850s, wafers began to disappear. The last example I find in my reference collection (without claiming this as definitive) is on a Confederate letter sheet dated 1863.

Revised folios

More substantive revisions were apparently made by replacing a folio. A clear example of this is found in a break between pp. 194 and 195. The last two inches of p. 194 have uncharacteristically been left blank, and the top of the next page (before the heading for the next chapter) has three lines crossed out. This indicates that the folio ending with p. 194 was replaced. (If folios were replaced in the progress of writing, rather than later, there would not be such a gap to betray the fact.)

Some single leaves have been used, which fact further indicates the discarding and revising of text. One such single leaf is numbered pp. 11–12, having the seam mark of the paper-machine belt; that mark being absent from the preceding and succeeding pages shows necessarily that a single leaf is present from the folio that had been so marked. Also (as mentioned earlier) pp. 127–128 represent a single leaf as indicated by the fact that the stationers' embossment is different from that of the leaves before and after.

Simple arithmetic indicates there must be at least one more single leaf. After the first folio (the title page, followed in turn by a blank page, the preface, and another blank page), there are 302 pages (301 numbered pages plus a blank final page). The two single leaves already identified represent four pages, so

302 minus 4 equals 298, but that is not evenly divisible by four. However subtracting one more leaf (two pages) *would* give a number so divisible (296 ÷ 4 = 74 folios), so there must be one additional single leaf; or there could be three, five, etc. The halving of a folio was probably done by slitting the fold with a paper knife (somewhat like the later letter opener only with a wider blade having a rounded tip—see Nickell 1990, pp. 106, 107), or again the pen knife could have been pressed into service.

8. BINDING

As will be clear from much of the foregoing, *The Bondwoman's Narrative* was composed not in a blank book but on sheets of stationery. Because of this the manuscript, subsequently bound, was not sewn in interfolded gatherings. The manuscript appears to have existed in two distinct forms: one without covers and one with.

Pre-cover "binding"

The decidedly soiled and abraded condition of the first and last page of the original manuscript (i.e., ignoring the flyleaves) is evidence that the manuscript was not bound immediately upon completion.

I find no evidence of the manuscript having been tied in a bundle with string or ribbon (as might have been indicated by damaged edges or a narrow, less-soiled crisscross area where ribbon or string had been).

Instead, although one conservation expert saw no obvious evidence of prior binding (Bowen 2001), I found what I believe is subtle evidence of it. Two sets of pinholes are seen in the interior margins of the pages (next to the book's "gutter"). These are within a few centimeters of the top and bottom and exist throughout the book (Figure 8.1). The pinholes penetrate the pasteovers whenever they intrude into the punched areas (e.g., on p. 222), indicating the holes were made after the narrative was effectively completed.

I considered but rejected the hypothesis that the pinholes were mis-punchings by the later bookbinder. The holes have occasionally been enlarged by tearing (e.g., the lower one on p. 97 and adjacent pages). This indicates that the holes had been threaded and the improvised volume subjected to some handling at that time.

Because the extraneous pinholes are located too far from the edge, the fastening would have obscured some of the text. They are also out of alignment and may represent two different attempts at an amateurish binding, probably by the author. (This was perhaps somewhat like Emily Dickinson did with groups of her poems, written on similarly folded sheets of stationery: "When the copying was completed she stacked the sheets one on top of another, stabbed holes through them at the edge, and secured the booklets with string." Those poems are believed to date from about 1858 to early 1860 [Shurr 1983].)

In any event, on completing the manuscript—after replacing any folios and committing to final pagination—the author went through the work and numbered each page at the top with her quill pen and ink. Sometimes, when there was writing close to the top edge, she crowded in the page number as best she could (for example "135").

Professional binding

As indicated, evidence shows that the present binding was done after some elapse of time. Kenneth Rendell (2001) had so suggested, and he stated: "The black cover of this type"—referring to the black-cloth-covered pasteboard binding—"is much more commonly seen on books and bound albums late in the nineteenth century. I don't recall seeing one this size earlier than about 1880."

Conservationist Craigen W. Bowen (2001) had noted that some "pages were slightly stuck together in the gutter as though adhesive had been applied, perhaps for reason of repair." Indeed visual and ultraviolet examination showed traces of what appeared to be paste, and I obtained and tested a sample (using a cotton swab moistened with distilled water to remove a trace and applying iodine reagent to it). This yielded a positive indication of starch, consistent with a flour paste. I suspect it is the "wheat paste" of bookbinders and that it was used to help consolidate the pages, particularly considering the presence of single leaves. (I do not think the author did the pasting: If she had a paste-pot, one wonders why she did not use it for the paste-over slips rather than utilize wafers.)

The pasting was probably done before the sewing. It appears to me that small groups of stacked folios may have been stuck together in sort of quasi-gatherings and then each sewn, stitching through the fold of one of the folios. (If desired, an expert on books and binding could be consulted, although I think little would be added relevant to the major issues [the author's identity and date of composition].)

The volume was almost certainly put in a book press, because the halved paste wafers, being somewhat thick, have left their half-moon shapes embossed into adjacent pages. I believe this would only occur to the extent seen with such pressing. (The effect proved a nuisance in studying the stationer's embossed crests, since the wafer imprints sometimes coincided with and partially obliterated them.)

9. TEXTUAL MATTERS

In addition to the writing materials, the text of *The Bondwoman's Narrative* offers considerable information about the author and the date of composition.

Vocabulary and spelling

The narrative is not that of an unread person. Polysyllabic words—like *magnanimity* (p. 78), *obsequious* (p. 23), *vicissitudes* (p. 7), *sagacity* (p. 28), *demoniacal* (p. 105), *unfathomable* (p. 115), *implacable* (p. 161), *ascertained* (p. 33), and *incipient* (p. 235)—flow from the author's pen.

To be sure, there are many misspellings: "incumber" for *encumber*, "excelent" for *excellent* (p. 9), "secresy" for *secrecy* (p. 49), "meloncholy" for *melancholy* (p. 51), "inseperable" for *inseparable* (p. 97), "hedious" for hideous (p. 214), "benumed" for *benumbed* (p. 232), and others, including "your" for *you're* (p. 109).

But some apparent misspellings—e.g. "connexions" (p. 13) and "life-time" (p. 19)—were actually appropriate at the time of writing (the mid-nineteenth century) as indicated by the *Oxford English Dictionary*. And some—like "recognised" (p. 10) and "defence" (p. 78)—may be owing to the author's reading of English literary works (frequently acknowledged by her epigraphs at the beginning of chapters).

The admixture of good vocabulary skills and occasional poor

spelling would seem consistent with someone who had struggled to learn. In the course of the manuscript, the narrator progresses from illiterate slave girl to keeper of "a school for colored children"—a progression that, if fictionalized, nevertheless seems a credible personal achievement (as witness, for example, the accomplishments of Frederick Douglass [1845]).

Readability level

The readability level of *The Bondwoman's Narrative* is relatively high. This can be shown by analyzing a rather typical passage (like this one, p. 17, describing the protagonist's visit to a gallery of ancestral portraits in the mansion of Lindendale):

> Though filled with superstitious awe I was in no has-
> -te to leave the room; for there surrounded by mysteri-
> -ous associations I seemed suddenly to have grown old,
> to have entered a new world of thoughts, and feel-
> -ings and sentiments I was not a slave with these
> pictured memorials of the past They could not en
> -force drudgery, or condemn me on account of my color
> to a life of servitude As their companion I could
> think and speculate In their presence my mind seem
> -ed to run riotous and exult in its freedom as a rat
> -tional being, and one destined for something higher and
> better than this world can afford

I applied a common readability formula (from Bovée and Thill 1989) that is based on the number of polysyllabic words in combination with the average sentence length. The readability level for the above passage is eleventh grade. Although this applies to the potential reader rather than the writer, it does naturally suggest that the latter has achieved at least that level of reading ability.

The readability scale, however, perhaps does not quite do justice to the impressive range of the author's seeming erudition. She refers to "the laws of the Medes and Persians" (p. 22), suggests appearances that "were enough to have provoked a smile on the lip of Heraclitus" (p. 143), and speaks of "the meaning of nature's various hieroglyphical symbols" (p. 206). She uses alliteration—"two weak[,] weary [,] wandering women" (p. 60)—and many other literary devices and conventions. If she has indeed become a schoolteacher, as her account says, that would certainly have further motivated her to read historical, literary, and other works.

Fictionalization

A full discussion of the narrative's content is beyond the scope of this report, but there are many indications that the work is a novel, despite the protestations in the Preface that "Being the truth it makes no pretensions to romance. . . ." There are gothic elements, for example, in the shadowy gloom of the mansion, the "legend of the linden" with its reputed curse, and the suggestion of various supernatural elements. In contrast is the true slave narrative of Frederick Douglass (1845) which, while containing the occasional quotation, lacks the lengthy exchanges of dialogue common to *The Bondwoman's Narrative,* as well as the elaborate scene-setting descriptions and other conventions.

However, the novel may be based on actual experiences. There are changes that may be due to fictionalization of real persons or events, such as the change of "Charlotte" to "Susan" (pp. 47 and 48). More telling, perhaps, is the fact that the name

"Wheeler" in the narrative was first written cryptically, for example as "Mr Wh——r" and "Mrs Wh——r," but then later was overwritten with the missing letters "eele" in each case to complete the name.

Beyond the fictionalization, geographical references may be evidential. Such phrases as "educated at the north" (p. 10), "in the southern states" (p. 53), "the North" (p. 152), and "A northern woman" (p. 154) indicate a southern perspective that would be appropriate for the mid-nineteenth century. References to Virginia—notably, mention of "the shores of the Old Dominion" (p. 16) and "the steamboat landing on the James River" (p. 50)—suggest familiarity with that state, as mention of "the public slave market in Wilmington" (p. 212) suggests knowledge of North Carolina.

Date indications

Numerous words and phrases throughout the narrative that seem odd or quaint by today's usage are in fact quite correct for the mid-nineteenth century (according to the *Oxford English Dictionary*, 1971). For example, "superscription," meaning the name and address on a letter (p. 41), was used by Thackeray in 1840; "converse" for conversation (p. 8), was employed by George Eliot in 1863; "apartments" to describe single rooms (pp. 14–17) was used by various writers, e.g. in 1824 and 1879; "Madras handkerchiefs," describing colorful silk-and-cotton kerchiefs worn by West Indian blacks as headdresses (p. 26), was in common use from at least 1833 to 1881; "the piazza" as used, erroneously, for a colonnade (p. 150), was so employed from 1638 and as late as 1861 and 1864 (the latter source acknowledging it as "a misnomer"); and so on and on.

A reflection of the time period in which Hannah was supposedly in Washington—which she refers to credibly as "the Capital" (p. 154), "the Federal Capital" (p. 155), and "Washington, the Federal City" (p. 161)—comes from the descriptions of talk by office seekers. They "would have a rail-road to the Pacific, and a ship Canal across the Isthmus," and "would quell the Indians and oust the Mormons . . ." (p. 202). In fact, railway construction westward from the Mississippi River began in 1851, and transcontinental travel was eventually made possible in 1869 ("Railways" 1860); focus on the Isthmus grew after the discovery of gold in California in 1848 ("Panama Canal" 1960); and the Mormons became especially controversial after their clashes with settlers in Illinois in 1846 (*World* 1999). Similarly, the mention of "vagabond Irishmen" (p. 203) might well have been prompted by the increased immigration that resulted from the great Irish famine of 1846–1847 (*World* 1999).

Throughout the narrative, references to slavery are in the present tense (as in the Preface's mention of "that institution whose curse rests" over the nation). This would make no sense if written after the war. Neither would the author's claim to being "A Fugitive Slave" who had "Recently Escaped from North Carolina." Mentions of "a deed of manumission" (p. 46), "a slave state" (p. 86), and "an Abolitionist" (p. 286) are all correct for the pre–Civil War period. To have omitted any mention of secession or the outbreak of the war itself would have been counterproductive if written after 1861. Following the war, the story would have seemed passé, perhaps thus helping to explain why it went unpublished.

Had the author wished to publish it as a retrospective, then surely she would have at least rewritten the title page and preface accordingly. Doubtless the same would be true even if the novel were actually composed after the war (which the evidence anyway strongly argues against).

A very specific date indicator—mention of "the equestrian

statue of Jackson" in Washington (p. 201)—provides a date before which the narrative could not have been completed. According to an internet source (http://thatman.homestead.com/jackson.html), that sculpture was done by Clark Mills in 1853.

Considering all this evidence, a date of circa 1853–1861 is indicated, consistent with the evidence from the writing materials.

Authorial indications

The author's point of view and insights as a woman, a black, and a Christian ring true. As indicated earlier, the handwriting is consistent with that of a relatively young person writing at the middle of the nineteenth century.

If I am correct in identifying the impressions over the wafers (at the corners of the pasteovers) as those of a thimble, and in suggesting that the scissors used were perhaps sewing scissors and that needle and thread were employed in an amateurish earlier binding by the author—if indeed these speculations are correct, they offer further evidence that the writer was a woman.

She seems often to be writing out of her own experience. Interestingly, she tells of an unusual dream (pp. 228–229) following the death of a fellow escaped slave. She relates the characteristics of what is known as a "waking dream"—i.e. a hypnopompic hallucination that occurs in the twilight between being asleep and awake. She experiences the bizarre imagery typical of such waking dreams (people often see ghosts, demons, angels, extraterrestrials, etc.) together with "sleep paralysis" (she specifically says she is "unable to move"). So accurately does she describe such a waking dream that it seems likely she actually experienced one. (For a discussion of the phenomenon, see Baker and Nickell 1992.)

SUMMARY

The Bondwoman's Narrative, a bound 301-page manuscript about 20 x 25 cm high is ostensibly "By Hannah Crafts / A Fugitive Slave / Recently Escaped from North Carolina" according to its title page. Its provenance can be reliably traced back to the 1940s.

Examination by a variety of techniques reveals it was written in modified round-hand script (a style of ca. 1840–1865) in a natural, if not notably elegant or swift fashion. It was written with a quill pen, using an ordinary iron-gall ink, on machine-made rag paper consisting of four types of stationery folios (folded sheets). Two of these bear an embossment of the Southworth paper manufacturing company, one type known in examples of 1856 and 1860.

Extraneous pinholes in the inside margins represent an apparent early attempt at binding, probably with ordinary needle and thread by the author. Originally this amateur binding lacked covers, because the first (title) page and the last are soiled and abraded. Much later the manuscript was professionally bound, not in the usual gatherings but—due to the writing having been done on a stack of folios—these were apparently consolidated with paste and then sewn, with covers affixed consisting of black cloth over pasteboard.

The manuscript was a work in progress and contained many revisions. There are numerous "wipe erasures" (the wet ink having been wiped off with the little finger), erasures made with an ink-eraser knife (occasional resulting blobs being blotted with sand), and pasteovers (scissors-cut slips affixed with halved, vermilion-colored paste wafers, the paper over which was impressed with, apparently, a thimble). As well, a few folios were replaced and there are a few single leaves.

Regarding textual matters, the narrative employs many polysyllabic words, artistic phrasings, and classical allusions, and yields a readability level of eleventh grade (by today's standards) although there are occasional spelling errors. There is evidence of fictionalization, despite the authorial preface denying any "pretensions to romance."

Nevertheless, southern geographical and other references seem to ring true, as does the pre–Civil War setting. Mention of "the equestrian statue of Jackson" demonstrates the narrative could not have been completed earlier than 1853, and the omission of any reference to secession or war—together with the preface's phrase "Fugitive Slave Recently Escaped . . ."—makes no sense unless written by 1861. Also credible is the author's point of view and insights as a young, Christian, African-American woman.

CONCLUSIONS

Considerable evidence indicates that *The Bondwoman's Narrative* is an authentic manuscript of circa 1853–1861. A specific mention of "the equestrian statue of Jackson" in Washington demonstrates that the work could not have been completed before 1853, and the omission of any reference to secession or the Civil War makes no logical sense unless it was written prior to those events. Other references in the text as well as indications from the language are also consistent with this period. No anachronisms were found to point to a later time of composition.

It was apparently written by a relatively young, African-

American woman who was deeply religious and had obvious literary skills, although eccentric punctuation and occasional misspellings suggest someone who struggled to become educated. Her handwriting is a serviceable rendering of a period-style script known as modified round hand (the fashion of ca. 1840–1865). She wrote more for legibility than speed, and was right handed.

Her writing accoutrements are also consistent with the 1850s. They included quill pens and a pen knife, iron-gall ink, stationery folios (i.e. folded sheets, including those with embossments from the Southworth paper company), an ink-eraser knife (unless she did double duty with her pen knife), a sander or sand-box (filled with common sand) used to blot ink, a box of vermilion wafers (paste discs) used to attach correction slips, that were usually cut from discarded leaves with small scissors. She probably had a paper knife (to slit an occasional folded sheet into two leaves). Apparently lacking a seal (to impress the paper over wafers to make a better bond), she seems to have employed a thimble for the purpose (leaving a distinctive pattern of raised dots). Finally, she seems to have used an ordinary needle and thread to sew the pages together (the volume's current professional binding having been done much later).

The combination of writing materials and apparent sewing tools used in the manuscript suggests they were kept in close proximity, as at the desk or sewing table or possibly in a portable writing box. These became popular to Victorian ladies in the 1850–1860 period. The common type of the latter, known as a lap desk, opened to provide a sloped writing surface and compartments for matching inkwell and sander, pens, etc. (See photograph in Nickell 1990, p. 149). There were even combined writing and sewing boxes for ladies, as well as multi-purpose "trinket" and "work" boxes (Jenkins 1963).

RECOMMENDATIONS

The findings in this report should be viewed in light of additional historical investigation that is being conducted externally by Professor Gates. Although I am confident of the 1853–1861 date estimate, should documentary evidence seem to conflict with it then both should subsequently be reevaluated to determine the true facts.

If a document should come to light that is thought to bear the signature or other handwriting of "Hannah Crafts," it should be compared with the writing of the narrative to determine whether they are indeed by the same person. This comparison must be done by an expert familiar with the handwriting of the period, since lay persons typically mistake *class* characteristics for *individual* ones (Nickell 1996, pp. 25–29).

The Bondwoman's Narrative is a valuable manuscript and should be preserved. Subject to the expert opinion of a professional conservationist, I recommend placing a loose sheet of acid-buffering paper inside both the front and back of the volume, inserted between the flyleaf and title page in the first place and between the last page of the original manuscript and flyleaf in the second instance. This would be to prevent the flyleaves—which are probably wood-pulp paper and quite acidic—from further degrading the historic manuscript.

APPENDIX

Recovered Text from the Underside of a Pasteover Slip

On the verso of a pasted-over slip on page 138 are the following seven lines (with unreadable portions indicated by ellipsis points):

1. Their misfortunes are nothing to me except I can take
2. advantage of them to promote my own views[.] I have
3. not [ma]de the laws under the operation of which . . .
4. -ful men may be sold like sheep[.] I only con . . . to . . .
5. the . . . duce them to practice[.] If such women . . .
6. sold is rather the fault of the law that permits
7. than of me who may perchance buy or even sell . . .

Note the similarity to text on pp. 122–123.

REFERENCES

Baker, Robert A., and Joe Nickell. 1992. *Missing Pieces: How to Investigate Ghosts, UFOs, Psychics, & Other Mysteries.* Buffalo, N.Y.: Prometheus Books, 226–227.

Bowen, Craigen W. 2001. Letter report (from Straus Center for Conservation, Harvard University Art Museum) to Henry L. Gates, April 5.

Bovée, Courtland L., and John V. Thill. 1989. *Business Communication Today*, second ed. New York: Random House, pp. 125–126.

Cahoon, Herbert, Thomas V. Lange, and Charles Ryskamp. 1977. *American Literary Autographs from Washington Irving to Henry James.* New York: Dover.

The Chicago Manual of Style, fourteenth ed. 1993. Chicago: The University of Chicago Press, p. 325ff.

Feigen, Michelle. 2001. "African-Americana Sales a Stunner at Swann's and Other Dealers," *The Manuscript Society News*, Vol. XXII, No. 2, pp. 56–59.

Douglass, Frederick. 1845. *Narrative of the Life of Frederick Douglass an American Slave Written by Himself.* Reprinted and edited by Benjamin Quarles, Cambridge, Mass.: The Belknap Press of Harvard University Press, 1979.

Jenkins, Dorothy H. 1963. *A Fortune in the Junk Pile: A Guide to Valuable Antiques that May Be Found in Attics, Cellars, etc.* New York: Crown Publishers, pp. 343–346.

Kennedy, Ed. 2001. Southworth Paper representative, interviewed by Henry Louis Gates Jr., April 30.

Nickell, Joe. 1990. *Pen, Ink & Evidence: A Study of Writing and Writing Materials for the Penman, Collector, and Document Detective.* Reprinted New Castle, Delaware: Oak Knoll Press, 2000.

———. 1991. "Erasures and Corrections in Historic Documents: An Overview," paper presented to 49th Annual Conference of the

American Society of Questioned Document Examiners, Lake Buena Vista, Fla., August 3–8.

———. 1993. "Stationers' Crests: A Catalog of More than 200 Embossed Paper Marks 1835–1901," *Manuscripts*, vol. XLV, No. 3, Summer, pp. 199–216.

———. 1996. *Detecting Forgery: Forensic Investigation of Documents.* Lexington, Ky.: University Press of Kentucky.

The Oxford English Dictionary, The Compact Edition of. 1971. New York: Oxford University Press.

"Panama Canal." 1960. *Encyclopaedia Britannica.*

"Railways." 1960. *Encyclopaedia Britannica.*

Rendell, Kenneth W. 2001. Letter report to Laurence Kirshbaum, Chairman, Time Warner Trade Publishing, April 26.

Shurr, William H. 1983. *The Marriage of Emily Dickinson.* Lexington, Ky.: The University Press of Kentucky, pp. 1–2.

The World Almanac and Book of Facts. 1999. Mahwah, New Jersey: World Almanac Books, p. 516.

APPENDIX B

Testimony of Jane Johnson

Version I

"I can't tell my exact age; I guess I am about 25; I was born in Washington City; lived there this New-Year's, if I shall live to see it, two years; I came to Philadelphia about two months ago.

I came with Col. Wheeler; I brought my two children, one aged 10, and the other a year or so younger; we went to Mr. Sully's and got something to eat; we then went to the wharf, then into the hotel.

Col. Wheeler told me to stay on the upper porch and did not let me go to dinner, and sent by the servants some dinner to me, but I did not desire any; after dinner he asked me if I had dinner; I told him I wanted none; while he was at dinner I saw a colored woman, and went to her and told her I was a slave woman traveling with a very curious gentleman, who did not want me to have anything to do or say to colored persons; she said she was sorry for me; I said nothing more; then I went back and took my seat where I had been ordered by Col. Wheeler; he had told me not to talk to colored persons; to tell everybody I was traveling with a minister going to Nicaragua; he seemed to think I might be led off; he did not tell me I could be free if I wanted to when I got to Philadelphia; on the boat he said he would give me my freedom; he never said so before; I had made preparations before leaving Washington to get my freedom in New York; I made a suit to disguise myself in—they had never seen me wear it—to escape in when I got to New York; Mr. Wheeler has that suit in his possession, in my trunk; I wasn't willing to come without my children; for I wanted to free them; I have been in Col. Wheeler's family nearly two years; he bought me from a gentleman of Richmond—a Mr. Crew; he was not a member of Col. Wheeler's family; Col. Wheeler was not more than half an hour at dinner; he came to look at me from the dinner-table, and found me where he had left me; I did not ask leave of absence at Bloodgood's Hotel; while Col. Wheeler went on board the boat a colored man asked me did I want to go with Col. W.; I told him "No, I do not;" at 9 o'clock that night he said he would touch the telegraph for me and some one [sic] would meet me at New York; I said I was obliged to him; no more was said then; I had never seen the man before; when Col. Wheeler took me on board he took me on the upper deck and sat us down alongside of him. While sitting there I saw a colored man and a white one; the white man beckoned me to come to him; the colored man asked did I desire my freedom; the white man approached Mr. W. and said he desired to tell me my rights; Mr. W. said, "My woman knows her rights;" they told me to go with them; he held out his hand but did not touch mine, and I immediately arose to go with him; I took my oldest boy by the hand; the youngest was picked up by some people and became very alarmed, and I proceeded off the boat as quickly as I could, being perfectly willing and desirous to go; Mr. Wheeler tried to stop me, no one else; he tried to get before me as though he wanted to talk to me; I wanted to get off the boat, and didn't listen to what he had to say. I did not say I did not want my freedom; I have always wanted it; I did not say I wanted to go with my master; I went very willingly to the carriage, I was very glad to go; the little boy said he wanted to go to his massa, he was frightened; I did not say I wanted to go to Col. Wheeler; there was no outcry of any kind, my little boy made all the noise that was made."

(*The Case of Passmore* Williamson, 1855)

Version II

"Jane Johnson being sworn, makes oath and says—"My name is Jane—Jane Johnson; I was the slave of Mr. Wheeler of Washington; he bought me and my two children, about two years ago, of Mr. Cornelius Crew, of Richmond, Va.; my youngest child is between six and seven years old, the other between ten and eleven; I have one other child only, and he is in Richmond; I have not seen him for about two years; never expect to see him again; Mr. Wheeler brought me and my two children to Philadelphia, on the way to Nicaragua, to wait on his wife; I didn't want to go without my two children, and he consented to take them; we came to Philadelphia by the cars; stopped at Mr. Sully's, Mr. Wheeler's father-in-law, a few moments; then went to the steamboat for New York at 2 o'clock, but were too late; we went into Bloodgood's Hotel; Mr. Wheeler went to dinner; Mr. Wheeler had told me in Washington to have nothing to say to colored persons, and if any of them spoke to me, to say I was a free woman traveling with a minister; we staid [sic] at Bloodgood's till 5 o'clock; Mr. Wheeler kept his eye on me all the time except when he was at dinner; he left his dinner to come and see if I was safe, and then went back again; while he was at dinner, I saw a colored woman and told her I was a slave woman, that my master had told me not to speak to colored people, and that if any of them spoke to me to say that I was

free; but I am not free; but I want to be free; she said: 'poor thing, I pity you;' after that I saw a colored man and said the same thing to him, he said he would telegraph to New York, and two men would meet me at 9 o'clock and take me with them; after that we went on board the boat, Mr. Wheeler sat beside me on the deck; I saw a colored gentleman come on board, he beckoned to me; I nodded my head, and could not go; Mr. Wheeler was beside me and I was afraid; a white gentleman then came and said to Mr. Wheeler, 'I want to speak to your servant, and tell her of her rights;' Mr. Wheeler rose and said, 'If you have anything to say, say it to me—she knows her rights;' the white gentleman asked me if I wanted to be free; I said 'I do, but I belong to this gentleman and I can't have it;' he replied, 'Yes, you can, come with us, you are as free as your master, if you want your freedom come now; if you go back to Washington you may never get it;' I rose to go, Mr. Wheeler spoke, and said, 'I will give you your freedom,' but he had never promised it before, and I knew he would never give it to me; the white gentleman held out his hand and I went toward him; I was ready for the word before it was given me; I took the children by the hands, who both cried, for they were frightened, but both stopped when they got on shore; a colored man carried the little one, I led the other by the hand. We walked down the street till we got to a hack; nobody forced me away; nobody pulled me, and nobody led me; I went away of my own free will; I always wished to be free and meant to be free when I came North; I hardly expected it in Philadelphia, but I thought I should get free in New York; I have been comfortable and happy since I left Mr. Wheeler, and so are the children; I don't want to go back; I could have gone in Philadelphia if I had wanted to; I could go now; but I had rather die than go back. I wish to make this statement before a magistrate, because I understand that Mr. Williamson is in prison on my account, and I hope the truth may be of benefit to him."

Jane [her mark] Johnson

(William Still, *The Underground Railroad,* pp. 94–95)

APPENDIX C

John Hill Wheeler's Library Catalogue
Compiled by Bryan C. Sinche

Wheeler compiled a catalogue of his books at his North Carolina home on June 10, 1850. Wheeler had six cases of books, each containing more than 180 volumes. The first case he catalogued contained primarily belletristic and philosophical works; other cases included law, history, classics, politics, and other assorted volumes. Besides the 1,200 volumes contained within Wheeler's library, he kept a selection of books in his parlor. These few titles were most likely for the women in his home; they cover topics such as needlepoint and homemaking.

The list below contains the legible titles from the belletristic portion of Wheeler's library. Wheeler does not list authors in his catalogue, except in a few instances; therefore, most publication data for the works in his library is speculative. I have used Wheeler's titles and the cutoff date of 1850 to locate possible authors and publishers for the works.

This list has been assembled using the Library of Congress catalogue, the National Union catalogue, and the OCLC catalogue. I have focused on editions published in Philadelphia and New York since Wheeler frequented those cities (especially Philadelphia). For the three works for which I have been unable to locate any possible publication data in any catalogue, I have simply listed the title as it appears in Wheeler's own catalogue.

Selection from Case One:
1. *Biography of Eminent Men, Statesmen, Heroes, Authors, Artists and Men of Science, of Europe and America.* Samuel Griswold Goodrich, ed. New York: Nafis and Cornish, 1846. This title is part of Peter Parley's Select Library.
2. Wheeler records *Literature and Literary Men* as a title. Though there is no exact match for such a title, this volume is likely one of the following:
> Gilfillan, George. *Sketches of Modern Literature, and Eminent Literary Men, (Being a Gallery of Literary Portraits).* 2 vols. New York: D. Appleton & Co.; Philadelphia: Geo. S. Appleton, 1846.
>
> Gilfillan, George. *Modern Literature and Literary Men: Being a Second Gallery of Literary Portraits.* New York: Appleton, 1850.

3. Phillips, Charles, *Curran and His Contemporaries.* Edinburgh and London: W. Blackwood and Sons, 1850.
4. *American Female Poets.* Rufus Wilmot Griswold, ed. (Running title: *Gems from American Female Poets.*) Bound with his *Gems from the American Poets.* Philadelphia: Porter and Coates, 1844.
5. *Marshal Book of Oratory.*
6. Hedge, Frederic Henry. *Prose Writers of Germany.* Philadelphia: Carey and Hart, 1848.
7. Kennedy, John Pendleton. *Swallow Barn.* Philadelphia: Carey and Lea, 1832.
8. The title *Lives of the Signers of the Declaration of Independence* could be one of the following:
> Dwight, Nathaniel. *The Lives of the Signers of the Declaration of Independence.* New York: Harper & Brothers, 1840.
>
> Goodrich, Charles A. *Lives of the Signers of the Declaration of*

Independence. New York: W. Reed & Co., 1829. (Also, New York: T. Mather, 1832.)

9. Wheeler records *Wiley Reader* as a title. This volume is most likely Wiley and Putnam. *Wiley & Putnam's Library of Choice Reading.* New York: Wiley and Putnam, 1846.

10. Wheeler records *Lives of the Poets* as a title, which suggests Samuel Johnson's work. However, he makes a notation that the volume is "by Howett." There is no work by such an author. One possibility for a *Lives of the Poets* not by Johnson is

Sanford, Ezekiel and Robert Walsh. *Works of the British Poets with Lives of the Authors.* 23 vols. Philadelphia: P. A. Mitchell, Ames and White, 1819.

11. Starling, Elizabeth. *Noble Deeds of American Women, or, Examples of Female Courage and Virtue.* Philadelphia: Carey, Lea and Blanchard, 1836.

12. Wheeler records *Poets of America and Europe* as a title. There is no work with this title in the LOC, OCLC, or *National Union* catalogues. A work with this title embedded in its complete title is

Hall, William. *Encyclopedia of English Grammar: Designed for the Use of Schools, Academics, and Private Learners. Embracing Grammar, Elocution, Rhetoric, Logic and Music, upon a New Plan Not Before Introduced, with Copious Exercises in Prose and Selections from the Most Distinguished Poets of Europe and America.* Columbus, Ohio: Scott & Bascom, 1850.

13. Nunes, Joseph A. *Aristocracy: or, Life among the "Upper Ten."* Philadelphia: T. B. Peterson, 1848.

14. Wheeler records *Women, or Virgin, Wife and Mother* as a title. Though there is no such title in the LOC, OCLC, or *National Union* catalogues, a similar title is

The True History of Henrietta de Belgrave: a Woman Born to Great Calamities, a Distressed Virgin, Unhappy Wife, and Most Afflicted Mother, Her Intended Voyage with Her Parents to the East Indies . . . London: Printed and sold at Bailey's Printing Office, 1750.

15. Johnson, Samuel. *The Rambler with a Historical and Biographical Preface by Alex Chalmers.* Philadelphia: J. J. Woodward, 1827. (This is one of seventy-five pre-1850 editions—the other Philadelphia edition published during Wheeler's life is *The Rambler, to Which is Prefixed an Essay on the Life and Genius of Dr. Johnson, by Arthur Murphy, Esq.* Philadelphia: H. Cowperthwait, 1828.

16. Moore, Thomas. *Works of Thomas Moore.* 4th ed. 2 vols. Philadelphia: Washington Press, 1827–28.

17. Scott, Sir Walter. *Works of Sir Walter Scott.* Philadelphia: Pomeroy, 1824. 7 vols. (There were ten pre-1850 American editions of Scott's *Works*—the other Philadelphia editions published during Wheeler's lifetime were by Carey and Hart, 1845 and 1847. Each edition contained ten volumes.)

18. Scott, Sir Walter. *Beauties of the Waverly Novels.* Boston: Samuel G. Goodrich, 1829.

19. Byron, Lord (George Gordon). *Works of Lord Byron.* 2 vols. Philadelphia: Moses Thomas, 1816. (Includes a sketch of Byron's life by J. W. Lake.)

20. Walpole, Horace. *Reminiscences.* Boston: Wells and Lilly, 1820. (This is the only American edition. J. Sharpe of London published *Reminiscences* in 1819.)

21. Burns, Robert. *Letters.* 2 vols. in 1. Boston: Wells and Lilly, 1820. (J. Sharpe of London published *Letters* in 1819.)

22. Gray, Thomas. *Letters.* Boston: Wells and Lilly, 1820.

23. Goldsmith, Oliver. *Essays by Dr. Goldsmith.* Philadelphia: B. Davies, 1802. (Part of the Select British Classics Series.) Though there are numerous editions of Goldsmith's *Essays*, this is the only one with the same title Wheeler recorded.

24. Bacon, Francis. *Essays, Moral, Economical and Political.* Philadelphia: R. Deseliver, etc., 1818.

25. Johnson, Samuel. *Sermons by Samuel Johnson LLD, Left for Publication by John Taylor.* Boston: Wells and Lilly, 1821. (J. Sharpe of London published *Sermons* in 1819.)

26. Reynold, Sir Joshua. *Discourses at the Royal Academy by Sir Joshua Reynolds.* Boston: Wells and Lilley, 1821.
27. Chesterfield, Philip Dormer Stanhope. *Lord Chesterfield's Letters to His Son.* Baltimore: John Kingston. Printed by A. Miltenberger, 1813.
28. Wheeler records *Poets and Artists of Great Britain*, which is most likely
> Hall, S. C. *The Book of Gems. The Poets and Artists of Great Britain.* London; Saunders and Otley, 1836; Philadelphia: T. Wardle, 1838.

29. Wheeler records *Years of Consolation* "by Mrs. Burton." This may be
> Butler, Mrs. Fanny Kemble. "Year of Consolation," in *Littell's Living Age 15* (1847).

30. Dwight, Theodore. *The Father's Book, or, Suggestions for the Government and Instruction of Young Children, on Principles Appropriate to a Christian Country.* Springfield, Mass.: G. and C. Merriam, 1834.
31. *Beauties of British Classics: Containing the Best Selections of Entertaining and Instructive Essays . . .* Baltimore: T. W. Cleland, 1826.
32. Warne, Joseph A. *Phrenology in the Family. Or, the Utility of Phrenology in Early Domestic Education . . .* Philadelphia: G. W. Donohue, 1839.
33. Goldsmith, Oliver. *Goldsmith's Poems. Consisting of The Traveller, The Deserted Village, Edwin and Angelina, Retaliation, Double Transformation, and A New Simile.* Philadelphia: Printed by H. Maxwell, for Mathew Carey, 1800. (Though there are numerous editions of Goldsmith's poems, this is the only one with this title.)
34. *Calliope, a Collection of English Ballads.* Baltimore: Edward J. Coale; J. Robinson, printer, 1814.
36. Swift, Jonathan. *Gulliver's Travels.* 2 vols. Philadelphia: Printed for Mathew Carey, 1808–09. (This is the first full, dated, American edition, but it is titled *Travels into Several Remote Regions of the World, by Lemuel Gulliver.* Later editions ignore Swift's pseudonymic title,

and the first American edition titled *Gulliver's Travels* was New York: Dixon and Silkels, 1827.)

37. Shakespeare, William. *Beauties of Shakespeare Regularly Selected from Each Play.* Boston: T. Bedlington, 1827.

38. Appears to be *Wanderer of Livitzen*. No such title appears in the Library of Congress catalogue. There is an entry for

    Waterston, George. *Wanderer in Washington.* Printed at the Washington Press by Jonathan Elliot, 1827.

39. Dickens, Charles. *Old Curiosity Shop.* Philadelphia: Lea and Blanchard, 1841, 1842, 1849.

40. *Wills' Poems.* Though there are no titles in the OCLC or LOC catalogue by this name, two possibilities are

    Willis, Nathaniel Parker. *The Poems, Sacred, Passionate and Humorous of Nathaniel Parker Willis.* New York: Clark and Austin, 1844.

    Willis, Nathaniel Parker. *Poems of Early and After Years.* Philadelphia: Carey and Hart, 1848.

41. Scott, Sir Walter. *Waverly Novels.* 5 vols. Philadelphia: Carey and Hart, 1839, 1844–49.

42. Dickens, Charles. *Barnaby Rudge.* Philadelphia: Lea and Blanchard, 1842.

43. Lever, Charles J. *Charles O'Malley.* Philadelphia: Carey and Hart, 1840–49. Five editions published in this span.

44. *Legends and Stories of Ireland; Containing the Dead Boxer and Other Tales.* Philadelphia: J. B. Perry; New York: Nafis and Cornish, 1820.

45. Hazlitt, William. *Characters of Shakespeare's Plays.* New York: Wiley and Putnam, 1845.

46. Brontë, Charlotte. *Jane Eyre.* New York: Harper, 1847.

47. Brontë, Emily. *Wuthering Heights.* London: Newby, 1847. (There are two American editions published prior to 1850; however, both are wrongly attributed to the "author of *Jane Eyre*.")

48. Warren, Samuel. *Now and Then . . .* Edinburgh and London: W. Blackwood and Sons, 1847?.

49. Brontë, Charlotte. New York: Harper, 1850. (Part of a three-volume collection entitled *The Brontë Novels*.)

50. Wheeler records this title as *Temptation*, and there are several possibilities in the OCLC catalogue, though this volume may be one of a series with *Voluptuousness, Pride, and Envy* (51–53).

    Other possibilities are

        Gascoigne, Caroline. *Temptation, or, a Wife's Perils*. London: H. Colburn, 1839.

        Kidder, Daniel Parish. *The Temptation, or, Henry Thornton. Showing the Progress and Fruits of Intemperance*. Boston: King, Saxton and Pierce, 1841.

        Sue, Eugène. *The Temptation; or, The Watch Tower of Koat-Vën: A Romantic Tale*. New York: Burgess, Stringer & Co., 1848.

        Temptation, or, Henry Morland. Boston: Bowles and Dearborn, Press of Isaac R. Butts and Co., 1827.

        Townsend, William Thompson. *Temptation, or, The Fatal Brand*. London: T. H. Lacy, 1800.

51. *Voluptuousness*.

52. Wheeler records this title as *Envy*. A possibility for this entry is

        Champion, Joseph. *Envy: A Poem, to General R. Smith*. London: printed for W. Davis, 1776.

53. Wheeler records this title as *Pride*. Though there is no such title in the LOC catalogue, some possibilities are

        Arthur, Timothy Shay. *Pride or Principle, Which Makes the Lady?* Philadelphia: R. G. Benford, 1844.

        Austen, Jane. *Pride and Prejudice: A Novel*. London: Printed for T. Egerton, 1813.

        Rusticus, Nicholas. *Pride, or, A Touch at the Times: A Satirical Poem, Addressed to All Genuine Reformers in This Glorious Age of Anti-ism*. Boston: John Marsh & Co., 1830.

        Soane, George. *Pride Shall Have a Fall; A Comedy, in Five Acts—with Songs*. London: Hurst, Robinson, & Co., 1824.

54. Dickens, Charles. *American Notes.* New York: Wilson and Company, 1842.
55. Lever, Charles J. *The Knight of Gwynne.* Philadelphia: T. B. Peterson and Bros., 1844.
56. Lever, Charles J. *Arthur O'Leary.* Philadelphia: Carey and Hart, 1847. (Also New York: W. H. Colyer, 1847.)
57. Gore, Mrs. (Catherine Grace Frances Gore). *The Banker's Wife; or, Court and City, A Novel* . . . New York: Harper, 1843.
58. Grey, Mrs. (Elizabeth Caroline). *The Gambler's Wife. A Novel.* New York: Harper, 1845.
59. Grey, Mrs. (Elizabeth Caroline). *The Little Wife. A Record of Matrimonial Life* . . . *Complete in One Volume.* Philadelphia: T. B. Peterson, 1840.
60. Grey, Mrs. (Elizabeth Caroline). *The Duke and the Cousin.* Philadelphia: T. B. Peterson, 1850.
61. Grey, Mrs. (Elizabeth Caroline). *Fanny Thornton, or Marriage, a Lottery.* New York: W. H. Graham, 1849.
62. Wheeler records *Sketches of Everyday Life* as a title. This is most likely

> Dickens, Charles. *Sketches by Boz, Illustrative of Everyday Life and Every-day people.* London: Chapman and Hall, 1850.

63. Scott, Harriett Anne. *The Hen-pecked Husband.* New York: H. Long and Brothers, 1848.
64. Wheeler records this title as *Nina Brewer.* Though no such titles appear in the LOC, OCLC, or *National Union* catalogues, some possibilities for this entry are

> Brewer, Nicholas. *A narrative of the life and sufferings of Nicholas Brewer, of the town of Cardiff, in the county of Glamorgan, master mariner, and of the oppressions he has suffered at the hands of the Custom House officers of the said town of Cardiff, by their wrongfully seizing and detaining his vessel, under the false and malicious pretence of her bowsprit being longer than by law allowed, whereas it was upwards of three feet under the length prescribed by the act: to-*

gether with copies of correspondence between the said Brewer, and the Hon. the Commissioners of Customs, the secretary to the Right Hon. the Lords of the Treasury, &c.: also, a copy of the case as laid before Samuel Marriott, Esq. and his opinion thereon. England: s.n., 1823.

Female marine. *The Adventures of Lucy Brewer, Alias Louisa Baker.* Boston: Printed for N. Coverly, 1816. (This book was published in over twenty-five American editions.)

65. Oxenford, John, tr. *Tales from the German, Comprising Specimens from the Most Celebrated Authors.* Translated by John Oxenford and C. A. Feiling. New York: Harper & Brothers, 1844.

66. Wheeler records *The Jew* as a title. Some possibilities for this record are

Cumberland, Richard. *The Jew, a Comedy, in Five Acts.* Philadelphia: T. H. Palmer, 1823.

The Jew, At Home and Abroad. Revised by the Committee of Publication. Philadelphia: American Sunday-School Union, 1845.

The Jew, by the author of "The Egyptian." Philadelphia: James Callen & Sons [date unknown, but is between 1844 and 1858]. (This is a juvenile book.)

Spindler, Carl tr. *The Jew: Translated from the German.* New York: Harper & Bros., 1844.

67. Mayhew, Horace. *Whom to Marry and How to Get Married, or, the Adventures of a Lady in Search of a Good Husband.* London: D. Bogue, 1847–48. (Published at the office of the *New York World* in 1848.)

68. Blanchard, Jerrold and Hablot Knight Browne. *The Disgrace to the Family, a Story of Social Distinctions.* London: Darton and Co., 1848.

69. À Beckett, Gilbert Abbott and George Cruikshank. *The Comic Blackstone.* Philadelphia: Carey and Hart, 1844.

70. *Texas and Her President.*

71. Grey, Mrs. (Elizabeth Caroline). *The Belle of the Family.* Philadelphia: T. B. Peterson, 1843.

72. Brackenridge, Hugh Henry. *Modern Chivalry, Containing the Adventures of Captain Farrago and Teague O'Regan.* Philadelphia: Printed and sold by John M'Culloch, 1792–97.

73. Wheeler records *Animal Magnetism* as a title. Some possibilities for this entry are

    Animal Magnetism: Its History to the Present Time. London: Dyer, 1841.

    Animal Magnetizer, or History, Phenomena and Curative Effects of Animal Magnetism, with Instruction for Conducting the Magnetic Operation by a Physician. Philadelphia: J. Kav. Jun. and Brother, 1841.

    Bell, John. *Animal Magnetism: Past Fictions—Present Science.* Philadelphia: Haswell, 1837.

    Inchbald, Elizabeth Simpson. *Animal Magnetism: A Farce, in Three Acts.* Philadelphia: Neal and Mackenzie, Mifflin and Parry, printers, 1828.

    Lang, William and Chauncey Hare Townshend. *Animal Magnetism; or, Mesmerism; Its History, Phenomena, and Present Condition; Containing Practical Instructions and the Latest Discoveries in the Science.* New York: Mowatt, 1844.

    Leger, Theodore. *Animal Magnetism; or, Psycodunamy.* New York: D. Appleton: Philadelphia: G. S. Appleton; 1846.

74. Wheeler records *Love and Marriage* as a title. Some possibilities for this entry include

    Buckston, John Baldwin. *The Rake and His Pupil, or, Folly, Love, and Marriage, A Comedy in Three Acts.* London: W. Strange, 1834.

    Hale, Sarah. "The love marriage," in *The Token.* New York: Edwards, 1842.

    Snyder, George. *Love, Courtship and Marriage.* Baltimore: F. P. Audoun, 1829.

75. Philipon, Charles, Louis Huart and Eugène Sue. *The Comic Wandering Jew.* New York: Dick & Fitzgerald, 1840.

BRYAN C. SINCHE is currently a doctoral student in early-American literature and American studies at the University of North Carolina at Chapel Hill; he also holds a B.A. in English from the University of Michigan. He is the managing editor of *a/b: Auto/Biography Studies* and conducts research in nineteenth-century American life writing.

A NOTE ON CRAFTS'S LITERARY INFLUENCES

Henry Louis Gates Jr.

Bryan Sinche's compilation of the belletristic texts in John Hill Wheeler's library provides a rare opportunity for scholars to trace with great specificity the echoes, allusions, and borrowings that this ex-slave drew upon to construct her novel. Among the authors that Crafts appropriated and revised, Dickens seems to have been second to none.

Wheeler's library, as of June 10, 1850, included three books by Dickens—*The Old Curiosity Shop, Barnaby Rudge, American Notes*, and probably, *Sketches by Boz*. It is quite likely that Wheeler obtained a copy of *Bleak House* when it was published in America in 1853, after being serialized in 1852 and 1853. As Hollis Robbins, a graduate student at Princeton, pointed out to me, Dickens—and *Bleak House* in particular—was a fertile source for Hannah Crafts. For example, *The Bondwoman's Narrative* contains several borrowings from *Bleak House*, some verbatim or nearly so, as in the following two examples:

Bondwoman's Narrative	Bleak House
Gloom everywhere. Gloom up the Potomac; where it rolls among meadows no longer green, and by splendid country seats. Gloom down the Potomac where it washes the sides of huge war-ships. Gloom on the marshes, the fields, and heights. Gloom settling steadily down over the sumptuous habitations of the rich, and creeping through the cellars of the poor. Gloom arresting the steps of grave and reverend Senators; for with fog, and drizzle, and a sleety driving mist the night has come at least two hours before its time...	Fog everywhere. Fog up the river, where it flows among green aits and meadows; fog down the river, where it rolls defiled among the tiers of shipping, and the waterside pollutions of a great (and dirty) city. Fog on the Essex marshes, fog on the Kentish heights. Fog creeping into the cabooses of collier-brigs; fog lying out on the yards, and hovering in the rigging of great ships; fog drooping on the gunwales of barges and small boats. Fog in the eyes and throats of ancient Greenwich pensioners....Most of the shops lighted two hours before their time... (Chapter 1)
Is it a stretch of imagination to say that by night they contained a swarm of misery, that crowds of foul existence crawled in out of gaps in walls and boards, or coiled themselves to sleep on nauseous heaps of straw fetid with human perspiration and where the rain drips in, and the damp airs of midnight fatch and carry malignant fevers....	Now, these tumbling tenements contain, by night, a swarm of misery. As on the ruined human wretch, vermin parasites appear, so, these ruined shelters have bred a crowd of foul existence that crawls in and out of gaps in walls and boards; and coils itself to sleep, in maggot numbers, where the rain drips in; and comes and goes, fetching and carrying fever.... (Chapter 16)

No doubt further investigation of the works listed above will unearth additional example of Crafts's influences and borrowings, and lead to a richer understanding of the sources from the canon of American and English literature that inspired a fugitive slave to dare to tell her tale.

BIBLIOGRAPHY

Allibone, S. Austin, ed. *Critical Dictionary of English Literature and British and American Authors.* Philadelphia: J. B. Lippincott, 1897.

Andrews, William L. *To Tell a Free Story: The First Century of Afro-American Autobiography.* Urbana: University of Illinois, 1986.

Anonymous. *The Sisters of Orleans: A Tale of Race and Social Conflict.* New York: Putnam, 1871.

Arnim, Ludwig Achim, Freiherr von. *Isabella von Ägypten.* 1812.

Bigelow, Harriet Hamline. *The Curse Entailed.* Boston: Wentworth, 1857.

Blassingame, John W. *Slave Testimony: Two Centuries of Letters, Speeches, Interviews, and Autobiographies.* Baton Rouge: Louisiana State University Press, 1977.

Brown, William Wells. *Clotel.* London: Partridge and Oakley, 1853.

Burkett, Randall and Nancy and Henry Louis Gates Jr. *The Black Biographical Dictionary Index.* Alexandria, Va.: Chadwyck Healy, 1985.

The Case of Passmore Williamson. Philadelphia: Pennsylvania Anti-Slavery Society, 1855.

Cathey, Cornelius Oliver. *Agricultural Developments in North Carolina.* Chapel Hill: University of North Carolina Press, 1956.

Child, Lydia Maria. *The Romance of the Republic.* Boston: Ticknor and Fields, 1867.

Clemens, Samuel L. *Pudd'nhead Wilson.* Hartford: American Publishing Co., 1894.

Davis, David Brion. "The Enduring Legacy of the South's Civil War Victory." *New York Times,* August 26, 2001.

Denison, Mary. *Old Hepsy.* New York: A. B. Burdick, 1858.

Dictionary of American Biography. New York: Charles Scribner's Sons, 1928–58.

Douglass, Frederick. *Narrative of the Life of Frederick Douglass, an American Slave.* Boston: Anti-Slavery Office, 1845.

———. *The Heroic Slave.* Boston: Jewett, 1853.

Elwin, Lizzy M. *Millie, the Quadroon.* Clyde, Ohio: Ames' Publishing Co., 1888.

Fabian, Ann. *The Unvarnished Truth: Personal Narratives in Nineteenth-Century America.* Berkeley: University of California Press, 2000.

Findling, John E., ed. *Dictionary of American Diplomatic History,* 2d ed., rev. and expanded. New York: Greenwood Press, 1989.

Foster, Frances Smith. *Written by Herself: Literary Production by African American Women, 1746–1892.* Bloomington: Indiana University Press, 1993.

———. *Witnessing Slavery: The Development of Ante-Bellum Slave Narratives.* 2d ed. Madison: University of Wisconsin Press, 1994.

———, ed. *Minnie's Sacrifice, Sowing and Reaping, Trial and Triumph: Three Rediscovered Novels by Frances E. W. Harper* (Boston: Beacon Press, 1994).

Frazier, E. Franklin. *Black Bourgeoisie.* Glencoe, Ill.: Free Press, 1957.

Griffith, Mattie. *Autobiography of a Female Slave.* Jackson: University of Mississippi, 1998 [1856].

Hegel, Georg Wilhelm Friedrich. *Phenomenology of Spirit.* New York: Oxford University Press, 1979.

Hildreth, Richard. *The Slave: or Memoirs of Archy Moore.* Boston: J. H. Eastburn, 1836.

———. *The White Slave: or, Memoirs of a Fugitive.* London: Ingram, Cooke and Company, 1852.

Ingraham, Joseph Holt. *The Quadroone; or, St. Michael's Day.* New York: Harper, 1841.

Jacobs, Harriet. *Incidents in the Life of a Slave Girl*. Edited by Jean Fagan Yellin. Cambridge: Harvard University Press, 1987.

Keckley, Elizabeth. *Behind the Scenes, or Thirty Years a Slave, and Four Years in the White House*. New York: G. W. Carleton, 1868.

Klauprect, Emil. *Cincinnati, or The Mysteries of the West*. [New York: Peter Lang, 1996], 1857.

Larsen, Nella. *Quicksand* (New York: Alfred A. Knopf, 1928).

Morgan, Joseph H. *Morgan's History of the New Jersey Conference of the A.M.E. Church*. Camden, N.J.: S. Chew, 1887.

Morrison, Toni. *Beloved*. New York: Knopf, 1998.

Newman, Richard. *Words Like Freedom*. Westport, Conn.: Locust Hill Press, 1996.

Nickell, Joe. *Pen, Ink & Evidence: A Study of Writing and Writing Materials for the Penman, Collector, and Document Detective*. New Castle, Del.: Oak Knoll Press, 1990.

———. *Detecting Forgery: Forensic Investigation of Documents*. Lexington: University Press of Kentucky, 1996.

Peacocke, James S. *The Creole Orphans*. New York: Derby & Jackson, 1856.

Perinchiet, Elizabeth M. *History of the Cemeteries in Burlington County, New Jersey, 1687–1975*. n.p., 1978.

Richmond, Legh. *The Negro Servant: An Authentic and Interesting Narrative*. Boston: Lincoln & Edmonds, 1815.

Rohrbach, Augusta. *Truth Stranger than Fiction: Race, Realism, and the U.S. Marketplace*. New York: Palgrave, 2002.

Sollors, Werner. *Neither Black Nor White Yet Both: Thematic Explorations of Interracial Literature*. Cambridge: Harvard University Press, 1997.

Still, William. *The Underground Railroad*. Philadelphia: Porter and Coates, 1872.

Stowe, Harriet Beecher. *Dred*. Boston: Phillips, Sampson, 1856.

———. *The Key to Uncle Tom's Cabin: Presenting the Original Facts and Documents Upon Which the Story Is Founded*. Boston: Jewett, 1853.

———. *Uncle Tom's Cabin.* Boston: Jewett, 1852.
Sundquist, Eric. *To Wake the Nation: Race in the Making of American Literature.* Cambridge: Harvard University Press, 1993.
Thomas à Kempis. *The Imitation of Christ.* Totowa, N.J.: Catholic Book Publishing Co., 1988.
Walpole, Horace. *Castle of Otranto.* New York: Oxford University Press, 1998.
Wheeler, John Hill. *Historical Sketches of North Carolina from 1584 to 1851.* Philadelphia: Lippincott, Grambo and Co., 1851.
———. *A Legislative Manual of North Carolina.* 1874.
———. *Reminiscences and Memoirs of North Carolina and Eminent North Carolinians.* Columbus, Ohio: Columbus Print Works, 1884.
———, ed. *The Narrative of Colonel David Fanning.* Richmond, Va.: privately printed, 1861.
Williams, James. *Narrative of James Williams.* New York: American Anti-Slavery Society, 1838.
Wilson, Harriet E. *Our Nig.* New York: Random House, 1983 [1859].
Wilson, James Grant and John Fiske, eds. *Appleton's Cyclopaedia of American Biography.* New York: Appleton, 1888.
Wright, Giles R. *Afro-Americans in New Jersey.* Trenton: New Jersey Historical Commission, 1988.
———. "New Jersey," in *Encyclopedia of African-American Culture and History,* edited by Jack Salzman, David Lionel Smith, and Cornel West. New York: Macmillan, 1996.
Wright, Richard. *Native Son.* New York: Harper & Brothers, 1940.
Yellin, Jean Fagan. *The Intricate Knot: Black Figures in American Literature, 1776–1863.* New York: New York University Press, 1992.

ACKNOWLEDGMENTS

Several colleagues generously assisted in the search for Hannah Crafts. Richard Newman attended the Swann auction to bid for Crafts's manuscript on my behalf. Nina Kollars typed the manuscript, which she and Newman proofed orally. Kollars also prepared a list of the novel's characters, and suggested that I search the censuses for Hannah Vincent. Newman was especially helpful in researching the history of the African Methodist Episcopal Church in New Jersey. Wyatt Houston Day, Kenneth Rendell, Dr. Joe Nickell, Leslie Morris, and Craigen Bowen shared their expert opinions about the date of Hannah Crafts's manuscript. Nina Kollars and Kevin Rabener searched the Internet for signs of Crafts, combing genealogical websites and CD-ROM databases.

Lisa Finder, Esme Bahn, Paul Abruzzo, and Claudia Hill painstakingly researched census records in the National Archives; Lisa Finder and Tim Bingaman expertly researched various records available only at the Mormon Family History Library; Esme Bahn and Nina Kollars pursued various leads at the Library of Congress, where Kollars photocopied John Hill Wheeler's entire diary by hand. Sheldon Cheek and Brian Sinche transcribed and searched Wheeler's diary and chronology for the years 1854–1861; Sinche pointed out the presence of a slave named "Esther" in one of Wheeler's 1857 entries, and Cheek analyzed points of overlap between the diary and the novel.

My colleagues William L. Andrews, Nina Baym, Sterling Bland, Rudolph Byrd, Lawrence Buell, Vincent Carretta, Karen Dalton, David Brion Davis, Ann Fabian, Frances Smith Foster, Evelyn Brooks Higginbotham, Gene Jarrett, Matthew Lee, David Levering Lewis, Robert E. May, Nellie Y. McKay, Richard Newman, Susan O'Donovan, Terri Oliver, Tom Parramore, Augusta Rohrbach, Bryan Sinche, Werner Sollors, and Jean Fagan Yellin read the manuscript of *The Bondwoman's Narrative,* shared their theories about its origin, and patiently tolerated my phone calls during which we would brainstorm about possible avenues of research. Terri Oliver analyzed the novel's plot elements and assisted with the annotation of the text. Richard Newman offered an analysis of the representation of black characters in *Uncle Tom's Cabin.*

Joanne Kendall, my expert and devoted secretary, typed several drafts of my introduction, the textual annotations, notes, and appendixes. Professor Arthur R. Miller, the Bruce Bromley Professor of Law at Harvard, offered keen advice about copyright law governing an unpublished nineteenth-century manuscript. My editor, Jamie Raab, brought enormous sensitivity to a very complex editorial process.

Tina Bennett, my agent, believed in this project from the day I purchased the manuscript at auction. Laurence Kirshbaum expressed tremendous enthusiasm and encouragement for this project from the first day I discussed it with him, introduced me to Kenneth Rendell and Dr. Joe Nickell, and engaged their services to authenticate Hannah Crafts's manuscript.

Sharon Adams, Henry Finder, Tina Bennett, William Andrews, Angela De Leon, and Richard Newman read and critiqued various drafts of my account of the quest to find Hannah Crafts. My indebtedness to each will be difficult to repay.

Finally, I would also like to thank Linda Duggins, Shelley Fisher Fishkin, Katherine Flynn, Catherine Keyser, Richard J. Powell, Hollis Robbins, Deborah H. Roberts, Ruby Saunders, William Shields, George Stevenson, Diana Trudell, and Mario Valdes.

ABOUT THE AUTHORS

∞

Henry Louis Gates Jr. is the Alphonse Fletcher University Professor and Director of the Hutchins Center for African and African American Research at Harvard University. An award-winning filmmaker, literary scholar, journalist, cultural critic, and institution builder, Professor Gates has authored or coauthored books including *Stony the Road*, *The Black Church*, and *The Black Box*, and created documentary films such as his groundbreaking genealogy series *Finding Your Roots*. His six-part PBS documentary, *The African Americans: Many Rivers to Cross*, earned an Emmy Award, a Peabody Award, and an NAACP Image Award. This series and his PBS documentary series *Reconstruction: America after the Civil War* were both honored with the Alfred I. duPont-Columbia University Award.

Gregg Hecimovich is a professor of English at Furman University in Greenville, South Carolina, and a Non-Resident Fellow of the Hutchins Center at Harvard University. He received his PhD in English from Vanderbilt University and has received fellowships from the National Endowment for the Humanities and elsewhere. He is the author of *The Life and Times of Hannah Crafts*, winner of the *Los Angeles Times* Book Prize for Biography and a finalist for the National Book Critics Circle Award for Biography.